PENGU

PENGUIN SEL
GENERAL EDITOR: CHRISTOPHER RICKS

CHRISTOPHER SMART: SELECTED POEMS

Christopher Smart was born in 1722 in Shipbourne, Kent, the son of a steward on the estate of Lord Vane. When he was eleven, his father died and he was sent to Durham School and became the protégé of Lord Barnard of Raby Castle. In 1739 he entered Pembroke College, Cambridge, where he became well known for his Latin verses, graduating with a BA in 1744. At this time he began publishing English verse but also earned a reputation for wildness and extravagance and was arrested for debt in 1747. He left Cambridge in 1749 to become a writer in London, where he scraped a living working for John Newbery and editing his periodicals, *The Student, or, the Oxford and Cambridge Miscellany* and *The Midwife, or, the Old Woman's Magazine*. In 1752 he published his first collection, *Poems on Several Occasions*, and, in the same year, married Anna Maria Carnan, the step-daughter of John Newbery. They had two daughters. In 1756 he published his *Hymn to the Supreme Being, on Recovery from a Dangerous Fit of Illness* and about that year began to suffer from a form of religious mania. Until January 1763, with one brief intermission, he was confined: first in St Luke's Hospital, then in Mr Potter's madhouse in Bethnal Green. This led to the irreparable breakdown of his marriage, but he continued to write poetry with even greater fertility until his death. These later writings, such as *A Song to David* and *Hymns for the Amusement of Children*, now recognized as his finest and most original work, passed almost unnoticed at the time. In April 1770 he was imprisoned for debt. He died in the following year.

Karina Williamson was educated at Frensham Heights School, Surrey, and Lady Margaret Hall, Oxford, where she gained a BA in English, followed by a B.Litt. She taught at the universities of Uppsala (in Sweden), Edinburgh and Oxford, and was Fellow of St Hilda's College, Oxford, from 1977 to 1988. She is now Supernumerary Fellow of St Hilda's and lives in Edinburgh. Her publications include numerous articles on English and Caribbean literature, and she is editor, with Marcus Walsh, of the OUP *Poetical Works of*

Christopher Smart. She is at present writing a book on poetry and science in the eighteenth century. She has one daughter and two sons by her first husband, Colin Williamson, who died in 1983. She is now married to Angus McIntosh.

Marcus Walsh was born in Leeds in 1947. He was educated at Temple Moor Grammar School, Leeds, and at Exeter College, Oxford, where he gained a BA in English in 1969, followed by a B.Phil. in 1971. In 1975 he gained a Ph.D. from the University of Toronto and is now Senior Lecturer in English at the University of Birmingham where he has been a lecturer since 1976. He is editor, with Karina Williamson, of the OUP *Poetical Works of Christopher Smart*. He has written numerous articles on Christopher Smart, as well as on biblical interpretation, textual editing and textual theory in the late-seventeenth and eighteenth centuries.

CHRISTOPHER SMART
SELECTED POEMS

EDITED BY KARINA WILLIAMSON
AND MARCUS WALSH

PENGUIN BOOKS

PENGUIN BOOKS

Published by the Penguin Group
27 Wrights Lane, London w8 5tz, England
Viking Penguin Inc., 40 West 23rd Street, New York, New York 10010, USA
Penguin Books Australia Ltd, Ringwood, Victoria, Australia
Penguin Books Canada Ltd, 2801 John Street, Markham Ontario, Canada l3r 1b4
Penguin Books (NZ) Ltd, 182–190 Wairau Road, Auckland 10, New Zealand

Penguin Books Ltd, Registered Offices: Harmondsworth, Middlesex, England

This edition first published 1990
1 3 5 7 9 10 8 6 4 2

Filmset in 10 on 12pt Sabon
Made and printed in Great Britain by
Cox & Wyman Ltd, Reading

CONTENTS

PREFACE

Unless otherwise indicated in the Notes, copy-text for the miscellaneous poems throughout is the earliest printed text, collated with later authorial versions where available. The text of *On Gratitude* is from Smart's holograph in the Berg Collection, New York Public Library. The text of *Jubilate Agno* follows the manuscript in the Houghton Library, Harvard University, with minor corrections of punctuation, spelling, omitted particles, and so on. A few emendations are recorded in the Notes. Copy-texts for the *Hymns and Spiritual Songs* and *Translation of the Psalms of David* are those printed in the volume entitled *A Translation of the Psalms of David* (1765); no further edition of either work was published in Smart's lifetime. Collation has been made with texts of individual hymns and psalms printed in the various advance *Proposals* for this subscription-published volume. Copy-text of *A Song to David* is the first edition, 1763, collated with the second edition printed in *A Translation of the Psalms of David*. Copy-text for the translations of Horace is *The Works of Horace, Translated into Verse* (1767), the only complete edition ever published. Copy-text for *Hymns for the Amusement of Children* is the first edition (1771), collated with the Dublin edition (1772) and the two surviving London editions of 1775 and 1786.

Margaret Anne Doody has claimed, of the Augustans, that 'no poets ever paid more attention to the sound of their words, or their appearance on the page in relation to each other', and that to modernize their spelling and capitalization is to deprive us of 'keys to reading' (*The Daring Muse,* Cambridge, 1985, p. 223). The argument is compelling for many poets of the mid-eighteenth century.

Smart, to a greater degree than most of his contemporaries, is a problematic case for modernization. The 'peculiarity' (the word is Smart's own) of his linguistic consciousness and practice is clear from his approving discussion of the Horatian *curiosa felicitas* in his Preface to the verse *Horace* (1767), from the *Jubilate Agno*, and from the published poetry especially of the last decade of his life. Very often this 'peculiarity' manifests itself in the form and spelling of words. In a number of the later works, especially those published by subscription, it is clear that Smart exercised a greater degree of control over his text than would have been normal in the mid-eighteenth century. A high proportion of orthographical 'peculiarities' are likely to be authorial, rather than printing-house practice. Distinctive orthography very often occurs in rhyme words ('wilk' [whelk]/milk; 'controul'/'soul'); to tamper with such occurrences would clearly be damaging, particularly given Smart's stated interest in the rhyming relationships of words (see *Jubilate Agno*, B582–600).

It has been our aim to present a text which reflects Smart's distinctive poetic methods, but which reduces to a minimum difficulties and unfamiliarities that arise not from particular and authorial causes but from general eighteenth-century spelling convention and printing-house custom. We have attempted to make this discrimination on the following principles. Older or irregular forms are retained in the case of:

i) clear manuscript evidence, or repeated use in a variety of printed texts, indicating Smart's preference: 'intitled', 'inclosure', etc.; 'controul', 'loadstone', 'couslip', 'shew', 'ax', etc.

ii) variant spelling indicating a variant pronunciation: 'accordant', 'grutch', 'largess', 'quadrupede', etc. Inconsistency in the printed text in the usage of, for example, 'grutch' and 'grudge', 'Cedron' and 'Kidron', is for this reason not normalized in this edition.

iii) variant spellings indicating emphasis, especially in rhyme-words: 'furr', 'excell', etc.

iv) variant spelling with semantic significance: 'holyday', 'fault'ring', 'landskip', etc.

v) spelling drawing attention to a word's etymology or derivation: 'oeconomy', 'aera', 'terras', 'phrenzy'.

vi) proper names: 'Forbisher', 'Spencer', 'Jehudah' (for 'Judah'), etc. Proper names and capitalized nouns in *Jubilate Agno* pose a special problem, in view of the importance attached to names and their precise written shapes in the manuscript. The principle followed here is to retain variant spellings (regardless of occasional inconsistencies, e.g., 'Tyger'/'tiger', 'Esau'/'Esaw') where they might have semantic significance, as in 'Rock' (roc) and 'Muscle' (mussel), or where they simply reflect spellings attested elsewhere in English or Latin usage. Variants that appear to be mere spelling mistakes or lapses of memory ('Jamim' for 'Jamin', 'Chichister' for 'Chichester', 'Myrcus' for 'Myrus', etc.) have been corrected.

Where no good case can be made on these grounds, older spellings are modernized: 'croud', 'brouse,' 'dispise', 'persue', 'icie', 'stedfast', 'chearful', 'groupe', 'expence', etc. Smart's -ick endings are normally modernized to -ic (except where 'musick' implies the older sense – 'a company of musicians' – or the word carries special emphasis). 'Wou'd' and 'woud' become 'would' throughout. Where printed or manuscript sources show a mixture of dialect and standard forms of a word ('destribution'/'distribution'; 'pilgramage'/'pilgrimage') we give the standard form throughout.

Elided forms, which have a metrical function, are retained ('priz'd', 'dev'ls'); inconsistencies are normalized ('sweetners' becomes 'sweet'ners', 'clustring' becomes 'clust'ring'). Punctuation is corrected on the very few occasions where it is necessary to clarify the sense. Capitalization of whole words is retained; this is almost certainly authorial, and has considerable semantic weight. Initial capitals are generally authorial, in the later poetry especially, and are also retained. Capitalization has been modernized, however, where copy-text is from the *Midwife*, in which all nouns were printed with initial capitals. The few footnotes Smart himself supplied to his poems are printed on the page.

Any modernized text is of course an editorial construction.

Readers wishing to see an unmodernized text may consult the Oxford English Texts edition of the *Poetical Works*.

The poems from Smart's earlier career have been chosen to demonstrate both his versatility and his accomplishment in the handling of popular forms of poetry. The Seatonian poems are printed in full because of their importance in his development as well as their intrinsic interest.

The major achievements in Christian poetry of the last dozen years of Smart's life are printed in their entirety: *Jubilate Agno, Hymns and Spiritual Songs for the Fasts and Festivals of the Church of England, A Song to David,* and *Hymns for the Amusement of Children*. The selections from *A Translation of the Psalms of David* are examples of Smart's characteristic voice of praise and adoration, and include a number of the wide range of metrical forms he used.

Selections from the miscellaneous poems of Smart's final years show how his religious experience suffused even his secular writings. The translations from Horace display his suppleness, wit and creativity as a translator.

The Notes are designed to establish the essential contexts for the poems chosen, to resolve major interpretative difficulties and identify key allusions. Readers who require the line-by-line commentary that Smart's poetry (and especially *Jubilate Agno*) often demands will need to consult the Oxford English Texts edition of the *Poetical Works*.

TABLE OF DATES

1722   11 April: Christopher Smart born, Shipbourne, Kent. Son of Peter Smart, Steward of Lord Vane's estate of Fairlawn at Shipbourne.

1733   Father dies. Smart sent to Durham School. Holidays spent at Raby Castle in Staindrop, the home of the family of Henry Vane.

1739   Leaves Durham School. Enters Pembroke College, Cambridge, as a sizar.

1742   Awarded Craven Scholarship.

1743   Latin translation of Pope's *Ode on St Cecilia's Day*.

1744   Graduates BA. Friendship with Charles Burney begins.

1745   Elected Fellow of Pembroke College. College Prae-lectorship in Philosophy.

1746   College Praelectorship in Rhetoric. Graduates MA.

1747   April: Writes, produces, and acts in *A Trip to Cambridge, or, the Grateful Fair*, a comedy performed at Pembroke College.

        November: Arrested for debt.

1749   Leaves Cambridge, to become a writer in London.

1750   April: *On the Eternity of the Supreme Being*, first of Smart's five winning entries for the Seatonian Prize at Cambridge University.

        June: *Horatian Canons of Friendship* published by John Newbery, for whom Smart was to work until 1756.

1750–51   Writes in and edits *The Student, or, the Oxford and Cambridge Miscellany*.

1750–53   Writes in and edits *The Midwife, or, the Old Woman's Magazine*.

1751   April: *On the Immensity of the Supreme Being*.
1751–2   Involved in 'Mrs Midnight's Oratory', a variety show at the Haymarket Theatre (first performance 27 December 1751).
1752   June: *Poems on Several Occasions*, the first collection of Smart's poems.
            November: *On the Omniscience of the Supreme Being*.
            Marries Anna Maria Carnan, John Newbery's step-daughter. Moves to Canonbury House, Islington.
1753–6   Writing for London theatres and periodicals.
1753   February: *The Hilliad, an Epic Poem*, written with Arthur Murphy.
            Daughter Marianne born.
1754   January: *On the Power of the Supreme Being*.
            Daughter Elizabeth born.
1755   Signs ninety-nine-year contract with Thomas Gardner to write for the *Universal Visiter*.
1756   *The Works of Horace, Translated Literally into English Prose* (publication announced December 1755).
            March: *On the Goodness of the Supreme Being*. Serious illness, mental or febrile. Samuel Johnson and others take on smart's responsibilities to the *Universal Visiter*.
            June: *Hymn to the Supreme Being on Recovery from a Dangerous Fit of Illness*.
1757   March: Application for admission to St Luke's Hospital for the Insane made on his behalf. Admitted in May. Main symptom of illness a compulsion to pray in public.
1758   May: discharged. Sometime before January 1759 admitted to Mr Potter's madhouse in Bethnal Green. Anna Maria Smart moves to Dublin, then in 1761 to Reading. Marriage now irretrievably broken down.
1759   Benefit performance of Aaron Hill's *Merope* put on for Smart by David Garrick.

FURTHER READING

EDITIONS

The Poetical Works of Christopher Smart, 5 vols., Oxford, 1980–
   Vol. 1: *Jubilate Agno*, ed. Karina Williamson, 1980
   Vol. 2: *Religious Poetry 1763–1771*, ed. Marcus Walsh and Karina Williamson, 1983
   Vol. 3: *A Translation of the Psalms of David*, ed. Marcus Walsh, 1987
   Vol. 4: *Miscellaneous Poems English and Latin*, ed. Karina Williamson, 1987
   Vol. 5: *Translations of Horace and Phaedrus*, ed. Karina Williamson (forthcoming)
Robert Brittain, ed., *Poems by Christopher Smart*, Princeton, 1950 (Brittain's Introduction and Notes are still unsurpassed as a general critical account of Smart's poetical works.)
W. H. Bond, ed., *Christopher Smart: Jubilate Agno*, Cambridge, Mass., 1954
Arthur Sherbo, ed., *Christopher Smart's Verse Translation of Horace's Odes*, Victoria, British Columbia, 1979

BIBLIOGRAPHY

Robert Mahony and Betty W. Rizzo, *Christopher Smart: An Annotated Bibliography, 1743–1983*, New York, 1984

BIOGRAPHY

Christopher Devlin, *Poor Kit Smart*, London, 1961
Arthur Sherbo, *Christopher Smart: Scholar of the University*, East Lansing, 1967

CRITICISM AND SCHOLARSHIP

Robert Brittain, 'An Early Model for *A Song to David*', *Publications of the Modern Language Association*, 56 (1941), pp. 165–74 (An important article; but see the corrections by P. R. Wikelund, *ELH*, 9 (1942), pp. 136–40, and A. D. McKillop, *Publications of the Modern Language Association*, 58 (1943), p. 582)

Donald Davie, 'Christopher Smart: Some Neglected Poems', *Eighteenth-Century Studies*, 3 (1970), pp. 242–64

Moira Dearnley, *The Poetry of Christopher Smart*, London, 1968

Christopher M. Dennis, 'A Structural Conceit in Smart's *Song to David*', *Review of English Studies*, NS 29 (1978), pp. 257–66

Allan J. Gedalof, 'The Rise and Fall of Smart's David', *Philological Quarterly*, 60 (1981), pp. 369–86

D. J. Greene, 'Smart, Berkeley, the Scientists and the Poets', *Journal of the History of Ideas*, 14 (1953), pp. 327–52

Harriet Guest, *A Form of Sound Words: The Religious Poetry of Christopher Smart*, Oxford, 1989

Geoffrey H. Hartman, 'Christopher Smart's "Magnificat": Toward a Theory of Representation', *ELH*, 41 (1974), pp. 429–54

A. D. Hope, 'The Apocalypse of Christopher Smart', *Studies in the Eighteenth Century*, ed. R. F. Brissenden, Canberra, 1968, pp. 269–84

A. J. Kuhn, 'Christopher Smart: The Poet as Patriot of the Lord', *ELH*, 30 (1963), pp. 121–36

Eli Mandel, 'Theories of Voice in Eighteenth-Century Poetry: Thomas Gray and Christopher Smart', *Fearful Joy: Papers from the Thomas Gray Bicentenary Conference at Carleton University*, eds. James Downey and Ben Jones, Montreal, 1974, pp. 103–18

David B. Morris, *The Religious Sublime: Christian Poetry and Critical Tradition in 18th-Century England*, Lexington, 1972. See especially ch. 5

Patricia Meyer Spacks, *The Poetry of Vision: Five Eighteenth-Century Poets*, Cambridge, Mass., 1967

R. C. Tennant, 'Christopher Smart and *The Whole Duty of Man*', *Eighteenth-Century Studies*, 13 (1979), pp. 63–78

Roberta E. Tovey, ' "I speak for all": Smart's Conversion of the Hebrew Psalm', *Philological Quarterly*, 62 (1983), pp. 315–33

Karina Williamson, 'Smart's *Principia*: Science and Anti-Science in *Jubilate Agno*', *Review of English Studies*, 30 (1979), pp. 409–22

To Ethelinda

On her doing my Verses the honour of
wearing them in her bosom.
Written at Thirteen.

Happy verses! that were prest
In fair Ethelinda's breast!
Happy muse, that didst embrace
The sweet, the heav'nly-fragrant place!
Tell me, is the omen true,   5
Shall the bard arrive there too?

Oft thro' my eyes my soul has flown,
And wanton'd on that ivory throne:
There with ecstatic transport burn'd,
And thought it was to heav'n return'd.   10
Tell me, is the omen true,
Shall the body follow too?

When first at nature's early birth,
Heav'n sent a man upon the earth,
Ev'n Eden was more fruitful found,   15
When Adam came to till the ground:
Shall then those breasts be fair in vain,
And only rise to fall again?

No, no, fair nymph – for no such end
Did heav'n to thee its bounty lend;   20
That breast was ne'er design'd by fate,
For verse, or things inanimate;

Then throw them from that downy bed,
And take the poet in their stead.

On Taking a Batchelor's Degree

In allusion to Horace, Book iii, Ode 30

Exegi monumentum aere perennius, &c.

'Tis done:—I tow'r to that degree,
    And catch such heav'nly fire,
That HORACE ne'er could rant like me,
    Nor is King's-chapel higher.
My name in sure recording page   5
    Shall time itself o'erpow'r,
If no rude mice with envious rage
    The buttery books devour.
A *title too, with added grace,
    My name shall now attend,   10
Till to the church with silent pace
    A nymph and priest ascend.
Ev'n in the schools I now rejoice,
    Where late I shook with fear,
Nor heed the Moderator's voice   15
    Loud thund'ring in my ear.
Then with Aeolian flute I blow
    A soft Italian lay,
Or where Cam's scanty waters flow,
    Releas'd from lectures, stray.   20
Meanwhile, friend †BANKS, my merits claim
    Their just reward from you,
For HORACE bids us challenge fame,
    When once that fame's our due.
Invest me with a graduate's gown,   25
    Midst shouts of all beholders,

* BATCHELOR.
† A celebrated tailor.

My head with ample square-cap crown,
And deck with hood my shoulders.

On an Eagle Confined in a College-Court

Imperial bird, who wont to soar
  High o'er the rolling cloud,
Where Hyperborean mountains hoar
  Their heads in Ether shroud; –
Thou servant of almighty JOVE,   5
Who, free and swift as thought, could'st rove
  To the bleak north's extremest goal; –
Thou, who magnanimous could'st bear
The sovereign thund'rer's arms in air,
  And shake thy native pole! –   10

Oh cruel fate! what barbarous hand,
  What more than Gothic ire,
At some fierce tyrant's dread command,
  To check thy daring fire,
Has plac'd thee in this servile cell,   15
Where Discipline and Dulness dwell,
  Where Genius ne'er was seen to roam;
Where ev'ry selfish soul's at rest,
Nor ever quits the carnal breast,
  But lurks and sneaks at home!   20

Tho' dim'd thine eye, and clipt thy wing,
  So grov'ling! once so great!
The grief-inspired Muse shall sing
  In tend'rest lays thy fate.
What time by thee scholastic Pride   25
Takes his precise, pedantic stride,
  Nor on thy mis'ry casts a care,
The stream of love ne'er from his heart
Flows out, to act fair pity's part;
  But stinks, and stagnates there.   30

Yet useful still, hold to the throng –
   Hold the reflecting glass, –
That not untutor'd at thy wrong
   The passenger may pass:
Thou type of wit and sense confin'd,   35
Cramp'd by the oppressors of the mind,
   Who study downward on the ground;
Type of the fall of Greece and Rome;
While more than mathematic gloom,
   Envelopes all around!   40

To Miss H—— with Some Music

Written by a poet outrageously in love.

Incomparable Harriot, loveliest fair,
That e'er breath'd sweetness on the vital air,
Whose matchless form to us below is giv'n,
As a bright pattern of the rest of heav'n,
Blest with a face, a temper, and a mind   5
To please, to soothe, and to instruct mankind!
Accept these notes – the warbling song begin,
And with your voice complete the cherubin;
Swift with your iv'ry fingers wake the keys,
And make e'en ——'s desolation please.   10
O would some God but listen to my pray'r,
And waft me to thee thro' the fields of air,
Thrown at thy feet a suppliant I'd reveal,
Each wish, each anguish, that my thoughts conceal,
In whisp'ring kisses I'd confess the whole,   15
And musically murmur out my soul.
May all the pow'rs that on fair virgins wait,
Heap on thee all that's happy, good, and great,
All that of earthly bliss you can conceive,
Your hopes can image, or your faith believe!   20
But vain are pray'rs, and all my wishes vain,
You are already all that I can feign.

With that sweet mind, to that fair body giv'n,
You must be blest – for all are blest in heav'n.
But you from *Time* th' improving form receive,   25
And he, alas! can take as well as give,
But that exalted soul which you enjoy,
Is what nor *Time* can give – nor can destroy.

Ode to Lady Harriot

To Harriot all accomplish'd fair,
Begin, ye Nine, a grateful air;
Ye Graces join her worth to tell,
And blazon what you can't excell.

Let Flora rifle all her bow'rs,   5
For fragrant shrubs, and painted flow'rs,
And, in her vernal robes array'd,
Present them to the noble maid.

Her breath shall give them new perfume,
Her blushes shall their dyes outbloom;   10
The lily now no more shall boast
Its whiteness, in her bosom lost.

See yon delicious woodbines rise
By oaks exalted to the skies,
So view in Harriot's matchless mind   15
Humility and greatness join'd.

To paint her dignity and ease,
Form'd to command, and form'd to please,
In wreaths expressive be there wove
The birds of Venus and of Jove.   20

There where th' immortal laurel grows,
And there, where blooms the crimson rose,
Be with this line the chaplet bound,
That beauty is with virtue crown'd.

Inscriptions on an Aeolian Harp

On one end
Partem aliquam, O venti, divum referatis ad aures!
VIRG.

On one side
Salve, quae fingis proprio modulamine carmen,
  Salve, Memnoniam vox imitata lyram!
Dulce O divinumque sonas sine pollicis ictu,
  Dives naturae simplicis, artis inops!   5
Talia, quae incultae dant mellea labra puellae,
  Talia sunt, faciles quae modulantur aves.

On the other side
Hail heav'nly harp, where Memnon's skill is shewn,
That charm'st the ear with music all thine own!
Which, tho' untouch'd, canst rapt'rous strains impart,
O rich of genuine nature, free from art!
Such the wild warblings of the sylvan throng,
So simply sweet the untaught virgin's song.   5

On the other end
Christopherus Smart Henrico Bell Armigero.

The Author Apologizes to a Lady, for His being a Little Man

Natura nusquam magis, quam in minimis tota est. PLIN.
Ολιγον τε φιλον τε. HOM.

Yes, contumelious fair, you scorn
  The amorous dwarf, that courts you to his arms,
But ere you leave him quite forlorn,
  And to some youth gigantic yield your charms,
Hear him – oh hear him, if you will not try,   5
And let your judgment check th' ambition of your eye.

Say, is it carnage makes the man?
Is to be monstrous really to be great?
Say, is it wise or just to scan
Your lover's worth by quantity, or weight?   10
Ask your mamma and nurse, if it be so;
Nurse and mamma, I ween, shall jointly answer, no.

The less the body to the view,
The soul (like springs in closer durance pent)
Is all exertion, ever new,   15
Unceasing, unextinguish'd, and unspent;
Still pouring forth executive desire,
As bright, as brisk, and lasting, as the vestal fire.

Does thy young bosom pant for fame;
Would'st thou be of posterity the toast?   20
The poets shall ensure thy name,
Who magnitude of *mind* not *body* boast.
Laurels on bulky bards as rarely grow,
As on the sturdy oak the virtuous misletoe.

Look in the glass, survey that cheek –   25
Where Flora has with all her roses blush'd;
The shape so tender, – looks so meek, –
The breasts made to be press'd, not to be crush'd –
Then turn to me, – turn with obliging eyes,
Nor longer Nature's works, in miniature, despise.   30

Young Ammon did the world subdue,
Yet had not more external man than I;
Ah! charmer, should I conquer you,
With him in fame, as well as size, I'll vie.
Then, scornful nymph, come forth to yonder grove,   35
Where I defy, and challenge, all thy utmost love.

To My Worthy Friend, Mr T. B. One of the People Called Quakers

Written in his Garden, July 1752.

Free from the proud, the pompous, and the vain,
How simply neat and elegantly plain,
Thy rural villa lifts its modest head,
Where fair convenience reigns in fashion's stead;
Where sober plenty does its bliss impart,   5
And glads thine hospitable, honest heart,
Mirth without vice, and rapture without noise,
And all the decent, all the manly joys!
Beneath a shadowy bow'r, the summer's pride,
Thy darling *Tullia sitting by my side;   10
Where light and shade in varied scenes display
A contrast sweet, like friendly *Yea* and *Nay*,
My hand, the secretary of my mind,
Left thee these lines upon the *poplar*'s rind.

* Mr B—'s daughter.

To the Rev. Mr Powell

On the Non-performance of a Promise he made the author of a Hare.

Friend, with regard to this same hare,
Am I to hope, or to despair?
By punctual post the letter came,
With P***LL's hand, and P***LL's name;
Yet there appear'd, for love or money,   5
Nor hare, nor leveret, nor coney.
Say, my dear Morgan, has my lord,
Like other great ones kept his word?
Or have you been deceiv'd by 'squire?

Or has your poacher lost his wire?   10
Or in some unpropitious hole,
Instead of puss, trepann'd a mole?
Thou valiant son of great Cadwallader,
Hast thou a hare, or hast thou swallow'd her?
    But now, methinks, I hear you say,   15
(And shake your head) 'Ah, well-a-day!
Painful pre-em'nence to be wise,
We wits have such short memories.
Oh, that the Act was not in force!
A horse! – my kingdom for a horse!   20
To love – yet be deny'd the sport!
Oh! for a friend or two at court!
God knows, there's scarce a man of quality
In all our peerless principality – '
    But hold – for on his country joking,   25
To a warm Welchman's most provoking.
As for poor puss, upon my honour,
I never set my heart upon her.
But any gift from friend to friend,
Is pleasing in its aim and end.   30
I, like the cock, would spurn a jewel,
Sent by th' unkind, th' unjust, and cruel.
But honest P***LL! – Sure from him
A barley-corn would be a gem.
Pleas'd therefore had I been, and proud,   35
And prais'd thy generous heart aloud,
If 'stead of hare (but do not blab it)
You'd sent me only a Welch rabbit.

Apollo and Daphne

AN EPIGRAM

When Phoebus was am'rous, and long'd to be rude,
Miss Daphne cry'd Pish! and ran swift to the wood,

And rather than do such a naughty affair,
She became a fine laurel to deck the God's hair.

The nymph was, no doubt, of a cold constitution;   5
For sure to turn tree was an odd resolution!
Yet in this she behav'd like a true modern spouse,
For she fled from his arms to distinguish his brows.

The Miser and the Mouse

AN EPIGRAM FROM THE GREEK

To a Mouse says a Miser 'my dear Mr Mouse,
Pray what may you please for to want in my house?'
Says the Mouse 'Mr Miser, pray keep yourself quiet,
You are safe in your person, your purse, and your diet:
A lodging I want, which ev'n you may afford,   5
But none would come here to beg, borrow, or board.'

Disertissime Romuli Nepotum

Imitated after Dining with Mr Murray.

O Thou, of British Orators the chief
That *were*, or are in *being*, or belief;
All eminence and goodness as thou art,
Accept the gratitude of POET SMART,
The meanest of the tuneful train as far,   5
As thou transcend'st the brightest at the bar.

Care and Generosity

A FABLE

Old Care with Industry and Art,
At length so well had play'd his Part;
He heap'd up such an ample store,
That Av'rice could not sigh for more:
Ten thousand flocks his shepherd told,   5
His coffers overflow'd with Gold;
The land all round him was his own,
With corn his crowded granaries groan.
In short so vast his charge and gain,
That to possess them was a pain;   10
With happiness oppress'd he lies,
And much too prudent to be wise.
Near him there liv'd a beauteous maid,
With all the charms of youth array'd;
Good, amiable, sincere and free,   15
Her name was Generosity.
'Twas hers the largess to bestow
On rich and poor, on friend and foe.
Her doors to all were open'd wide,
The pilgrim there might safe abide: 20
For th' hungry and the thirsty crew,
The bread she broke, the drink she drew;
There Sickness laid her aching head,
And there Distress could find a bed. –
Each hour with an all-bounteous hand,   25
Diffus'd she blessings round the land:
Her gifts and glory lasted long,
And numerous was th' accepting throng.
At length pale Penury seiz'd the dame,
And Fortune fled, and Ruin came,   30
She found her riches at an end,
And that she had not made one friend. –
All curs'd her for not giving more,
Nor thought on what she'd done before;

She wept, she rav'd, she tore her hair,   35
When lo! to comfort her came Care. –
And cry'd, my dear, if you will join
Your hand in nuptial bonds with mine;
All will be well – you shall have store,
And I be plagu'd with Wealth no more. –   40
Tho' I restrain your bounteous heart,
You still shall act the generous part. –
The Bridal came – great was the feast,
And good the pudding and the priest;
The bride in nine moons brought him forth   45
A little maid of matchless worth:
Her face was mix'd of Care and Glee,
They christen'd her Oeconomy;
And styled her fair Discretion's Queen,
The mistress of the golden mean.   50
Now Generosity confin'd,
Is perfect easy in her mind;
She loves to give, yet knows to spare,
Nor wishes to be free from Care.

The Country Squire and the Mandrake

The sun had rais'd above the mead,
His glorious horizontal head;
Sad Philomela left her thorn;
The lively linnets hymn'd the morn,
And nature, like a waking bride,   5
Her blushes spread on ev'ry side;
The cock as usual crow'd up Tray,
Who nightly with his master lay;
The faithful spaniel gave the word,
Trelooby at the signal stirr'd,   10
And with his gun, from wood to wood
The man of prey his course pursu'd;
The dew and herbage all around,

Like pearls and emeralds on the ground;
Th' uncultur'd flowers that rudely rise,   15
Where smiling freedom art defies;
The lark, in transport, tow'ring high,
The crimson curtains of the sky,
Affected not Trelooby's mind –
For what is beauty to the blind?   20
Th' amorous voice of *silvan* love,
Form'd charming concerts in the grove;
Sweet zephyr sigh'd on Flora's breast,
And drew the black-bird from his nest;
Whistling he leapt from leaf to leaf;   25
But what is music to the deaf?
    At length while poring on the ground,
With monumental look profound,
A curious vegetable caught
His – something similar to thought: 30
Wond'ring, he ponder'd, stooping low,
(Trelooby always lov'd a show)
And on the Mandrake's vernal station,
Star'd with prodigious observation.
Th' affronted Mandrake with a frown,   35
Address'd in rage the wealthy clown.
    'Proud member of the rambling race,
That vegetate from place to place,
Pursue the leveret at large,
Nor near thy blunderbuss discharge.   40
Disdainful tho' thou look'st on me,
What art thou, or what canst thou be?
Nature, that mark'd thee as a fool,
Gave no materials for the school.
In what consists thy work and fame?   45
The preservation of the Game. –
For what? thou avaricious elf,
But to destroy it all thyself;
To lead a life of drink and feast,
T' oppress the poor, and cheat the priest,   50
Or triumph in a virgin lost,

Is all the manhood thou canst boast. –
Pretty, in nature's various plan,
To see a weed that's like a man;
But 'tis a grievous thing indeed,   55
To see a man so like a weed.'

A Story of a Cock and a Bull

Yes – we excel in arts and arms,
In learning's lore, and beauty's charms;
The sea's wide empire we engross,
All nations hail the British cross;
The land of liberty we tread,   5
And woe to his devoted head,
Who dares the contrary advance,
One Englishman's worth ten of France.
These, these are truths what man won't write for,
Won't swear, won't bully, and won't fight for?   10
Yet (tho' perhaps I speak thro' vanity)
Would we'd a little more humanity!
Too far, I fear, I've drove the jest,
So leave to Cock and Bull the rest.
    A Bull who'd listen'd to the vows   15
Of above fifteen hundred cows,
And serv'd his master fresh and fresh,
With hecatombs of special flesh,
Like to a hermit, or a dervise,
Grown old and feeble in the service,   20
Now left the meadow's green parade,
And sought a solitary shade.
The cows proclaim'd by mournful mooing
The Bull's deficiency in wooing,
And to their disappointed master   25
All told the terrible disaster.
    Is this the case (quoth Hodge) O rare!
But hold, to-morrow is the fair:

Thou to thy doom, old boy, art fated
To-morrow – and thou shalt be baited –   30
The deed was done – Curse on the wrong!
Bloody description, hold thy tongue –
Victorious yet the Bull return'd,
And with stern silence inly mourn'd.
    A vet'ran, brave, majestic Cock,   35
Who serv'd for hour-glass, guard and clock,
Who crow'd the mansion's first relief,
Alike from goblin and from thief;
Whose youth escap'd the Christmas skillet,
Whose vigour brav'd the Shrovetide billet,   40
Had just return'd in wounds and pain,
Triumphant from the barbarous main.
By riv'lets brink, with trees o'ergrown,
He heard his fellow-suff'rer moan,
And greatly scorning wounds and smart,   45
Gave him three cheers, with all his heart.
    'Rise, neighbour, from that pensive attitude,
Brave witness of vile man's ingratitude,
And let us both with spur and horn
The cruel reasoning monster scorn –   50
Methinks at ev'ry dawn of day,
When first I chant my blithsome lay,
Methinks I hear from out the sky
"All will be better by and by."
When bloody, base, degenerate man,   55
Who deviates from his maker's plan,
Who Nature and her work abuses,
And thus his fellow-servants uses,
Shall greatly, and yet justly, want
The mercy he refused to grant.   60
And, when his heart, his conscience purges,
Shall wish to be the brute he scourges.'

'Hail, Energeia! hail, my native tongue'

Hail, Energeia! hail, my native tongue,
Concisely full, and musically strong!
Thou, with the pencil, hold'st a glorious strife,
And paints the passions greater than the life:
In thunders now tremendously array'd,   5
Now soft as murmurs of the melting maid:
Now piercing loud, and as the clarion clear,
And now resounding rough to rouse the ear:
Now quick as light'ning in its rapid flow,
Now, in its stately march, magnificently slow.   10
    Hail, Energeia! hail, my native tongue,
    Concisely full, and musically strong!
    Thou, with the pencil, hold'st a glorious strife,
    And paints the passions greater than the life.

SEATONIAN POEMS

On the Eternity of the Supreme Being

Conamur tenues grandia –
Nec Dis, nec viribus aequis –

Hail, wond'rous Being, who in pow'r supreme
Exists from everlasting, whose great Name
Deep in the human heart, and every atom
The Air, the Earth, or azure Main contains
In undecipher'd characters is wrote –   5
INCOMPREHENSIBLE! – O what can words
The weak interpreters of mortal thoughts,
Or what can thoughts (tho' wild of wing they rove
Thro' the vast concave of th' aetherial round)
If to the Heav'n of Heavens they'd win their way   10
Advent'rous, like the birds of night they're lost,
And delug'd in the flood of dazzling day. –
  May then the youthful, uninspired Bard
Presume to hymn th' Eternal; may he soar
Where Seraph, and where Cherubin on high   15
Resound th' unceasing plaudits, and with them
In the grand Chorus mix his feeble voice?
  He may – if Thou, who from the witless babe
Ordainest honor, glory, strength and praise,
Uplift th' unpinion'd Muse, and deign t' assist,   20
GREAT POET OF THE UNIVERSE, his song.
  Before this earthly Planet wound her course
Round Light's perennial fountain, before Light
Herself 'gan shine, and at th' inspiring word
Shot to existence in a blaze of day,   25
Before 'the Morning-Stars together sang'

And hail'd Thee Architect of countless worlds –
Thou art – all-glorious, all-beneficent,
All Wisdom and Omnipotence thou art.
   But is the aera of Creation fix'd   30
At when these Worlds began? Could ought retard
Goodness, that knows no bounds, from blessing ever,
Or keep th' immense Artificer in sloth?
Avaunt the dust-directed crawling thought,
That Puissance immeasurably vast,   35
And Bounty inconceivable could rest
Content, exhausted with one week of action –
No – in th' exertion of thy righteous pow'r,
Ten thousand times more active than the Sun,
Thou reign'd, and with a mighty hand compos'd   40
Systems innumerable, matchless all,
All stampt with thine uncounterfeited seal.
   But yet (if still to more stupendous heights
The Muse unblam'd her aching sense may strain)
Perhaps wrapt up in contemplation deep,   45
The best of Beings on the noblest theme
Might ruminate at leisure, Scope immense
Th' eternal Pow'r and Godhead to explore,
And with itself th' omniscient mind replete.
This were enough to fill the boundless All,   50
This were a Sabbath worthy the Supreme!
Perhaps enthron'd amidst a choicer few,
Of Spirits inferior, he might greatly plan
The two prime Pillars of the Universe,
Creation and Redemption – and a while   55
Pause – with the grand presentiments of glory.
   Perhaps – but all's conjecture here below,
All ignorance, and self-plum'd vanity –
O Thou, whose ways to wonder at's distrust,
Whom to describe's presumption (all we can, –   60
And all we may –) be glorified, be prais'd.
   A Day shall come, when all this Earth shall perish,
Nor leave behind ev'n Chaos; it shall come
When all the armies of the elements

Shall war against themselves, and mutual rage   65
To make Perdition triumph; it shall come,
When the capacious atmosphere above
Shall in sulphureous thunders groan, and die,
And vanish into void; the earth beneath
Shall sever to the center, and devour   70
Th' enormous blaze of the destructive flames.
Ye rocks, that mock the raving of the floods,
And proudly frown upon th' impatient deep,
Where is your grandeur now? Ye foaming waves,
That all along th' immense Atlantic roar,   75
In vain ye swell; will a few drops suffice
To quench the inextinguishable fire?
Ye mountains, on whose cloud-crown'd tops the cedars
Are lessen'd into shrubs, magnific piles,
That prop the painted chambers of the heav'ns   80
And fix the earth continual; Athos, where;
Where, Tenerif's thy stateliness to-day?
What, Aetna, are thy flames to these? – No more
Than the poor glow-worm to the golden Sun.

      Nor shall the verdant valleys then remain   85
Safe in their meek submission; they the debt
Of nature and of justice too must pay.
Yet I must weep for you, ye rival fair,
Arno and Andalusia; but for thee
More largely and with filial tears must weep,   90
O Albion, O my Country; Thou must join,
In vain dissever'd from the rest, must join
The terrors of th' inevitable ruin.

      Nor thou, illustrious monarch of the day;
Nor thou, fair queen of night; nor you, ye stars,   95
Tho' million leagues and million still remote,
Shall yet survive that day; Ye must submit
Sharers, not bright spectators of the scene.

      But tho' the Earth shall to the center perish,
Nor leave behind ev'n Chaos; tho' the air   100
With all the elements must pass away,
Vain as an idiot's dream; tho' the huge rocks,

That brandish the tall cedars on their tops,
With humbler vales must to perdition yield;
Tho' the gilt Sun, and silver-tressed Moon   105
With all her bright retinue, must be lost;
Yet Thou, Great Father of the world, surviv'st
Eternal, as thou wert: Yet still survives
The soul of man immortal, perfect now,
And candidate for unexpiring joys.   110
    He comes! He comes! the awful trump I hear;
The flaming sword's intolerable blaze
I see; He comes! th' Archangel from above.
'Arise, ye tenants of the silent grave,
Awake incorruptible and arise: 115
From east to west, from the antarctic pole
To regions hyperborean, all ye sons,
Ye sons of Adam, and ye heirs of Heav'n –
Arise, ye tenants of the silent grave,
Awake incorruptible and arise.'   120
    'Tis then, nor sooner, that the restless mind
Shall find itself at home; and like the ark
Fix'd on the mountain-top, shall look aloft
O'er the vague passage of precarious life;
And, winds and waves and rocks and tempests past,   125
Enjoy the everlasting calm of Heav'n:
'Tis then, nor sooner, that the deathless soul
Shall justly know its nature and its rise:
'Tis then the human tongue new-tun'd shall give
Praises more worthy the eternal ear.   130
Yet what we can, we ought; – and therefore, Thou,
Purge thou my heart, Omnipotent and Good!
Purge thou my heart with hyssop, lest like Cain
I offer fruitless sacrifice, and with gifts
Offend and not propitiate the Ador'd.   135
Tho' gratitude were bless'd with all the pow'rs
Her bursting heart could long for, tho' the swift,
The firey-wing'd imagination soar'd
Beyond ambition's wish – yet all were vain
To speak Him as he is, who is INEFFABLE.   140

Yet still let reason thro' the eye of faith
View Him with fearful love; let truth pronounce,
And adoration on her bended knee
With Heav'n-directed hands confess His reign.
And let th' Angelic, Archangelic band   145
With all the Hosts of Heav'n, Cherubic forms,
And forms Seraphic, with their silver trumps
And golden lyres attend: – 'For Thou art holy,
For thou art One, th' Eternal, who alone
Exerts all goodness, and transcends all praise.'   150

On the Immensity of the Supreme Being

Once more I dare to rouse the sounding string
The Poet of my God – Awake my glory,
Awake my lute and harp – my self shall wake,
Soon as the stately night-exploding bird
In lively lay sings welcome to the dawn.   5
   List ye! how nature with ten thousand tongues
Begins the grand thanksgiving, Hail, all hail,
Ye tenants of the forest and the field!
My fellow subjects of th' eternal King,
I gladly join your Mattins, and with you   10
Confess his presence, and report his praise.
   O Thou, who or the Lambkin, or the Dove
When offer'd by the lowly, meek, and poor,
Prefer'st to Pride's whole hecatomb, accept
This mean Essay, nor from thy treasure-house   15
Of Glory' immense the Orphan's mite exclude.
   What tho' th' Almighty's regal throne be rais'd
High o'er yon azure Heav'n's exalted dome
By mortal eye unken'd – where East nor West
Nor South, nor blust'ring North has breath to blow;   20
Albeit He there with Angels, and with Saints
Hold conference, and to his radiant host
Ev'n face to face stand visibly confest:

Yet know that nor in Presence or in Pow'r
Shines He less perfect here; 'tis Man's dim eye   25
That makes th' obscurity. He is the same,
Alike in all his Universe the same.
   Whether the mind along the spangled Sky
Measures her pathless walk, studious to view
Thy works of vaster fabric, where the Planets   30
Weave their harmonious rounds, their march directing
Still faithful, still inconstant to the Sun;
Or where the Comet thro' space infinite
(Tho' whirling worlds oppose and globes of fire)
Darts, like a javelin, to his destin'd goal.   35
Or where in Heav'n above the Heav'n of Heav'ns
Burn brighter Suns, and goodlier Planets roll
With Satellites more glorious – Thou art there.
   Or whether on the Ocean's boist'rous back
Thou ride triumphant, and with out-stretch'd arm   40
Curb the wild winds and discipline the billows,
The suppliant Sailor finds Thee there, his chief,
His only help – When Thou rebuk'st the storm –
It ceases – and the vessel gently glides
Along the glassy level of the calm.   45
   Oh! could I search the bosom of the sea,
Down the great depth descending; there thy works
Would also speak thy residence; and there
Would I thy servant, like the still profound,
Astonish'd into silence muse thy praise!   50
Behold! behold! th' unplanted garden round
Of vegetable coral, sea-flow'rs gay,
And shrubs of amber from the pearl-pav'd bottom
Rise richly varied, where the finny race
In blithe security their gambols play: 55
While high above their heads Leviathan
The terror and the glory of the main
His pastime takes with transport, proud to see
The ocean's vast dominion all his own.
   Hence thro' the genial bowels of the earth   60
Easy may fancy pass; till at thy mines

Gani or Raolconda she arrive,
And from the adamant's imperial blaze
Form weak ideas of her maker's glory.
Next to Pegu or Ceylon let me rove,   65
Where the rich ruby (deem'd by Sages old
Of Sovereign virtue) sparkles ev'n like Sirius
And blushes into flames. Thence will I go
To undermine the treasure-fertile womb
Of the huge Pyrenean, to detect   70
The Agate and the deep-intrenched gem
Of kindred Jasper – Nature in them both
Delights to play the Mimic on herself;
And in their veins she oft portrays the forms
Of leaning hills, of trees erect, and streams   75
Now stealing softly on, now thund'ring down
In desperate cascade with flow'rs and beasts
And all the living landskip of the vale:
In vain thy pencil Claudio, or Poussin,
Or thine, immortal Guido, would essay   80
Such skill to imitate – it is the hand
Of God himself – for God himself is there.
   Hence with the ascending springs let me advance,
Thro' beds of magnets, minerals and spar,
Up to the mountain's summit, there t' indulge   85
Th' ambition of the comprehensive eye,
That dares to call th' Horizon all her own.
Behold the forest, and the expansive verdure
Of yonder level lawn, whose smooth-shorn sod
No object interrupts, unless the oak   90
His lordly head uprears, and branching arms
Extends – Behold in regal solitude,
And pastoral magnificence he stands
So simple! and so great! the under-wood
Of meaner rank an awful distance keep.   95
Yet Thou art there, yet God himself is there
Ev'n on the bush (tho' not as when to Moses
He shone in burning Majesty reveal'd)
Nathless conspicuous in the Linnet's throat

Is his unbounded goodness – Thee her Maker,   100
Thee her Preserver chants she in her song;
While all the emulative vocal tribe
The grateful lesson learn – no other voice
Is heard, no other sound – for in attention
Buried, ev'n babbling *Echo* holds her peace.   105
   Now from the plains, where th' unbounded prospect
Gives liberty her utmost scope to range,
Turn we to yon enclosures, where appears
Chequer'd variety in all her forms,
Which the vague mind attract and still suspend   110
With sweet perplexity. What are yon tow'rs
The work of lab'ring man and clumsy art
Seen with the ring-dove's nest – on that tall beech
Her pensile house the feather'd Artist builds –
The rocking winds molest her not; for see,   115
With such due poise the wond'rous fabric's hung,
That, like the compass in the bark, it keeps
True to itself and steadfast ev'n in storms.
Thou idiot that asserts, there is no God,
View and be dumb for ever –   120
Go bid Vitruvius or Palladio build
The bee his mansion, or the ant her cave –
Go call Correggio, or let Titian come
To paint the hawthorn's bloom, or teach the cherry
To blush with just vermilion – hence away –   125
Hence ye profane! for God himself is here.
Vain were th' attempt, and impious to trace
Thro' all his works th' Artificer Divine –
And tho' nor shining sun, nor twinkling star
Bedeck'd the crimson curtains of the sky;   130
Tho' neither vegetable, beast, nor bird
Were extant on the surface of this ball,
Nor lurking gem beneath; tho' the great sea
Slept in profound stagnation, and the air
Had left no thunder to pronounce its maker;   135
Yet man at home, within himself, might find
The Deity immense, and in that frame

So fearfully, so wonderfully made,
See and adore his providence and pow'r –
I see, and I adore – O God most bounteous!   140
O infinite of Goodness and of Glory!
The knee, that thou hast shap'd, shall bend to Thee,
The tongue, which thou hast tun'd, shall chant thy praise,
And, thine own image, the immortal soul,
Shall consecrate herself to Thee for ever.   145

On the Omniscience of the Supreme Being

Arise, divine Urania, with new strains
To hymn thy God, and thou, immortal Fame,
Arise, and blow thy everlasting trump.
All glory to th' Omniscient, and praise,
And pow'r, and domination in the height!   5
And thou, cherubic Gratitude, whose voice
To pious ears sounds silverly so sweet,
Come with thy precious incense, bring thy gifts,
And with thy choicest stores the altar crown.
Thou too, my Heart, whom he, and he alone   10
Who all things knows, can know, with love replete,
Regenerate, and pure, pour all thyself
A living sacrifice before his throne:
And may th' eternal, high mysterious tree,
That in the center of the arched Heav'ns   15
Bears the rich fruit of Knowledge, with some branch
Stoop to my humble reach, and bless my toil!
    When in my mother's womb conceal'd I lay
A senseless embryo, then my soul thou knewst,
Knewst all her future workings, every thought,   20
And every faint idea yet unform'd.
When up the imperceptible ascent
Of growing years, led by thy hand, I rose,
Perception's gradual light, that ever dawns
Insensibly to day, thou didst vouchsafe,   25

And taught me by that reason thou inspir'dst,
That what of knowledge in my mind was low,
Imperfect, incorrect – in Thee is wondrous,
Uncircumscrib'd, unsearchably profound,
And estimable solely by itself.   30
   What is that secret pow'r, that guides the brutes,
Which Ignorance calls instinct? 'Tis from Thee,
It is the operation of thine hands
Immediate, instantaneous; 'tis thy wisdom,
That glorious shines transparent thro' thy works.   35
Who taught the Pye, or who forewarn'd the Jay
To shun the deadly nightshade? tho' the cherry
Boasts not a glossier hue, nor does the plum
Lure with more seeming sweets the amorous eye,
Yet will not the sagacious birds, decoy'd   40
By fair appearance, touch the noxious fruit.
They know to taste is fatal, whence alarm'd
Swift on the winnowing winds they work their way.
Go to, proud reas'ner philosophic Man,
Hast thou such prudence, thou such knowledge? – No.   45
Full many a race has fell into the snare
Of meretricious looks, of pleasing surface,
And oft in desert isles the famish'd pilgrim
By forms of fruit, and luscious taste beguil'd,
Like his forefather Adam, eats and dies.   50
For why? his wisdom on the leaden feet
Of slow experience, dully tedious, creeps,
And comes, like vengeance, after long delay.
   The venerable Sage, that nightly trims
The learned lamp, t'investigate the pow'rs   55
Of plants medicinal, the earth, the air,
And the dark regions of the fossil world,
Grows old in following, what he ne'er shall find;
Studious in vain! till haply, at the last
He spies a mist, then shapes it into mountains,   60
And baseless fabrics from conjecture builds.
While the domestic animal, that guards
At midnight hours his threshold, if oppress'd

By sudden sickness, at his master's feet
Begs not that aid his services might claim,   65
But is his own physician, knows the case,
And from th'emetic herbage works his cure.
Hark from afar the *feather'd matron screams,
And all her brood alarms, the docile crew
Accept the signal one and all, expert   70
In th' art of nature and unlearn'd deceit:
Along the sod, in counterfeited death,
Mute, motionless they lie; full well appriz'd
That the rapacious adversary's near.
But who inform'd her of th' approaching danger,   75
Who taught the cautious mother, that the hawk
Was hatcht her foe, and liv'd by her destruction?
Her own prophetic soul is active in her,
And more than human providence her guard.
    When Philomela, ere the cold domain   80
Of crippled winter gins t'advance, prepares
Her annual flight, and in some poplar shade
Takes her melodious leave, who then's her pilot?
Who points her passage thro' the pathless void
To realms from us remote, to us unknown?   85
Her science is the science of her God.
Not the magnetic index to the North
E'er ascertains her course, nor buoy, nor beacon.
She heav'n-taught voyager, that sails in air,
Courts nor coy West nor East, but instant knows   90
What † Newton, or not sought, or sought in vain.
    Illustrious name, irrefragable proof
Of man's vast genius, and the soaring soul!
Yet what wert thou to him, who knew his works,
Before creation form'd them, long before   95
He measur'd in the hollow of his hand
Th' exulting ocean, and the highest Heav'ns
He comprehended with a span, and weigh'd

* The Hen Turkey.
† The Longitude.

The mighty mountains in his golden Scales:
Who shone supreme, who was himself the light,   100
Ere yet Refraction learn'd her skill to paint,
And bend athwart the clouds her beauteous bow.
   When Knowledge at her father's dread command
Resign'd to Israel's king her golden key,
Oh to have join'd the frequent auditors   105
In wonder and delight, that whilom heard
Great Solomon descanting on the brutes.
Oh how sublimely glorious to apply
To God's own honour, and good will to man,
That wisdom he alone of men possess'd   110
In plenitude so rich, and scope so rare.
How did he rouse the pamper'd silken sons
Of bloated ease, by placing to their view
The sage industrious ant, the wisest insect,
And best œconomist of all the field!   115
Tho' she presumes not by the solar orb
To measure times and seasons, nor consults
Chaldean calculations, for a guide;
Yet conscious that December's on the march
Pointing with icy hand to want and woe,   120
She waits his dire approach, and undismay'd
Receives him as a welcome guest, prepar'd
Against the churlish winter's fiercest blow.
For when, as yet the favourable Sun
Gives to the genial earth th' enlivening ray,   125
Not the poor suffering slave, that hourly toils
To rive the groaning earth for ill-sought gold,
Endures such trouble, such fatigue, as she;
While all her subterraneous avenues,
And storm-proof cells with management most meet   130
And unexampled housewif'ry she forms:
Then to the field she hies, and on her back,
Burden immense! she bears the cumbrous corn.
Then many a weary step, and many a strain,
And many a grievous groan subdued, at length   135
Up the huge hill she hardly heaves it home:

Nor rests she here her providence, but nips
With subtle tooth the grain, lest from her garner
In mischievous fertility it steal,
And back to day-light vegetate its way.   140
Go to the Ant, thou sluggard, learn to live,
And by her wary ways reform thine own.
But, if thy deaden'd sense, and listless thought
More glaring evidence demand; behold,
Where yon pellucid populous hive presents   145
A yet uncopied model to the world!
There Machiavel in the reflecting glass
May read himself a fool. The Chemist there
May with astonishment invidious view
His toils outdone by each plebeian Bee,   150
Who, at the royal mandate, on the wing
From various herbs, and from discordant flow'rs
A perfect harmony of sweets compounds.
    Avaunt Conceit, Ambition take thy flight
Back to the Prince of vanity and air!   155
Oh 'tis a thought of energy most piercing;
Form'd to make pride grow humble; form'd to force
Its weight on the reluctant mind, and give her
A true but irksome image of herself.
Woeful vicissitude! when Man, fall'n Man,   160
Who first from Heav'n from gracious God himself
Learn'd knowledge of the Brutes, must know by Brutes
Instructed and reproach'd, the scale of being;
By slow degrees from lowly steps ascend,
And trace Omniscience upwards to its spring!   165
Yet murmur not, but praise – for tho' we stand
Of many a Godlike privilege amerc'd
By Adam's dire transgression, tho' no more
Is Paradise our home, but o'er the portal
Hangs in terrific pomp the burning blade;   170
Still with ten thousand beauties blooms the Earth
With pleasures populous, and with riches crown'd.
Still is there scope for wonder and for love
Ev'n to their last exertion – show'rs of blessings

Far more than human virtue can deserve,   175
Or hope expect, or gratitude return.
Then O ye People, O ye Sons of men,
Whatever be the colour of your lives,
Whatever portion of itself his Wisdom
Shall deign t'allow, still patiently abide,   180
And praise him more and more; nor cease to chant
ALL GLORY TO TH' OMNISCIENT, AND PRAISE,
AND POW'R, AND DOMINATION IN THE
    HEIGHT!
And thou, cherubic Gratitude, whose voice
To pious ears sounds silverly so sweet,   185
Come with thy precious incense, bring thy gifts,
And with thy choicest stores the altar crown.

                    ΤΩ ΘΕΩ ΔΟΞΑ.

On the Power of the Supreme Being

'Tremble, thou earth! th' anointed poet said,
At God's bright presence, tremble, all ye mountains
And all ye hillocks on the surface bound.'
Then once again, ye glorious thunders roll,
The Muse with transport hears ye, once again   5
Convulse the solid continent, and shake,
Grand musick of omnipotence, the isles.
'Tis thy terrific voice, thou God of power,
'Tis thy terrific voice; all Nature hears it
Awaken'd and alarm'd; she feels its force,   10
In every spring she feels it, every wheel,
And every movement of her vast machine.
Behold! quakes Apennine, behold! recoils
Athos, and all the hoary-headed Alps
Leap from their bases at the godlike sound.   15
But what is this, celestial tho' the note,
And proclamation of the reign supreme,

Compar'd with such as, for a mortal ear
Too great, amaze the incorporeal worlds?
Should ocean to his congregated waves   20
Call in each river, cataract, and lake,
And with the wat'ry world down an huge rock
Fall headlong in one horrible cascade,
'Twere but the echo of the parting breeze,
When Zephyr faints upon the lily's breast,   25
'Twere but the ceasing of some instrument,
When the last ling'ring undulation
Dies on the doubting ear, if nam'd with sounds
So mighty! so stupendous! so divine!
    But not alone in the aërial vault   30
Does he the dread theocracy maintain:
For oft, enrag'd with his intestine thunders,
He harrows up the bowels of the earth,
And shocks the central magnet. – Cities then
Totter on their foundations, stately columns,   35
Magnific walls, and heav'n-assaulting spires.
What tho' in haughty eminence erect
Stands the strong citadel, and frowns defiance
On adverse hosts, tho' many a bastion jut
Forth from the rampart's elevated mound,   40
Vain the poor providence of human art,
And mortal strength how vain! while underneath
Triumphs his mining vengeance in th' uproar
Of shatter'd towers, riven rocks, and mountains,
With clamour inconceivable uptorn,   45
And hurl'd adown th' abyss. Sulphureous pyrites
Bursting abrupt from darkness into day,
With din outrageous and destructive ire
Augment the hideous tumult, while it wounds
Th' afflicted ear, and terrifies the eye,   50
And rends the heart in twain. Twice have we felt,
Within Augusta's walls twice have we felt
They threaten'd indignation, but ev'n Thou,
Incens'd Omnipotent, art gracious ever,
Thy goodness infinite but mildly warn'd us   55

With mercy-blended wrath; O spare us still,
Nor send more dire conviction: we confess
That thou art He, th' Almighty: we believe.
For at thy righteous power whole systems quake,
For at thy nod tremble ten thousand worlds.   60
   Hark! on the winged Whirlwind's rapid rage,
Which is and is not in a moment – hark!
On th' hurricane's tempestuous sweep he rides
Invincible, and oaks and pines and cedars
And forests are no more. For conflict dreadful!   65
The West encounters East, and Notus meets
In his career the Hyperborean blast.
The lordly lions shudd'ring seek their dens,
And fly like tim'rous deer; the king of birds,
Who dar'd the solar ray, is weak of wing   70
And faints and falls and dies; – while He supreme
Stands steadfast in the center of the storm.
   Wherefore, ye objects terrible and great,
Ye thunders, earthquakes, and ye fire-fraught wombs
Of fell Volcanos, whirlwinds, hurricanes,   75
And boiling billows hail! in chorus join
To celebrate and magnify your Maker,
Who yet in works of a minuter mould
Is not less manifest, is not less mighty.
   Survey the magnet's sympathetic love,   80
That woos the yielding needle; contemplate
Th' attractive amber's pow'r, invisible
Ev'n to the mental eye; or when the blow
Sent from th' electric sphere assaults thy frame,
Shew me the hand, that dealt it! – baffled here   85
By his omnipotence Philosophy
Slowly her thoughts inadequate revolves,
And stands, with all his circling wonders round her,
Like heavy Saturn in th' etherial space
Begirt with an inexplicable ring.   90
   If such the operations of his power,
Which at all seasons and in ev'ry place
(Rul'd by establish'd laws and current nature)

Arrest th' attention! Who? O Who shall tell
His acts miraculous, when his own decrees   95
Repeals he, or suspends, when by the hand
Of Moses or of Joshua, or the mouths
Of his prophetic seers, such deeds he wrought,
Before th' astonish'd Sun's all seeing eye,
That Faith was scarce a virtue. Need I sing   100
The fate of Pharaoh and his numerous band
Lost in the reflux of the wat'ry walls,
That melted to their fluid state again?
Need I recount how Sampson's warlike arm
With more than mortal nerves was strung t' o'erthrow   105
Idolatrous Philistia? shall I tell
How David triumph'd, and what Job sustain'd?
– But, O supreme, unutterable mercy!
O love unequal'd, mystery immense,
Which angels long t' unfold! 'tis man's redemption   110
That crowns thy glory, and thy pow'r confirms,
Confirms the great, th' uncontroverted claim.
When from the Virgin's unpolluted womb
Shone forth the Sun of Righteousness reveal'd,
And on benighted reason pour'd the day;   115
Let there be peace (he said) and all was calm
Amongst the warring world – calm as the sea,
When O be still, ye boisterous Winds, he cry'd,
And not a breath was blown, nor murmur heard.
His was a life of miracles and might,   120
And charity and love, ere yet he taste
The bitter draught of death, ere yet he rise
Victorious o'er the universal foe,
And Death and Sin and Hell in triumph lead.
His by the right of conquest is mankind,   125
And in sweet servitude and golden bonds
Were ty'd to him for ever. – O how easy
Is his ungalling yoke, and all his burdens
'Tis ecstasy to bear! Him blessed Shepherd
His flocks shall follow thro' the maze of life   130
And shades that tend to Day-spring from on high;

And as the radiant roses after fading
In fuller foliage and more fragrant breath
Revive in smiling spring, so shall it fare
With those that love him – for sweet is their savour,   135
And all eternity shall be their spring.
Then shall the gates and everlasting doors,
At which the *King of Glory* enters in,
Be to the Saints unbarr'd: and there, where pleasure
Boasts an undying bloom, where dubious hope   140
Is certainty, and grief-attended love
Is freed from passion – there we'll celebrate
With worthier numbers, him, who is, and was,
And in immortal prowess King of Kings
Shall be the Monarch of all worlds for ever.   145

On the Goodness of the Supreme Being

Orpheus, for* so the Gentiles call'd thy name,
Israel's sweet Psalmist, who alone couldst wake
Th' inanimate to motion; who alone
The joyful hillocks, the applauding rocks,
And floods with musical persuasion drew;   5
Thou who to hail and snow gav'st voice and sound,
And mad'st the mute melodious! – greater yet
Was thy divinest skill and rul'd o'er more
Than art and nature; for thy tuneful touch
Drove trembling Satan from the heart of Saul,   10
And quell'd the evil Angel: – in this breast
Some portion of thy genuine spirit breathe,
And lift me from myself each thought impure
Banish; each low idea raise, refine,
Enlarge, and sanctify; – so shall the muse   15
Above the stars aspire, and aim to praise

* See this conjecture strongly supported by Delany, in his *Life of David*.

Her God on earth, as he is prais'd in heaven.
  Immense Creator! whose all-pow'rful hand
Fram'd universal Being, and whose Eye
Saw like thyself, that all things form'd were good;   20
Where shall the tim'rous bard thy praise begin,
Where end the purest sacrifice of song,
And just thanksgiving? – The thought-kindling light,
Thy prime production, darts upon my mind
Its vivifying beams, my heart illumines,   25
And fills my soul with gratitude and Thee.
Hail to the cheerful rays of ruddy morn,
That paint the streaky East, and blithsome rouse
The birds, the cattle, and mankind from rest!
Hail to the freshness of the early breeze,   30
And Iris dancing on the new-fall'n dew!
Without the aid of yonder golden globe
Lost were the garnet's lustre, lost the lily,
The tulip and auricula's spotted pride;
Lost were the peacock's plumage, to the sight   35
So pleasing in its pomp and glossy glow.
O thrice-illustrious! were it not for thee
Those pansies, that reclining from the bank,
View thro' th' immaculate, pellucid stream
Their portraiture in the inverted heaven,   40
Might as well change their triple boast, the white,
The purple, and the gold, that far outvie
The Eastern monarch's garb, ev'n with the dock,
Ev'n with the baneful hemlock's irksome green.
Without thy aid, without thy gladsome beams   45
The tribes of woodland warblers would remain
Mute on the bending branches, nor recite
The praise of him, who, ere he form'd their flight,
Their voices tun'd to transport, wing'd their flight,
And bade them call for nurture, and receive;   50
And lo! they call; the blackbird and the thrush,
The woodlark, and the redbreast jointly call;
He hears and feeds their feather'd families,
He feeds his sweet musicians, – nor neglects

Th' invoking ravens in the greenwood wide;   55
And tho' their throats coarse ruttling hurt the ear,
They mean it all for music, thanks and praise
They mean, and leave ingratitude to man; –
But not to all, – for hark! the organs blow
Their swelling notes round the cathedral's dome,   60
And grace th' harmonious choir, celestial feast
To pious ears, and med'cine of the mind;
The thrilling trebles and the manly base
Join in accordance meet, and with one voice
All to the sacred subject suit their song: 65
While in each breast sweet melancholy reigns
Angelically pensive, till the joy
Improves and purifies; – the solemn scene
The Sun thro' storied panes surveys with awe,
And bashfully with-holds each bolder beam.   70
Here, as her home, from morn to eve frequents
The cherub Gratitude; – behold her Eyes!
With love and gladness weepingly they shed
Ecstatic smiles; the incense, that her hands
Uprear, is sweeter than the breath of May   75
Caught from the nectarine's blossom, and her voice
Is more than voice can tell; to him she sings,
To him who feeds, who clothes and who adorns,
Who made and who preserves, whatever dwells
In air, in steadfast earth, or fickle sea.   80
O He is good, he is immensely good!
Who all things form'd, and form'd them all for man;
Who mark'd the climates, varied every zone,
Dispensing all his blessings for the best
In order and in beauty: – rise, attend,   85
Attest, and praise, ye quarters of the world!
Bow down, ye elephants, submissive bow
To him, who made the mite; tho' Asia's pride,
Ye carry armies on your tow'r-crown'd backs,
And grace the turban'd tyrants, bow to him   90
Who is as great, as perfect and as good
In his less-striking wonders, till at length

The eye's at fault and seeks th' assisting glass.
Approach and bring from Araby the blest
The fragrant cassia, frankincense and myrrh,   95
And meekly kneeling at the altar's foot
Lay all the tributary incense down.
Stoop, sable Africa, with rev'rence stoop,
And from thy brow take off the painted plume;
With golden ingots all thy camels load   100
T' adorn his temples, hasten with thy spear
Reverted and thy trusty bow unstrung,
While unpursu'd thy lions roam and roar,
And ruin'd tow'rs, rude rocks and caverns wide
Remurmur to the glorious, surly sound.   105
And thou, fair Indian, whose immense domain
To counterpoise the Hemisphere extends,
Haste from the West, and with thy fruits and flow'rs,
Thy mines and med'cines, wealthy maid, attend.
More than the plenteousness so fam'd to flow   110
By fabling bards from Amalthea's horn
Is thine; thine therefore be a portion due
Of thanks and praise: come with thy brilliant crown
And vest of furr; and from thy fragrant lap
Pomegranates and the rich *ananas pour.   115
But chiefly thou, Europa, seat of grace
And Christian excellence, his goodness own,
Forth from ten thousand temples pour his praise;
Clad in the armour of the living God
Approach, unsheath the spirit's flaming sword;   120
Faith's shield, Salvation's glory, – compass'd helm
With fortitude assume, and o'er your heart
Fair truth's invulnerable breast-plate spread;
Then join the general chorus of all worlds,
And let the song of charity begin   125
In strains seraphic, and melodious pray'r.
    'O all-sufficient, all-beneficent,
Thou God of Goodness and of glory, hear!

* Ananas the Indian name for Pine-Apples.

Thou, who to lowliest minds dost condescend,
Assuming passions to enforce thy laws,   130
Adopting jealousy to prove thy love:
Thou, who resign'd humility uphold,
Ev'n as the florist props the drooping rose,
But quell tyrannic pride with peerless pow'r,
Ev'n as the tempest rives the stubborn oak: 135
O all-sufficient, all-beneficent,
Thou God of goodness and of glory hear!
Bless all mankind, and bring them in the end
To heav'n, to immortality, and THEE!'

Hymn to the Supreme Being

On Recovery from a dangerous Fit of Illness

When *Israel's ruler on the royal bed
    In anguish and in perturbation lay,
The down reliev'd not his anointed head,
    And rest gave place to horror and dismay.
Fast flow'd the tears, high heav'd each gasping sigh   5
When God's own prophet thunder'd – MONARCH,
    THOU MUST DIE.

And must I go, th' illustrious mourner cry'd,
    I who have serv'd thee still in faith and truth,
Whose snow-white conscience no foul crime has dy'd
    From youth to manhood, infancy to youth,   10
Like David, who have still rever'd thy word
The sovereign of myself and servant of the Lord!

The judge Almighty heard his suppliant's moan,
    Repeal'd his sentence, and his health restor'd;
The beams of mercy on his temples shone,   15
    Shot from that heaven to which his sighs had soar'd;

* Hezekiah vide Isaiah xxxviii.

The *sun retreated at his maker's nod
And miracles confirm the genuine work of God.

But, O immortals! What had I to plead
   When death stood o'er me with his threat'ning lance,   20
When reason left me in the time of need,
   And sense was lost in terror or in trance,
My sick'ning soul was with my blood inflam'd,
And the celestial image sunk, defac'd and maim'd.

I sent back memory, in heedful guise,   25
   To search the records of preceding years;
Home, like the †raven to the ark, she flies,
   Croaking bad tidings to my trembling ears.
O Sun, again that thy retreat was made,
And threw my follies back into the friendly shade!   30

But who are they, that bid affliction cease! –
   Redemption and forgiveness, heavenly sounds!
Behold the dove that brings the branch of peace,
   Behold the balm that heals the gaping wounds –
Vengeance divine's by penitence supprest –   35
She ‡struggles with the angel, conquers, and is blest.

Yet hold, presumption, nor too fondly climb,
   And thou too hold, O horrible despair!
In man humility's alone sublime,
   Who diffidently hopes he's Christ's own care –   40
O all-sufficient Lamb! in death's dread hour
Thy merits who shall slight, or who can doubt thy power?

But soul-rejoicing health again returns,
   The blood meanders gently in each vein,
The lamp of life renew'd with vigour burns,   45
   And exil'd reason takes her seat again –
Brisk leaps the heart, the mind's at large once more,
To love, to praise, to bless, to wonder and adore.

* Isaiah, chap. xxxviii.
† Gen. viii. 7.
‡ Gen. xxxii. 24, 25, 26, 27, 28.

The virtuous partner of my nuptial bands,
   Appear'd a widow to my frantic sight;   50
My little prattlers lifting up their hands,
   Beckon me back to them, to life, and light;
I come, ye spotless sweets! I come again,
Nor have your tears been shed, nor have ye knelt in vain.

All glory to th' ETERNAL, to th' IMMENSE,   55
   All glory to th' OMNISCIENT and GOOD,
Whose power's uncircumscrib'd, whose love's intense;
   But yet whose justice ne'er could be withstood,
Except thro' him – thro' him, who stands alone,
Of worth, of weight allow'd for all Mankind t' atone!   60

He rais'd the lame, the lepers he made whole,
   He fix'd the palsied nerves of weak decay,
He drove out Satan from the tortur'd soul,
   And to the blind gave or restor'd the day, –
Nay more, – far more unequal'd pangs sustain'd,   65
Till his lost fallen flock his taintless blood regain'd.

My feeble feet refus'd my body's weight,
   Nor would my eyes admit the glorious light,
My nerves convuls'd shook fearful of their fate,
   My mind lay open to the powers of night.   70
He pitying did a second birth bestow
A birth of joy – not like the first of tears and woe.

Ye strengthen'd feet, forth to his altar move;
   Quicken, ye new-strung nerves, th' enraptur'd lyre;
Ye heav'n-directed eyes, o'erflow with love;   75
   Glow, glow, my soul, with pure seraphic fire;
Deeds, thoughts, and words no more his mandates break,
But to his endless glory work, conceive, and speak.

O! penitence, to virtue near allied,
   Thou can'st new joys e'en to the blest impart;   80
The list'ning angels lay their harps aside
   To hear the music of thy contrite heart;

And heav'n itself wears a more radiant face,
When charity presents thee to the throne of grace.

*Chief of metallic forms is regal gold;   85
    Of elements, the limpid fount that flows;
Give me 'mongst gems the brilliant to behold;
    O'er Flora's flock imperial is the rose:
Above all birds the sov'reign eagle soars;
And monarch of the field the lordly lion roars.   90

What can with great Leviathan compare,
    Who takes his pastime in the mighty main?
What, like the *Sun*, shines thro' the realms of air,
    And gilds and glorifies th' ethereal plain –
Yet what are these to man, who bears the sway?   95
For all was made for him – to serve and to obey.

Thus in high heaven charity is great,
    Faith, hope, devotion hold a lower place;
On her the cherubs and the seraphs wait,
    Her, every virtue courts, and every grace;   100
See! on the right, close by th' Almighty's throne,
In him she shines confest, who came to make her known.

Deep-rooted in my heart then let her grow,
    That for the past the future may atone;
That I may act what thou hast giv'n to know,   105
    That I may live for THEE and THEE alone,
And justify those sweetest words from heav'n,
    'THAT HE SHALL LOVE THEE MOST
        †TO WHOM THOU'ST MOST FORGIVEN.'

* Pind. Olymp. 1.
† Luke vii. 41, 42, 43.

JUBILATE AGNO

Fragment A

Rejoice in God, O ye Tongues; give the glory to the Lord, and the Lamb.

Nations, and languages, and every Creature, in which is the breath of Life.

Let man and beast appear before him, and magnify his name together.

Let Noah and his company approach the throne of Grace, and do homage to the Ark of their Salvation.

Let Abraham present a Ram, and worship the God of his Redemption. 5

Let Isaac, the Bridegroom, kneel with his Camels, and bless the hope of his pilgrimage.

Let Jacob, and his speckled Drove adore the good Shepherd of Israel.

Let Esau offer a scape Goat for his seed, and rejoice in the blessing of God his father.

Let Nimrod, the mighty hunter, bind a Leopard to the altar, and consecrate his spear to the Lord.

Let Ishmael dedicate a Tyger, and give praise for the liberty, in which the Lord has let him at large. 10

Let Balaam appear with an Ass, and bless the Lord his people and his creatures for a reward eternal.

Let Anah, the son of Zibion, lead a Mule to the temple, and bless God, who amerces the consolation of the creature for the service of Man.

Let Daniel come forth with a Lion, and praise God with all his might through faith in Christ Jesus.

Let Naphthali with an Hind give glory in the goodly words of Thanksgiving.

Let Aaron, the high priest, sanctify a Bull, and let him go free to the Lord and Giver of Life.

Let the Levites of the Lord take the Beavers of the brook alive into the Ark of the Testimony.

Let Eleazar with the Ermine serve the Lord decently and in purity.

Let Ithamar minister with a Chamois, and bless the name of Him, which clotheth the naked.

Let Gershom with an Pygarg (Hart) bless the name of Him, who feedeth the hungry.

Let Merari praise the wisdom and power of God with the Coney, who scoopeth the rock, and archeth in the sand.

Let Kohath serve with the Sable, and bless God in the ornaments of the Temple.

Let Jehoida bless God with an Hare, whose mazes are determined for the health of the body and to parry the adversary.

Let Ahitub humble himself with an Ape before Almighty God, who is the maker of variety and pleasantry.

Let Abiathar with a Fox praise the name of the Lord, who balances craft against strength and skill against number.

Let Moses, the Man of God, bless with a Lizard, in the sweet majesty of good-nature, and the magnanimity of meekness.

Let Joshua praise God with an Unicorn – the swiftness of the Lord, and the strength of the Lord, and the spear of the Lord mighty in battle.

Let Caleb with an Ounce praise the Lord of the Land of beauty and rejoice in the blessing of his good Report.

Let Othniel praise God with the Rhinoceros, who put on his armour for the reward of beauty in the Lord.

Let Tola bless with the Toad, which is the good creature of God, tho' his virtue is in the secret, and his mention is not made.

Let Barak praise with the Pard – and great is the might of the faithful and great is the Lord in the nail of Jael and in the sword of the Son of Abinoam.   30

Let Gideon bless with the Panther – the Word of the Lord is invincible by him that lappeth from the brook.

Let Jotham praise with the Urchin, who took up his parable and provided himself for the adversary to kick against the pricks.

Let Boaz, the Builder of Judah, bless with the Rat, which dwelleth in hardship and peril, that they may look to themselves and keep their houses in order.

Let Obed-Edom with a Dormouse praise the Name of the Lord God his Guest for increase of his store and for peace.

Let Abishai bless with the Hyaena – the terror of the Lord, and the fierceness, of his wrath against the foes of the King and of Israel.   35

Let Ethan praise with the Flea, his coat of mail, his piercer, and his vigour, which wisdom and providence have contrived to attract observation and to escape it.

Let Heman bless with the Spider, his warp and his woof, his subtlety and industry, which are good.

Let Chalcol praise with the Beetle, whose life is precious in the sight of God, tho' his appearance is against him.

Let Darda with a Leech bless the Name of the Physician of body and soul.

Let Mahol praise the Maker of Earth and Sea with the Otter, whom God has given to dive and to burrow for his preservation.   40

Let David bless with the Bear — The beginning of victory to
the Lord — to the Lord the perfection of excellence —
Hallelujah from the heart of God, and from the hand of
the artist inimitable, and from the echo of the heavenly
harp in sweetness magnifical and mighty.

Let Solomon praise with the Ant, and give the glory to the
Fountain of all Wisdom.

Let Romamti-ezer bless with the Ferret — The Lord is a
rewarder of them, that diligently seek him.

Let Samuel, the Minister from a child, without ceasing
praise with the Porcupine, which is the creature of
defence and stands upon his arms continually.

Let Nathan with the Badger bless God for his retired fame,   45
and privacy inaccessible to slander.

Let Joseph, who from the abundance of his blessing may
spare to him, that lacketh, praise with the Crocodile,
which is pleasant and pure, when he is interpreted, tho'
his look is of terror and offence.

Let Esdras bless Christ Jesus with the Rose and his people,
which is a nation of living sweetness.

Let Mephibosheth with the Cricket praise the God of
cheerfulness, hospitality, and gratitude.

Let Shallum with the Frog bless God for the meadows of
Canaan, the fleece, the milk and the honey.

Let Hilkiah praise with the Weasel, which sneaks for his   50
prey in craft, and dwelleth at ambush.

Let Job bless with the Worm — the life of the Lord is in
Humiliation, the Spirit also and the truth.

Let Elihu bless with the Tortoise, which is food for praise
and thanksgiving.

Let Hezekiah praise with the Dromedary — the zeal for the
glory of God is excellence, and to bear his burden is
grace.

Let Zadok worship with the Mole — before honour is
humility, and he that looketh low shall learn.

Let Gad with the Adder bless in the simplicity of the   55
preacher and the wisdom of the creature.

Let Tobias bless Charity with his Dog, who is faithful,
vigilant, and a friend in poverty.

Let Anna bless God with the Cat, who is worthy to be
presented before the throne of grace, when he has
trampled upon the idol in his prank.

Let Benaiah praise with the Asp — to conquer malice is
nobler, than to slay the lion.

Let Barzillai bless with the Snail — a friend in need is as the
balm of Gilead, or as the slime to the wounded bark.

Let Joab with the Horse worship the Lord God of Hosts.   60

Let Shemaiah bless God with the Caterpiller — the minister
of vengeance is the harbinger of mercy.

Let Ahimelech with the Locust bless God from the tyranny
of numbers.

Let Cornelius with the Swine bless God, which purifyeth all
things for the poor.

Let Araunah bless with the Squirrel, which is a gift of
homage from the poor man to the wealthy and
increaseth good will.

Let Bakbakkar bless with the Salamander, which feedeth   65
upon ashes as bread, and whose joy is at the mouth of
the furnace.

Let Jabez bless with Tarantula, who maketh his bed in the
moss, which he feedeth, that the pilgrim may take heed
to his way.

Let Jakim with the Satyr bless God in the dance. —

Let Iddo praise the Lord with the Moth — the writings of
man perish as the garment, but the Book of God
endureth for ever.

Let Nebuchadnezzar bless with the Grashopper – the pomp
and vanities of the world are as the herb of the field, but
the glory of the Lord increaseth for ever.

Let Naboth bless with the Canker-worm – envy is cruel   70
and killeth and preyeth upon that which God has given
to aspire and bear fruit.

Let Lud bless with the Elk, the strenuous asserter of his
liberty, and the maintainer of his ground.

Let Obadiah with the Palmer-worm bless God for the
remnant that is left.

Let Agur bless with the Cockatrice – The consolation of the
world is deceitful, and temporal honour the crown of
him that creepeth.

Let Ithiel bless with the Baboon, whose motions are regular
in the wilderness, and who defendeth himself with a staff
against the assailant.

Let Ucal bless with the Cameleon, which feedeth on the   75
Flowers and washeth himself in the dew.

Let Lemuel bless with the Wolf, which is a dog without a
master, but the Lord hears his cries and feeds him in the
desert.

Let Hananiah bless with the Civet, which is pure from
benevolence.

Let Azarias bless with the Reindeer, who runneth upon the
waters, and wadeth thro' the land in snow.

Let Mishael bless with the Stoat – the praise of the Lord
gives propriety to all things.

Let Savaran bless with the Elephant, who gave his life for   80
his country that he might put on immortality.

Let Nehemiah, the imitator of God, bless with the Monkey,
who is work'd down from Man.

Let Manasses bless with the Wild-Ass – liberty begetteth
insolence, but necessity is the mother of prayer.

Let Jebus bless with the Camelopard, which is good to
  carry and to parry and to kneel.

Let Huz bless with the Polypus – lively subtlety is
  acceptable to the Lord.

Let Buz bless with the Jackall – but the Lord is the Lion's   85
  provider.

Let Meshullam bless with the Dragon, who maketh his den
  in desolation and rejoiceth amongst the ruins.

Let Enoch bless with the Rackoon, who walked with God
  as by the instinct.

Let Hashbadana bless with the Catamountain, who stood
  by the Pulpit of God against the dissensions of the
  Heathen.

Let Ebed-Melech bless with the Mantiger, the blood of the
  Lord is sufficient to do away the offence of Cain, and
  reinstate the creature which is amerced.

Let A Little Child with a Serpent bless Him, who ordaineth   90
  strength in babes to the confusion of the Adversary.

Let Huldah bless with the Silkworm – the ornaments of the
  Proud are from the bowels of their Betters.

Let Susanna bless with the Butterfly – beauty hath wings,
  but chastity is the Cherub.

Let Sampson bless with the Bee, to whom the Lord hath
  given strength to annoy the assailant and wisdom to his
  strength.

Let Amasiah bless with the Chaffer – the top of the tree is
  for the brow of the champion, who has given the glory to
  God.

Let Hashum bless with the Fly, whose health is the honey   95
  of the air, but he feeds upon the thing strangled, and
  perisheth.

Let Malchiah bless with the Gnat – it is good for man and
  beast to mend their pace.

Let Pedaiah bless with the Humble-Bee, who loves himself in solitude and makes his honey alone.

Let Maaseiah bless with the Drone, who with the appearance of a Bee is neither a soldier nor an artist, neither a swordsman nor smith.

Let Urijah bless with the Scorpion, which is a scourge against the murmurers – the Lord keep it from our coasts.

Let Anaiah bless with the Dragon-fly, who sails over the pond by the wood-side and feedeth on the cresses. 100

Let Zorobabel bless with the Wasp, who is the Lord's architect, and buildeth his edifice in armour.

Let Jehu bless with the Hornet, who is the soldier of the Lord to extirpate abomination and to prepare the way of peace.

Let Mattithiah bless with the Bat, who inhabiteth the desolations of pride and flieth amongst the tombs.

Let Elias which is the innocency of the Lord rejoice with the Dove.

Let Asaph rejoice with the Nightingale – The musician of the Lord! and the watchman of the Lord! 105

Let Shema rejoice with the Glowworm, who is the lamp of the traveller and mead of the musician.

Let Jeduthun rejoice with the Woodlark, who is sweet and various.

Let Chenaniah rejoice with Chloris, in the vivacity of his powers and the beauty of his person.

Let Gideoni rejoice with the Goldfinch, who is shrill and loud, and full withal.

Let Giddalti rejoice with the Mocking-bird, who takes off the notes of the Aviary and reserves his own. 110

Let Jogli rejoice with the Linnet, who is distinct and of mild delight.

Let Benjamin bless and rejoice with the Redbird, who is
    soft and soothing.

Let Dan rejoice with the Blackbird, who praises God with
    all his heart, and biddeth to be of good cheer.

Fragment B

Let Elizur rejoice with the Partridge, who is a prisoner of
    state and is proud of his keepers.
*For I am not without authority in my jeopardy, which I
    derive inevitably from the glory of the name of the Lord.*

Let Shedeur rejoice with Pyrausta, who dwelleth in a
    medium of fire, which God hath adapted for him.
*For I bless God whose name is Jealous – and there is a zeal
    to deliver us from everlasting burnings.*

Let Shelumiel rejoice with Olor, who is of a goodly savour,
    and the very look of him harmonizes the mind.
*For my existimation is good even amongst the slanderers
    and my memory shall arise for a sweet savour unto the
    Lord.*

Let Jael rejoice with the Plover, who whistles for his live,
    and foils the marksmen and their guns.
*For I bless the PRINCE of PEACE and pray that all the
    guns may be nail'd up, save such as are for the rejoicing
    days.*

Let Raguel rejoice with the Cock of Portugal – God send   5
    good Angels to the allies of England!
*For I have abstained from the blood of the grape and that
    even at the Lord's table.*

Let Hobab rejoice with Necydalus, who is the Greek of a
    Grub.
*For I have glorified God in GREEK and LATIN, the
    consecrated languages spoken by the Lord on earth.*

Let Zurishaddai with the Polish Cock rejoice – The Lord
    restore peace to Europe.
*For I meditate the peace of Europe amongst family
    bickerings and domestic jars.*

Let Zuar rejoice with the Guinea Hen – The Lord add to
    his mercies in the WEST!
*For the HOST is in the WEST – the Lord make us thankful
    unto salvation.*

Let Chesed rejoice with Strepsiceros, whose weapons are
    the ornaments of his peace.
*For I preach the very GOSPEL of CHRIST without
    comment and with this weapon shall I slay envy.*

Let Hagar rejoice with Gnesion, who is the right sort of   10
    eagle, and towers the highest.
*For I bless God in the rising generation, which is on my
    side.*

Let Libni rejoice with the Redshank, who migrates not but
    is translated to the upper regions.
*For I have translated in the charity, which makes things
    better and I shall be translated myself at the last.*

Let Nahshon rejoice with the Seabreese, the Lord gives the
    sailors of his Spirit.
*For he that walked upon the sea, hath prepared the floods
    with the Gospel of peace.*

Let Helon rejoice with the Woodpecker – the Lord
    encourage the propagation of trees!
*For the merciful man is merciful to his beast, and to the
    trees that give them shelter.*

Let Amos rejoice with the Coote – prepare to meet thy
    God, O Israel.
*For he hath turned the shadow of death into the morning,
    the Lord is his name.*

Let Ephah rejoice with Buprestis, the Lord endue us with   15
    temperance and humanity, till every cow have her mate!
*For I am come home again, but there is nobody to kill the
    calf or to pay the music.*

Let Sarah rejoice with the Redwing, whose harvest is in the
frost and snow.
*For the hour of my felicity, like the womb of Sarah, shall
come at the latter end.*

Let Rebekah rejoice with Iynx, who holds his head on one
side to deceive the adversary.
*For I should have avail'd myself of waggery, had not
malice been multitudinous.*

Let Shuah rejoice with Boa, which is the vocal serpent.
*For there are still serpents that can speak – God bless my
head, my heart and my heel.*

Let Ehud rejoice with Onocrotalus, whose braying is for
the glory of God, because he makes the best music in his
power.
*For I bless God that I am of the same seed as Ehud, Mutius
Scaevola, and Colonel Draper.*

Let Shamgar rejoice with Otis, who looks about him for   20
the glory of God, and sees the horizon complete at once.
*For the word of God is a sword on my side – no matter
what other weapon a stick or a straw.*

Let Bohan rejoice with the Scythian Stag – he is beef and
breeches against want and nakedness.
*For I have adventured myself in the name of the Lord, and
he hath mark'd me for his own.*

Let Achsah rejoice with the Pigeon who is an antidote to
malignity and will carry a letter.
*For I bless God for the Postmaster general and all
conveyancers of letters under his care especially Allen
and Shelvock.*

Let Tohu rejoice with the Grouse – the Lord further the
cultivating of heaths and the peopling of deserts.
*For my grounds in New Canaan shall infinitely compensate
for the flats and mains of Staindrop Moor.*

Let Hillel rejoice with Ammodytes, whose colour is
deceitful and he plots against the pilgrim's feet.
*For the praise of God can give to a mute fish the notes of a
nightingale.*

Let Eli rejoice with Leucon – he is an honest fellow, which 25
is a rarity.
For I have seen the White Raven and Thomas Hall of
Willingham and am my self a greater curiosity than both.

Let Jemuel rejoice with Charadrius, who is from the
HEIGHT and the sight of him is good for the jaundice.
For I look up to heaven which is my prospect to escape
envy by surmounting it.

Let Pharaoh rejoice with Anataria, whom God permits to
prey upon the ducks to check their increase.
For if Pharaoh had known Joseph, he would have blessed
God and me for the illumination of the people.

Let Lotan rejoice with Sauterelle. Blessed be the name of
the Lord from the Lote-tree to the Palm.
For I pray God to bless improvements in gardening till
London be a city of palm-trees.

Let Dishon rejoice with the Landrail, God give his grace to
the society for preserving the game.
For I pray to give his grace to the poor of England, that
Charity be not offended and that benevolence may
increase.

Let Hushim rejoice with the King's Fisher, who is of royal 30
beauty, tho' plebeian size.
For in my nature I quested for beauty, but God, God hath
sent me to sea for pearls.

Let Machir rejoice with Convolvulus, from him to the ring
of Saturn, which is the girth of Job; to the signet of God
– from Job and his daughters BLESSED BE JESUS.
For there is a blessing from the STONE of JESUS which is
founded upon hell to the precious jewel on the right
hand of God.

Let Atad bless with Eleos, the nightly Memorialist ελεησον
κυριε.
For the nightly Visitor is at the window of the impenitent,
while I sing a psalm of my own composing.

Let Jamin rejoice with the Bittern – blessed be the name of Jesus for Denver Sluice, Ruston, and the draining of the fens.

For there is a note added to the scale, which the Lord hath made fuller, stronger and more glorious.

Let Ohad rejoice with Byturos who eateth the vine and is a minister of temperance.

For I offer my goat as he browses the vine, bless the Lord from chambering and drunkeness.

Let Zohar rejoice with Cychramus who cometh with the quails on a particular affair.

For there is a traveling for the glory of God without going to Italy or France.

Let Serah, the daughter of Asher, rejoice with Ceyx, who maketh his cabin in the Halcyon's hold.

For I bless the children of Asher for the evil I did them and the good I might have received at their hands.

Let Magdiel rejoice with Ascarides, which is the life of the bowels – the worm hath a part in our frame.

For I rejoice like a worm in the rain in him that cherishes and from him that tramples.

Let Becher rejoice with Oscen who terrifies the wicked, as trumpet and alarm the coward.

For I am ready for the trumpet and alarm to fight, to die and to rise again.

Let Shaul rejoice with Circos, who hath clumsy legs, but he can wheel it the better with his wings. –

For the banish'd of the Lord shall come about again, for so he hath prepared for them.

Let Hamul rejoice with the Crystal, who is pure and translucent.

For sincerity is a jewel which is pure and transparent, eternal and inestimable.

Let Ziphion rejoice with the Tit-Lark who is a groundling, but he raises the spirits.

For my hands and my feet are perfect as the sublimity of Naphtali and the felicity of Asher.

Let Mibzar rejoice with the Cadess, as is their number, so
  are their names, blessed be the Lord Jesus for them all.
For the names and number of animals are as the name and
  number of the stars. –

Let Jubal rejoice with Caecilia, the woman and the slow-
  worm praise the name of the Lord.
For I pray the Lord Jesus to translate my MAGNIFICAT
  into verse and represent it.

Let Arodi rejoice with the Royston Crow, there is a society
  of them at Trumpington and Cambridge.
For I bless the Lord Jesus from the bottom of Royston
  Cave to the top of King's Chapel.

Let Areli rejoice with the Criel, who is a dwarf that   45
  towereth above others.
For I am a little fellow, which is intitled to the great mess
  by the benevolence of God my father.

Let Phuvah rejoice with Platycerotes, whose weapons of
  defence keep them innocent.
For I this day made over my inheritance to my mother in
  consideration of her infirmities.

Let Shimron rejoice with the Kite, who is of more value
  than many sparrows.
For I this day made over my inheritance to my mother in
  consideration of her age.

Let Sered rejoice with the Wittal – a silly bird is wise unto
  his own preservation.
For I this day made over my inheritance to my mother in
  consideration of her poverty.

Let Elon rejoice with Attelabus, who is the Locust without
  wings.
For I bless the thirteenth of August, in which I had the
  grace to obey the voice of Christ in my conscience.

Let Jahleel rejoice with the Woodcock, who liveth upon   50
  suction and is pure from his diet.
For I bless the thirteenth of August, in which I was willing
  to run all hazards for the sake of the name of the Lord.

Let Shuni rejoice with the Gull, who is happy in not being
  good for food.
For I bless the thirteenth of August, in which I was willing
  to be called a fool for the sake of Christ.

Let Ezbon rejoice with Musimon, who is from the ram and
  she-goat.
For I lent my flocks and my herds and my lands at once
  unto the Lord.

Let Barkos rejoice with the Black Eagle, which is the least
  of his species and the best-natured.
For nature is more various than observation tho' observers
  be innumerable.

Let Bedan rejoice with Ossifrage – the bird of prey and the
  man of prayer.
For Agricola is Γηουργος.

Let Naomi rejoice with Pseudosphece who is between a   55
  wasp and a hornet.
For I pray God to bless POLLY in the blessing of Naomi
  and assign her to the house of DAVID.

Let Ruth rejoice with the Tumbler – it is a pleasant thing to
  feed him and be thankful.
For I am in charity with the French who are my foes and
  Moabites because of the Moabitish woman.

Let Ram rejoice with the Fieldfare, who is a good gift from
  God in the season of scarcity.
For my Angel is always ready at a pinch to help me out and
  to keep me up.

Let Manoah rejoice with Cerastes, who is a Dragon with
  horns.
For CHRISTOPHER must slay the Dragon with a
  PHEON's head.

Let Talmai rejoice with Alcedo, who makes a cradle for its
  young, which is rock'd by the winds.
For they have separated me and my bosom, whereas the
  right comes by setting us together.

Let Bukki rejoice with the Buzzard, who is clever, with the   60
    reputation of a silly fellow.
For silly fellow! silly fellow! is against me and belongeth
    neither to me nor my family.

Let Michal rejoice with Leucrocuta who is a mixture of
    beauty and magnanimity.
For he that scorneth the scorner hath condescended to my
    low estate.

Let Abiah rejoice with Morphnus who is a bird of passage
    to the Heavens.
For Abiah is the father of Joab and Joab of all Romans and
    English Men.

Let Hur rejoice with the Water-wag-tail, who is a
    neighbour, and loves to be looked at.
For they pass by me in their tour, and the good Samaritan
    is not yet come. –

Let Dodo rejoice with the purple Worm, who is clothed
    sumptuously, tho' he fares meanly.
For I bless God in the behalf of TRINITY COLLEGE in
    CAMBRIDGE and the society of PURPLES in
    LONDON –

Let Ahio rejoice with the Merlin who is a cousin german of   65
    the hawk.
For I have a nephew CHRISTOPHER to whom I implore
    the grace of God.

Let Joram rejoice with the Water-Rail, who takes his
    delight in the river.
For I pray God praise the CAM – Mr HIGGS and Mr and
    Mrs WASHBOURNE as the drops of the dew.

Let Chileab rejoice with Ophion who is clean made, less
    than an hart, and a Sardinian.
For I pray God bless the king of Sardinia and make him an
    instrument of his peace.

Let Shephatiah rejoice with the little Owl, which is the
    winged Cat.
For I am possessed of a cat, surpassing in beauty, from
    whom I take occasion to bless Almighty God.

Let Ithream rejoice with the great Owl, who understandeth
that which he professes.
For I pray God for the professors of the University of
Cambridge to attend and to amend.

Let Abigail rejoice with Lethophagus – God be gracious to 70
the widows indeed.
For the Fatherless Children and widows are never deserted
of the Lord.

Let Anathoth bless with Saurix, who is a bird of
melancholy.
For I pray God be gracious to the house of Stuart and
consider their afflictions.

Let Shammua rejoice with the Vultur who is strength and
fierceness.
For I pray God be gracious to the seed of Virgil, to Mr
GOODMAN SMITH of King's and Joseph STUD.

Let Shobab rejoice with Evech who is of the goat kind
which is meditation and pleasantry.
For I give God the glory that I am a son of ABRAHAM a
PRINCE of the house of my fathers.

Let Ittai the Gittite rejoice with the Gerfalcon – amicus
certus in re incerta cernitur.
For my brethren have dealt deceitfully as a brook, and as
the stream of brooks that pass away.

Let Ibhar rejoice with the Pochard – a child born in 75
prosperity is the chiefest blessing of peace.
For I bless God for my retreat at CANBURY, as it was the
place of the nativity of my children.

Let Elishua rejoice with Cantharis – God send bread and
milk to the children.
For I pray God to give them the food which I cannot earn
for them any otherwise than by prayer.

Let Chimham bless with Drepanis who is a passenger from
the sea to heaven.
For I pray God bless the Chinese which are of ABRAHAM
and the Gospel grew with them at the first.

Let Toi rejoice with Percnopteros which haunteth the sugar-fens.
For I bless God in the honey of the sugar-cane and the milk of the cocoa.

Let Nepheg rejoice with Cenchris which is the spotted serpent.
For I bless God in the libraries of the learned and for all the booksellers in the world.

Let Japhia rejoice with Buteo who hath three testicles. 80
For I bless God in the strength of my loins and for the voice which he hath made sonorous.

Let Gibeon rejoice with the Puttock, who will shift for himself to the last extremity.
For 'tis no more a merit to provide for oneself, but to quit all for the sake of the Lord.

Let Elishama rejoice with Mylaecos Ισχετε χειρα μυλαιου αλιτριδες. ευδετε μακρα.
For there is no invention but the gift of God, and no grace like the grace of gratitude.

Let Elimelech rejoice with the Horn-Owl who is of gravity and amongst my friends in the tower.
For grey hairs are honourable and tell every one of them to the glory of God.

Let Eliada rejoice with the Gier-eagle who is swift and of great penetration.
For I bless the Lord Jesus for the memory of GAY, POPE and SWIFT.

Let Eliphalet rejoice with Erodius who is God's good creature, which is sufficient for him. 85
For all good words are from GOD, and all others are cant.

Let Jonathan, David's nephew, rejoice with Oripelargus who is noble by his ascent.
For I am enobled by my ascent and the Lord hath raised me above my Peers.

Let Sheva rejoice with the Hobby, who is the service of the
    great.
For I pray God bless my lord CLARENDON and his seed
    for ever.

Let Ahimaaz rejoice with the Silver-Worm who is a living
    mineral.
For there is silver in my mines and I bless God that it is
    rather there than in my coffers.

Let Shobi rejoice with the Kastrel – blessed be the name
    JESUS in falconry and in the MALL.
For I blessed God in St James's Park till I routed all the
    company.

Let Elkanah rejoice with Cymindis – the Lord illuminate us   90
    against the powers of darkness.
For the officers of the peace are at variance with me, and
    the watchman smites me with his staff.

Let Ziba rejoice with Glottis whose tongue is wreathed in
    his throat.
For I am the seed of the WELCH WOMAN and speak the
    truth from my heart.

Let Micah rejoice with the spotted Spider, who counterfeits
    death to effect his purposes.
For they lay wagers touching my life. – God be gracious to
    the winners.

Let Rizpah rejoice with the Eyed Moth who is beautiful in
    corruption.
For the piety of Rizpah is imitable in the Lord – wherefore
    I pray for the dead.

Let Naharai, Joab's armour-bearer rejoice with Rock who
    is a bird of stupendous magnitude.
For the Lord is my ROCK and I am the bearer of his
    CROSS.

Let Abiezer, the Anethothite, rejoice with Phrynos who is   95
    the scaled frog.
For I am like a frog in the brambles, but the Lord hath put
    his whole armour upon me.

Let Nachon rejoice with Pareas who is a serpent more
innocent than others.
*For I was a Viper-catcher in my youth and the Lord
delivered me from his venom.*

Let Lapidoth with Percnos – the Lord is the builder of the
wall of CHINA – REJOICE.
*For I rejoice that I attribute to God, what others vainly
ascribe to feeble man.*

Let Ahinoam rejoice with Prester – The seed of the woman
hath bruised the serpent's head.
*For I am ready to die for his sake – who lay down his life
for all mankind.*

Let Phurah rejoice with Penelopes, the servant of Gideon
with the fowl of the brook.
*For the son of JOSHUA shall prevail against the servant of
Gideon – Good men have their betters.*

Let Jether, the son of Gideon, rejoice with Ecchetae which   100
are musical grashoppers.
*For my seed shall worship the Lord JESUS as numerous
and musical as the grashoppers of Paradise.*

Let Hushai rejoice with the Ospray who is able to parry the
eagle.
*For I pray God to turn the council of Ahitophel into
foolishness.*

Let Eglah rejoice with Phalaris who is a pleasant object
upon the water.
*For the learning of the Lord increases daily, as the sun is an
improving angel.*

Let Haggith rejoice with the white Weasel who devoureth
the honey and its maker.
*For I pray God for a reformation amongst the women and
the restoration of the veil.*

Let Abital rejoice with Ptyas who is arrayed in green and
gold.
*For beauty is better to look upon than to meddle with and
tis good for a man not to know a woman.*

Let Maacah rejoice with Dryophyte who was blessed of the 105
Lord in the valley.
*For the Lord Jesus made him a nosegay and blessed it and
he blessed the inhabitants of flowers.*

Let Zabud Solomon's friend rejoice with Oryx who is a
frolicsome mountaineer.
*For a faithful friend is the medicine of life, but a neighbour
in the Lord is better than he.*

Let Adoniram the receiver general of the excise rejoice with
Hypnale the sleepy adder.
*For I stood up betimes in behalf of LIBERTY,
PROPERTY and NO EXCISE.*

Let Pedahel rejoice with Pityocampa who eateth his house
in the pine.
*For they began with grubbing up my trees and now they
have excluded the planter.*

Let Ibzan rejoice with the Brandling – the Lord further the
building of bridges and making rivers navigable.
*For I am the Lord's builder and free and accepted MASON
in CHRIST JESUS.*

Let Gilead rejoice with the Gentle – the Lord make me a 110
fisher of men.
*For I bless God in all gums and balsams and every thing
that ministers relief to the sick.*

Let Zelophehad rejoice with Ascalabotes who casteth not
his coat till a new one is prepared for him.
*For the Sun's at work to make me a garment and the Moon
is at work for my wife.*

Let Mahlah rejoice with Pellos who is a tall bird and
stately.
*For tall and stately are against me, but humiliation on
humiliation is on my side.*

Let Tirzah rejoice with Tylus which is the Cheeslip and
food for the chicken.
*For I have a providential acquaintance with men who bear
the names of animals.*

Let Hoglah rejoice with Leontophonos who will kill the
   lion, if he is eaten.
*For I bless God to Mr Lion Mr Cock Mr Cat Mr Talbot
   Mr Hart Mrs Fysh Mr Grub, and Miss Lamb.*

Let Milcah rejoice with the Horned Beetle who will strike a 115
   man in the face.
*For they throw my horns in my face and reptiles make
   themselves wings against me.*

Let Noah rejoice with Hibris who is from a wild boar and
   a tame sow.
*For I bless God for the immortal soul of Mr Pigg of
   DOWNHAM in NORFOLK.*

Let Abdon rejoice with the Glede who is very voracious
   and may not himself be eaten.
*For I fast this day even the 31st of August N.S. to prepare
   for the SABBATH of the Lord.*

Let Zuph rejoice with Dipsas, whose bite causeth thirst.
*For the bite of an Adder is cured by its grease and the
   malice of my enemies by their stupidity.*

Let Schechem of Manasseh rejoice with the Green Worm
   whose livery is of the field.
*For I bless God in SHIPBOURNE FAIRLAWN the
   meadows the brooks and the hills.*

Let Gera rejoice with the Night Hawk – blessed are those 120
   who watch when others sleep.
*For the adversary hath exasperated the very birds against
   me, but the Lord sustain'd me.*

Let Anath rejoice with Rauca who inhabiteth the root of
   the oak.
*For I bless God for my Newcastle friends, the voice of the
   raven and heart of the oak.*

Let Cherub rejoice with the Cherub who is a bird and a
   blessed Angel.
*For I bless God for every feather from the wren in the
   sedge to the CHERUBS and their MATES.*

*

LET PETER rejoice with the MOON FISH who keeps up
the life in the waters by night.
FOR I pray the Lord JESUS that cured the LUNATIC to
be merciful to all my brethren and sisters in these houses.

Let Andrew rejoice with the Whale, who is array'd in
beauteous blue and is a combination of bulk and activity.
For they work me with their harping-irons, which is a
barbarous instrument, because I am more unguarded
than others.

Let James rejoice with the Skuttle-Fish, who foils his foe by   125
the effusion of his ink.
For the blessing of God hath been on my epistles, which I
have written for the benefit of others.

Let John rejoice with Nautilus who spreads his sail and
plies his oar, and the Lord is his pilot.
For I bless God that the CHURCH of ENGLAND is one
of the SEVEN ev'n the candlestick of the Lord.

Let Philip rejoice with Boca, which is a fish that can speak.
For the ENGLISH TONGUE shall be the language of the
WEST.

Let Bartholomew rejoice with the Eel, who is pure in
proportion to where he is found and how he is used.
For I pray Almighty CHRIST to bless the MAGDALEN
HOUSE and to forward a National purification.

Let Thomas rejoice with the Sword-Fish, whose aim is
perpetual and strength insuperable.
For I have the blessing of God in the three POINTS of
manhood, of the pen, of the sword, and of chivalry.

Let Matthew rejoice with Uranoscopus, whose eyes are   130
lifted up to God.
For I am inquisitive in the Lord, and defend the philosophy
of the scripture against vain deceit.

Let James the less, rejoice with the Haddock, who brought
the piece of money for the Lord and Peter.
For the nets come down from the eyes of the Lord to fish
up men to their salvation.

Let Jude bless with the Bream, who is of melancholy from
   his depth and serenity.
*For I have a greater compass both of mirth and melancholy
   than another.*

Let Simon rejoice with the Sprat, who is pure and
   innumerable.
*For I bless the Lord JESUS in the innumerables, and for
   ever and ever.*

Let Matthias rejoice with the Flying-Fish, who has a part
   with the birds, and is sublimity in his conceit.
*For I am redoubted, and redoubtable in the Lord, as is
   THOMAS BECKET my father.*

Let Stephen rejoice with Remora – The Lord remove all   135
   obstacles to his glory.
*For I have had the grace to GO BACK, which is my
   blessing unto prosperity.*

Let Paul rejoice with the Seale, who is pleasant and faithful,
   like God's good ENGLISHMAN.
*For I paid for my seat in St PAUL's, when I was six years
   old, and took possession against the evil day.*

Let Agrippa, which is Agricola, rejoice with Elops, who is a
   choice fish.
*For I am descended from the steward of the island –
   blessed be the name of the Lord Jesus king of England.*

Let Joseph rejoice with the Turbut, whose capture makes
   the poor fisher-man sing.
*For the poor gentleman is the first object of the Lord's
   charity and he is the most pitied who hath lost the most.*

Let Mary rejoice with the Maid – blessed be the name of
   the immaculate CONCEPTION.
*For I am in twelve HARDSHIPS, but he that was born of a
   virgin shall deliver me out of all.*

Let John, the Baptist, rejoice with the Salmon – blessed be   140
   the name of the Lord Jesus for infant Baptism.
*For I am safe, as to my head, from the female dancer and
   her admirers.*

Let Mark rejoice with the Mullet, who is John Dore, God
  be gracious to him and his family.
For I pray for CHICHESTER to give the glory to God, and
  to keep the adversary at bay.

Let Barnabas rejoice with the Herring – God be gracious to
  the Lord's fishery.
For I am making to the shore day by day, the Lord Jesus
  take me.

Let Cleopas rejoice with the Mackerel, who cometh in a
  shoal after a leader.
For I bless the Lord JESUS upon RAMSGATE PIER – the
  Lord forward the building of harbours.

Let Abiud of the Lord's line rejoice with Murex, who is
  good and of a precious tincture.
For I bless the Lord JESUS for his very seed, which is in my
  body.

Let Eliakim rejoice with the Shad, who is contemned in his   145
  abundance.
For I pray for R and his family, I pray for Mr Becher, and I
  bean for the Lord JESUS.

Let Azor rejoice with the Flounder, who is both of the sea
  and of the river.
For I pray to God for Nore, for the Trinity house, for all
  light-houses, beacons and buoys.

Let Sadoc rejoice with the Bleak, who playeth upon the
  surface in the Sun.
For I bless God that I am not in a dungeon, but am
  allowed the light of the Sun.

Let Achim rejoice with the Miller's Thumb, who is a
  delicious morsel for the water fowl.
For I pray God for the PYGMIES against their feather'd
  adversaries, as a deed of charity.

Let Eliud rejoice with Cinaedus, who is a fish yellow all
  over.
For I pray God for all those, who have defiled themselves
  in matters inconvenient.

Let Eleazar rejoice with the Grampus, who is a pompous   150
spouter.
For I pray God be gracious to CORNELIUS MATTHEWS
name and connection.

Let Matthan rejoice with the Shark, who is supported by
multitudes of small value.
For I am under the same accusation with my Saviour – for
they said, he is besides himself.

Let Jacob rejoice with the Gold Fish, who is an eye-trap.
For I pray God for the introduction of new creatures into
this island.

Let Jairus rejoice with the Silver Fish, who is bright and
lively.
For I pray God for the ostriches of Salisbury Plain, the
beavers of the Medway and silver fish of Thames.

Let Lazarus rejoice with Torpedo, who chills the life of the
assailant through his staff.
For Charity is cold in the multitude of possessions, and the
rich are covetous of their crumbs.

Let Mary Magdalen rejoice with the Place, whose goodness   155
and purity are of the Lord's making.
For I pray to be accepted as a dog without offence, which
is best of all.

Let Simon the leper rejoice with the Eel-pout, who is a
rarity on account of his subtlety.
For I wish to God and desire towards the most High,
which is my policy.

Let Alpheus rejoice with the Whiting, whom God hath
bless'd in multitudes, and his days are as the days of
PURIM.
For the tides are the life of God in the ocean, and he sends
his angel to trouble the great DEEP.

Let Onesimus rejoice with the Cod – blessed be the name
of the Lord Jesus for a miraculous draught of men.
For he hath fixed the earth upon arches and pillars, and the
flames of hell flow under it.

Let Joses rejoice with the Sturgeon, who saw his maker in
the body and obtained grace.
For *the grosser the particles the nearer to the sink, and the
nearer to purity, the quicker the gravitation.*

Let Theophilus rejoice with the Folio, who hath teeth, like   160
the teeth of a saw.
For *MATTER is the dust of the Earth, every atom of which
is the life.*

Let Bartimeus rejoice with the Quaviver – God be gracious
to the eyes of him, who prayeth for the blind.
For *MOTION is as the quantity of life direct, and that
which hath not motion, is resistance.*

Let CHRISTOPHER, who is Simon of Cyrene, rejoice with
the Rough – God be gracious to the CAM and to DAVID
· CAM and his seed for ever.
For *Resistance is not of GOD, but he – hath built his
works upon it.*

Let Timeus rejoice with the Ling – God keep the English
Sailors clear of French bribery.
For *the Centripetal and Centrifugal forces are GOD
SUSTAINING and DIRECTING.*

Let Salome rejoice with the Mermaid, who hath the
countenance and a portion of human reason.
For *Elasticity is the temper of matter to recover its place
with vehemence.*

Let Zacharias rejoice with the Gudgeon, who improves in   165
his growth till he is mistaken.
For *Attraction is the earning of parts, which have a
similitude in the life.*

Let Campanus rejoice with the Lobster – God be gracious
to all the CAMPBELLs especially John.
For *the Life of God is in the Loadstone, and there is a
magnet, which pointeth due EAST.*

Let Martha rejoice with the Skallop – the Lord revive the
exercise and excellence of the Needle.
For *the Glory of God is always in the East, but cannot be
seen for the cloud of the crucifixion.*

Let Mary rejoice with the Carp – the ponds of Fairlawn
and the garden bless for the master.
For due East is the way to Paradise, which man knoweth
not by reason of his fall.

Let Zebedee rejoice with the Tench – God accept the good
son for his parents also.
For the Longitude is (nevertheless) attainable by steering
angularly notwithstanding.

Let Joseph of Arimathea rejoice with the Barbel – a good   170
coffin and a tomb-stone without grudging!
For Eternity is a creature and is built upon Eternity
καταβολη επι τη διαβολη.

Let Elizabeth rejoice with the Crab – it is good, at times, to
go back.
For Fire is a mixed nature of body and spirit, and the body
is fed by that which hath not life.

Let Simeon rejoice with the Oyster, who hath the life
without locomotion.
For Fire is exasperated by the Adversary, who is Death,
unto the detriment of man.

Let Jona rejoice with the Wilk – Wilks, Wilkie, and
Wilkinson bless the name of the Lord Jesus.
For an happy Conjecture is a miraculous cast by the Lord
Jesus.

Let Nicodemus rejoice with the Muscle, for so he hath
provided for the poor.
For a bad Conjecture is a draught of stud and mud.

Let Gamaliel rejoice with the Cockle – I will rejoice in the   175
remembrance of mercy.
For there is a Fire which is blandishing, and which is of
God direct.

Let Agabus rejoice with the Smelt – The Lord make me
serviceable to the HOWARDs.
For Fire is a substance and distinct, and purifyeth ev'n in
hell.

Let Rhoda rejoice with the Sea-Cat, who is pleasantry and
    purity.
For the Shears is the first of the mechanical powers, and to
    be used on the knees.

Let Elmodam rejoice with the Chubb, who is wary of the
    bait and thrives in his circumspection.
For if Adam had used this instrument right, he would not
    have fallen.

Let Jorim rejoice with the Roach – God bless my throat
    and keep me from things strangled.
For the power of the Shears is direct as the life.

Let Addi rejoice with the Dace – It is good to angle with   180
    meditation.
For the power of the WEDGE is direct as its altitude by
    communication of Almighty God.

Let Luke rejoice with the Trout – Blessed be Jesus in Aa, in
    Dee and in Isis.
For the Skrew, Axle and Wheel, Pulleys, the Lever and
    inclined Plane are known in the Schools.

Let Cosam rejoice with the Perch, who is a little tyrant,
    because he is not liable to that, which he inflicts.
For the Centre is not known but by the application of the
    members to matter.

Let Levi rejoice with the Pike – God be merciful to all
    dumb creatures in respect of pain.
For I have shown the Vis Inertiae to be false, and such is all
    nonsense.

Let Melchi rejoice with the Char, who cheweth the cud.
For the Centre is the hold of the Spirit upon the matter in
    hand.

Let Joanna rejoice with the Anchovy – I beheld and lo! a   185
    great multitude!
For FRICTION is inevitable because the Universe is FULL
    of God's works.

Let Neri rejoice with the Keeling Fish, who is also called
   the Stock Fish.
For the PERPETUAL MOTION is in all the works of
   Almighty GOD.

Let Janna rejoice with the Pilchard – the Lord restore the
   seed of Abishai.
For it is not so in the engines of man, which are made of
   dead materials, neither indeed can be.

Let Esli rejoice with the Soal, who is flat and spackles for
   the increase of motion.
For the Moment of bodies, as it is used, is a false term –
   bless God ye Speakers on the Fifth of November.

Let Nagge rejoice with the Perriwinkle – 'for the rain it
   raineth every day.'
For Time and Weight are by their several estimates.

Let Anna rejoice with the Porpus, who is a joyous fish and   190
   of good omen.
For I bless GOD in the discovery of the LONGITUDE
   direct by the means of GLADWICK.

Let Phanuel rejoice with the Shrimp, which is the children's
   fishery.
For the motion of the PENDULUM is the longest in that it
   parries resistance.

Let Chuza rejoice with the Sea-Bear, who is full of sagacity
   and prank.
For the WEDDING GARMENTS of all men are prepared
   in the SUN against the day of acceptation.

Let Susanna rejoice with the Lamprey, who is an eel with a
   title.
For the Wedding Garments of all women are prepared in
   the MOON against the day of their purification.

Let Candace rejoice with the Craw-fish – How hath the
   Christian minister renowned the Queen.
For CHASTITY is the key of knowledge as in Esdras, Sir
   Isaac Newton and now, God be praised, in me.

Let The Eunuch rejoice with the Thorn-Back – It is good to   195
be discovered reading the BIBLE.
*For Newton nevertheless is more of error than of the truth,
but I am of the WORD of GOD.*

Let Simon the Pharisee rejoice with the Grigg – the Lord
bring up Issachar and Dan.
*For WATER is not of solid constituents, but is dissolved
from precious stones above.*

Let Simon the converted Sorcerer rejoice with the Dab
quoth Daniel.
*For the life remains in its dissolvent state, and that in great
power.*

Let Joanna, of the Lord's line, rejoice with the Minnow,
who is multiplied against the oppressor.
*For WATER is condensed by the Lord's FROST, tho' not
by the FLORENTINE experiment.*

Let Jonas rejoice with the Sea-Devil, who hath a good
name from his Maker.
*For GLADWICK is a substance growing on hills in the
East, candied by the sun, and of diverse colours.*

Let Alexander rejoice with the Tunny – the worse the time   200
the better the eternity.
*For it is neither stone nor metal but a new creature, soft to
the ax, but hard to the hammer.*

Let Rufus rejoice with the Needle-fish, who is very good in
his element.
*For it answers sundry uses, but particularly it supplies the
place of Glass.*

Let Matthat rejoice with the Trumpet-fish – God revive the
blowing of the TRUMPETS.
*For it giveth a benign light without the fragility, malignity
or mischief of Glass.*

Let Mary, the mother of James, rejoice with the Sea-Mouse
– it is good to be at peace.
*For it attracteth all the colours of the GREAT BOW which
is fixed in the EAST.*

Let Prochorus rejoice with Epodes, who is a kind of fish
with Ovid who is at peace in the Lord.
For the FOUNTAINS and SPRINGS are the life of the
waters working up to God.

Let Timotheus rejoice with the Dolphin, who is of
benevolence.
For they are in SYMPATHY with the waters above the
Heavens, which are solid.

Let Nicanor rejoice with the Skeat – Blessed be the name of
the Lord Jesus in fish and in the Shewbread, which ought
to be continually on the altar, now more than ever, and
the want of it is the Abomination of Desolation spoken
of by Daniel.
For the Fountains, springs and rivers are all of them from
the sea, whose water is filtrated and purified by the earth.

Let Timon rejoice with Crusion – The Shew-Bread in the
first place is gratitude to God to shew who is bread,
whence it is, and that there is enough and to spare.
For there is Water above the visible surface in a
spiritualizing state, which cannot be seen but by
application of a CAPILLARY TUBE.

Let Parmenas rejoice with the Mixon – Secondly it is to
prevent the last extremity, for it is lawful that rejected
hunger may take it.
For the ASCENT of VAPOURS is the return of
thanksgiving from all humid bodies.

Let Dorcas rejoice with Dracunculus – blessed be the name
of the Lord Jesus in the Grotto.
For the RAIN WATER kept in a reservoir at any altitude,
suppose of a thousand feet, will make a fountain from a
spout of ten feet of the same height.

Let Tychicus rejoice with Scolopendra, who quits himself
of the hook by voiding his intrails.
For it will ascend in a stream two thirds of the way and
afterwards prank itself into ten thousand agreeable
forms.

205

210

Let Trophimus rejoice with the Sea-Horse, who should
　　have been to Tychicus the father of Yorkshiremen.
For *the SEA is a seventh of the Earth – the spirit of the*
　　Lord by Esdras.

Let Tryphena rejoice with Fluta – Saturday is the Sabbath
　　for the mouth of God hath spoken it.
For *MERCURY is affected by the AIR because it is of a*
　　similar subtlety.

Let Tryphosa rejoice with Acarne – With such a
　　preparation the Lord's Jubile is better kept.
For *the rising in the BAROMETER is not effected by*
　　pressure but by sympathy.

Let Simon the Tanner rejoice with Alausa – Five days are
　　sufficient for the purposes of husbandry.
For *it cannot be separated from the creature with which it*
　　is intimately and eternally connected.

Let Simeon Niger rejoice with the Loach – The blacks are　　215
　　the seed of Cain.
For *where it is stinted of air there it will adhere together*
　　and stretch on the reverse.

Let Lucius rejoice with Corias – Some of Cain's seed was
　　preserved in the loins of Ham at the flood.
For *it works by balancing according to the hold of the*
　　spirit.

Let Manaen rejoice with Donax. My DEGREE is good
　　even here, in the Lord I have a better.
For *QUICK-SILVER is spiritual and so is the AIR to all*
　　intents and purposes.

Let Sergius Paulus rejoice with Dentex – Blessed be the
　　name of Jesus for my teeth.
For *the AIR-PUMP weakens and dispirits but cannot*
　　wholly exhaust.

Let Silas rejoice with the Cabot – the philosophy of the
　　times ev'n now is vain deceit.
For *SUCKTION is the withdrawing of the life, but life will*
　　follow as fast as it can.

Let Barsabas rejoice with Cammarus – Newton is ignorant 220
for if a man consult not the WORD how should he
understand the WORK? –

*For there is infinite provision to keep up the life in all the
parts of Creation.*

Let Lydia rejoice with Attilus – Blessed be the name of him
which eat the fish and honey comb.

For the AIR is contaminated by curses and evil language.

Let Jason rejoice with Alopecias, who is subtlety without
offence.

*For poisonous creatures catch some of it and retain it or ere
it goes to the adversary.*

Let Dionysius rejoice with Alabes who is peculiar to the
Nile.

*For IRELAND was without these creatures, till of late,
because of the simplicity of the people.*

Let Damaris rejoice with Anthias – The fountain of the
Nile is known to the Eastern people who drink it.

*For the AIR is purified by prayer which is made aloud and
with all our might.*

Let Apollos rejoice with Astacus, but St Paul is the Agent 225
for England.

*For loud prayer is good for weak lungs and for a vitiated
throat.*

Let Justus rejoice with Crispus in a Salmon-Trout – the
Lord look on the soul of Richard Atwood.

*For SOUND is propagated in the spirit and in all
directions.*

Let Crispus rejoice with Leviathan – God be gracious to the
soul of HOBBES, who was no atheist, but a servant of
Christ, and died in the Lord – I wronged him God
forgive me.

For the VOICE of a figure is complete in all its parts.

Let Aquila rejoice with Beemoth who is Enoch, no fish but
a stupendous creeping Thing.

*For a man speaks HIMSELF from the crown of his head to
the sole of his feet.*

Let Priscilla rejoice with Cythera. As earth increases by
  Beemoth so the sea likewise enlarges.
For a LION roars HIMSELF complete from head to tail.

Let Tyrannus rejoice with Cephalus who hath a great head.   230
*For all these things are seen in the spirit which makes the
  beauty of prayer.*

Let Gaius rejoice with the Water-Tortoise – Paul and
  Tychicus were in England with Agricola my father.
*For all whispers and unmusical sounds in general are of the
  Adversary.*

Let Aristarchus rejoice with Cynoglossus – The Lord was
  at Glastonbury in the body and blessed the thorn.
*For 'I will hiss saith the Lord' is God's denunciation of
  death.*

Let Alexander rejoice with the Sea-Urchin – The Lord was
  at Bristol and blessed the waters there.
*For applause or the clapping of the hands is the natural
  action of man on the descent of the glory of God.*

Let Sopater rejoice with Elacate – The waters of Bath were
  blessed by St Matthias.
*For EARTH which is an intelligence hath a voice and a
  propensity to speak in all her parts.*

Let Secundus rejoice with Echeneis who is the sea-lamprey.   235
*For ECHO is the soul of the voice exerting itself in hollow
  places.*

Let Eutychus rejoice with Cnide – Fish and honeycomb are
  blessed to eat after a recovery. –
*For ECHO cannot act but when she can parry the
  adversary.*

Let Mnason rejoice with Vulvula a sort of fish – Good
  words are of God, the cant from the Devil.
*For ECHO is greatest in Churches and where she can assist
  in prayer.*

Let Claudius Lysias rejoice with Coracinus who is black
and peculiar to Nile.
*For a good voice hath its Echo with it and it is attainable
by much supplication.*

Let Bernice rejoice with Corophium which is a kind of
crab.
*For the VOICE is from the body and the spirit – and it is a
body and a spirit.*

Let Phebe rejoice with Echinometra who is a beautiful   240
shellfish red and green.
*For the prayers of good men are therefore visible to second-
sighted persons.*

Let Epenetus rejoice with Erythrinus who is red with a
white belly.
For HARPSICHORDS are best strung with gold wire.

Let Andronicus rejoice with Esox, the Lax, a great fish of
the Rhine.
For HARPS and VIOLS are best strung with Indian weed.

Let Junia rejoice with the Faber-Fish – Broil'd fish and
honeycomb may be taken for the sacrament.
*For the GERMAN FLUTE is an indirect – the common
flute good, bless the Lord Jesus BENJAMIN HALLET.*

Let Amplias rejoice with Garus, who is a kind of Lobster.
*For the feast of TRUMPETS should be kept up, that being
the most direct and acceptable of all instruments.*

Let Urbane rejoice with Glanis, who is a crafty fish who   245
bites away the bait and saves himself.
*For the TRUMPET of God is a blessed intelligence and so
are all the instruments in HEAVEN.*

Let Stachys rejoice with Glauciscus, who is good for
Women's milk.
*For GOD the father Almighty plays upon the HARP of
stupendous magnitude and melody.*

Let Apelles rejoice with Glaucus – behold the seed of the
brave and ingenious how they are saved!
*For innumerable Angels fly out at every touch and his tune
is a work of creation.*

Let Aristobulus rejoice with Glycymerides who is pure and
sweet.
*For at that time malignity ceases and the devils themselves
are at peace.*

Let Herodion rejoice with Holothuria which are prickly
fishes.
*For this time is perceptible to man by a remarkable stillness
and serenity of soul.*

Let Narcissus rejoice with Hordeia – I will magnify the   250
Lord who multiplied the fish.
For the Aeolian harp is improveable into regularity.

Let Persis rejoice with Liparis – I will magnify the Lord
who multiplied the barley loaves.
*For when it is so improved it will be known to be the
SHAWM.*

Let Rufus rejoice with Icthyocolla of whose skin a water-
glue is made.
*For it would be better if the LITURGY were musically
performed.*

Let Asyncritus rejoice with Labrus who is a voracious fish.
*For the strings of the SHAWM were upon a cylinder which
turned to the wind.*

Let Phlegon rejoice with the Sea-Lizard – Bless Jesus
THOMAS BOWLBY and all the seed of Reuben.
*For this was spiritual music altogether, as the wind is a
spirit.*

Let Hermas rejoice with Lamyrus who is of things creeping   255
in the sea.
For there is nothing but it may be played upon in delight.

Let Patrobas rejoice with Lepas, all shells are precious.
For the flames of fire may be blown thro' musical pipes.

Let Hermes rejoice with Lepus, who is a venomous fish.
For it is so higher up in the vast empyrean.

Let Philologus rejoice with Ligarius – shells are all parries
to the adversary.
For nothing is so real as that which is spiritual.

Let Julia rejoice with the Sleeve-Fish – Blessed be Jesus for
all the TAYLERS.
*For an IGNIS FATUUS is either the fool's conceit or a blast
from the adversary.*

Let Nereus rejoice with the Calamary – God give success to   260
our fleets.
*For SHELL-FIRE or ELECTRICAL is the quick air when
it is caught.*

Let Olympas rejoice with the Sea-Lantern, which glows
upon the waters.
*For GLASS is worked in the fire till it partakes of its
nature.*

Let Sosipater rejoice with Cornuta. There are fish for the
Sea-Night-Birds that glow at bottom.
*For the electrical fire is easily obtain'd by the working of
glass.*

Let Lucius rejoice with the Cackrel Fish. God be gracious
to JM^s FLETCHER who has my tackling.
For all spirits are of fire and the air is a very benign one.

Let Tertius rejoice with Maia which is a kind of crab.
*For the MAN in VACUO is a flat conceit of preposterous
folly.*

Let Erastus rejoice with Melandry which is the largest   265
Tunny.
For the breath of our nostrils is an electrical spirit.

Let Quartus rejoice with Mena. God be gracious to the
immortal soul of poor Carte, who was barbarously and
cowardly murder'd – the Lord prevent the dealers in
clandestine death.
*For an electrical spirit may be exasperated into a malignant
fire.*

Let Sosthenes rejoice with the Winkle – all shells like the parts of the body are good kept for those parts.
For it is good to quicken in paralytic cases being the life applied unto death.

Let Chloe rejoice with the Limpin – There is a way to the terrestrial Paradise upon the knees.
For the method of philosophizing is in a posture of Adoration.

Let Carpus rejoice with the Frog-Fish – A man cannot die upon his knees.
For the School-Doctrine of Thunder and Lightning is a Diabolical Hypothesis.

Let Stephanas rejoice with Mormyra who is a fish of divers　270
colours.
For it is taking the nitre from the lower regions and directing it against the Infinite of Heights.

Let Fortunatus rejoice with the Burret – it is good to be born when things are crossed.
For THUNDER is the voice of God direct in verse and music.

Let Lois rejoice with the Angel-Fish – There is a fish that swims in the fluid Empyrean.
For LIGHTNING is a glance of the glory of God.

Let Achaicus rejoice with the Fat-Back – The Lord invites his fishers to the WEST INDIES.
For the Brimstone that is found at the times of thunder and lightning is worked up by the Adversary.

Let Sylvanus rejoice with the Black-Fish – Oliver Cromwell himself was the murderer in the Mask.
For the voice is always for infinite good which he strives to impede.

Let Titus rejoice with Mys – O Tite siquid ego adjuero　275
curamve levasso!
For the Devil can work coals into shapes to afflict the minds of those that will not pray.

Let Euodias rejoice with Myrus – There is a perfumed fish I
   will offer him for a sweet savour to the Lord.
*For the coffin and the cradle and the purse are all against a
   man.*

Let Syntyche rejoice with Myax – There are shells in the
   earth which were left by the FLOOD.
*For the coffin is for the dead and death came by
   disobedience.*

Let Clement rejoice with Ophidion – There are shells again
   in earth at sympathy with those in sea.
*For the cradle is for weakness and the child of man was
   originally strong from the womb.*

Let Epaphroditus rejoice with Opthalmias – The Lord
   increase the Cambridge collection of fossils.
*For the purse is for money and money is dead matter with
   the stamp of human vanity.*

Let Epaphras rejoice with Orphus – God be gracious to the   280
   immortal soul of Dr Woodward.
*For the adversary frequently sends these particular images
   out of the fire to those whom they concern.*

Let Justus rejoice with Pagrus – God be gracious to the
   immortal soul of Dr Middleton.
*For the coffin is for me because I have nothing to do with
   it.*

Let Nymphas rejoice with Pagurus – God bless Charles
   Mason and all Trinity College.
*For the cradle is for me because the old Dragon attacked
   me in it and I overcame in Christ.*

Let Archippus rejoice with Nerita whose shell swimmeth.
*For the purse is for me because I have neither money nor
   human friends.*

Let Eunice rejoice with Oculata who is of the Lizard kind.
*For LIGHT is propagated at all distances in an instant
   because it is actuated by the divine conception.*

Let Onesiphorus rejoice with Orca, who is a great fish.   285
*For the Satellites of the planet prove nothing in this matter
    but the glory of Almighty God.*

Let Eubulus rejoice with Ostrum the scarlet – God be
    gracious to Gordon and Groat.
For the SHADE is of death and from the adversary.

Let Pudens rejoice with Polypus – The Lord restore my
    virgin!
*For Solomon said vanity of vanities, vanity of vanities all is
    vanity.*

Let Linus rejoice with Ozaena who is a kind of Polype –
    God be gracious to Lyne and Anguish.
*For Jesus says verity of verities, verity of verities all is
    verity.*

Let Claudia rejoice with Passer – the purest creatures
    minister to wantoness by unthankfulness.
*For Solomon said THOU FOOL in malice from his own
    vanity.*

Let Artemas rejoice with Pastinaca who is a fish with a   290
    sting.
*For the Lord reviled not at all in hardship and temptation
    unutterable.*

Let Zenas rejoice with Pecten – The Lord obliterate the
    laws of man!
*For Fire hath this property that it reduces a thing till finally
    it is not.*

Let Philemon rejoice with Pelagia – The laws and
    judgement are impudence and blindness.
*For all the filth of wicked men shall be done away by fire in
    Eternity.*

Let Apphia rejoice with Pelamis – The Lord Jesus is man's
    judgement.
*For the furnace itself shall come up at the last according to
    Abraham's vision.*

Let Demetrius rejoice with Peloris, who is greatest of Shell-Fishes.

For the Convex of Heaven shall work about on that great event.

Let Antipas rejoice with Pentadactylus — A papist hath no 295
sentiment — God bless CHURCHILL.

For the ANTARTICK POLE is not yet but shall answer in the Consummation.

For the devil hath most power in winter, because darkness prevails.

For the Longing of Women is the operation of the Devil upon their conceptions.

For the marking of their children is from the same cause both of which are to be parried by prayer.

For the laws of King James the first against Witchcraft were wise, had it been of man to make laws.

For there are witches and wizards even now who are 300
spoken to by their familiars.

For the visitation of their familiars is prevented by the Lord's incarnation.

For to conceive with intense diligence against one's neighbour is a branch of witchcraft.

For to use pollution, exact and cross things and at the same time to think against a man is the crime direct.

For prayer with music is good for persons so exacted upon.

For before the NATIVITY is the dead of the winter and 305
after it the quick.

For the sin against the HOLY GHOST is INGRATITUDE.

For stuff'd guts make no music; strain them strong and you shall have sweet melody.

For the SHADOW is of death, which is the Devil, who can make false and faint images of the works of Almighty God.

For *every man beareth death about him ever since the transgression of Adam, but in perfect light there is no shadow.*

For *all Wrath is Fire, which the adversary blows upon and* 310 *exasperates.*

For *SHADOW is a fair Word from God, which is not returnable till the furnace comes up.*

For *the ECLIPSE is of the adversary – blessed be the name of Jesus for Whisson of Trinity.*

For *the shadow is his and the penumbra is his and his the perplexity of the phenomenon.*

For *the eclipses happen at times when the light is defective.*

For *the more the light is defective, the more the powers of* 315 *darkness prevail.*

For *deficiencies happen by the luminaries crossing one another.*

For *the SUN is an intelligence and an angel of the human form.*

For *the MOON is an intelligence and an angel in shape like a woman.*

For *they are together in the spirit every night like man and wife.*

For *Justice is infinitely beneath Mercy in nature and office.* 320

For *the Devil himself may be just in accusation and punishment.*

For *HELL is without eternity from the presence of Almighty God.*

For *Volcanos and burning mountains are where the adversary hath most power.*

For *the angel GRATITUDE is my wife – God bring me to her or her to me.*

For the propagation of light is quick as the divine
   Conception.   325

For FROST is damp and unwholesome air candied to fall
   to the best advantage.

For I am the Lord's News-Writer – the scribe-evangelist –
   Widow Mitchel, Gun and Grange bless the Lord Jesus.

For Adversity above all other is to be deserted of the grace
   of God.

For in the divine Idea this Eternity is complete and the
   Word is a making many more.

For there is a forlorn hope ev'n for impenitent sinners   330
   because the furnace itself must be the crown of Eternity.

For my hope is beyond Eternity in the bosom of God my
   saviour.

For by the grace of God I am the Reviver of
   ADORATION amongst ENGLISH-MEN.

For being desert-ed is to have desert in the sight of God
   and intitles one to the Lord's merit.

For things that are not in the sight of men are thro' God of
   infinite concern.

For envious men have exceeding subtlety quippe qui in –   335
   vident.

For avaricious men are exceeding subtle like the soul
   separated from the body.

For their attention is on a sinking object which perishes.

For they can go beyond the children of light in matters of
   their own misery.

For Snow is the dew candied and cherishes.

For TIMES and SEASONS are the Lord's – Man is no   340
   CHRONOLOGER.

For there is a CIRCULATION of the SAP in all vegetables.

For SOOT is the dross of Fire.

For the CLAPPING of the hands is naught unless it be to
   the glory of God.

For God will descend in visible glory when men begin to
   applaud him.

For all STAGE-Playing is Hypocrisy and the Devil is the   345
   master of their revels.

For the INNATATION of corpuscles is solved by the Gold-
   beater's hammer – God be gracious to Christopher
   Peacock and to all my God-Children.

For the PRECESSION of the Equinoxes is improving
   nature – something being gained every where for the
   glory of God perpetually.

For the souls of the departed are embodied in clouds and
   purged by the Sun.

For the LONGITUDE may be discovered by attending the
   motions of the Sun. Way 2d.

For you must consider the Sun as dodging, which he does   350
   to parry observation.

For he must be taken with an Astrolabe, and consider'd
   respecting the point he left.

For you must do this upon your knees and that will secure
   your point.

For I bless God that I dwell within the sound of Success,
   and that it is well with ENGLAND this blessed day.
   NATIVITY of our LORD N.S. 1759.

For a Man is to be looked upon in that which he excells as
   on a prospect.

For there be twelve cardinal virtues – three to the East –   355
   Greatness, Valour, Piety.

For there be three to the West – Goodness, Purity and
   Sublimity.

For there be three to the North – Meditation, Happiness,
   Strength.

For there be three to the South – Constancy, Pleasantry
   and Wisdom.

For the Argument A PRIORI is GOD in every man's
   CONSCIENCE.

For the Argument A POSTERIORI is God before every   360
   man's eyes.

For the Four and Twenty Elders of the Revelation are Four
   and Twenty Eternities.

For their Four and Twenty Crowns are their respective
   Consummations.

For a CHARACTER is the votes of the Worldlings, but the
   seal is of Almighty GOD alone.

For there is no music in flats and sharps which are not in
   God's natural key.

For where Accusation takes the place of encouragement a   365
   man of Genius is driven to act the vices of a fool.

For the Devil can set a house on fire, when the inhabitants
   find combustibles.

For the old account of time is the true – Decr 28th
   1759–60 –

For Faith as a grain of mustard seed is to believe, as I do,
   that an Eternity is such in respect to the power and
   magnitude of Almighty God.

For a DREAM is a good thing from GOD.

For there is a dream from the adversary which is terror.   370

For the phenomenon of dreaming is not of one solution,
   but many.

For Eternity is like a grain of mustard as a growing body
   and improving spirit.

For the malignancy of fire is owing to the Devil's hiding of
    light, till it became visible darkness.

For the Circle may be SQUARED by swelling and
    flattening.

For the Life of God is in the body of man and his spirit in   375
    the Soul.

For there was no rain in Paradise because of the delicate
    construction of the spiritual herbs and flowers.

For the Planet Mercury is the WORD DISCERNMENT.

For the Scotchman seeks for truth at the bottom of a well,
    the Englishman in the Heaven of Heavens.

For the Planet Venus is the WORD PRUDENCE or
    providence.

For GOD nevertheless is an extravagant BEING and   380
    generous unto loss.

For there is no profit in the generation of man and the loss
    of millions is not worth God's tear.

For this is the twelfth day of the MILLENNIUM of the
    MILLENNIUM foretold by the prophets – give the glory
    to God ONE THOUSAND SEVEN HUNDRED AND
    SIXTY –

For the Planet Mars is the word FORTITUDE.

For to worship naked in the Rain is the bravest thing for
    the refreshing and purifying the body.

For the Planet Jupiter is the WORD DISPENSATION.   385

For Tully says to be generous you must be first just, but the
    voice of Christ is distribute at all events.

For Kittim is the father of the Pygmies, God be gracious to
    Pigg his family.

For the Soul is divisible and a portion of the Spirit may be
    cut off from one and applied to another.

For NEW BREAD is the most wholesome especially if it be
     leaven'd with honey.

For a NEW SONG also is best, if it be to the glory of God; 390
     and taken with the food like the psalms.

For the Planet Saturn is the word TEMPERANCE or
     PATIENCE.

For Jacob's Ladder are the steps of the Earth graduated
     hence to Paradise and thence to the throne of God.

For a good wish is well but a faithful prayer is an eternal
     benefit.

For SPICA VIRGINIS is the star that appeared to the wise
     men in the East and directed their way before it was yet
     insphered.

For an IDEA is the mental vision of an object.   395

For Lock supposes that an human creature, at a given time
     may be an atheist i.e. without God, by the folly of his
     doctrine concerning innate ideas.

For it is not lawful to sell poison in England any more than
     it is in Venice, the Lord restrain both the finder and
     receiver.

For the ACCENTS are the invention of the Moabites, who
     learning the GREEK tongue marked the words after
     their own vicious pronunciation.

For the GAULS (the now-French and original Moabites)
     after they were subdued by Caesar became such Grecians
     at Rome.

For the Gaullic manuscripts fell into the hands of the   400
     inventors of printing.

For all the inventions of man, which are good, are the
     communications of Almighty God.

For all the stars have satellites, which are terms under their
     respective words.

For *tiger is a word and his satellites are Griffin, Storgis, Cat and others.*

For *my talent is to give an impression upon words by punching, that when the reader casts his eye upon 'em, he takes up the image from the mould which I have made.*

For *JOB was the son of Issachar and patience is the child of strength.*   405

For *the Names of the DAYS, as they now stand, are foolish and abominable.*

For *the Days are the First, Second, Third, Fourth, Fifth, Sixth and Seventh.*

For *the names of the months are false – the Hebrew appellatives are of God.*

For *the Time of the Lord's temptation was in early youth and imminent danger.*

For *an equivocal generation is a generation and no generation.*   410

For *putrifying matter nevertheless will yield up its life in diverse creatures and combinations of creatures.*

For *a TOAD can dwell in the centre of a stone, because – there are stones whose constituent life is of those creatures.*

For *a Toad hath by means of his eye the most beautiful prospects of any other animal to make him amends for his distance from his Creator in Glory.*

For *FAT is the fruit of benevolence, therefore it was the Lord's in the Mosaic sacrifices.*

For *the very particular laws of Moses are the determinations of CASES that fell under his cognizance.*   415

For *the Devil can make the shadow thicker by candlelight by reason of his pow'r over malignant fire.*

For the Romans clipped their words in the Augustan thro'
idleness and effeminacy and paid foreign actors for
speaking them out.

For when the weight and the pow'r are equivalent the prop
is of none effect.

For shaving of the beard was an invention of the people of
Sodom to make men look like women.

For the ends of the world are the accomplishment of great   420
events, and the consummation of periods.

For ignorance is a sin because illumination is to be
obtained by prayer.

For Preferment is not from the East, West or South, but
from the North, where Satan has most power.

For the ministers of the Devil set the hewer of wood over
the head of God's free Man.

For this is inverting God's good order, edifice and
edification, and appointing place, where the Lord has not
appointed.

For the Ethiopian question is already solved in that the   425
Blacks are the children of Cain.

For the phenomenon of the horizontal moon is the truth —
she appears bigger in the horizon because she actually is
so.

For it was said of old 'can the Ethiopian change his skin?'
the Lord has answer'd the question — by his merit and
death he shall. —

For the moon is magnified in the horizon by Almighty God,
and so is the Sun.

For she has done her day's-work and the blessing of God
upon her, and she communicates with the earth.

For when she rises she has been strength'ned by the Sun,   430
who cherishes her by night.

For *man is born to trouble in the body, as the sparks fly upwards in the spirit.*

For *man is between the pinchers while his soul is shaping and purifying.*

For *the* ENGLISH *are the seed of Abraham and work up to him by Joab, David, and Naphtali. God be gracious to us this day. General Fast March 14th 1760.*

For *the Romans and the English are one people the children of the brave man who died at the altar praying for his posterity, whose death was the type of our Saviour's.*

For *the* WELCH *are the children of Mephibosheth and*   435
    Ziba with a mixture of David in the Jones's.

For *the Scotch are the children of Doeg with a mixture of Cush the Benjamite, whence their innate antipathy to the English.*

For *the* IRISH *are the children of Shimei and Cush with a mixture of something lower – the Lord raise them!*

For *the* FRENCH *are Moabites even the children of Lot.*

For *the* DUTCH *are the children of Gog.*

For *the Poles are the children of Magog.*   440

For *the Italians are the children of Samuel and are the same as the Grecians.*

For *the Spaniards are the children of Abishai Joab's brother, hence is the goodwill between the two nations.*

For *the Portuguese are the children of Ammon – God be gracious to Lisbon and send good angels amongst them!*

For *the Hottentots are the children of Gog with a Black mixture.*

For *the Russians are the Children of Ishmael.*   445

For *the Turks are the children of Esaw, which is Edom.*

For the Wallachians are the children of Huz. God be
   gracious to Elizabeth Hughes, as she was.

For the Germans are the children of the Philistins even the
   seed of Anak.

For the Prussians are the children of Goliah – but the
   present, whom God bless this hour, is a Campbell of the
   seed of Phinees.

For the Hanoverians are Hittites of the seed of Uriah. God   450
   save the king.

For the Hessians are Philistines with a mixture of Judah.

For the Saxons are Benjamites, men of great subtlety and
   Marshal Saxe was direct from Benjamin.

For the Danes are of the children of Zabulon.

For the Venetians are the children of Mark and Romans.

For the Swiss are Philistins of a particular family. God be   455
   gracious to Jonathan Tyers his family and to all the
   people at Vaux Hall.

For the Sardinians are of the seed of David – The Lord
   forward the Reformation amongst the good seed first. –

For the Mogul's people are the children of Phut.

For the Old Greeks and the Italians are one people, which
   are blessed in the gift of Music by reason of the song of
   Hannah and the care of Samuel with regard to divine
   melody.

For the Germans and the Dutch are the children of the
   Goths and Vandals who did a good in destruction of
   books written by heathen Free-Thinkers against God.

For there are Americans of the children of Toi. –   460

For the Laplanders are the children of Gomer.

For the Phenomena of the Diving Bell are solved right in
   the schools.

For NEW BREAD is the most wholesome — God be
gracious to Baker.

For the English are the children of Joab, Captain of the
host of Israel, who was the greatest man in the world to
GIVE and to ATCHIEVE.

For TEA is a blessed plant and of excellent virtue. God   465
give the Physicians more skill and honesty!

For nutmeg is exceeding wholesome and cherishing, neither
does it hurt the liver.

For The Lightning before death is God's illumination in the
spirit for preparation and for warning.

For Lavender Cotton is exceeding good for the teeth. God
be gracious to Windsmore.

For the Fern is exceeding good and pleasant to rub the
teeth.

For a strong preparation of Mandragora is good for the   470
gout.

For the Bark was a communication from God and is
sovereign.

For the method of curing an ague by terror is exaction.

For Exaction is the most accursed of all things, because it
brought the Lord to the cross, his betrayers and
murderers being such from their exaction.

For an Ague is the terror of the body, when the blessing of
God is with'eld for a season.

For benevolence is the best remedy in the first place and the   475
bark in the second.

For, when the nation is at war, it is better to abstain from
the punishment of criminals especially, every act of
human vengeance being a check to the grace of God.

For the letter ϡ which signifies GOD by himself is on the
fibre of some leaf in every Tree.

For ⸱ is the grain of the human heart and on the network of the skin.

For ⸱ is in the veins of all stones both precious and common.

For ⸱ is upon every hair both of man and beast. 480

For ⸱ is in the grain of wood.

For ⸱ is in the ore of all metals.

For ⸱ is on the scales of all fish.

For ⸱ is on the petals of all flowers.

For ⸱ is upon all shells. 485

For ⸱ is in the constituent particles of air.

For ⸱ is on the mite of the earth.

For ⸱ is in the water yea in every drop.

For ⸱ is in the incomprehensible ingredients of fire.

For ⸱ is in the stars the sun and in the Moon. 490

For ⸱ is upon the Sapphire Vault.

For the doubling of flowers is the improvement of the gard'ner's talent.

For the flowers are great blessings.

For the Lord made a Nosegay in the meadow with his disciples and preached upon the lily.

For the angels of God took it out of his hand and carried it 495
to the Height.

For a man cannot have public spirit, who is void of private benevolence.

For there is no Height in which there are not flowers.

For flowers have great virtues for all the senses.

For the flower glorifies God and the root parries the adversary.

For *the flowers have their angels even the words of God's*   500
   Creation.

For *the warp and woof of flowers are worked by perpetual*
   moving spirits.

For *flowers are good both for the living and the dead.*

For *there is a language of flowers.*

For *there is a sound reasoning upon all flowers.*

For *elegant phrases are nothing but flowers.*   505

For *flowers are peculiarly the poetry of Christ.*

For *flowers are medicinal.*

For *flowers are musical in ocular harmony.*

For *the right names of flowers are yet in heaven. God make*
   gard'ners better nomenclators.

For *the Poorman's nosegay is an introduction to a Prince.*   510

For *it were better for the SERVICE, if only select psalms*
   were read.

For *the Lamentations of Jeremiah, Songs from other*
   scriptures, and parts of Esdras might be taken to supply
   the quantity.

For *A is the beginning of learning and the door of heaven.*

For *B is a creature busy and bustling.*

For *C is a sense quick and penetrating.*   515

For *D is depth.*

For *E is eternity – such is the power of the English letters*
   taken singly.

For *F is faith.*

For *G is God – whom I pray to be gracious to Livemore*
   my fellow prisoner.

For *H is not a letter, but a spirit – Benedicatur Jesus*   520
   Christus, sic spirem!

For *I is identity. God be gracious to Henry Hatsell.*

For K is king.

For L is love. God in every language.

For M is music and Hebrew מ is the direct figure of God's harp.

For N is new.   525

For O is open.

For P is power.

For Q is quick.

For R is right.

For S is soul.   530

For T is truth. God be gracious to Jermyn Pratt and to Harriote his Sister.

For U is unity, and his right name is Uve to work it double.

For W is word.

For ᴕG is hope – consisting of two check G – God be gracious to Anne Hope.

For Y is yea. God be gracious to Bennet and his family!   535

For Z is zeal.

For in the education of children it is necessary to watch the words, which they pronounce with difficulty, for such are against them in their consequences.

For A is awe, if pronounced full. Stand in awe and sin not.

For B pronounced in the animal is bey importing authority.

For C pronounced hard is ke importing to shut.   540

For D pronounced full is day.

For E is east particularly when formed little e with his eye.

For F in its secondary meaning is fair.

For G in a secondary sense is good.

For H is heave.   545

For I is the organ of vision.

For K is keep.

For L is light, and ⟩ is the line of beauty.

For M is meet.

For N is nay.   550

For O is over.

For P is peace.

For Q is quarter.

For R is rain, or thus reign, or thus rein.

For S is save.   555

For T is take.

For V is veil.

For W is world.

For ⊃G beginneth not, but connects and continues.

For Y is young – the Lord direct me in the better way of   560
    going on in the Fifth year of my jeopardy June the 17th
    N.S. 1760. God be gracious to Dr YOUNG.

For Z is zest. God give us all a relish of our duty.

For Action and Speaking are one according to God and the
    Ancients.

For the approaches of Death are by illumination.

For a man cannot have Public Spirit, who is void of private
    benevolence.

For the order of Alamoth is first three, second six, third   565
    eighteen, fourth fifty four, and then the whole band.

For the order of Sheminith is first ten, second twenty, third
    thirty and then the whole band.

For the first entrance into Heaven is by complement.

For Flowers can see, and Pope's Carnations knew him.

For the devil works upon damps and lowth and causes
    agues.

For *Ignorance is a sin, because illumination is to be had by* 570
prayer.

For *many a genius being lost at the plough is a false*
thought – the divine providence is a better manager.

For *a man's idleness is the fruit of the adversary's diligence.*

For *diligence is the gift of God, as well as other good*
things.

For *it is a good NOTHING in one's own eyes and in the*
eyes of fools.

For *aera in its primitive sense is but a weed amongst corn.* 575

For *there is no knowing of times and seasons, in submitting*
them to God stands the Christian's Chronology.

For *Jacob's brown sheep wore the Golden fleece.*

For *Shaving of the face was the invention of the Sodomites*
to make men look like women.

For *God has given us a language of monosyllables to*
prevent our clipping.

For *a toad enjoys a finer prospect than another creature to* 580
compensate his lack.
  Tho' toad I am the object of man's hate.
  Yet better am I than a reprobate. (who has the worst
    of prospects).

For *there are stones, whose constituent particles are little*
toads.

For *the spiritual music is as follows.*

For *there is the thunder-stop, which is the voice of God*
direct.

For *the rest of the stops are by their rhymes.*

For *the trumpet rhymes are sound bound, soar more and* 585
the like.

For *the Shawm rhymes are lawn fawn moon boon and the*
like.

For the harp rhymes are sing ring string and the like.

For the cymbal rhymes are bell well toll soul and the like.

For the flute rhymes are tooth youth suit mute and the like.

For the dulcimer rhymes are grace place beat heat and the   590
like.

For the Clarinet rhymes are clean seen and the like.

For the Bassoon rhymes are pass, class and the like. God be
gracious to Baumgarden.

For the dulcimer are rather van fan and the like and grace
place &c are of the bassoon.

For the beat heat, weep peep &c are of the pipe.

For every word has its marrow in the English tongue for   595
order and for delight.

For the dissyllables such as able table &c are the fiddle
rhymes.

For all dissyllables and some trissyllables are fiddle rhymes.

For the relations of words are in pairs first.

For the relations of words are sometimes in oppositions.

For the relations of words are according to their distances   600
from the pair.

For there be twelve cardinal virtues the gifts of the twelve
sons of Jacob.

For Reuben is Great. God be gracious to Lord Falmouth.

For Simeon is Valiant. God be gracious to the Duke of
Somerset.

For Levi is Pious. God be gracious to the Bishop of
London.

For Judah is Good. God be gracious to Lord Granville.   605

For Dan is Clean — neat, dextrous, apt, active, compact.
God be gracious to Draper.

For Naphtali is sublime — God be gracious to Chesterfield.

For Gad is Contemplative – God be gracious to Lord
  Northampton.

For Ashur is Happy – God be gracious to George Bowes.

For Issachar is strong – God be gracious to the Duke of   610
  Dorsett.

For Zabulon is Constant – God be gracious to Lord Bath.

For Joseph is Pleasant – God be gracious to Lord
  Bolingbroke.

For Benjamin is Wise – God be gracious to Honeywood.

For all Foundation is from God depending.

For the two Universities are the Eyes of England.   615

For Cambridge is the right and the brightest.

For Pembroke Hall was founded more in the Lord than
  any College in Cambridge.

For mustard is the proper food of birds and men are bound
  to cultivate it for their use.

For they that study the works of God are peculiarly
  assisted by his Spirit.

For all the creatures mention'd by Pliny are somewhere or   620
  other extant to the glory of God.

For Rye is food rather for fowls than men.

For Rye-bread is not taken with thankfulness.

For the lack of Rye may be supplied by Spelt.

For languages work into one another by their bearings.

For the power of some animal is predominant in every   625
  language.

For the power and spirit of a CAT is in the Greek.

For the sound of a cat is in the most useful preposition xατ'
  ευχην.

For the pleasantry of a cat at pranks is in the language ten
  thousand times over.

For JACK UPON PRANCK is in the performance of περι together or separate.

For Clapperclaw is in the grappling of the words upon one 630 another in all the modes of versification.

For the sleekness of a Cat is in his αγλαιηφι.

For the Greek is thrown from heaven and falls upon its feet.

For the Greek when distracted from the line is sooner restored to rank and rallied into some form than any other.

For the purring of a Cat is his τρυζει.

For his cry is in οναι, which I am sorry for. 635

For the Mouse (Mus) prevails in the Latin.

For Edi-mus, bibi-mus, vivi-mus — ore-mus.

For the Mouse is a creature of great personal valour.

For – this is a true case – Cat takes female mouse from the company of male – male mouse will not depart, but stands threat'ning and daring.

For this is as much as to challenge, if you will let her go, I 640 will engage you, as prodigious a creature as you are.

For the Mouse is of an hospitable disposition.

For bravery and hospitality were said and done by the Romans rather than others.

For two creatures the Bull and the Dog prevail in the English.

For all the words ending in -ble are in the creature. Invisi-ble, Incomprehensi-ble, ineffa-ble, A-ble.

For the Greek and Latin are not dead languages, but taken 645 up and accepted for the sake of him that spoke them.

For can is (canis) is cause and effect a dog.

For the English is concise and strong. Dog and Bull again.

For Newton's notion of colours is αλογος unphilosophical.

For the colours are spiritual.

For WHITE is the first and the best.   650

For there are many intermediate colours, before you come
     to SILVER.

For the next colour is a lively GREY.

For the next colour is BLUE.

For the next is GREEN of which there are ten thousand
     distinct sorts.

For the next is YELLOW which is more excellent than red, 655
     tho' Newton makes red the prime. God be gracious to
     John Delap.

For RED is the next working round the Orange.

For Red is of sundry sorts till it deepens to BLACK.

For black blooms and it is PURPLE.

For purple works off to BROWN which is of ten thousand
     acceptable shades.

For the next is PALE. God be gracious to William   660
     Whitehead.

For pale works about to White again.

NOW that colour is spiritual appears inasmuch as the
     blessing of God upon all things descends in colour.

For the blessing of health upon the human face is in colour.

For the blessing of God upon purity is in the Virgin's
     blushes.

For the blessing of God in colour is on him that keeps his   665
     virgin.

For I saw a blush in Staindrop Church, which was of God's
     own colouring.

For it was the benevolence of a virgin shewn to me before
     the whole congregation.

For the blessing of God upon the grass is in shades of
Green visible to a nice observer as they light upon the
surface of the earth.

For the blessing of God unto perfection in all bloom and
fruit is by colouring.

For from hence something in the spirit may be taken off by   670
painters.

For Painting is a species of idolatry, tho' not so gross as
statuary.

For it is not good to look with earning upon any dead
work.

For by so doing something is lost in the spirit and given
from life to death.

For BULL in the first place is the word of Almighty God.

For he is a creature of infinite magnitude in the height.   675

For there is the model of every beast of the field in the
height.

For they are blessed intelligences and all angels of the living
God.

For there are many words under Bull.

For Bul the Month is under it.

For Sea is under Bull.   680

For Brook is under Bull. God be gracious to Lord
Bolingbroke.

For Rock is under Bull.

For Bullfinch is under Bull. God be gracious to the Duke of
Cleveland.

For God, which always keeps his work in view has painted
a Bullfinch in the heart of a stone. God be gracious to
Gosling and Canterbury.

For the Bluecap is under Bull.   685

For the Humming Bird is under Bull.

For Beetle is under Bull.

For Toad is under bull.

For Frog is under Bull, which he has a delight to look at.

For the Pheasant-eyed Pink is under Bull. Blessed Jesus   690
    RANK EL.

For Bugloss is under Bull.

For Bugle is under Bull.

For Oxeye is under Bull.

For Fire is under Bull.

For I will consider my Cat Jeoffry.   695

For he is the servant of the Living God duly and daily
    serving him.

For at the first glance of the glory of God in the East he
    worships in his way.

For is this done by wreathing his body seven times round
    with elegant quickness.

For then he leaps up to catch the musk, which is the
    blessing of God upon his prayer.

For he rolls upon prank to work it in.   700

For having done duty and received blessing he begins to
    consider himself.

For this he performs in ten degrees.

For first he looks upon his fore-paws to see if they are
    clean.

For secondly he kicks up behind to clear away there.

For thirdly he works it upon stretch with the fore-paws   705
    extended.

For fourthly he sharpens his paws by wood.

For fifthly he washes himself.

For Sixthly he rolls upon wash.

For *Seventhly he fleas himself, that he may not be
interrupted upon the beat.*

For *Eighthly he rubs himself against a post.*   710

For *Ninthly he looks up for his instructions.*

For *Tenthly he goes in quest of food.*

For *having consider'd God and himself he will consider his
neighbour.*

For *if he meets another cat he will kiss her in kindness.*

For *when he takes his prey he plays with it to give it*   715
chance.

For *one mouse in seven escapes by his dallying.*

For *when his day's work is done his business more properly
begins.*

For *he keeps the Lord's watch in the night against the
adversary.*

For *he counteracts the powers of darkness by his electrical
skin and glaring eyes.*

For *he counteracts the Devil, who is death, by brisking*   720
about the life.

For *in his morning orisons he loves the sun and the sun
loves him.*

For *he is of the tribe of Tiger.*

For *the Cherub Cat is a term of the Angel Tiger.*

For *he has the subtlety and hissing of a serpent, which in
goodness he suppresses.*

For *he will not do destruction, if he is well-fed, neither will*   725
he spit without provocation.

For *he purrs in thankfulness, when God tells him he's a
good Cat.*

For *he is an instrument for the children to learn
benevolence upon.*

For *every house is incomplete without him and a blessing is lacking in the spirit.*

For *the Lord commanded Moses concerning the cats at the departure of the Children of Israel from Egypt.*

For *every family had one cat at least in the bag.*   730

For *the English Cats are the best in Europe.*

For *he is the cleanest in the use of his fore-paws of any quadrupede.*

For *the dexterity of his defence is an instance of the love of God to him exceedingly.*

For *he is the quickest to his mark of any creature.*

For *he is tenacious of his point.*   735

For *he is a mixture of gravity and waggery.*

For *he knows that God is his Saviour.*

For *there is nothing sweeter than his peace when at rest.*

For *there is nothing brisker than his life when in motion.*

For *he is of the Lord's poor and so indeed is he called by*   740
benevolence perpetually – Poor Jeoffry! poor Jeoffry! the rat has bit thy throat.

For *I bless the name of the Lord Jesus that Jeoffry is better.*

For *the divine spirit comes about his body to sustain it in complete cat.*

For *his tongue is exceeding pure so that it has in purity what it wants in music.*

For *he is docile and can learn certain things.*

For *he can set up with gravity which is patience upon*   745
approbation.

For *he can fetch and carry, which is patience in employment.*

For he can jump over a stick which is patience upon proof positive.

For he can spraggle upon waggle at the word of command.

For he can jump from an eminence into his master's bosom.

For he can catch the cork and toss it again. 750

For he is hated by the hypocrite and miser.

For the former is afraid of detection.

For the latter refuses the charge.

For he camels his back to bear the first notion of business.

For he is good to think on, if a man would express himself 755 neatly.

For he made a great figure in Egypt for his signal services.

For he killed the Ichneumon-rat very pernicious by land.

For his ears are so acute that they sting again.

For from this proceeds the passing quickness of his attention.

For by stroking of him I have found out electricity. 760

For I perceived God's light about him both wax and fire.

For the Electrical fire is the spiritual substance, which God sends from heaven to sustain the bodies both of man and beast.

For God has blessed him in the variety of his movements.

For, tho' he cannot fly, he is an excellent clamberer.

For his motions upon the face of the earth are more than 765 any other quadrupede.

For he can tread to all the measures upon the music.

For he can swim for life.

For he can creep.

Fragment C

Let Ramah rejoice with Cochineal.
For H is a spirit and therefore he is God.

Let Gaba rejoice with the Prickly Pear, which the Cochineal
feeds on.
For I is person and therefore he is God.

Let Nebo rejoice with the Myrtle-Leaved-Sumach as with
the Skirret Jub. 2d.
For K is king and therefore he is God.

Let Magbish rejoice with the Sage-Tree Phlomis as with the
Goats-beard Jub. 2d.
For L is love and therefore he is God.

Let Hashum rejoice with Moon-Trefoil.   5
For M is music and therefore he is God.

Let Netophah rejoice with Cow-Wheat.
For N is novelty and therefore he is God.

Let Chephirah rejoice with Millet.
For O is over and therefore he is God.

Let Beeroth rejoice with Sea-Buckthorn.
For P is power and therefore he is God.

Let Kirjath-arim rejoice with Cacalianthemum.
For Q is quick and therefore he is God.

Let Hadid rejoice with Capsicum Guiney Pepper.   10
For R is right and therefore he is God.

Let Senaah rejoice with Bean Caper.
For S is soul and therefore he is God.

Let Kadmiel rejoice with Hemp-Agrimony.
For T is truth and therefore he is God.

Let Shobai rejoice with Arbor Molle.
For U is union and therefore he is God.

Let Hatita rejoice with Millefolium Yarrow.
For W is worth and therefore he is God.

Let Ziha rejoice with Mitellia.
For X has the pow'r of three and therefore he is God.

Let Hasupha rejoice with Turkey Balm.
For Y is yea and therefore he is God.

Let Hattil rejoice with Xeranthemum.
For Z is zeal and therefore he is God, whom I pray to be gracious to the Widow Davis and Davis the Bookseller.

Let Bilshan rejoice with the Leek. David for ever! God bless the Welch March 1st 1761 N.S.
For Christ being A and Ω is all the intermediate letters without doubt.

Let Sotai rejoice with the Mountain Ebony.
For there is a mystery in numbers.

Let Sophereth rejoice with White Hellebore.   20
For One is perfect and good being at unity in himself.

Let Darkon rejoice with the Melon-Thistle.
For Two is the most imperfect of all numbers.

Let Jaalah rejoice with Moly wild garlic.
For every thing infinitely perfect is Three.

Let Ami rejoice with the Bladder Sena in season or out of season bless the name of the Lord.
For the Devil is two being without God.

Let Pochereth rejoice with Fleabane.
For he is an evil spirit male and female.

Let Keros rejoice with Tree Germander.   25
For he is called the Duce by foolish invocation on that account.

Let Padon rejoice with Tamnus Black Briony.
For Three is the simplest and best of all numbers.

Let Mizpar rejoice with Stickadore.
For Four is good being square.

Let Baanah rejoice with Napus the French Turnip.
For Five is not so good in itself but works well in combination.

Let Reelaiah rejoice with the Sea-Cabbage.
For Five is not so good in itself as it consists of two and
three.

Let Parosh rejoice with Cacubalus Chickweed.   30
For Six is very good consisting of twice three.

Let Hagab rejoice with Serpyllum Mother of Thyme.
    Hosanna to the memory of Q. Anne. March 8th
    N.S. 1761 – God be gracious to old Windsmore.
For Seven is very good consisting of two complete
numbers.

Let Shalmai rejoice with Meadow Rue. –
For Eight is good for the same reason and propitious to me
Eighth of March 1761 hallelujah.

Let Habaiah rejoice with Asteriscus Yellow Starwort.
For Nine is a number very good and harmonious.

Let Tel-harsa rejoice with Aparine Clivers.
For Cipher is a note of augmentation very good.

Let Rehoboam rejoice with Polium Montanum. God give   35
    grace to the Young King.
For innumerable ciphers will amount to something.

Let Hanan rejoice with Poley of Crete.
For the mind of man cannot bear a tedious accumulation of
nothing without effect.

Let Sheshbazzar rejoice with Polygonatum Solomon's seal.
For infinite upon infinite they make a chain.

Let Zeboim rejoice with Bastard Dittany.
For the last link is from man very nothing ascending to the
first Christ the Lord of All.

Let The Queen of Sheba rejoice with Bulapathon Herb
    Patience.
For the vowel is the female spirit in the Hebrew consonant.

Let Cyrus rejoice with Baccharis Plowman's Spikenard.   40
    God be gracious to Warburton.
For there are more letters in all languages not
communicated.

Let Lebanah rejoice with the Golden Wingged Flycatcher a
Mexican Small Bird of Passage.
*For there are some that have the power of sentences. O
rare thirteenth of march 1761.*

Let Hagabah rejoice with Orchis. Blessed be the name of
the Lord Jesus for my seed in eternity.
For St Paul was caught up into the third heavens.

Let Siaha rejoice with the Razor-Fish. God be gracious to
John Bird and his wife.
*For there he heard certain words which it was not possible
for him to understand.*

Let Artaxerxes rejoice with Vanelloes. Palm Sunday 1761.
The Lord Strengthen me.
For they were constructed by uncommunicated letters.

Let Bishlam rejoice with the Cotton-bush.   45
*For they are signs of speech too precious to be
communicated for ever.*

Let Mithridath rejoice with Balsam of Tolu.
*For after ה there follows another letter in the Hebrew
tongue.*

Let Tabeel rejoice with the Carob-tree.
For his name is Wau and his figure is thus ﭏ.

Let Ariel rejoice with Balsam of Peru, which sweats from a
tree, that flowers like the Foxglove.
*For the Aeolians knew something of him in the spirit, but
could not put him down.*

Let Ebed rejoice with Balsam of Gilead. God be gracious to
Stede.
*For the figures were first communicated to Esaw. God be
gracious to Musgrave.*

Let Jarib rejoice with Balsam of Capivi. The Lord   50
strengthen my reins.
For he was blest as a merchant.

Let Shimshai rejoice with Stelis Missletoe on Fir.
*For the blessing of Jacob was in the spirit and Esau's for
temporal thrift.*

Let Joiarib rejoice with Veronica Fluellen or Speedwell.
For the story of Orpheus is of the truth.

Let Tatnai rejoice with the Barbadoes Wild Olive.
For there was such a person a cunning player on the harp.

Let Ezra rejoice with the Reed. The Lord Jesus make music
of it. Good Friday 1761.
*For he was a believer in the true God and assisted in the
spirit.*

Let Josiphiah rejoice with Tower-Mustard. God be   55
gracious to Durham School.
*For he play'd upon the harp in the spirit by breathing upon
the strings.*

Let Shether-boznai rejoice with Turnera. End of Lent 1761.
No. 5.
*For this will affect every thing that is sustain'd by the spirit,
even every thing in nature.*

Let Jozadak rejoice with Stephanitis a vine growing
naturally into chaplets.
*For it is the business of a man gifted in the word to
prophesy good.*

Let Jozabad rejoice with the Lily-Daffodil. Easter Day 22nd
March 1761.
*For it will be better for England and all the world in a
season, as I prophesy this day.*

Let Telem rejoice with Hart's Penny-royal.
*For I prophesy that they will obey the motions of the spirit
descended upon them as at this day.*

Let Abdi rejoice with Winter-green. God be gracious to   60
Abdy.
*For they have seen the glory of God already come down
upon the trees.*

Let Binnui rejoice with Spotted Lungwort or Couslip of
  Jerusalem. God give blessing with it.
For I prophesy that it will descend upon their heads also.

Let Aziza rejoice with the Day Lily.
*For I prophesy that the praise of God will be in every
  man's mouth in the Public streets.*

Let Zabbai rejoice with Buckshorn Plaintain Coronopus.
*For I prophesy that there will be Public worship in the
  cross ways and fields.*

Let Ramoth rejoice with Persicaria.
*For I prophesy that the general salutation will be: The
  Lord Jesus prosper you. I wish you good luck in the
  name of the Lord Jesus!*

Let Athlai rejoice with Bastard Marjoram.   65
For I prophesy that there will be more mercy for criminals.

Let Uel rejoice with Lysimachia Loose-strife which drinks
  of the brook by the way.
*For I prophesy that there will be less mischief concerning
  women.*

Let Kelaiah rejoice with Hermannia.
*For I prophesy that they will be cooped up and kept under
  due controul.*

Let Elasah rejoice with Olibanum White or Male
  Frankincense from an Arabian tree, good against
  Catarrhs and Spitting blood from which Christ Jesus
  deliver me.
*For I prophesy that there will be full churches and empty
  play-houses.*

Let Adna rejoice with Gum Opopanax from the wounded
  root of a species of panace, Heracleum, a tall plant
  growing to be two or three yards high with many large
  wings of a yellowish green – good for old coughs and
  asthmas.
*For I prophesy that they will learn to take pleasure in
  glorifying God with great cheerfulness.*

Let Bedeiah rejoice with Gum Sagapenum flowing from a   70
    species of Ferula which grows in Media. Lord have
    mercy on my breast.
For I prophesy that they will observe the Rubric with
    regard to days of Fasting and Abstinence.

Let Ishijah rejoice with Sago gotten from the inward pith of
    the bread-tree. The Lord Jesus strengthen my whole
    body.
For I prophesy that the clergy in particular will set a better
    example.

Let Chelal rejoice with Apios Virginian Liquorice Vetch.
For I prophesy that they will not dare to imprison a
    brother or sister for debt.

Let Miamin rejoice with Mezereon. God be gracious to
    Polly and Bess and all Canbury.
For I prophesy that hospitality and temperance will revive.

Let Zebida rejoice with Tormentil good for haemorrhages
    in the mouth – even so Lord Jesus.
For I prophesy that men will be much stronger in the body.

Let Shemaria rejoice with Riciasides.   75
For I prophesy that the gout, and consumptions will be
    curable.

Let Jadau rejoice with Flixweed.
For I prophesy that man will be as good as a Lupine.

Let Shimeon rejoice with Squills.
For the Lupine professes his Saviour in Grain.

Let Sheal rejoice with Scorpioides. God be gracious to
    Legg.
For the very Hebrew letter is fairly graven upon his Seed.

Let Ramiah rejoice with Water-Germander.
For with diligence the whole Hebrew Alphabet may be
    found in a parcel of his seed.

Let Jeziah rejoice with Viper's Grass.   80
For this is a stupendous evidence of the communicating
    God in externals.

Let Machnadebai rejoice with the Mink, a beast.
For I prophesy that they will call the days by better names.

Let Meremoth rejoice with the Golden Titmouse of
  Surinam.
For the Lord's day is the first.

Let Mattenai rejoice with Hatchet Vetch.
For the following is the second.

Let Chelluh rejoice with Horehound.
For so of the others untill the seventh.

Let Jaasau rejoice with Bird's foot.   85
*For the seventh day is the Sabbath according to the word of
  God direct for ever and ever.*

Let Maadai rejoice with Golden Rod.
*For I prophesy that the King will have grace to put the
  crown upon the altar.*

Let Sharai rejoice with Honey-flower.
*For I prophesy that the name of king in England will be
  given to Christ alone.*

Let Shashai rejoice with Smyrnium.
*For I prophesy that men will live to a much greater age.
  This ripens apace God be praised.*

Let Hananiah the son of an apothecary rejoice with
  Bdellium.
For I prophesy that they will grow taller and stronger.

Let Hassenaah rejoice with the White Beet. God be   90
  gracious to Hasse and all musicians.
*For degeneracy has done a great deal more than is in
  general imagined.*

Let Hachaliah rejoice with Muscus Arboreus.
For men in David's time were ten feet high in general.

Let Sanballat rejoice with Ground Moss found sometimes
  on human skulls.
*For they had degenerated also from the strength of their
  fathers.*

Let Col-hozeh rejoice with Myrobalans, Bellerica, Chebula,
Citrina, Emblica and Indica.
*For I prophesy that players and mimes will not be named
amongst us.*

Let Meah rejoice with Variae, a kind of streaked panther.
April 8th praise the name of the Lord.
*For I prophesy in the favour of dancing which in mutual
benevolence is for the glory of God.*

Let Eliashib rejoice with Shepherd's Purse.   95
*For I prophesy that the exactions of Moab will soon be at
an end.*

Let Azbuk rejoice with Valerianella Corn Sallet.
*For the Moabites even the French are in their chastisement
for humiliation.*

Let Geshem (which is Rain) rejoice with Kneeholm. Blessed
be the name of the Lord Jesus for Rain and his family
and for the plenteous rain this day. April 9th 1761. N.S.
*For I prophesy that the Reformation will make way in
France when Moab is made meek by being well drubbed
by the English.*

Let Bavai rejoice with Calceolus Ladies Slipper.
*For I prophesy that the Reformation will make great way
by means of the Venetians.*

Let Henadad rejoice with Cacalianthemum.
*For the Venetian will know that the Englishman is his
brother.*

Let Shallum rejoice with Mullein Tapsus barbatus, good   100
for the breast.
For the Liturgy will obtain in all languages.

Let Ophel rejoice with Camara.
For England is the head and not the tail.

Let Meshezabeel rejoice with Stephanomelis. Old April
bless the name of the Lord Jesus.
For England is the head of Europe in the spirit.

Let Zadok the son of Baana rejoice with Viburnum.
For Spain, Portugal and France are the heart.

Let Vaniah rejoice with Pug in a pinner. God be gracious to
the house of Vane especially Anne.
For Holland and Germany are the middle.

Let Besodeiah rejoice with the Nettle.   105
For Italy is one of the legs.

Let Melatiah rejoice with Adonis Bird's eye.
*For I prophesy that there will not be a meetinghouse within
two miles of a church.*

Let Jadon rejoice with Borrage.
For I prophesy that schismatics will be detected.

Let Palal rejoice with the female Balsamime. God be
gracious to my wife.
For I prophesy that men will learn the use of their knees.

Let Ezer rejoice with Basella Climbing Nightshade.
*For every thing that can be done in that posture (upon the
knees) is better so done than otherwise.*

Let Uzai rejoice with Meadow Sweet.   110
*For I prophesy that they will understand the blessing and
virtue of the rain.*

Let Zalaph rejoice with Rose-bay.
For rain is exceedingly good for the human body.

Let Halohesh rejoice with Ambrosia, that bears a fruit like
a club.
*For it is good therefore to have flat roofs to the houses, as
of old.*

Let Malchiah Son of Rechab rejoice with the Rose-colour'd
flow'ring Rush.
*For it is good to let the rain come upon the naked body
unto purity and refreshment.*

Let Sia rejoice with Argemone Prickly Poppy.
For I prophesy that they will respect decency in all points.

Let Lebana rejoice with Amaranthoides Globe Amaranth.   115
For they will do it in conceit, word, and motion.

Let Rephaiah the Son of Hur rejoice with the Berry-bearing
    Angelica.
For they will go forth afield.

Let Harhaiah of the Goldsmiths rejoice with Segullum, the
    earth that detects the mine.
*For the Devil can work upon stagnating filth to a very great
    degree.*

Let Harumaph rejoice with the Upright Honeysuckle.
For I prophesy that we shall have our horns again.

Let Hashabniah rejoice with the Water Melon. Blessed be
    the manuscripts of Almighty God.
*For in the day of David Man as yet had a glorious horn
    upon his forehead.*

Let Phaseah rejoice with the Cassioberry Bush.   120
*For this horn was a bright substance in colour and
    consistence as the nail of the hand.*

Let Nephishesim rejoice with Cannacorus Indian Reed.
*For it was broad, thick and strong so as to serve for
    defence as well as ornament.*

Let Tamah rejoice with Cainito Star-Apple – God be
    praised for this Eleventh of April o.s. in which I enter
    into the Fortieth Year of my age. Blessed. Blessed.
    Blessed!
*For it brighten'd to the Glory of God, which came upon
    the human face at morning prayer.*

Let Siloah rejoice with Guidonia with a Rose-Colour'd-
    Flower.
For it was largest and brightest in the best men.

Let Benjamin a Rebuilder of Jerusalem rejoice with the
    Rock-Rose. Newton, bless!
For it was taken away all at once from all of them.

Let Malchijah Son of Harim rejoice with Crysanthemoides. 125
*For this was done in the divine contempt of a general
    pusillanimity.*

Let Besai rejoice with Hesperis Queen's Gilly-Flow'r.
*For this happened in a season after their return from the
    Babylonish captivity.*

Let Perida rejoice with Podded Fumitory.
*For their spirits were broke and their manhood impair'd by
    foreign vices for exaction.*

Let Tabbaoth rejoice with Goldy Locks. God be merciful to
    my wife.
*For I prophesy that the English will recover their horns the
    first.*

Let Bakbuk rejoice with Soft Thistle.
*For I prophesy that all the nations in the world will do the
    like in turn.*

Let Hodevah rejoice with Coronilla.   130
*For I prophesy that all Englishmen will wear their beards
    again.*

Let Tobiah rejoice with Crotolaria. God be praised for his
    infinite goodness and mercy.
For a beard is a good step to a horn.

Let Mehetabeel rejoice with Haemanthus the Blood Flower.
    Blessed be the name of the Blood of the Lord Jesus.
*For when men get their horns again, they will delight to go
    uncovered.*

Let Bazlith rejoice with the Horned Poppy.
For it is not good to wear any thing upon the head.

Let Hagaba rejoice with the Turnsole. God be gracious to
    Cutting.
*For a man should put no obstacle between his head and the
    blessing of Almighty God.*

Let Shalmai rejoice with Lycopersicum Love-Apple. God be 135
    gracious to Dunn.
*For a hat was an abomination of the heathen. Lord have
    mercy upon the Quakers.*

Let Arah rejoice with Fritillaria the Chequer'd Tulip.
For the ceiling of the house is an obstacle and therefore we
pray on the house-top.

Let Raamiah rejoice with the Double Sweetscented Pione.
For the head will be liable to less disorders on the recovery
of its horn.

Let Hashub Son of Pahath-moab rejoice with the French
Honeysuckle.
For the horn on the forehead is a tower upon an arch.

Let Ananiah rejoice with the Corn-Flag.
For it is a strong munition against the adversary, who is
sickness and death.

Let Nahamani rejoice with the May-apple. God give me   140
fruit to this month.
For it is instrumental in subjecting the woman.

Let Mispereth rejoice with the Ring Parakeet.
For the insolence of the woman has increased ever since
Man has been crest-fallen.

Let Nehum rejoice with the Artichoke.
For they have turned the horn into scoff and derision
without ceasing.

Let Ginnethon rejoice with the Bottle Flower.
For we are amerced of God, who has his horn.

Let Zidkijah rejoice with Mulberry Blight. God be gracious
to Gum my fellow Prisoner.
For we are amerced of the blessed angels, who have their
horns.

Let Malluch rejoice with Methonica Superb Lily.   145
For when they get their horns again they will put them
upon the altar.

Let Jeremiah rejoice with Hemlock, which is good in
outward application.
For they give great occasion for mirth and music.

Let Bilgai rejoice with Tamalapatra Indian Leaf.
*For our Blessed Saviour had not his horn upon the face of
    the earth.*

Let Maaziah rejoice with Chick Pease. God be gracious to
    Harris White 5th of May 1761.
*For this was in meekness and condescension to the
    infirmities of human nature at that time.*

Let Kelita rejoice with Xiphion the Bulbous Iris.
For at his second coming his horn will be exalted in glory.

Let Pelaiah rejoice with Cloud-Berries. God be gracious to   150
    Peele and Ferry.
For his horn is the horn of Salvation.

Let Azaniah rejoice with the Water Lily.
For Christ Jesus has exalted my voice to his own glory.

Let Rehob rejoice with Caucalis Bastard Parsley.
*For he has answered me in the air as with a horn from
    Heaven to the ears of many people.*

Let Sherebiah rejoice with Nigella, that bears a white
    flower.
For the horn is of plenty.

Let Beninu rejoice with Heart-Pear. God be gracious to
    George Bening.
For this has been the sense of all ages.

Let Bunni rejoice with Bulbine – leaves like leek, purple   155
    flower.
For Man and Earth suffer together.

Let Zatthu rejoice with the Wild Service.
*For when Man was amerced of his horn, earth lost part of
    her fertility.*

Let Hizkijah rejoice with the Dwarf American Sun-Flower.
For the art of Agriculture is improving.

Let Azzur rejoice with the Globe-Thistle.
For this is evident in flowers.

Let Hariph rejoice with Summer Savoury.
For it is more especially manifest in double flowers.

Let Nebai rejoice with the Wild Cucumber.   160
*For earth will get it up again by the blessing of God on the
    industry of man.*

Let Magpiash rejoice with the Musk.
For the horn is of plenty because of milk and honey.

Let Hezir rejoice with Scorpion Sena.
*For I pray God be gracious to the Bees and the Beeves this
    day.*

Fragment D

Let Dew, house of Dew rejoice with Xanthenes a precious
    stone of an amber colour.

Let Round, house of Round rejoice with Myrmecites a gem
    having an Emmet in it.

Let New, house of New rejoice with Nasamonites a gem of
    a sanguine colour with black veins.

Let Hook, house of Hook rejoice with Sarda a Cornelian –
    blessed be the name of the Lord Jesus by hook.

Let Crook, house of Crook rejoice with Ophites black   5
    spotted marble – Blessed be the name of the Lord Jesus
    by crook. The Lord enable me to shift.

Let Lime, house of Lime rejoice with Sandareses a kind of
    gem in Pliny's list.

Let Linnet, house of Linnet rejoice with Tanos, which is a
    mean sort of Emerald.

Let Hind, house of Hind rejoice with Paederos Opal – God
    be gracious to Mrs Hind, that lived at Canbury.

Let Tyrrel, house of Tyrrel rejoice with Sardius Lapis an
    Onyx of a black colour. God speed Hawke's Fleet.

Let Moss, house of Moss rejoice with the Pearl-Oyster
behold how God has consider'd for him that lacketh.

Let Ross, house of Ross rejoice with the Great Flabber
Dabber Flat Clapping Fish with hands. Vide Anson's
Voyage and Psalm 98th ix.

Let Fisher, house of Fisher rejoice with Sandastros a kind
of burning stone with gold drops in the body of it. God
be gracious to Fisher of Cambridge and to all of his
name and kindred.

Let Fuller, house of Fuller rejoice with Perileucos a precious
stone with a white thread descending from its face to the
bottom.

Let Thorpe, house of Thorpe rejoice with Xystios an
ordinary stone of the Jasper-kind.

Let Alban, house of Alban rejoice with Scorpites a precious
stone in some degree of the creatures.

Let Wand, house of Wand rejoice with Synochitis a gem
supposed by Pliny to have certain magical effects.

Let Freeman, house of Freeman rejoice with Carcinias a
precious stone the colour of a sea-crab. The Lord raise
the landed interest.

Let Quince, house of Quince rejoice with Onychipuncta a
gem of the Jasper-kind.

Let Manly, house of Manly rejoice with the Booby a
tropical bird.

Let Fage, house of Fage rejoice with the Fiddlefish – Blessed
be the name of the Lord Jesus in the fish's mouth.

Let Benning, house of Benning rejoice with the Sea-Egg.
Lord have mercy on the soul of Benning's wife.

Let Singleton, house of Singleton rejoice with the Hog-
Plumb. Lord have mercy on the soul of Lord Vane.

Let Thickness, house of Thickness rejoice with The Papah a
fruit found at Chequetan.

Let Heartly, house of Heartly rejoice with the Drummer-
Fish. God be gracious to Heartly of Christ, to Marsh,
Hingeston and Bill.

Let Sizer, house of Sizer rejoice with Trichros a precious   25
stone black at bottom, white atop and blood-red in the
middle.

Let Chetwind, house of Chetwind rejoice with
Hammocrysos, a gem with gold sands on it.

Let Branch, house of Branch rejoice with Haematites –
Blessed be the name of the Lord Jesus THE BRANCH.

Let Dongworth, house of Dongworth rejoice with Rhymay
the Bread-fruit. God be gracious to the immortal soul of
Richard Dongworth.

Let Randall, house of Randall rejoice with Guavoes. God
give Randall success.

Let Osborne, house of Osborne rejoice with Lithizontes a   30
sort of carbuncle. God be gracious to the Duke of Leeds
and his family.

Let Oldcastle, house of Oldcastle rejoice with
Leucopthalmos. God put it in heart of king to repair and
beautify Dover Castle.

Let Beeson, house of Beeson rejoice with Pyropus,
carbuncle opal. God be gracious to Masters of Yoke's
Place.

Let Salmon, house of Salmon rejoice with Sapinos a kind of
Amethyst.

Let Crutenden, house of Crutenden rejoice with Veneris
Gemma a kind of amethyst.

Let Bridges, house of Bridges rejoice with Jasponyx, which   35
is the Jasper-Onyx.

Let Lane, house of Lane rejoice with Myrmecias a precious
stone with little knots in it.

Let Cope, house of Cope rejoice with Centipedes. God give
me strength to cope with all my adversaries.

Let Sutton, house of Sutton rejoice with Cholos a gem of
the Emerald kind.

Let Pelham, house of Pelham rejoice with Callimus in
Taphiusio one stone in the body of another. God bless
the Duke of Newcastle.

Let Holles, house of Holles rejoice with Pyriasis a black   40
stone that burns by friction. The Lord kindle amongst
Englishmen a sense of their name.

Let Lister, house of Lister rejoice with Craterites a very
hard stone. The Lord hear my prayer even as I attend
unto his commandments.

Let Ash, house of Ash rejoice with Callaica a green gem.
God be gracious to Miss Leroche my fellow traveller
from Calais.

Let Baily, house of Baily rejoice with Catopyrites of
Cappadocia. God be gracious to the immortal soul of
Lewis Baily author of the Practice of Piety.

Let Glover, house of Glover rejoice with Capnites a kind of
Jasper – blessed be the memory of Glover the martyr.

Let Egerton, house of Egerton rejoice with Sphragis, green   45
but not pellucid.

Let Reading, house of Reading rejoice with Synodontites
found in the fish Synodontes, 27th July N.S. 1762 Lord
Jesus have mercy on my soul.

Let Bolton, house of Bolton rejoice with Polygrammos, a
kind of Jasper with white streaks.

Let Paulet, house of Paulet rejoice with Chalcites, a
precious stone of the colour of Brass.

Let Stapleton, house of Stapleton rejoice with Scythis a
precious stone – the Lord rebuild the old houses of
England.

Let Newdigate, house of Newdigate rejoice with   50
Sandaserion a stone in India like Green Oil.

Let Knightly, house of Knightly rejoice with Zoronysios a gem supposed by the ancients to have magical effects. Star – word – herb – gem.

Let Fellows, house of Fellows rejoice with Syrites a gem found in a Wolf's bladder.

Let Ascham, house of Ascham rejoice with Thyitis a precious stone remarkably hard. God be gracious to Bennet.

Let Mowbray, house of Mowbray rejoice with The Black and Blue Creeper a beautiful small bird of Brazil.

Let Aldrich, house of Aldrich rejoice with the Trincalo or Tricolor, a leaf without a flower or the flower of a leaf. 55

Let Culmer, house of Culmer rejoice with Phloginos a gem of a fire-colour.

Let Catesby, house of Catesby rejoice with Cerites a precious stone like wax.

Let Atterbury, house of Atterbury rejoice with Eurotias a black stone with the appearance of mould on it.

Let Hoare, house of Hoare rejoice with Crysopis a precious stone of a gold-colour. God be gracious to John Rust.

Let Fane, house of Fane rejoice with Chalcedonius Lapis a 60
sort of onyx called a Chalcedony.

Let Lorman, house of Lorman rejoice with Cheramites, a sort of precious stone.

Let Flexney, house of Flexney rejoice with Triopthalmos – God be gracious to Churchill, Loyd and especially to Sheels.

Let Gavel, house of Gavel rejoice with Phlogites a precious stone of a various flame-colour.

Let Hederick, house of Hederick rejoice with Pyritis a precious stone which held in the hand will burn it; this is fixed fire.

Let Pleasant, house of Pleasant rejoice with The Carrier   65
Fish – God be gracious to Dame Fysh.

Let Tayler, house of Tayler rejoice with the Flying Mole –
God keep him from the poor man's garden. God be
gracious to William Tayler Sen and Junr.

Let Grieve, house of Grieve rejoice with Orites a precious
stone perfectly round. Blessed be the name of the Man of
Melancholy, for Jacob Grieve.

Let Bowes, house of Bowes rejoice with the Dog Fly. Lord
have mercy upon me and support me in all my plagues
and temptations.

Let Alberton, house of Alberton rejoice with Paneros a
precious stone good against barrenness.

Let Morgan, house of Morgan rejoice with Prasius Lapis of   70
a Leek-green colour.

Let Powell, house of Powell rejoice with Synochitis a
precious stone abused by the ancient sorcerers.

Let Howell, house of Howell rejoice with Ostracias a gem
like an oyster.

Let Close, house of Close rejoice with Chalcophonos a gem
sounding like brass. O all ye gems of the mine bless ye
the Lord, praise him and magnify him for ever.

Let Johnson, house of Johnson rejoice with Omphalocarpa
a kind of bur. God be gracious to Samuel Johnson.

Let Hopgood, house of Hopgood rejoice with Nepenthes   75
an herb which infused in wine drives away sadness –
very likely.

Let Hopwood, house of Hopwood rejoice with Aspalathus
the Rose of Jerusalem.

Let Benson, house of Benson rejoice with Sea-Ragwort or
Powder'd Bean. Lord have mercy on the soul of Dr
Benson Bsp. of Gloucester.

Let Marvel, house of Marvel rejoice with Brya a little shrub
like birch.

Let Hull, house of Hull rejoice with Subis a bird called the Spight which breaks the Eagle's eggs.

Let Mason, house of Mason rejoice with Suberies the 80
Capitol Cork Tree. Lord be merciful to William Mason.

Let Fountain, house of Fountain rejoice with Syriacus Rephanus a sweet kind of Radish.

Let Scroop, house of Scroop rejoice with Fig-Wine – Palmi primarium vinum. Not so – Palmi-primum is the word.

Let Hollingstead, house of Hollingstead rejoice with Sissitietaeris herb of good fellowship. Praise the name of the Lord September 1762.

Let Moyle, house of Moyle rejoice with Phlox a flame-colour'd flower without smell. tentanda via est. Via, veritas, vita sunt Christus.

Let Mount, house of Mount rejoice with Anthera a 85
flowering herb. The Lord lift me up.

Let Dowers, house of Dowers rejoice with The American Nonpareil a beautiful small-bird.

Let Cudworth, house of Cudworth rejoice with the Indian Jaca Tree, which bears large clusters of fruit like apples.

Let Cuthbert, house of Cuthbert rejoice with Phyllandrian a good herb growing in marshes – Lord have mercy on the soul of Cornelius Harrison.

Let Chillingworth, house of Chillingworth rejoice with Polygonoides an herb with leaves like laurel, long and thick, good against serpents.

Let Conworth, house of Conworth rejoice with Nenuphar 90
a kind of Water Lily.

Let Ransom, house of Ransom rejoice with Isidos Plocamos a sea shrub of the Coral kind, or rather like Coral.

Let Ponder, house of Ponder rejoice with Polion an herb, whose leaves are white in the morning, purple at noon, and blue in the evening.

Let Woodward, house of Woodward rejoice with Nerium
the Rose-Laurel – God make the professorship of fossils
in Cambridge a useful thing.

Let Spincks, house of Spinks rejoice with Struthiomela a
little sort of Quinces – The Lord Jesus pray for me.

Let Peacock, house of Peacock rejoice with Engalacton an   95
herb good to breed milk.

Let Nason, house of Nason rejoice with Errhinum a
medicine to clear the nose.

Let Bold, house of Bold rejoice with the Hop-Hornbeam.
God send me a neighbour this September.

Let Spriggings, house of Spriggings rejoice with Eon the
Tree of which Argo was built.

Let Bear, house of Bear rejoice with Gelotophyllis an herb
which drank in wine and myrrh causes excess of
laughter.

Let Sloper, house of Sloper rejoice with Gelotophye   100
another laughing plant.

Let Tollfree, house of Tollfree rejoice with Fern of Trees –
Lord stave off evil this day.

Let Clare, house of Clare rejoice with Galeotes a kind of
Lizard at enmity with serpents. Lord receive the soul of
Dr Wilcox Master of Clare Hall.

Let Wilmot, house of Wilmot rejoice with Epipetros an
herb coming up spontaneous (of the seed of the earth)
but never flowers.

Let Anstey, house of Anstey rejoice with Eumeces a kind of
balm. Lord have mercy on Christopher Anstey and his
kinswoman.

Let Ruston, house of Ruston rejoice with Fulviana Herba,   105
ab inventore, good to provoke urine. Lord have mercy
upon Roger Pratt and his family.

Let Atwood, house of Atwood rejoice with Rhodora with leaves like a nettle and flower like a rose. God bless all benefactors of Pembroke Hall.

Let Shield, house of Shield rejoice with Reseda an herb dissolving swelling, and imposthumes.

Let Atkins, house of Atkins rejoice with Salicastrum Wild Wine upon willows and osiers.

Let Pearson, house of Pearson rejoice with the American Aloe. I pray for the soul of Frances Burton.

Let Hough, house of Hough rejoice with Pegasus The Flying Horse – there be millions of them in the air. God bless the memories of Bsp. Hough and of Peter.

Let Evelyn, house of Evelyn rejoice with Phu a Plinian shrub sweet-scented. I pray God for trees enough in the posterities.

Let Wing, house of Wing rejoice with Phlomos a sort of Rush. I give the glory to God, thro' Christ, for taking the Havannah. Septr 30th 1762.

Let Chace, house of Chace rejoice with Papyrus. God be gracious to Sr Richard and family.

Let Pulteney, house of Pulteney rejoice with Tragion a shrub like Juniper.

Let Abdy, house of Abdy rejoice with Ecbolia a medicine to fetch a dead child out of the womb. God give me to bless for Gulstone and Halford.

Let Hoadley, house of Hoadley rejoice with Dryos Hyphear which is the Oak-Missletoe.

Let Free, house of Free rejoice with Thya a king of Wild Cypress.

Let Pink, house of Pink rejoice with Trigonum a herb used in garlands – the Lord succeed my pink borders.

Let Somner, house of Somner rejoice with the Blue Daisie – God be gracious to my neighbour and his family this day, 7th Octr 1762.

Let Race, house of Race rejoice with Osiritis Dogshead.   120
    God be praised for the eighth of October 1762.

Let Trowell, house of Trowell rejoice with Teuchites a kind
    of sweet rush.

Let Tilson, house of Tilson rejoice with Teramnos a kind of
    weed. Lord have mercy on the soul of Tilson, Fellow of
    Pembroke Hall.

Let Loom, house of Loom rejoice with Colocasia, an
    Egyptian Bean of whose leaves they made cups and pots.

Let Knock, house of Knock rejoice with Condurdon which
    bears red flowers in July and worn about the neck is
    good for scrophulous cases.

Let Case, house of Case rejoice with Coctanum a Syrian   125
    Fig. The Lord cure my cough.

Let Tomlyn, house of Tomlyn rejoice with Tetralyx a kind
    of herb.

Let Bason, house of Bason rejoice with Thelypteris which is
    Sea-Fern.

Let Joslyn, house of Joslyn rejoice with Cotonea a Venetian
    herb.

Let Mace, house of Mace rejoice with Adipsos a kind of
    Green Palm with the smell of a quince.

Let Potts, house of Potts rejoice with Ulex an herb like   130
    rosemary with a quality of attracting gold.

Let Bedingfield, house of Bedingfield rejoice with Zygia,
    which is a kind of maple.

Let Tough, house of Tough rejoice with Accipitrina. N.B.
    The hawk beat the raven St Luke's day 1762.

Let Balsam, house of Balsam rejoice with Chenomycon an
    herb the sight of which terrifies a goose. Lord have mercy
    on William Hunter his family.

Let Graves, house of Graves rejoice with Cinnaris the
    Stag's antidote – the persecuted Christian is as the
    hunted stag.

Let Tombs, house of Tombs rejoice with Acesis Water Sage   135
— God be gracious to Christopher Charles Tombs.

Let Addy, house of Addy rejoice with Crysippea a kind of
herb so called from the discoverer.

Let Jump, house of Jump rejoice with Zoster a Sea-Shrub.
Blessed be the name of Christ for the Anniversary of the
Battle of Agincourt 1762.

Let Bracegirdle, house of Bracegirdle rejoice with Xiris a
kind of herb with sharp leaves.

Let Girdlestone, house of Girdlestone rejoice with
Crysocarpum a kind of Ivy.

Let Homer, house of Homer rejoice with Cinnabar which   140
makes a red colour.

Let Lenox, house of Lenox rejoice with Achnas the Wild
Pear Tree. God be gracious to the Duke of Richmond.

Let Altham, house of Altham rejoice with the Everlasting
Apple-Tree.

Let Travell, house of Travell rejoice with Ciborium The
Egyptian Bean.

Let Tyers, house of Tyers rejoice with Aegilops a kind of
bulbous root. God give good will to Jonathan Tyers and
his family this day. All Saints. N.S. 1762.

Let Clever, house of Clever rejoice with Calathiana a sort   145
of Autumnal flower.

Let Bones, house of Bones rejoice with The Red-Crested
Black and Blue Bird of Surinam.

Let Pownall, house of Pownall rejoice with the Murrion a
creature of the Beaver kind.

Let Fig, house of Fig rejoice with Fleawort. The Lord
magnify the idea of Smart singing hymns on this day in
the eyes of the whole University of Cambridge. Novr 5th
1762. N.S.

Let Codrington, house of Codrington rejoice with
    Thelyphonon an herb whose root kills scorpions.

Let Butler, house of Butler rejoice with Theombrotios a   150
    Persian herb. God be gracious to the immortal Soul of
    the Duke of Ormond.

Let Bodley, house of Bodley rejoice with Tetragnathius a
    creature of the Spider kind.

Let Acton, house of Acton rejoice with Theangelis an herb
    used by the Ancients for magical purposes.

Let Peckwater, house of Peckwater rejoice with Tettigonia
    a small kind of Grashopper.

Let Sheldon, house of Sheldon rejoice with Teucrion an
    herb like Germander.

Let Brecknock, house of Brecknock rejoice with   155
    Thalassegle an herb. God be merciful to Timothy
    Brecknock.

Let Plank, house of Plank rejoice with the Sea Purslain –
    God be gracious to Thomas Rosoman and family.

Let Goosetree, house of Goosetree rejoice with Hippophaes
    a kind of teazle used in the dressing of cloth. God exalt
    the Soul of Captain Goosetree.

Let Baimbridge, house of Baimbridge rejoice with
    Hippophaestum of the same kind. Horses should be
    cloth'd in winter. – Bambridge praise the name of the
    Lord.

Let Metcalf, house of Metcalf rejoice with Holcus Wall-
    Barley – God give grace to my adversaries to ask council
    of Abel.

Let Graner, house of Graner rejoice with Hircules Bastard   160
    Nard. The Lord English Granier and his family.

Let Cape, house of Cape rejoice with Orgament an herb.

Let Oram, house of Oram rejoice with Halus an herb like
    unto Orgament.

Let Sykes, house of Sykes rejoice with Hadrobolum a kind
of sweet gum.

Let Plumer, house of Plumer rejoice with Hastula Regia an
herb resembling a spear.

Let Digby, house of Digby rejoice with Glycryhiza   165
Sweetroot. God be gracious to Sr Digby Legard his Son
and family.

Let Otway, house of Otway rejoice with Hippice an herb
which being held in an horse's mouth keeps him from
hunger.

Let Cecil, house of Cecil rejoice with Gnaphalium an herb
bleached by nature white and soft for the purpose of
flax. God bless Lord Salisbury.

Let Rogers, house of Rogers rejoice with Hypelates a kind
of Laurel – God be gracious to Rogers and Spilsbury
with their families.

Let Cambden, house of Cambden rejoice with
Glischromargos a kind of white marl.

Let Conduit, house of Conduit rejoice with Graecula a kind 170
of Rose. God be gracious to the immortal soul of Sr Isaac
Newton.

Let Hands, house of Hands rejoice with Hadrosphaerum a
kind of Spikenard with broad leaves.

Let Snipe, house of Snipe rejoice with Haemotimon a kind
of red glass. Blessed be the name of Jesus for the 29th of
Novr.

Let Aylesworth, house of Aylesworth rejoice with Glinon
which is a kind of Maple.

Let Aisley, house of Aisley rejoice with Halicastrum which
is a kind of bread corn.

Let Ready, house of Ready rejoice with Junco The Reed   175
Sparrow. Blessed be the name of Christ Jesus Voice and
Instrument.

Let Bland, house of Bland rejoice with Lacta a kind of
Cassia. God be gracious to Bland of Durham and the
Widow George.

Let Abington, house of Abington rejoice with Lea a kind of
Colewort – praise him upon the sound of the trumpet.

Let Adcock, house of Adcock rejoice with Lada a shrub,
which has gummy leaves.

Let Snow, house of Snow rejoice with Hysginum a plant
dying Scarlet.

Let Wardell, house of Wardell rejoice with Leiostreum a   180
smooth oyster. God give grace to the black trumpeter
and have mercy on the soul of Scipio.

Let Herring, house of Herring rejoice with Iberica a kind of
herb. Blessed be the name of the Lord Jesus for Miss
Herring.

Let Dolben, house of Dolben rejoice with Irio Winter
Cresses, Rock Gentle or Rock Gallant.

Let Oakley, house of Oakley rejoice with the Skink a little
amphibious creature found upon Nile.

Let Owen, house of Owen rejoice with the Shag-green a
beast from which the skin so called is taken.

Let Twist, house of Twist rejoice with Neottophora a little   185
creature that carries its young upon its back.

Let Constant, house of Constant rejoice with the Musk-
Goat – I bless God for two visions of Anne Hope's being
in charity with me.

Let Amos, house of Amos rejoice with The Avosetta a bird
found at Rome.

Let Humphreys, house of Humphreys rejoice with The
Beardmanica a curious bird.

Let Busby, house of Busby rejoice with The Ganser a bird.
God prosper Westminster-School.

Let Alured, house of Alured rejoice with the Book-Spider –   190
I refer the people of both Universities to the Bible for
their morality.

Let Lidgate, house of Lidgate rejoice with The Flammant a
curious large bird on the coast of Cuba. God make us
amends for the restoration of the Havannah.

Let Cunningham, house of Cunningham rejoice with The
Bohemian Jay. I pray for Peace between the K. of Prussia
and Empress Queen.

Let Thornhill, house of Thornhill rejoice with The Albicore
a Sea Bird. God be gracious to Hogarth his wife. Blessed
be the name of the Lord Jesus at Adgecomb.

Let Dawn, house of Dawn rejoice with The Frigate Bird
which is found upon the coasts of India.

Let Horton, house of Horton rejoice with Birdlime –   195
Blessed be the name of the Lord Jesus against the
destruction of Small Birds.

Let Arne, house of Arne rejoice with The Jay of Bengal.
God be gracious to Arne his wife, to Michael and
Charles Burney.

Let Westbrooke, house of Westbrooke rejoice with the
Quail of Bengal. God be gracious to the people of
Maidstone.

Let Allcock, house of Allcock rejoice with The King of the
Wavows a strange fowl. I pray for the whole University
of Cambridge especially Jesus College this blessed day.

Let Audley, house of Audley rejoice with The Green Crown
Bird. The Lord help on with the hymns.

Let Bloom, house of Bloom rejoice with Hecatompus a fish   200
with an hundred feet.

Let Beacon, house of Beacon rejoice with Amadavad a fine
bird in the East Indies.

Let Blomer, house of Blomer rejoice with Halimus a Shrub
   to hedge with. Lord have mercy upon poor labourers this
   bitter frost Decr 29 N.S. 1762.

Let Merrick, house of Merrick rejoice with Lageus a kind
   of Grape. God all-sufficient bless and forward the
   Psalmist in the Lord Jesus.

Let Appleby, house of Appleby rejoice with Laburnum a
   shrub whose blossom is disliked by bees.

Let Waite, house of Waite rejoice with the Shittah-Tree –   205
   blessed be the name of the Lord Jesus for the musicians
   and dancers this holiday-time.

Let Stedman, house of Stedman rejoice with Jacobaea St
   James's Wort. God be merciful to the house of Stuart.

Let Poet, house of Poet rejoice with Hedychrum a kind of
   ointment of a sweet smelling savour. God speed the New
   Year thro' Christ 1763.

Let Jesse, house of Jesse rejoice with the Lawrey a kind of
   bird. God forward my version of the psalms thro' Jesus
   Christ our Lord.

Let Clemison, house of Clemison rejoice with Helix a kind
   of Ivy. God be praised for the vision of the Redcap and
   packet.

Let Crockatt, house of Crockatt rejoice with Emboline an   210
   Asiatic Shrub with small leaves, an antidote. I pray for
   the soul of Crockatt the bookseller the first to put me
   upon a version of the Psalms.

Let Oakley, house of Oakley rejoice with Haliphaeus a tree
   with such bitter fruit that nothing but swine will touch it.

Let Preacher, house of Preacher rejoice with Helvella a
   small sort of cabbage. God be merciful to the immortal
   soul of Stephen the Preacher.

Let Heron, house of Heron rejoice with the Tunal-Tree on
   which the Cochineal feeds.

Let Kitcat, house of Kitcat rejoice with Copec the Pitch-
  Stone. Janry 8th 1763 Hallelujah.

Let Gisbourne, house of Gisbourne rejoice with   215
  Isocinnamon an herb of a sweet smelling savour.

Let Poor, house of Poor rejoice with Jasione a kind of
  Withwind — Lord have mercy on the poor this hard
  weather. Jan: 10th 1763.

Let Eccles, house of Eccles rejoice with Heptapleuros a
  kind of Plantain. I pray for a musician or musicians to
  set the new psalms.

Let Moseley, house of Moseley rejoice with Spruce — I bless
  God for Old Foundation Day at Pemb. Hall.

Let Pass, house of Pass rejoice with Salt — The Lord pass
  the last year's accounts in my conscience thro' the merits
  of Jesus Christ. New Year by Old Stile 1763.

Let Forward, house of Forward rejoice with Immussulus a   220
  kind of bird — the Lord forward my translation of the
  psalms this year.

Let Quarme, house of Quarme rejoice with Thyosiris
  yellow Succory — I pray God bless all my Subscribers.

Let Larkin, house of Larkin rejoice with Long-wort or
  Torch-herb — God give me good riddance of my present
  grievances.

Let Halford, house of Halford rejoice with Siren a musical
  bird. God consider thou me for the baseness of those I
  have served very highly.

Let Ayerst, house of Ayerst rejoice with the Wild Beet —
  God be gracious to Smith, Cousins, Austin, Cam and
  Kingsley and Kinleside.

Let Decker, house of Decker rejoice with Sirpe a Cyrenian 225
  plant yielding an odoriferous juice.

Let Cust, house of Cust rejoice with Margaris a date like
  unto a pearl.

Let Usher, house of Usher rejoice with Condurdon an herb
with a red flower worn about the neck for the scurvy.

Let Slingsby, house of Slingsby rejoice with Midas a little
worm breeding in beans.

Let Farmer, house of Farmer rejoice with Merois an herb
growing at Meroe, leaf like lettuce and good for dropsy.

Let Affleck, house of Affleck rejoice with The Box-thorn.   230
Blessed be the name of the Lord Jesus Emanuel.

Let Arnold, house of Arnold rejoice with Leucographis a
simple good against spitting of blood.

Let Morris, house of Morris rejoice with Lepidium a
Simple of the Cress kind.

Let Crane, house of Crane rejoice with Libanotis an herb
that smells like Frankincense.

Let Arden, house of Arden rejoice with Mew an herb with
the stalk and leaves like Anise.

Let Joram, house of Joram rejoice with Meliphylla Balm   235
Gentle. God be gracious to John Sherrat.

Let Odwell, house of Odwell rejoice with Lappago Maiden
Lips. Blessed be the name of Jesus in singularities and
singular mercies.

Let Odney, house of Odney rejoice with Canaria a simple
called Hound's-grass.

HYMNS AND SPIRITUAL SONGS FOR THE FASTS AND FESTIVALS OF THE CHURCH OF ENGLAND

Te decet Hymnus

שירו לו זמרו לו שיחו בכל
נפלאתיו

Hymn 1: New Year

WORD of endless adoration,
   Christ, I to thy call appear;
On my knees in meek prostration
   To begin a better year.

Spirits in eternal waiting,   5
   *Special ministers of pray'r,
Which our welcome antedating,
   Shall the benediction bear.

Which, the type of vows completed,
   Shall the wreathed garland send,   10
While new blessings are intreated,
   And communicants attend.

Emblem of the hopes beginning,
   Who the budding rods shall bind,
Way from guiltless natures winning,   15
   In good-will to human kind.

Ye that dwell with cherub-turtles
   Mated in that upmost light,
Or parade† amongst the myrtles,
   On your steeds of speckl'd white.   20

* Tobit, xii. 15.
† Zec.i. 8.

Ye that sally from the portal
  Of yon everlasting bow'rs,
Sounding symphonies immortal,
  Years, and months, and days, and hours.

But nor myrtles, nor the breathing   25
  Of the never-dying grove,
Nor the chaplets sweetly wreathing,
  And by hands angelic wove;

Not the music or the mazes
  Of those spirits aptly tim'd,   30
Can avail like pray'r and praises
  By the Lamb himself sublim'd.

Take ye therefore what ye give him,
  Of his fulness grace for grace,
Strive to think him, speak him, live him,   35
  Till you find him face to face.

Sing like David, or like Hannah,
  As the spirit first began,
To the God of heights hosanna!
  Peace and charity to man.   40

Christ his blessing universal
  On th'arch-patriarch's seed bestow,
Which attend to my rehearsal
  Of melodious pray'r below.

Hymn 2: Circumcision

When Abraham was bless'd,
And on his face profess'd
  The Saviour Christ hereafter born,
'Thou pilgrim and estrang'd,
Thy name,' said God, 'is chang'd,   5
  Thy lot secur'd from want and scorn.

'O Abraham, my friend,
My covenant attend,
    Which Shilo's self shall not repeal,
Chastise from carnal sin   10
Thy house and all thy kin,
    Thy faith by circumcision seal.'

The promis'd Shilo came,
And then receiv'd the name
    Of Jesus, Saviour of the soul;   15
As he the law fulfill'd
Which checks the fleshly-will'd,
    And o'er the passion gives controul.

O clean and undefil'd!
Thou shalt not be beguil'd   20
    By youthful heat and female art,
To thee the strains belong
Of that mysterious song
    Where none but virgins bear a part.

Come every purer thought,   25
By which the mind is wrought
    From man's corruption, nature's dust;
Away each vain desire,
And all the fiends that fire
    The soul to base and filthy lust.   30

Ye swans that sail and lave
In Jordan's hallow'd wave,
    Ah sweet! ah pensive! ah serene!
Thou rose of maiden flush,
Like Joseph's guiltless blush,   35
    And herb of ever-grateful green;

Ye lilies of perfume,
That triumph o'er the loom,
    And gaudy greatness far outshine;
And thou the famous tree,   40
Whose name is chastity,
    And all the brilliants of the mine;

Ye doves of silver down
That plume the seraph's crown,
    All, all the praise of Jesus sing,   45
The joy of heav'n and earth,
And Christ's eternal worth,
    The pearl of God, the Father's ring.

Let elegance, the flow'r
Of words, in tune and pow'r,   50
    Find some device of cleanest choice
About that gem to place –
'This is my HEIR of GRACE,
    In whose perfections I rejoice.'

Hymn 3: Epiphany

Grace, thou source of each perfection,
    Favour from the height thy ray;
Thou the star of all direction,
    Child of endless truth and day.

Thou that bidst my cares be calmer,   5
    Lectur'd what to seek and shun,
Come, and guide a western palmer
    To the Virgin and her Son.

Lo! I travel in the spirit,
    On my knees my course I steer   10
To the house of might and merit
    With humility and fear.

Poor at least as John or Peter
    I my vows alone prefer;
But the strains of love are sweeter   15
    Than the frankincense and myrrh.

Neither purse nor scrip I carry,
    But the books of life and pray'r;
Nor a staff my foe to parry,
    'Tis the cross of Christ I bear.   20

From a heart serene and pleasant
    'Midst unnumber'd ills I feel,
I will meekly bring my present,
    And with sacred verses kneel.

Muse, through Christ the Word, inventive   25
    Of the praise so greatly due;
Heav'nly gratitude retentive
    Of the bounties ever new;

Fill my heart with genuine treasures,
    Pour them out before his feet,   30
High conceptions, mystic measures,
    Springing strong and flowing sweet.

Come, ye creatures of thanksgiving,
    Which are harmoniz'd to bless,
Birds that warble for your living,   35
    Beasts with ways of love express.

Thou the shepherd's faithful fellow,
    As he lies by Cedron's stream,
Where soft airs and waters mellow
    Take their Saviour for their theme.   40

Thou too gaily grave domestic,
    With whose young fond childhood plays,
Held too mean for verse majestic,
    First with me thy Maker praise.

Browsing kids, and lambkins grazing,   45
    Colts and younglings of the drove,
Come with all your modes of praising,
    Bounding through the leafless grove.

Ye that skill the flow'rs to fancy,
    And in just assemblage sort,   50
Pluck the primrose, pluck the pansy,
    And your prattling troop exhort.

'Little men, in Jesus mighty,
   And ye maids that go alone,
Bodies chaste, and spirits flighty,   55
   Ere the world and guilt are known.

'Breath so sweet, and cheeks so rosy —
   Put your little hands to pray,
Take ye ev'ry one a posy,
   And away to Christ, away.' —   60

Youth, benevolence, and beauty,
   In your Saviour's praise agree,
Which this day receives our duty,
   Sitting on the virgin's knee.

That from this day's institution   65
   Ev'ry penitent in deed,
At his hour of retribution,
   As a child, through him may speed.

Hymn 4: *Conversion of St Paul*

Thro' him, the chief, begot by Nun,
Controul'd the progress of the sun;
The shadow too, through him, retir'd
The ten degrees it had acquir'd.

The barren could her fruit afford,   5
The woman had her dead restor'd,
The statesman could himself demean
To seek the river, and be clean.

At his command, ev'n Christ I Am,
The cruse was fill'd, and iron swam;   10
The floods were dry'd to make a track,
And Jordan's wave was driven back.

All these in ancient days occurr'd,
The great atchievements of the Word,
By Joshua's hand, by Moses' rod,   15
By virtue of the men of God.

But greater is the mighty deed
To make a profligate recede,
And work a boist'rous madman mild,
To walk with Jesus like a child.   20

To give a heart of triple steel
The Lord's humanity to feel;
And there, where pity had no place,
To fill the measure of his grace;

To wash internal blackness white,   25
To call the worse than dead to light;
To make the fruitless soil to hold
Ten thousand times ten thousand fold.

To turn a servant of the times
From modish and ambitious crimes;   30
To pour down a resistless blaze,
'Go, persecutor, preach and praise.'

Hymn 5: King Charles the Martyr

The persecutor was redeem'd,
And preach'd the name he had blasphem'd;
But, ah! tho' worded for the best,
How subtle men his writings wrest.

Hence heresies and sects arose   5
According to the saint they chose,
All against Christ alike – but all
Of some distorted text of Paul.

Had not such reas'ners been at strife
With Christ's good doctrine and his life,   10
The land of God's selected sheep
Had 'scap'd this day to fast and weep.

Ah great unfortunate, the chief
Of monarchs in the tale of grief,
By marriage ill-advis'd, akin   15
To Moab and the man of sin!

When Christ was spitted on and slain,
The temple rent her veil in twain;
And in the hour that Charles was cast
The church had well nigh groan'd its last.   20

But now aloft her head she bears,
Accepted in his dying pray'rs; —
Great acts in human annals shine —
Great sufferings claim applause divine.

Hymn 6: The Presentation of Christ in the Temple

Preserver of the church, thy spouse,
    From sacrilege and wrong,
To whom the myriads pay their vows,
Give ear, and in my heart arouse
    The spirit of a nobler song.   5

When Hiero built, from David's plan,
    The house of godlike style,
And Solomon, the prosp'rous man,
Whose reign with wealth and fame began,
    O'erlaid with gold the glorious pile;   10

Great was the concourse of mankind
    The structure to review;
Such bulk with sweet proportion join'd
The labours of a vaster mind,
    In all directions grand and true.   15

And yet it was not true and grand
    The Godhead to contain;
By whom immensity is spann'd,
Which has eternal in his hand
    The globe of his supreme domain.   20

Tho' there the congregation knelt
  The daily debt to pay,
Tho' there superior glories dwelt,
Tho' there the host their blessings dealt,
  The highest GRACE was far away.   25

At length another fane arose,
  The fabric of the poor;
And built by hardship midst her foes,
One hand for work and one for blows,
  Made this stupendous blessing sure.   30

That God should in the world appear
  Incarnate – as a child –
That he should be presented here,
At once our utmost doubts to clear,
  And make our hearts with wonder wild.   35

Present ye therefore, on your knees,
  Hearts, hands resign'd and clean;
Ye poor and mean of all degrees,
If he will condescend and please
  To take at least what orphans glean –   40

I speak for all – for them that fly,
  And for the race that swim;
For all that dwell in moist and dry,
Beasts, reptiles, flow'rs and gems to vie
  When gratitude begins her hymn.   45

Praise him ye doves, and ye that pipe
  Ere buds begin to stir;
Ev'n every finch of every stripe,
And thou of filial love the type,
  O stork! that sit'st upon the fir.   50

Praise him thou sea, to whom he gave
  The shoal of active mutes;
(Fit tenants of thy roaring wave)
Who comes to still the fiends, that rave
  In oracles and school disputes.   55

By Jesus number'd all and priz'd,
  Praise him in dale and hill;
Ye beasts for use and peace devis'd,
And thou which patient and despis'd,
  Yet shalt a prophecy fulfill.   60

Praise him ye family that weave
  The crimson to be spread
There, where communicants receive,
And ye, that form'd the eye to grieve,
  Hid in green bush or wat'ry bed.   65

Praise him ye flow'rs that serve the swarm
  With honey for their cells;
Ere yet the vernal day is warm,
To call out millions to perform
  Their gambols on your cups and bells.   70

Praise him ye gems of lively spark,
  And thou the pearl of price;
In that great depth or caverns dark,
Nor yet are wrested from the mark,
  To serve the turns of pride and vice.   75

Praise him ye cherubs of his breast,
  The mercies of his love,
Ere yet from guile and hate profest,
The phoenix makes his fragrant nest
  In his own paradise above.   80

Hymn 7: Ash Wednesday. First Day of Lent

  O Charity! that couldst receive
    The dying thief's repentant pray'r;
  And didst upon the cross relieve
    Thy fellow-suff'rer there!

Tho' he revil'd among the rest –   5
   Before the point of utmost dread,
Grace unto pray'r was first imprest,
   And then forgiveness sped.

Alas! the more of us defraud
   The Lord of his most righteous due,   10
And live by guiding truth unaw'd,
   And vanities pursue.

The harlot vice with joy we clasp,
   Nor shun to meet her tainted breath;
And leave repentance to the gasp   15
   Of hope-retarded death;

Albeit there are appointed times
   For men to worship and to fast;
Then purge your conscience of its crimes
   At least while those shall last.   20

The words of vengeance threat the tree,
   And fix their axes to the helves –
Pray therefore – pray for such as flee
   Their Saviour and themselves.

Since some are but the more defil'd,   25
   As canons urge them to comply,
And Christ's example in the wild
   By thwarting texts deny;

Read on your knees the holy book
   That's penn'd to soothe despondent fears –   30
And if the Lord but deign a look,
   Remember Peter's tears.

Hymn 8: St Matthias

Hark! the cock proclaims the morning,
   Match the rhyme, and strike the strings;
Heav'nly muse, embrace the warning,
   Raise thy voice, and stretch thy wings.

Lo! the poor, alive and likely   5
　'Midst desertion and distress,
Teach the folk that deal obliquely,
　They had better bear and bless.

If we celebrate Matthias,
　Let us do it heart and soul;   10
Nor let worldly reasons bias
　Our conceptions from their goal.

As the fancy cools and rambles,
　Keep her constant, keep her chaste;
Ward from wine, and from the shambles,   15
　Sight and appetite, and taste.

Tho' thy craving bowels murmur
　And against thy pray'r rebell;
Yet be firmer still, and firmer
　In the work begun so well.   20

Sick and weakly, pris'ners, strangers,
　Cold in nakedness we lie;
Train'd in hunger, thirst and dangers,
　As in exercise to die.

All avail not to dispirit   25
　Toil, determin'd to succeed;
And we trust in Christ his merit,
　As we have his woes to plead.

Yea, our lot is fallen fairer
　Than the sons of wealth and pride;   30
While our Saviour is a sharer
　In all hardships that betide.

Hard and precious are together,
　Stripes and wounds are endless gain;
If with him the storm we weather,   35
　With him also we shall reign.

We shall take the traitors' places,
   And their forfeit office hold,
And to Christ shall show our faces,
   Not betray'd by us or sold.   40

Lord, our spirits disencumber,
   From the world our hearts dismiss;
Let us reckon to the number
   Of thy saints in fruitful bliss.

Let the few of Christ be hearty   45
   In the cause they bleed to win,
And religion make her party
   Good against the pow'r of sin.

Let us pray – by self-denial
   Every sense to Christ resign,   50
Till we from the fiery trial
   Pure as purity refine.

Hymn 9: The Annunciation of the Blessed Virgin

O Purity, thou test
Of love amongst the blest,
How excellent thou art,
The Lord Jehovah's heart,
   Whose sweet attributes embrace,   5
   Every virtue, praise and grace.

Thou fair and good dispos'd,
'Midst glories undisclos'd,
Inspire the notes to play
Upon the virgin's day;   10
   High above all females nam'd,
   And by Gabriel's voice proclaim'd.

Glad herald, ever sent
Upon some blest event,
But never sped to men   15
On such a charge till then –
   When his Saviour's feet he kiss'd,
   To promulge his birth dismiss'd.

Hail mystery! thou source
Of nature's plainest course,   20
How much this work transcends
Thine usual means and ends –
   Wherefore call'd, we shall not spare
   Louder praise, and oft'ner pray'r.

But if the work be new,   25
So should the song be too,
By every thought that's born
In freshness of the morn;
   Every flight of active wings,
   Every shift upon the strings.   30

To praise the mighty hand
By which the world was mann'd,
Which dealt to great and small
Their talents clear of all;
   Kind to kind by likeness linkt,   35
   Various all, and all distinct.

Praise him seraphic tone
Of instruments unknown,
High strains on golden wire,
Work'd by etherial fire;   40
   Blowing on unceasing chords,
   'King of kings, and lord of lords.'

Praise Hannah, of the three,
That sang in Mary's key;
With her that made her psalm   45
Beneath the bow'ring palm;
   With the dame – Bethulia's boast,
   Honour'd o'er th' Assyrian host.

Praise him faith, hope, and love
That tend Jehovah's dove;   50
By men from lust repriev'd
As females best conceiv'd;
   To remount the man and muse
   Far above all earthly views.

Hymn 10: *The Crucifixion of Our Blessed Lord*

The world is but a sorry scene,
Untrue, unhallow'd, and unclean,
   And hardly worth a man;
The fiend upon the land prevails,
And o'er the floods in triumph sails,   5
   Do goodness all she can.

How many works for such a day?
How glorious? that ye scourge and slay
   Ye blind, by blinder led;
All hearts at once devising bad,   10
Hands, mouths against their Maker mad,
   With Satan at the head –

Are these the race of saints profest,
That for authorities contest,
   And question and debate?   15
Yet in so foul a deed rebell,
Beyond example, ev'n from hell,
   To match its barb'rous hate.

Behold the man! the tyrant said,
As in the robes of scoff array'd,   20
   And crown'd with thorns he stood;
And feigning will to let him go
He chose Barabbas, open foe
   Of human kind and good.

And was it He, whose voice divine,   25
Could change the water into wine,
   And first his pow'r averr'd;
Which fed in Galilea's groves
The fainting thousands with the loaves
   And fishes of his word!   30

And was it He, whose mandate freed
The palsied suppliant, and in deed
   The sabbath-day rever'd;
Which bade the thankful dumb proclaim
The Lord omnipotent by name,   35
   Till loosen'd deafness heard!

And was it He, whose hand was such,
As lighten'd blindness at a touch,
   And made the lepers whole;
Could to the dropsy health afford,   40
And to the lunatic restor'd
   Serenity of soul!

The daughter that so long a term
By Satan's bonds had been infirm,
   Was rescued and receiv'd;   45
Yea, with the foes of faith and hope
His matchless charity could cope,
   When Malchus was reliev'd.

The woman in his garment's hem
Conceiv'd a prevalence to stem   50
   The sources of her pain;
He calls – the dead from death arise,
And as their legions he defies
   The dev'ls descend again.

His irresistible command   55
Convey'd the vessel to the land,
   As instant as his thought;
He caus'd the tempest to forget
Its rage, and into Peter's net,
   The wond'rous capture brought.   60

The roarings of the billows cease
To hear the gospel of his peace
  Upon the still profound –
He walk'd the waves – and at his will,
The fish to pay th' exactor's bill   65
  To Judah's coast was bound.

The wither'd hand he saw and cur'd,
And health from gen'ral ail secur'd
  Where'er disease was rife;
And was omniscient to tell   70
The woman at the patriarch's well
  The story of her life.

But never since the world was known,
One so stupendous as his own,
  And rich of vast event;   75
From love ador'd, as soon as seen,
Had not his hated message been
  To bid the world repent.

Ah, still desirous of a king,
To give voluptuous vice its swing   80
  With passions like a brute;
By Jesus Christ came truth and grace,
But none indulgence, pension, place,
  The slaves of SELF to suit.

The Lord on Gabbatha they doom,   85
Before the delegate of Rome,
  Deserted and exposed –
They might have thought on Israel's God,
Which on the sapphire pavement trod,
  To sev'nty seers disclos'd.   90

They might have thought upon the loss
Of Eden, and the dreadful cross
  That happen'd by a tree;
Ere yet with cursed throats they shout
To bring the dire event about,   95
  Tho' prophesy'd to be.

O God, the bonds of sin enlarge,
Lay not this horror to our charge,
   But as we fast and weep,
Pour out the streams of love profuse,   100
Let all the pow'rs of mercy loose,
   While wrath and vengeance sleep.

Hymn 11: Easter Day

Awake – arise – lift up thy voice,
   Which as a trumpet swell,
Rejoice in Christ – again rejoice,
   And on his praises dwell.

The muse at length, no more perplext   5
   In search of human wit,
Shall kneel her down, and take her text
   From lore of sacred writ.

My lot in holy ground was cast,
   And for the prize I threw;
And in the path by thousands past   10
   The Lord shall make me new.

O let the people, with the priest,
   Adorn themselves to pray,
And with their faces to the east   15
   Their adoration pay.

Let us not doubt, as doubted some,
   When first the Lord appear'd;
But full of faith and rev'rence come
   What time his voice is heard.   20

And ev'n as John, who ran so well,
   Confess upon our knees
The prince that locks up death and hell,
   And has himself the *keys.

* Rev. i. 18.

'Tis He that puts all hearts in tune   25
   With strings that never jar,
And they that rise to praise him soon,
   Shall win the *MORNING STAR.

The morning star, and pearl of price,
   And †stone of lucid white,   30
Are all provocatives from vice,
   To heav'n and true delight.

O GLADNESS! that suspend'st belief
   For fear that rapture dreams;
Thou also hast the tears of grief,   35
   And failst in wild extremes.

Tho' Peter make a clam'rous din,
   Will he thy doubts destroy?
Will little Rhoda let him in,
   Incredulous with joy?   40

And thus thro' gladness and surprise
   The saints their Saviour treat;
Nor will they trust their ears and eyes
   But by his hands and feet.

These hands of lib'ral love indeed   45
   In infinite degree,
Those feet still frank to move and bleed
   For millions and for me.

A watch, to slavish duty train'd,
   Was set by spiteful care,   50
Lest what the sepulchre contain'd
   Should find alliance there.

Herodians came to seal the stone
   With Pilate's gracious leave,
Lest dead and friendless, and alone,   55
   Should all their skill deceive.

* Rev. ii. 28.
† Rev. ii. 17.

O dead arise! O friendless stand
  By seraphim ador'd –
O solitude! again command
  Thy host from heav'n restor'd.   60

Watchmen sleep on, and take your rest,
  And wake when conscience stings;
For Christ shall make the grave his nest
  Till God return his wings.

He died – but death itself improv'd   65
  To triumph o'er the foe,
And preach'd, as God's great spirit mov'd,
  To sinners chain'd below.

The souls that perish'd in the flood
  He bid again to bliss;   70
And caus'd his rod with hope to bud
  From out the dread abyss.

The seventh day above the week
  Still would he keep and bless;
The pain'd to sooth, the lost to seek,   75
  And grievance to redress.

Yet never such a day before
  Of holy work was spent,
While hardship infinite he bore
  That malice might relent.   80

And whether from success exempt
  The story is not told;
But sure most glorious was th' attempt,
  Whose fame in heav'n's enroll'd.

And each man in his spirit knows   85
  That mercy has no bound;
And from that upmost zenith flows
  The lowest depth to sound.

And therefore David calls for praise
   From all the gulfs that yawn,   90
Our thoughts by greater strokes to raise
   Than e'er before were drawn.

Beyond the height that science kens,
   Where genius is at home;
And poets take their golden pens   95
   To fill th' immortal tome.

Ye that for psalmody contend,
   Exert your trilling throats;
And male and female voices blend
   With joy's divinest notes.   100

By fancy rais'd to Zion's top
   Your swelling organ join;
And praise the Lord on every stop
   Till all your faces shine.

With sweetest breath your trumpets fill'd,   105
   Shall forward strength and grace;
Then all your warbling measures build
   Upon the grounding bass.

The boxen pipe, for deepness form'd,
   Involve in strains of love,   110
And flutes, with inspiration warm'd,
   Shall imitate the dove.

Amongst the rest arouse the harp,
   And with a master's nail;
And from the quick vibrations carp   115
   The graces of the scale.

The flow'rs from every bed collect,
   And on the altar lift;
And let each silver vase be deckt
   With nature's graceful gift.   120

And from the steeple's summit stream
    The flag of golden gloss,
Exposing to the glancing beam
    The glorious English cross;

And let the lads of gladness born   125
    The ringers be renew'd;
And as they usher'd in the morn,
    Let them the day conclude.

Hymn 12: St Mark

Pull up the bell-flow'rs of the spring,
And let the budding greenwood ring
    With many a cheerful song;
All blessing on the human race,
From CHRIST, evangelist of grace,   5
    To whom these strains belong.

To whom belong the tribe that vie
In what is music to the eye,
    Whose voice is 'stoop to pray' –
While many colour'd tints attire   10
His fav'rites, like the golden wire,
    The beams on wind flow'rs play.

To whom belong the dress and airs
Of nature in her warbling pairs,
    And in her bloomy pride;   15
By whom the man of pray'r computes
His year, and estimates the fruits
    Of every time and tide.

To whom the sacred penman cries,
And as he heav'nwards lifts his eyes,   20
    With meekness kneels him down;
Then what inspiring truth indites,
His strengthen'd memory recites,
    The tale of God's renown.

O holy Mark! ordain'd in youth   25
To be historian of the truth
  From heav'n's first fountain brought;
And Christ his hand was on thy head,
To bless thee that thou shouldst be read,
  And in his churches taught.   30

And tho', as Peter's scribe and son,
Thou mightst a charity have done
  To cover his disgrace;
Yet strictly charg'd thou wouldst not spare
At large the treason to declare,   35
  And in its order place.

Thus in the church, to cleanse our sin,
By fair confession we begin,
  And in thanksgiving end;
And they that have the Lord deny'd,   40
Must not come there the crime to hide,
  But promise to amend.

Then let us not this day refuse,
With joy to give the Christian dues
  To Lazars at the door;   45
'O for the name and love of Christ
Spare one poor dole from all your grist,
  One mite from all your store!'

And those that in by-places lurk,
Invite with overpay to work,   50
  Thy garner'd hay to fill;
And worship on the new mown sod,
And active to the Lord thy God,
  Keep lust and conscience still.

Hymn 13: St Philip and St James

Now the winds are all composure,
  But the breath upon the bloom,
Blowing sweet o'er each inclosure,
  Grateful off'rings of perfume.

Tansy, calaminth and daisies,   5
  On the river's margin thrive;
And accompany the mazes
  Of the stream that leaps alive.

Muse, accordant to the season,
  Give the numbers life and air;   10
When the sounds and objects reason
  In behalf of praise and pray'r.

All the scenes of nature quicken,
  By the genial spirit fann'd;
And the painted beauties thicken   15
  Colour'd by the master's hand.

Earth her vigour repossessing
  As the blasts are held in ward;
Blessing heap'd and press'd on blessing,
  Yield the measure of the Lord.   20

Beeches, without order seemly,
  Shade the flow'rs of annual birth,
And the lily smiles supremely
  Mention'd by the Lord on earth.

Couslips seize upon the fallow,   25
  And the cardamine in white,
Where the corn-flow'rs join the mallow,
  Joy and health, and thrift unite.

Study sits beneath her arbour,
  By the bason's glossy side;   30
While the boat from out its harbour
  Exercise and pleasure guide.

Pray'r and praise be mine employment,
　　Without grudging or regret,
Lasting life, and long enjoyment,　　　　　　35
　　Are not here, and are not yet.

Hark! aloud, the black-bird whistles,
　　With surrounding fragrance blest,
And the goldfinch in the thistles
　　Makes provision for her nest.　　　　　　40

Ev'n the hornet hives his honey,
　　Bluecap builds his stately dome,
And the rocks supply the coney
　　With a fortress and an home.

But the servants of their Saviour,　　　　　　45
　　Which with gospel-peace are shod,
Have no bed but what the paviour
　　Makes them in the porch of God.

O thou house that hold'st the charter
　　Of salvation from on high,　　　　　　　50
Fraught with prophet, saint, and martyr,
　　Born to weep, to starve and die!

Great to-day thy song and rapture
　　In the choir of Christ and WREN
When two prizes were the capture　　　　　　55
　　Of the hand that fish'd for men.

To the man of quick compliance
　　Jesus call'd, and Philip came;
And began to make alliance
　　For his master's cause and name.　　　　　60

James, of title most illustrious,
　　Brother of the Lord, allow'd;
In the vineyard how industrious,
　　Nor by years nor hardship bow'd!

Each accepted in his trial, 65
 One the CHEERFUL one the JUST;
Both of love and self-denial,
 Both of everlasting trust.

Living they dispens'd salvation,
 Heav'n-endow'd with grace and pow'r; 70
And they dy'd in imitation
 Of their Saviour's final hour.

Who, for cruel traitors pleading,
 Triumph'd in his parting breath;
O'er all miracles preceding 75
 His inestimable death.

Hymn 14: *The Ascension of Our Lord Jesus Christ*

'And other wond'rous works were done
 No mem'ry can recall;
Which were they number'd every one,
Not all the space beneath the sun
 Could hold the fair detail of all.' 5

The text is full, and strong to do
 The glorious subject right;
But on the working mind's review
The letter's like the spirit true,
 And clear and evident as light. 10

For not a particle of space
 Where'er his glory beam'd,
With all the modes of site and place,
But were the better for his grace,
 And up to higher lot redeem'd. 15

For all the motley tribe that pair,
 And to their cover skim,
Became his more immediate care,
The raven urgent in his pray'r,
 And those that make the woodland hymn. 20

For every creature left at will
   The howling WASTE to roam,
Which live upon the blood they spill,
From his own hands receive their fill,
   What time the desert was his home.   25

They knew him well, and could not err,
   To him they all appeal'd;
The beast of sleek or shaggy fur,
And found their natures to recur
   To what they were in Eden's field.   30

For all that dwell in depth or wave,
   And ocean – every drop –
Confess'd his mighty pow'r to save,
When to the floods his peace he gave,
   And bade careering whirlwinds stop.   35

And all things meaner from the worm
   Probationer to fly;
To him that creeps his little term,
And countless rising from the sperm
   Shed by sea-reptiles, where they ply.   40

These all were bless'd beneath his feet,
   Approaching them so near;
Vast flocks that have no mouths to bleat,
With yet a spirit to intreat,
   And in their rank divinely dear.   45

For on some special good intent,
   Advancement or relief,
Or some great evil to prevent,
Or some perfection to augment,
   He held his life of tears and grief.   50

'Twas his the pow'rs of hell to curb,
   And men possess'd to free;
And all the blasting fiends disturb
From seed of bread, from flow'r and herb,
   From fragrant shrub and stately tree.   55

The song can never be pursu'd
   When Infinite's the theme —
For all to crown, and to conclude,
He bore and bless'd ingratitude,
   And insult in its worst extreme.   60

And having then such deeds atchiev'd
   As never man before,
From scorn and cruelty repriev'd,
In highest heav'n he was receiv'd,
   To reign with God for evermore.   65

Hymn 15: Whitsunday

King of sempiternal sway,
Thou hast kept thy word to-day,
That the COMFORTER should come,
That gainsayers should be dumb.
While the tongues of men transfus'd   5
With thy spirit should be loos'd,
And untutor'd Hebrew speak,
Latin, Arabic, and Greek.

That thy praises might prevail
On each note upon the scale,   10
In each nation that is nam'd,
On each organ thou hast fram'd;
Every speech beneath the sun,
Which from Babel first begun;
Branch or leaf, or flow'r or fruit   15
Of the Hebrew's ancient root.

This great miracle was wrought,
That the millions might be taught,
And themselves of hope assure
By the preaching of the poor —   20
O thou God of truth and pow'r
Bless all Englishmen this hour;
That their language may suffice
To make nations good and wise.

Yea, the God of truth and pow'r 25
Blesses Englishmen this hour;
That their language may suffice
To make nations good and wise –
Wherefore then no more success –
That so much is much to bless – 30
*Revelation is our own,
Secret things are God's alone.

* Deut. xxix. 29.

Hymn 16: Trinity Sunday

If Jesus be reveal'd,
There is no truth conceal'd
For honour or for awe,
That tends to drive or draw
  To the hope of heav'nly bliss, 5
  From the dread of hell's abyss.

If oracles be mute,
And every dull dispute
Of ostentatious gloom
In Athens or in Rome; 10
  We should, sure, amend our ways
  By submission, pray'r and praise.

O THREE! of blest account
To which all sums amount,
For if the church has two
The work of pray'r to do, 15
  God himself, th' Almighty word,
  Will be there to make the third.

One Lord, one faith, one font,
Are all good Christians want   20
To make the fiend retreat,
And build the saint complete;
   Where the Godhead self-allied,
   Faith, hope, charity reside.

Man, soul and angel join   25
To strike up strains divine;
O blessed and ador'd,
Thine aid from heav'n afford;
   HOLY, HOLY, HOLY THREE,
   Which in One, as One agree.   30

For angel, man and soul
Make up upon the whole,
One individual here,
And in the highest sphere;
   Where with God he shall repose,   35
   From whose image first he rose.

Ye books, that load the shelves,
To lead us from ourselves,
Where things, in doubt involv'd,
Are rather made than solv'd;   40
   Render to the dust and worm
   All ye question or affirm.

Ye poets, seers and priests,
Whose lore the spirit feasts,
And keep the banquet on,   45
From Moses ev'n to John;
   On your truth I will regale,
   'Which is great and must prevail.'

The Trinity is plain,
So David's psalms maintain,   50
– Who made not God his boast
But by the HOLY GHOST;
   Thence prophetic to record
   All the suff'rings of the Lord.

Yet all the Scriptures run   55
That God is great and one,
Or else there is no cause
Of nature or her laws;
   To controul and comprehend
   All beginning, course and end.   60

Hymn 17: *The King's Restoration*

Almighty Jesu! first and last,
   The sole original and cause
Of all heroic actions past,
   The God of patriot deeds, and gracious laws;
Which didst at sea this western empire found   5
The chief, the lords and people in thy love renown'd.

We thank thee that we were despis'd,
   And as unblest barbarians held;
For then and therefore thou devis'd
   All things in which we have the rest excell'd;   10
The progeny, that God's free woman bare,
In all their leagues and dealings faithful, just and fair.

We thank thee for the spacious stream,
   Thrice rolling thro' the sounding arch;
O'er which the dome of CHRIST supreme   15
   Sees George's gallant horse exalt their march,
And thence their prosp'rous embarkation speed,
Against the fraud and pride of Moab's spurious seed.

We thank thee for the naval sway
   Which o'er the subject seas we claim;   20
And for the homage nations pay,
   Submissive to the great Britannic fame;
Who soon as they thy precious cross discern,
Bow lowering to the staff on our imperial stern.

We thank thee for Eliza's reign,   25
   When to the realm thy spirit spake;
And for thy triumphs on the main
   By Howard, Forbisher, and glorious Drake;
Whose heart was offer'd, resolute and free,
To bleed for Englishmen, but that was done by thee.   30

We thank thee for thy pow'r divine,
   By which our ships were mann'd from heav'n;
What wonder then if three should join
   To play their destin'd balls and conquer seven,
That Forest, Suckling, Langdon should prevail,   35
When thou hadst weigh'd the combat in thy righteous scale.

The glory to thy name we yield,
   By which the vast exploit was done;
At Poictier's and in Cressey's field
   Against vain Moab must'ring ten to one,   40
'Enough to kill, to take and put to flight,'
By faith of Englishmen in God's redoubted might.

The glory to thy name for Cam,
   Immortal from the hour he bled,
Who stoutly fixt himself to dam   45
   The torrent, rushing on his LEADER's head;
The glory to thy name, for each and all,
Of Henry's gifted sword, or Edward's noble stall.

The glory to thy name for Ann,
   And for the houses that she built;   50
And for that great victorious man,
   Who ran profane oppression to the hilt;
Born HIS sublime atchievement to fulfill,
Which bids IMPOSSIBLE make speed to do his will.

The glory to thy name for Ann,   55
   Sweet princess, with thy grace endu'd;
And for that charitable plan,
   By which the poor may preach, and have his food;
And for the special pray'r that she preferr'd,
Which for the famous march of deathless Webb was heard. 60

The glory to thy name for Ann,
   Again a princess, and most sweet,
To meet her Saviour Christ she ran,
   And gently stoopt to wash the poor man's feet;
Queen of the wave, to cherish with her wing   65
A Russel, Shovel, Rook, a Benbow, and a Byng.

We give the glory for the means
   By which the reformation rose;
Thy grace to stop the bloody scenes
   Of pride and cruelty, thy deadly foes;   70
Whence now the church in dignity sublimes,
The simple truth of Christ, and praise of pristine times.

We give the glory for thy word,
   That it so well becomes our tongue;
And that thy spirit is transferr'd   75
   Upon the strains of old in Hebrew sung.
And for the services dispers'd abroad,
– The church her seemly course of practic pray'r and laud.

We give the glory for the eyes
   Of science, and the realm around;   80
The two great rivals for the prize,
   Ingenuous to a blessing on the sound.
Well may their schools and num'rous chapels teach,
'The word is very Christ, that we adore and preach.'

O fair possessions! ghostly wealth!   85
   Nigh laid and lost on Charles's block,
What time the constitution's health
   Was broke, and ruin'd by the general shock;
Till God was with the loyal pray'r implor'd,
And THIS DAY saw the heir acknowledg'd and restor'd.   90

On this day, therefore, we support
   The joy with such applause begun,
Which sounding from th' imperial fort,
   Redoubles clam'rous roar from gun to gun.
Controuling unto good the sulph'rous blaze,   95
And making Satan's wrath benevolent of praise.

List! – as ye bless at each discharge,
  Remember where the glory's due
(In every house, and bow'r and barge)
  To Christ his love for everlasting true.   100
Accordant to the prophecies express,
His people to redeem, revisit and redress.

Remember all the pious vows
  Made by our ancestors, for us,
That we should thus dispose the boughs,   105
  And wear the royal oak in triumph thus;
And to the skies, the caps of freedom hurl'd,
Should thus proclaim the queen of islands and the world.

Ye soldiers reverend with scars,
  Remember Chelsea's pleasant groves;   110
And you, ye students of the stars,
  Remov'd from seaman's toils to fair alcoves;
Remember Edward's children train'd in art,
Which now can con the card, and now can plan the chart.

Remember all ye may of good,   115
  Select the nosegay from the sod;
But leave the brambles in the wood –
  Remember charity is God –
Which, scorning custom, her illib'ral crowds
Brings virtue to the sun, while slips and crimes she clouds. 120

Hymn 18: St Barna bas

  Daring as the noon-tide ray
  On the summer's longest day,
    Is the truth of Christ supreme;
  Proving at its sacred touch,
  Whether Ophir's gold be such,   5
    Or a shift to seem.

Joses, who can doubt thee now,
Who will not thy faith allow,
    With thy lands, for Christ, at sale?
By foul lucre undefil'd,   10
In the spirit Jesus' child,
    Son of comfort, hail!

For a substance to endure
Hast thou listed with the poor,
    Triumph o'er thyself atchiev'd –   15
Thee thy Saviour God inrolls
In the calendar of souls,
    Sainted and receiv'd.

Heroes of the Christian cause,
Candidates for God's applause,   20
    – Leaving all for Christ his sake;
Scorning temporal reward,
Ready to confess the Lord
    At the cross or stake.

Shew your everlasting store   25
To one great believer more,
    And your ghostly gifts impart –
Grutching treasures for the moth,
To the Lord he pledg'd his troth,
    And ally'd his heart.   30

Hence instructed, let us learn
Heav'n and heav'nly things to earn,
    And with want by pray'r to cope;
To the Lord your wealth resign,
Distribution is divine,   35
    Misers have no hope.

Hymn 19: The Nativity of St John the Baptist

Great and bounteous BENEFACTOR,
   We thy gen'rous aid adjure,
Shield us from the foul exactor,
   And his sons, that grind the poor.

Lo the swelling fruits of summer,   5
   With inviting colours dy'd,
Hang, for ev'ry casual comer,
   O'er the fence projecting wide.

See the corn for plenty waving,
   Where the lark secur'd her eggs –   10
In the spirit then be saving,
   Give the poor that sings and begs.

Gentle nature seems to love us
   In each fair and finish'd scene,
All is beauteous blue above us,   15
   All beneath is cheerful green.

Now when warmer rays enlighten
   And adorn the lengthen'd time,
When the views around us brighten,
   Days a rip'ning from their prime,   20

She that was as barren reckon'd,
   Had her course completely run,
And her dumb-struck husband beckon'd
   For a pen to write a son.

JOHN, the child of Zacharias,   25
   Just returning to his earth,
Prophet of the Lord Messias,
   And fore-runner of his birth.

He too martyr'd, shall precede him,
   Ere he speed to heav'n again,
Ere the traitors shall implead him,   30
   And the priest his God arraign.

John beheld the great and holy,
   Hail'd the love of God supreme;
O how gracious, meek, and lowly,
   When baptiz'd in Jordan's stream!   35

If from honour so stupendous
   He the grace of pow'r deriv'd,
And to tyrants was tremendous,
   That at fraud and filth conniv'd;   40

If he led a life of rigour,
   And th' abstemious vow obey'd;
If he preach'd with manly vigour,
   Practis'd sinners to dissuade;

If his voice by fair confession   45
   Christ's supremacy avow'd;
If he check'd with due suppression
   Self-incitements to be proud;

Vice conspiring to afflict him
   To the death that ends the great,   50
Offer'd him a worthy victim
   For acceptance in the height.

Hymn 20: St Peter

High above the world's pursuit,
   Far beyond the fool's conceit,
Where the cherub plays her lute,
   Dwells the man of God complete.

Greatness here severely shunn'd,   5
   Falls in heav'n to virtue's share,
And the poor man finds a fund
   Of eternal treasures there.

To the Lord is not access
   But by magnitude above,   10
And exalted strength must bless
   In yon upper flights of love.

Peter from repentance rose
  To the magnitude requir'd,
First of all his master chose   15
  In celestial pomp attir'd.

But he is a stranger still
  To the Roman frauds and fees;
He nor sold to vice her will,
  Nor to Mammon left his keys.   20

Hence the practice, prais'd at Rome,
  Christian principle confounds –
What! at eminence presume,
  And not skill to know the grounds?

What! can pride and kingly pow'r,   25
  With the soldier kept in pay,
And a crown like Babel's tow'r,
  Suit the sons of YEA and NAY?

YEA is Christ avouch'd by truth,
  Sharing hardship with her prince,   30
Feed my lambs – instruct the youth –
  Feed my sheep – the old convince.

NAY is quit thy house and land,
  And all carnal things abjure;
NAY is neither rich nor grand,   35
  But refuses for the poor.

Peter, when with Christ he went,
  Made this excellence his plea –
'Here we are, and rest content,
  Quitting all, and tending thee.'   40

Wherefore he was worthy deem'd
  On the mountain-top to tread,
While surpassing glories beam'd
  On his master's hallow'd head.

Wherefore too this day we hold   45
   As of honourable note,
We of Christ's peculiar fold,
   That protest against the goat.

Wheresoe'er we are dispers'd,
   In the ocean, or ashore,   50
Still the service is rehears'd,
   Still we worship and adore.

Thanks to God we have a form
   Of sound words aboard the ship,
In the calm, or in the storm,   55
   To exalt him heart and lip.

There Jehovah's dove may perch
   On the topmast as she swims —
Ev'ry vessel is a church
   Meet for praise, for pray'r, and hymns.   60

Hymn 21: St James

Sure a seaman's lot is bless'd,
   Gen'rous, faithful, frank, and brave,
Since the Lord himself possess'd
   Of disciples from the wave.
Sure a realm, whose fame depends   5
On their deeds the rest transcends.

Yea, from fishers on the coast,
   Poor, and by the nations scorn'd,
With our navy's gallant host
   Seas are crowded and adorn'd,   10
Wheresoe'er the billows toss,
Bearing Christ's triumphant cross.

Lo! the Lord is on the cliff,
   Peter's partner, come away;
Leave thy tackle and thy skiff
   For a life to preach and pray —   15
James shall answer the command,
Soon as he can make the land.

Let the net no more be haul'd,
   Zebedee, thy sire neglect   20
Now, the son of thunder call'd,
   E'en the word of God direct —
Thou disputing sects shall foil,
And conviction bless thy toil.

Having now obtain'd release   25
   From thy low concerns and cares,
Go, and preach the Spaniard peace,
   Teach ambitious pomp her pray'rs,
Fav'ring still, in Jesus' stead,
God in England at the head.   30

O that all the human race
   In what region, clime, or zone,
Would the genuine faith embrace,
   As in these thy kingdoms' known;
Prosper thou the pilgrims sent   35
To prepare the great event.

Prosper thou, O God of light,
   Them which propagate thy word
In the realms that fiends benight —
   By no seas or toils deterr'd;   40
More and more in this employ
Thy cherubic guard convoy.

God of heartiness and strength,
   God of English pray'r and laud,
May good-nature speed at length,   45
   Join'd with grace, to foes abroad,
Thou that lend'st a special ear
To the simple and sincere.

Hymn 22: St Bartholomew

'Behold an Israelite indeed,
   In whom there is no guile,' –
Whom neither worldly ways mislead,
   Nor treach'rous thoughts defile.

SINCERITY, belov'd of Christ,   5
   For him herself has kept,
And neither purchas'd, nor intic't,
   With him has smil'd and wept.

Her Jesus in his arms infolds,
   And to his church ascribes –   10
She wears the precious ring that holds
   Each jewel of the tribes.

Gold is not very gold, nor myrrh
   True myrrh, nor rubies glow,
If first not try'd and prov'd by her   15
   That they indeed are so.

She is a fountain from the truth,
   And floods embracing all;
Hypocrisy shall gnash its tooth
   Whene'er it hears her call.   20

Who then amongst mankind can thrive
   That has such ghostly worth?
The saint must needs be flay'd alive,
   Possessing her on earth.

Come then, or sword, or fire, or ax,   25
   Devour me branch and stem,
I will not fail to pay the tax
   Of life for such a gem.

Hymn 23: St Matthew

Ev'n exactors of the toll,
   And the harlot of the stew,
   Sooner give the Lord his due
Than men disguis'd of soul.

Matthew made the Lord a feast,   5
   Wealth and business left behind,
   Of his tribe, and of his kind,
Among the worst and least.

Yet he had an eye to God
   Soon as Jesus Christ drew near,   10
   And with meekness, faith, and fear,
He worship'd to his nod.

Humbl'd therefore by the shame
   Of his worldly filth and guilt,
   By his hand the Lord has built   15
A pillar to his name.

One for ev'ry point are four,
   Matthew for an obvious praise,
   His in Hebrew chose to raise,
That easterns might adore.   20

Of a meaner order, Mark,
   As he would the north address,
   Yet his word of God express
Illuminates the dark.

Luke diffusive takes a sweep,   25
   Rising to command the west,
   And by Jesus Christ is blest,
Historic high and deep.

John, above the rest divine,
   In the church her southern isle,
   Stands of plain majestic style,   30
Where warmth and brightness join.

These combin'd the church sustain,
  But this day assigns to thee,
  Matthew, rather than the three,   35
The heav'n directed strain.

Sure the mother-tongue is great,
  Since it is what seraphs use;
  Since with that the cherub woos
To mutual praise his mate.   40

Hymn 24: *St Michael and All Angels*

Angelic natures, great in arms
  Against the dragon and his pow'rs,
Whom Michael's excellence alarms
  From highest heav'n's imperial tow'rs;

Ye that in Christ his church attend   5
  What time the services are sung,
And your propitious spirits blend
  With our united heart and tongue.

O come, celestial watch and ward,
  As in the closet I adore,   10
My fellow-servants of the Lord,
  To whom these measures I restore.

If Satan's malice was withstood
  Where Moses cold and breathless lay,
Give Michael, patient, meek, and good,   15
  Through Christ, the glory of the day.

If Tobit's charitable soul,
  A type of Jesus Christ to come,
Was blessed from the poor man's dole
  Ev'n to the social sparrow's crumb;   20

If to the living and the dead
  His hand was rich in deeds of love,
First Raphael from his Master fled
  By mandate in the heights above.

If Zacharias was inform'd   25
  That God his pious pray'rs should crown,
The barren womb to ripeness warm'd,
  'Twas Gabriel brought the tidings down.

Hail mighty princes in the height,
  Which o'er stupendous works preside   30
Of vast authority and weight –
  But there are other pow'rs beside.

These, one for every man, are sent
  God in the spirit to reveal,
To forward ev'ry good event,   35
  And each internal grief to heal.

Hymn 25: St Luke

Luke, physician of the wound,
  Where the troubl'd conscience stings,
Far beyond the skill profound
Of the graduates here renown'd,
  Or the costly springs.   5

Thy conversion soon is wrought,
  When thou seest thy Saviour's cures,
So surpassing human thought,
What thy books from Greece have taught,
  Or thy hope assures.   10

Henceforth, without scrip or purse,
  Go on embassage divine,
Med'cines of the soul disperse
To the wicked and perverse
  Thou wert wont to join.   15

Thee thy Saviour shall allot
  His great actions to relate,
And thy brethren's sins to blot;
Greater blessing there is not
  In a mortal state.   20

Thou shalt also tell the deeds
  Of that apostolic band,
While the happy convert reads
How in Christ the pris'ner pleads
  By a master's hand. 25

Sure thy skill in picture came
  To th' assistance of thy pen,
If she was of heav'nly flame,
That is now a sin and shame,
  By the frauds of men. 30

Her the hypocrites adore
  In the fane of modern Rome,
And from shadows aid implore,
That they may blaspheme the more,
  And the more presume. 35

Christ from such detested arts
  Guard thy church with watchful eyes,
Keep from Satan's snares and darts,
Innocent as doves our hearts,
  But as serpents wise. 40

Hymn 26: The Accession of King George III

By me, says Wisdom, monarchs reign,
  And princes right decree;
The conduct of the land and main
  Is minister'd by me.

Where neither Philip's son was sped, 5
  Nor Roman eagles flew,
The English standard rears its head,
  To storm and to subdue.

Our gallant fleets have won success,
  Christ Jesus at the helm, 10
And let us therefore kneel and bless
  The sovereign of the realm.

This day the youth began his race,
 With angels for allies,
And God shall give him strength and grace   15
 To claim the naval prize.

His righteous spirit he fatigu'd
 To speak the nation's peace;
Yet more and more the Papists leagu'd
 To mar the world's increase.   20

The Lord accept his good intent,
 And be his great defence,
And may his enemies repent
 At no prescrib'd expense.

As yet this isle the proof has stood,   25
 Which God from all disjoins;
O make him singularly good,
 And bless with fruit his loins.

His eastern, western bounds enlarge,
 Which swarms in vain contest,   30
And keep the people of his charge
 In wealth and godly rest.

Hymn 27: St Simon and St Jude

Peace be to the souls of those
 Which for Jesus Christ have bled,
Or that triumph'd o'er their foes
 With the coals upon their head.

Which for him have undergone   5
 Any other dread or death,
Crucify'd, or stabb'd, or sawn,
 Blessing to their latest breath.

Simon well may claim a place
 In our book of Common Pray'r;   10
Here he likewise planted grace
 By his apostolic care.

He his pilgrimage perform'd
    Far as the Britannic coast,
And the ready converts swarm'd   15
    To receive the Holy Ghost.

Fair sincerity's the ground
    For the Lord to sow his seed,
That will flourish and abound
    With a goodly crop indeed.   20

Christ is pow'rful to renew
    Men so quick his will to know,
Whence ten thousand churches grew,
    And ten thousand more shall grow.

Farther yet, and farther east,   25
    English sails shall be unfurl'd,
Wafting many a pious priest
    To protest against the world.

Farther yet, and farther west,
    We shall send the faith abroad,   30
Against nations to protest,
    That are still by Christ unaw'd.

We shall cite from holy Jude
    Wholesome texts to mend their way,
Whom our praise and pray'rs include   35
    In the duty of to-day.

He is full of just complaint,
    As foul deeds his wrath provoke;
And they massacred the saint
    For the cutting words he spoke.   40

Let us therefore well provide
    This good festival to hold,
Lest to us they be apply'd
    As to wand'rers from the fold.

Lo! the church herself attires   45
　For the work of pray'r and song;
To the strains that Christ inspires
　Crowds of either sex shall throng.

Hymn 28: All Saints

Many male and female names,
From the cross, the sword, and flames,
To their blessed Saviour dear,
Have escap'd memorial here.

These are all the Lord's elect,   5
Which the church must not neglect,
But appoints a day to raise
Anthems for a gen'ral praise.

Stars of the superior class,
Which in magnitude surpass,   10
From the time they rose and shone,
Have their names and places known.

Mazaroth his circuit runs,
With Arcturus and his sons;
Pleiad twinkles o'er the streams   15
Of Orion's bolder beams.

But what glories in array
Brighten all the milky way,
Where innumerables vie,
Told alone by God Most High!   20

Enoch of exceeding grace,
Abr'ham of unnumber'd race,
Jael bursting into fame,
Joab of stupendous name.

These the seers of God commit   25
To the rolls of holy writ,
With a multitude of note,
Which our children have by rote.

There are thousand thousands more,
Like the sand upon the shore,   30
Through the love of Christ reveal'd,
All in heav'n receiv'd and seal'd.

Hymn 29: *The Fifth of November*

What impression God and reason
  Had on some abandon'd times,
Was made evident by treason,
  And the most flagitious crimes.

England lay dissolv'd in slumber,   5
  Toil and emulation ceas'd,
Till the malice, strength, and number
  Of her foes were all increas'd.

Eat and drink, and die to-morrow,
  From the cottage to the helm,   10
Till the blessed man of sorrow
  Was not heard in all the realm.

This was deem'd a fit occasion
  For the Papists to be bold,
For the children of evasion   15
  To come sneaking from their hold.

What a plan of devastation,
  That the dev'l alone could start,
How at once to crush the nation
  In the bowels, head, and heart!   20

There is no such great perdition
  In the story of mankind,
Not by craft and superstition,
  Yea, and cruelty combin'd.

God, in a stupendous manner,   25
  Bade a spendthrift nation home –
Let us therefore fix the banner
  On the high cathedral's dome.

Play the music – call the singers –
    Open wide the prison door –   30
Make a banquet for the ringers –
    Give to poverty the store.

Fire away the joyful volley,
    Deck your houses, bless your wine;
Triumph o'er the Papists' folly,   35
    Who their God would undermine.

Hymn 30: St Andrew

O Lord, thou God of bliss,
    Which highest natures leave
To rectify the things amiss
    Amongst the sons of Eve.

From time to time they came   5
    To warn and to correct;
But ah! the dreadful sin and shame,
    With small or none effect.

At length no more with-held
    By seraph's tears and pray'r,   10
The God of heav'n himself compell'd
    This fleshly veil to wear.

But how to find a friend
    In poverty and woe,
Omnipotence must needs attend   15
    His steps where'er they go.

When John his Saviour spy'd,
    Behold the LAMB (said he).
If it be so, St Andrew cry'd,
    No more I follow thee.   20

His teacher he forsook,
    And on his face he fell,
And instantly himself betook
    To life's eternal well.

Then from a life reform'd,   25
    He spread example wide,
And multitudes with zeal he warm'd
    To take their Saviour's side.

At length the words prevail
    Which Christ prophetic spake,   30
And to the cross the saint they hale
    That ruffian traitors make.

Tormented, tried, and bound
    Two well-supported days,
His life his dying accents crown'd,   35
    E'en to their last essays.

His body was remov'd
    From Patrae to the Turk,
Where it, through Christ, shall be improv'd
    To do a glorious work.   40

The Spirit shall descend,
    And churches shall aspire,
– And they that now the mosques attend,
    Of Jesus shall inquire.

Yea Edom one and all   45
    Shall choose the Lord their chief;
And he shall finally recall
    The sons of unbelief.

Hymn 31: St Thomas

Ah! Thomas, wherefore wouldst thou doubt,
    And put the Lord in pain,
And mad'st his wounds to spout
    Anew from ev'ry vein?

Lo! those of God are blessed most,
    Which, simple and serene,   5
Believe the Holy Ghost,
    That operates unseen.

This is that great and prior proof
   Of God and of his Son,   10
Beneath whose sacred roof
   To-day the duty's done.

Tho' seventeen hundred years remote,
   We can perform our part,
And to the Lord devote   15
   The tribute of our heart.

O Lord, the slaves of sin release,
   Their ways in Christ amend,
Our faith and hope increase,
   Our charities extend.   20

Make thou our alter'd lives of use
   To all the skirts around,
And purge from each abuse
   Thy church, so much renown'd.

Enlarge from Mammon's spells her priests,   25
   And from all carnal cares,
And bid to ghostly feasts,
   To pure cherubic airs.

Thy people in that choir employ
   Whose business is above,   30
In gratitude and joy,
   In wonder, praise, and love.

Hymn 32: *The Nativity of Our Lord and Saviour Jesus Christ*

Where is this stupendous stranger,
   Swains of Solyma, advise,
Lead me to my Master's manger,
   Shew me where my Saviour lies?

O Most Mighty! O MOST HOLY!   5
   Far beyond the seraph's thought,
Art thou then so mean and lowly
   As unheeded prophets taught?

O the magnitude of meekness!
   Worth from worth immortal sprung;   10
O the strength of infant weakness,
   If eternal is so young!

If so young and thus eternal,
   Michael tune the shepherd's reed,
Where the scenes are ever vernal,   15
   And the loves be love indeed!

See the God blasphem'd and doubted
   In the schools of Greece and Rome;
See the pow'rs of darkness routed,
   Taken at their utmost gloom.   20

Nature's decorations glisten
   Far above their usual trim;
Birds on box and laurels listen,
   As so near the cherubs hymn.

Boreas now no longer winters   25
   On the desolated coast;
Oaks no more are riv'n in splinters
   By the whirlwind and his host.

Spinks and ouzles sing sublimely,
   'We too have a Saviour born;'   30
Whiter blossoms burst untimely
   On the blest Mosaic thorn.

God all-bounteous, all-creative,
   Whom no ills from good dissuade,
Is incarnate, and a native   35
   Of the very world he made.

Hymn 33: St Stephen

O Maker! of almighty skill,
Whose word all wonders can fulfill,
Where'er the sun, where'er the planets shine,
Exertion and effect at once are thine.

God! great and manifest around,   5
In earth, and air, and depth profound,
In every movement, animals that breathe,
And all the beauties visible beneath.

But nobler works about his throne,
And brighter glories are his own,   10
Where high o'er heav'n the loves his Spirit mates,
And virtues, graces, mercies he creates.

A saint is a stupendous thing,
Sublimest work of Christ the king;
For ere his blessed Saviour can succeed,   15
How many foes to foil, and veins to bleed!

Soon as the Lord resum'd the skies,
He put up his immortal prize,
And in a full maturity of soul,
Great Stephen ran the first, and past the goal.   20

His therefore is the champion's crown –
And his the firstlings of renown –
O GRACE, thou never rais'd a sweeter flow'r,
Which sprang, and gemm'd, and blossom'd in an hour.

Then welcome to a quick reward,   25
Ev'n in the bosom of the Lord,
To hear, 'Well done, thou good and faithful friend,
Receive thy Saviour's joy, that knows no end.

'Beyond the bliss of ear or eye,
Beyond the heart's conception high,   30
Beyond the topmost flight of mortal ken,
Hosanna! halelujah! and amen.' –

Hymn 34: St John the Evangelist

Hosanna! yet again,
  Another glorious day,
  Ye cherubs sing and play,
Ye seraphs swell the strain.

Hail! highly favour'd man,   5
  Thy name and lot transcend
  All praise that e'er was penn'd
Since first the verse began.

O dear to Christ supreme,
  His bosom friend declar'd,   10
  And yet for all he car'd
With tenderness extreme.

As Benjamin was blest,
  When he to Egypt came,
  By Joseph full of fame,
And honour'd o'er the rest.   15

But Christ was meek and poor,
  No chariot his to ride,
  No Goshen to divide,
No favours to procure.   20

Yet in his realms above,
  Which are the highest heav'n,
  First of th' elect elev'n,
Thou claim'st thy master's love.

Hymn 35: The Holy Innocents

Love and pity are ally'd,
So are cruelty and pride;
But they never met till now,
As in Herod's hellish vow.

Ev'ry tyrant of his time   5
Stands abash'd at such a crime;
Not a monster since the flood
Was in equal guilt of blood.

Rachael, with a mother's grief,
Sees the ruffians and their chief,   10
Piercing heav'n and earth with cries,
For her children's rescue tries.

'Cherubs lend your aid in air;
Seraphim, ye shall not dare
Such a scene as this to see,   15
And not succour God and me.'

Woman, speed thee back to bliss –
At a greater price than this,
Ere the plan of Christ we build,
Prophecies must be fulfill'd.   20

Blessed be the Lord's escape,
When the gulf began to gape,
And the fiends from hell were sent,
Man's salvation to prevent.

By the hope which prophets give,   25
By the psalmist 'he shall live',
Sav'd for a sufficient space
To perform his work of grace.

Though the heav'n and earth shall fail,
Yet his spirit shall prevail,   30
Till all nations have concurr'd
In the worship of the WORD.

A SONG TO DAVID

David the son of Jesse said, and the man who was raised
up on high, the anointed of the God of Jacob, and the
sweet psalmist of Israel, said,
The Spirit of the Lord spake by me, and his word was in
my tongue.

2 Sam. xxiii. 1, 2.

Contents

Invocation, ver. 1, 2, 3. – The excellence and lustre of David's
character in twelve points of view, ver. 4; proved from the
history of his life, to ver. 17. – He consecrates his genius for
consolation and edification. – The subjects he made choice of –
the Supreme Being – angels; men of renown; the works of nature
in all directions, either particularly or collectively considered, to
ver. 27. – He obtains power over infernal spirits, and the
malignity of his enemies; wins the heart of Michal, to ver. 30. –
Shews that the pillars of knowledge are the monuments of God's
works in the first week, to ver. 38. – An exercise upon the
decalogue, from ver. 40 to 49. – The transcendent virtue of
praise and adoration, ver. 50 and 51. – An exercise upon the
seasons, and the right use of them, from ver. 52 to 64. – An
exercise upon the senses, and how to subdue them, from ver. 65
to 71. – An amplification in five degrees, which is wrought up
to this conclusion, That the best poet which ever lived was
thought worthy of the highest honour which possibly can be
conceived, as *the Saviour of the world was ascribed to his house,
and called his son in the body.*

Christopher Smart

1

O Thou, that sit'st upon a throne,
With harp of high majestic tone,
  To praise the King of kings;
And voice of heav'n-ascending swell,
Which, while its deeper notes excell,   5
  Clear, as a clarion, rings:

2

To bless each valley, grove and coast,
And charm the cherubs to the post
  Of gratitude in throngs;
To *keep* the days on Zion's mount,   10
And send the year to his account,
  With dances and with songs:

3

O Servant of God's holiest charge,
The minister of praise at large,
  Which thou may'st now receive;   15
From thy blest mansion hail and hear,
From topmost eminence appear
  To this the wreath I weave.

4

Great, valiant, pious, good, and clean,
Sublime, contemplative, serene,   20
  Strong, constant, pleasant, wise!
Bright effluence of exceeding grace;
Best man! – the swiftness and the race,
  The peril, and the prize!

5

Great – from the lustre of his crown,   25
From Samuel's horn and God's renown,
  Which is the people's voice;
For all the host, from rear to van,
Applauded and embrac'd the man –
  The man of God's own choice.   30

6

Valiant – the word, and up he rose –
The fight – he triumph'd o'er the foes,
   Whom God's just laws abhor;
And arm'd in gallant faith he took
Against the boaster, from the brook,   35
   The weapons of the war.

7

Pious – magnificent and grand;
'Twas he the famous temple plann'd:
   (The seraph in his soul)
Foremost to give his Lord his dues,   40
Foremost to bless the welcome news,
   And foremost to condole.

8

Good – from Jehudah's genuine vein,
From God's best nature good in
grain,
   His aspect and his heart;   45
To pity, to forgive, to save,
Witness En-gedi's conscious cave,
   And Shimei's blunted dart.

9

Clean – if perpetual prayer be pure,
And love, which could itself inure   50
   To fasting and to fear –
Clean in his gestures, hands, and feet,
To smite the lyre, the dance complete,
   To play the sword and spear.

10

Sublime – invention ever young,   55
Of vast conception, tow'ring tongue,
   To God th' eternal theme;
Notes from yon exaltations caught,
Unrival'd royalty of thought,
   O'er meaner strains supreme.   60

11

Contemplative – on God to fix
His musings, and above the six
    The sabbath-day he blest;
'Twas then his thoughts self-conquest prun'd,
And heavenly melancholy tun'd,   65
    To bless and bear the rest.

12

Serene – to sow the seeds of peace,
Rememb'ring, when he watch'd the fleece,
    How sweetly Kidron purl'd –
To further knowledge, silence vice,   70
And plant perpetual paradise
    When God had calm'd the world.

13

Strong – in the Lord, who could defy
Satan, and all his powers that lie
    In sempiternal night;   75
And hell, and horror, and despair
Were as the lion and the bear
    To his undaunted might.

14

Constant – in love to God THE TRUTH,
Age, manhood, infancy, and youth –   80
    To Jonathan his friend
Constant, beyond the verge of death;
And Ziba, and Mephibosheth,
    His endless fame attend.

15

Pleasant – and various as the year;   85
Man, soul, and angel, without peer,
    Priest, champion, sage and boy;
In armour, or in ephod clad,
His pomp, his piety was glad;
    Majestic was his joy.   90

16

Wise — in recovery from his fall,
Whence rose his eminence o'er all,
   Of all the most revil'd;
The light of Israel in his ways,
Wise are his precepts, prayer and praise,   95
   And counsel to his child.

17

His muse, bright angel of his verse,
Gives balm for all the thorns that pierce,
   For all the pangs that rage;
Blest light, still gaining on the gloom,   100
The more than Michal of his bloom,
   Th' Abishag of his age.

18

He sung of God — the mighty source
Of all things — the stupendous force
   On which all strength depends;   105
From whose right arm, beneath whose eyes,
All period, pow'r, and enterprise
   Commences, reigns, and ends.

19

Angels — their ministry and meed,
Which to and fro with blessings speed,   110
   Or with their citterns wait;
Where Michael with his millions bows,
Where dwells the seraph and his spouse,
   The cherub and her mate.

20

Of man — the semblance and effect
Of God and Love — the Saint elect   115
   For infinite applause —
To rule the land, and briny broad,
To be laborious in his laud,
   And heroes in his cause.   120

21

The world – the clust'ring spheres he made,
The glorious light, the soothing shade,
  Dale, champaign, grove, and hill;
The multitudinous abyss,
Where secrecy remains in bliss,   125
  And wisdom hides her skill.

22

Trees, plants, and flow'rs – of virtuous root;
Gem yielding blossom, yielding fruit,
  Choice gums and precious balm;
Bless ye the nosegay in the vale,   130
And with the sweet'ners of the gale
  Enrich the thankful psalm.

23

Of fowl – e'en ev'ry beak and wing
Which cheer the winter, hail the spring,
  That live in peace or prey;   135
They that make music, or that mock,
The quail, the brave domestic cock,
  The raven, swan, and jay.

24

Of fishes – ev'ry size and shape,
Which nature frames of light escape,   140
  Devouring man to shun:
The shells are in the wealthy deep,
The shoals upon the surface leap,
  And love the glancing sun.

25

Of beasts – the beaver plods his task;   145
While the sleek tygers roll and bask,
  Nor yet the shades arouse:
Her cave the mining coney scoops;
Where o'er the mead the mountain stoops,
  The kids exult and browse.   150

26

Of gems – their virtue and their price,
Which hid in earth from man's device,
　　Their darts of lustre sheathe;
The jasper of the master's stamp,
The topaz blazing like a lamp   155
　　Among the mines beneath.

27

Blest was the tenderness he felt
When to his graceful harp he knelt,
　　And did for audience call;
When Satan with his hand he quell'd,   160
And in serene suspense he held
　　The frantic throes of Saul.

28

His furious foes no more malign'd
As he such melody divin'd,
　　And sense and soul detain'd;   165
Now striking strong, now soothing soft,
He sent the godly sounds aloft,
　　Or in delight refrain'd.

29

When up to heav'n his thoughts he pil'd,
From fervent lips fair Michal smil'd,   170
　　As blush to blush she stood;
And chose herself the queen, and gave
Her utmost from her heart, 'so brave,
　　And plays his hymns so good.'

30

The pillars of the Lord are sev'n,   175
Which stand from earth to topmost heav'n;
　　His wisdom drew the plan;
His WORD accomplish'd the design,
From brightest gem to deepest mine,
　　From CHRIST enthron'd to man.   180

31

Alpha, the cause of causes, first
In station, fountain, whence the burst
   Of light, and blaze of day;
Whence bold attempt, and brave advance,
Have motion, life, and ordinance,   185
   And heav'n itself its stay.

32

Gamma supports the glorious arch
On which angelic legions march,
   And is with sapphires pav'd;
Thence the fleet clouds are sent adrift,   190
And thence the painted folds, that lift
   The crimson veil, are wav'd.

33

Eta with living sculpture breathes,
With verdant carvings, flow'ry wreathes
   Of never-wasting bloom;   195
In strong relief his goodly base
All instruments of labour grace,
   The trowel, spade, and loom.

34

Next Theta stands to the Supreme –
Who form'd, in number, sign, and scheme,   200
   Th' illustrious lights that are;
And one address'd his saffron robe,
And one, clad in a silver globe,
   Held rule with ev'ry star.

35

Iota's tun'd to choral hymns   205
Of those that fly, while he that swims
   In thankful safety lurks;
And foot, and chapitre, and niche,
The various histories enrich
   Of God's recorded works.   210

36

Sigma presents the social droves,
With him that solitary roves,
   And man of all the chief;
Fair on whose face, and stately frame,
Did God impress his hallow'd name,   215
   For ocular belief.

37

OMEGA! GREATEST and the BEST,
Stands sacred to the day of rest,
   For gratitude and thought;
Which bless'd the world upon his pole,   220
And gave the universe his goal,
   And clos'd th' infernal draught.

38

O DAVID, scholar of the Lord!
Such is thy science, whence reward
   And infinite degree;   225
O strength, O sweetness, lasting ripe!
God's harp thy symbol, and thy type
   The lion and the bee!

39

There is but One who ne'er rebell'd,
But One by passion unimpell'd,   230
   By pleasures unintic't;
He from himself his semblance sent,
Grand object of his own content,
   And saw the God in CHRIST.

40

'Tell them I am,' JEHOVA said   235
To MOSES; while earth heard in dread,
   And smitten to the heart,
At once above, beneath, around,
All nature, without voice or sound,
   Replied, 'O Lord, THOU ART.'   240

41

Thou art – to give and to confirm,
For each his talent and his term;
   All flesh thy bounties share:
Thou shalt not call thy brother fool;
The porches of the Christian school   245
   Are meekness, peace, and pray'r.

42

Open, and naked of offence,
Man's made of mercy, soul, and sense;
   God arm'd the snail and wilk;
Be good to him that pulls thy plough;   250
Due food and care, due rest, allow
   For her that yields thee milk.

43

Rise up before the hoary head,
And God's benign commandment dread,
   Which says thou shalt not die: 255
'Not as I will, but as thou wilt,'
Pray'd He whose conscience knew no guilt;
   With whose bless'd pattern vie.

44

Use all thy passions! – love is thine,
And joy, and jealousy divine;   260
   Thine hope's eternal fort,
And care thy leisure to disturb,
With fear concupiscence to curb,
   And rapture to transport.

45

Act simply, as occasion asks;   265
Put mellow wine in season'd casks;
   Till not with ass and bull:
Remember thy baptismal bond;
Keep from commixtures foul and fond,
   Nor work thy flax with wool.   270

46

Distribute: pay the Lord his tithe,
And make the widow's heart-strings blithe;
   Resort with those that weep:
As you from all and each expect,
For all and each thy love direct,   275
   And render as you reap.

47

The slander and its bearer spurn,
And propagating praise sojourn
   To make thy welcome last;
Turn from old Adam to the New;   280
By hope futurity pursue;
   Look upwards to the past.

48

Controul thine eye, salute success,
Honour the wiser, happier bless,
   And for thy neighbour feel;   285
Grutch not of Mammon and his leaven,
Work emulation up to heaven
   By knowledge and by zeal.

49

O DAVID, highest in the list
Of worthies, on God's ways insist,   290
   *The genuine word repeat:
Vain are the documents of men,
And vain the flourish of the pen
   That keeps the fool's conceit.

* Ps. 119.

50

PRAISE above all – for praise prevails;   295
Heap up the measure, load the scales,
   And good to goodness add:
The gen'rous soul her Saviour aids,
But peevish obloquy degrades;
   The Lord is great and glad.   300

51

For ADORATION all the ranks
Of angels yield eternal thanks,
   And DAVID in the midst;
With God's good poor, which, last and least
In man's esteem, thou to thy feast,   305
   O blessed bride-groom, bidst.

52

For ADORATION seasons change,
And order, truth, and beauty range,
   Adjust, attract, and fill:
The grass the polyanthus cheques;   310
And polish'd porphyry reflects,
   By the descending rill.

53

Rich almonds colour to the prime
For ADORATION; tendrils climb,
   And fruit-trees pledge their gems;   315
And *Ivis with her gorgeous vest
Builds for her eggs her cunning nest,
   And bell-flowers bow their stems.

54

With vinous syrup cedars spout;
From rocks pure honey gushing out,   320
   For ADORATION springs:
All scenes of painting crowd the map
Of nature; to the mermaid's pap
   The scaled infant clings.

55

The spotted ounce and playsome cubs   325
Run rustling 'mongst the flow'ring shrubs,
   And lizards feed the moss;
For ADORATION †beasts embark,
While waves upholding halcyon's ark
   No longer roar and toss.   330

56

While Israel sits beneath his fig,
With coral root and amber sprig
   The wean'd advent'rer sports;
Where to the palm the jasmin cleaves,
For ADORATION 'mongst the leaves   335
   The gale his peace reports.

57

Increasing days their reign exalt,
Nor in the pink and mottled vault
   Th'opposing spirits tilt;
And, by the coasting reader spied,   340
The silverlings and crusions glide
   For ADORATION gilt.

58

For ADORATION rip'ning canes
And cocoa's purest milk detains
   The western pilgrim's staff;   345
Where rain in clasping boughs inclos'd,
And vines with oranges dispos'd,
   Embow'r the social laugh.

* Humming-bird.

† There is a large quadruped that preys upon fish, and provides himself
with a piece of timber for that purpose, with which he is very handy.

59

Now labour his reward receives,
For ADORATION counts his sheaves   350
    To peace, her bounteous prince;
The nectarine his strong tint imbibes,
And apples of ten thousand tribes,
    And quick peculiar quince.

60

The wealthy crops of whit'ning rice,   355
'Mongst thyine woods and groves of spice,
    For ADORATION grow;
And, marshall'd in the fenced land,
The peaches and pomegranates stand,
    Where wild carnations blow.   360

61

The laurels with the winter strive;
The crocus burnishes alive
    Upon the snow-clad earth:
For ADORATION myrtles stay
To keep the garden from dismay,   365
    And bless the sight from dearth.

62

The pheasant shows his pompous neck;
And ermine, jealous of a speck,
    With fear eludes offence:
The sable, with his glossy pride,   370
For ADORATION is descried,
    Where frosts the wave condense.

63

The cheerful holly, pensive yew,
And holy thorn, their trim renew;
    The squirrel hoards his nuts: 375
All creatures batten o'er their stores,
And careful nature all her doors
    For ADORATION shuts.

64

For ADORATION, DAVID's psalms
Lift up the heart to deeds of alms;   380
   And he, who kneels and chants,
Prevails his passions to controul,
Finds meat and med'cine to the soul,
   Which for translation pants.

65

For ADORATION, beyond match,   385
The scholar bulfinch aims to catch
   The soft flute's iv'ry touch;
And, careless on the hazel spray,
The daring redbreast keeps at bay
   The damsel's greedy clutch.   390

66

For ADORATION, in the skies,
The Lord's philosopher espies
   The Dog, the Ram, and Rose;
The planet's ring, Orion's sword;
Nor is his greatness less ador'd   395
   In the vile worm that glows.

67

For ADORATION *on the strings
The western breezes work their wings,
   The captive ear to sooth. –
Hark! 'tis a voice – how still, and small –   400
That makes the cataracts to fall,
   Or bids the sea be smooth.

* Aeolian harp.

68

For ADORATION, incense comes
From bezoar, and Arabian gums;
   And on the civet's furr.   405
But as for prayer, or ere it faints,
Far better is the breath of saints
   Than galbanum and myrrh.

69

For ADORATION from the down,
Of dam'sins to th' anana's crown,   410
   God sends to tempt the taste;
And while the luscious zest invites
The sense, that in the scene delights,
   Commands desire be chaste.

70

For ADORATION, all the paths   415
Of grace are open, all the baths
   Of purity refresh;
And all the rays of glory beam
To deck the man of God's esteem,
   Who triumphs o'er the flesh.   420

71

For ADORATION, in the dome
Of Christ the sparrows find an home;
   And on his olives perch:
The swallow also dwells with thee,
O man of God's humility,   425
   Within his Saviour CHURCH.

72

Sweet is the dew that falls betimes,
And drops upon the leafy limes;
   Sweet Hermon's fragrant air: 430
Sweet is the lily's silver bell,
And sweet the wakeful tapers smell
   That watch for early pray'r.

73

Sweet the young nurse with love intense,
Which smiles o'er sleeping innocence;
   Sweet when the lost arrive: 435
Sweet the musician's ardour beats,
While his vague mind's in quest of sweets,
   The choicest flow'rs to hive.

74

Sweeter in all the strains of love,
The language of thy turtle dove,   440
   Pair'd to thy swelling chord;
Sweeter with ev'ry grace endu'd,
The glory of thy gratitude,
   Respir'd unto the Lord.

75

Strong is the horse upon his speed;   445
Strong in pursuit the rapid glede,
   Which makes at once his game:
Strong the tall ostrich on the ground;
Strong thro' the turbulent profound
   Shoots *xiphias to his aim.   450

76

Strong is the lion – like a coal
His eye-ball – like a bastion's mole
   His chest against the foes:
Strong, the gier-eagle on his sail,
Strong against tide, th' enormous whale   455
   Emerges as he goes.

77

But stronger still, in earth and air,
And in the sea, the man of pray'r;
   And far beneath the tide;
And in the seat to faith assign'd,
Where ask is have, where seek is find,   460
   Where knock is open wide.

* The sword-fish.

78

Beauteous the fleet before the gale;
Beauteous the multitudes in mail,
   Rank'd arms and crested heads: 465
Beauteous the garden's umbrage mild,
Walk, water, meditated wild,
   And all the bloomy beds.

79

Beauteous the moon full on the lawn;
And beauteous, when the veil's withdrawn,   470
   The virgin to her spouse:
Beauteous the temple deck'd and fill'd,
When to the heav'n of heav'ns they build
   Their heart-directed vows.

80

Beauteous, yea beauteous more than these,   475
The shepherd king upon his knees,
   For his momentous trust;
With wish of infinite conceit,
For man, beast, mute, the small and great,
   And prostrate dust to dust.   480

81

Precious the bounteous widow's mite;
And precious, for extreme delight,
   *The largess from the churl:
Precious the ruby's blushing blaze,
And †alba's blest imperial rays,   485
   And pure cerulean pearl.

* Sam. xxv. 18.
† Rev. ii. 17.

82

Precious the penitential tear;
And precious is the sigh sincere,
  Acceptable to God:
And precious are the winning flow'rs,   490
In gladsome Israel's feast of bow'rs,
  Bound on the hallow'd sod.

83

More precious that diviner part
Of David, ev'n the Lord's own heart,
  Great, beautiful, and new: 495
In all things where it was intent,
In all extremes, in each event,
  Proof — answ'ring true to true.

84

Glorious the sun in mid career;
Glorious th' assembled fires appear;   500
  Glorious the comet's train:
Glorious the trumpet and alarm;
Glorious th' almighty stretch'd-out arm;
  Glorious th' enraptur'd main:

85

Glorious the northern lights astream;   505
Glorious the song, when God's the theme;
  Glorious the thunder's roar:
Glorious hosanna from the den;
Glorious the catholic amen;
  Glorious the martyr's gore: 510

86

Glorious — more glorious is the crown
Of Him that brought salvation down
  By meekness, call'd thy Son;
Thou at stupendous truth believ'd,
And now the matchless deed's atchiev'd,   515
  DETERMINED, DARED, and DONE.

FINIS.

FROM
A TRANSLATION OF
THE PSALMS OF DAVID

ATTEMPTED IN THE SPIRIT OF
CHRISTIANITY, AND ADAPTED TO
THE DIVINE SERVICE

Ταδε λεγει ὁ ἀγιος, ὁ αληθινος, ὁ εχων την κλειδα του Δαβιδ.

Rev. iii. 7.

In this translation, all expressions, that seem contrary to Christ, are omitted, and evangelical matter put in their room; – and as it was written with an especial view to the divine service, the reader will find sundry allusions to the rites and ceremonies of the Church of England, which are intended to render the work in general more useful and acceptable to congregations.

Psalm 18

Thee will I love, O Lord, my tow'r,
My Saviour of almighty pow'r
  Is God, in whom I dare;
By whom my conq'ring bands are led,
My buckler in the hour of dread,   5
  And refuge from despair.

I will invoke the great Supreme
Whose matchless merits are the theme
  Of everlasting praise;
So when the furious warriours chafe,   10
I shall command the battle safe
  From terror and amaze.

The sorrows of a death-like gloom,
And all the visions of the tomb
  Came threat'ning as at hand;   15
And blood in such profusion spilt
By swords extravagant of guilt
  My trembling heart unmann'd.

Hell with her agonizing pains,
And horror of eternal chains,   20
  My vestibule alarm'd;
And by my active health forsook,
A ghastly consternation shook,
  And all my strength disarm'd.

Thro' trouble when my members fail,   25
O Lord, I will myself avail
  Of thy most holy name;
To thee prefer my soul's complaint,
And from diseases and restraint
  Thy blest protection claim.   30

So that within thy sacred shrine
Thou shalt thy gracious ears incline,
  As I thy help beseech;
Thy psalmist to the height shall soar,
And up at Heaven's interior door   35
  Shall thine attention reach.

Strong dread redoubled to convulse
All nature's frame at every pulse,
  And from their topmost height,
Down to the bottom of their base,   40
The hills were shaken and gave place,
  Because his wrath was great.

Out in his presence issue wreathes
Of lucid smoke, and as he breathes
  Flames from his mouth transpire;   45
Which rage so vehement and fierce,
The bowels of the earth they pierce,
  And set her mines on fire.

The empyrean at his frown
Was humbled, and the heav'ns came down   50
  With all the host incens'd
Of Michael summon'd from his seat,
And gathering underneath his feet,
  The darkness was condens'd.

And on the innumerable flight   55
Of cherubims, the sons of light,
  He rode in grand career;
And bore on the stupendous force
And speed of winged winds his course,
  O'er vaulted space to steer.   60

A thick tremendous veil he made,
The glorious majesty to shade,
  Where in the midst he storm'd;
And his pavilion was a cloud
Of deepest water, which to shroud,   65
  His alter'd face he form'd.

But then the brightness which he beam'd,
As he the copious lustre stream'd,
    The dusky scene controuls;
And as the gloom around was clear'd,   70
From out the central blaze appear'd,
    Hail mixt with burning coals.

God also thunder'd – the most high
Pronounc'd his thunder in the sky,
    The rolling pomp to drive;   75
And at his omnipresent word,
Above, beneath, around occurr'd
    Hailstones and coals alive.

He from his loaded quiver drew
The forked arrows, and they flew   80
    To make obstruction void;
He bade the heathen wrath avast,
And with the lightning that he cast,
    Their menaces destroy'd.

The secret water springs the while   85
Were seen ev'n to the source of Nile,
    And in the world beneath,
The pillars of th' inferior arch
Stood naked at the fires that search,
    And his strong vengeance breathe.   90

His blessed angel he shall send
To fetch me, and in pow'r defend
    From his terrific scourge;
With which he visits all around,
And from the floods of the profound   95
    I shall to peace emerge.

He shall in love prevent my fall,
Till my worst enemy of all
    With guilty shame shall blush;
And save me from the gross disgust   100
Of men with ruffian rage robust,
    Whose furious weight would crush.

In that sad hour of pinching need,
They strove my progress to impede,
   And from my point debarr'd;   105
But Christ the Lord, to whom I pray,
Upheld my goings in the way,
   At once my guide and guard.

He saw my jeopardy discharg'd,
And freedom's ample walk enlarg'd,   110
   With plenty and content;
He set me in a spacious place,
Because I found peculiar grace,
   When kneeling to repent.

The Lord shall my reward prepare,   115
Because my dealings have been fair,
   And from all treach'ry free;
According to the spotless hue,
With which these harmless hands I shew,
   My recompense shall be.   120

For I with courage have abode
By God and truth, and kept the road
   Which goes to endless bliss;
Nor have deserted from his cause,
Like men that have not known his laws   125
   The godless and remiss.

Because with application strict
I to thy laws my mind addict,
   Their import to discern;
Nor poorly single out a part,   130
But keep them all with all my heart
   As of the last concern.

I likewise found myself intire,
And pure from every vain desire,
   Lascivious and unclean;   135
My former follies I eschew'd,
And all the past of life review'd,
   My thoughts from vice to wean:

Wherefore the Lord, whom thus I please,
And which my righteous dealing sees   140
  With his paternal eyes,
According as my hands are pure,
Shall to my soul in heav'n secure
  The blest immortal prize.

Where saints and holy angels dwell,   145
Thou shalt in holiness excell,
  And shalt have perfect peace;
Where perfected beyond the sketch
Of Nature, to their utmost stretch,
  Faith, hope and grace increase.   150

In living waters thou shalt bathe,
And God with purity shall swathe
  Thy loins as with a girth;
And with the clean and undefil'd,
Thou shalt be number'd as a child,   155
  In this thy second birth.

For thou shalt save the poor oppress'd,
And have his grievances redress'd,
  By thine immediate aid;
And pompous pride, that is above   160
The works of charity and love,
  Thou shalt to want degrade.

Thou shalt indulge a farther length
To David's life, and with new strength
  My blazing lamp shall burn;   165
Again my vessel shall embark,
And God shall dissipate the dark,
  And urge the day's return.

Thro' thee I shall maintain my post,
Nor of the fury of an host,   170
  Or numbers, make account;
And, as thy present help supports,
Shall leap o'er battlements and forts,
  And every bar surmount.

God's way is just, his word the same,   175
And proof against the sev'nfold flame,
   When challeng'd to the test;
He is the Saviour and the shield
Of all that in his truth reveal'd
   Their firm affiance rest.   180

For what is the Supreme, or who
But God Almighty, and all-true
   On his eternal throne;
What is this pow'r and strength of ours,
And what is strength, or what are pow'rs   185
   But God's, and God alone?

It is the Lord that girds my sword,
Whose grace and might their help afford,
   Calm thought with wrath to mix;
Against each giant foe of Gath,   190
'Tis he alone directs my path,
   His champion's fame to fix.

His mandates to my feet impart
The swiftness of the nimble hart,
   To run with them that fly;   195
He takes me up from off the ground,
On which with active speed I bound,
   And sets me up on high.

The Lord has with my forces fought,
And these my hardy members taught   200
   The battle to sustain;
My hands are practical and apt,
And with their vigour I have snapt
   A bow of steel in twain.

Thou'st plac'd salvation's glorious helm   205
Upon thy servant, and his realm
   E'en to remotest Dan;
I rise augmented from thy rod,
And thy kind chastisement, O God,
   Shall magnify the man.   210

Thou shalt enlarge me round about,
And wheresoe'er I take my rout,
   My pilgrimage equip;
By thee directed I shall move,
And thou shalt keep as in a groove   215
   My footsteps lest they slip.

With God and Israel's cause at stake,
I shall their armies overtake,
   Which our perdition seek;
Nor will my rapid courses slack,   220
Nor bring Jehudah's standard back,
   Till I have made them meek.

I will attack them sword in hand,
Nor shall they my sure stroke withstand,
   While God my arm uplifts;   225
One shall his thirst of glory glut
With hundreds vanquish'd—ten shall put
   Ten thousand to their shifts.

Thy pow'r shall gird and brace my loins,
Whene'er the fierce encounter joins,   230
   Thine angel shall aggrieve
The foe that Israel's coast alarms,
Till I by my victorious arms
   Immortal fame atchieve.

Thou'st made mine enemies retreat,   235
Nor could they, previous of defeat,
   My fair battalia front;
And I shall quell their boistrous boasts,
Invested by the Lord of Hosts,
   With brav'ry scorners want.   240

Their clamours shall ascend the skies,
But none shall stay to hear their cries
   Of angels or of men;
To God they shall address their suit,
Yet they shall have but little fruit,   245
   To their devotions then.

They came in number, like the dust,
Their weapons in our heart to thrust,
   Like dust they shall recede;
Or crumbled clay before the wind,   250
Nor shall an atom stay behind,
   To signify their deed.

Thou shalt preserve thy servant's life
From faction and domestic strife,
   However rais'd or spread;   255
And fresh from every clime and shore,
The heathen shall thy name adore,
   With David at their head.

My swelling sails shall be unfurl'd,
And to reform a distant world,   260
   Thou shall my fleets convoy;
And nations from thy word remote,
I to thine honour will devote,
   And in thy ways employ.

Soon as my precepts they imbibe,   265
They shall to their good truth subscribe,
   And their rude manners change;
Yea perjured hypocrites shall throng
To God and Jesus, whom they wrong
   As they themselves estrange.   270

The stranger shall be taken in,
Redeem'd from slavery and sin,
   Their Saviour to invoke —
Their nature shall no more despond
Of mercy, but embrace the bond   275
   Of peace and Christ his yoke.

The God of all perfection lives,
And reigns o'er all things, and he gives
   The laurel to my lance;
And I will bless him and applaud   280
His pow'rful succour, and his laud
   And magnitude advance.

E'en he whose holy angels wage
Their warfare with me, and engage
   Against the strength of stealth,   285
Of hate and falsehood, and confirms
My people in submissive terms
   By plenty, peace and wealth.

He shall my soul's salvation set
O'er those that cruel men abet,   290
   Still pouring fresh and fresh;
And for my safety shall provide
From every loud blasphemer's pride,
   And from an arm of flesh.

I therefore will my Saviour thank,   295
And from a faithful heart and frank
   The song of praise produce;
And to the Gentiles will I sing
Of him who guides the warrior's sling,
   Or fills the peaceful cruse.   300

Great things and prosperous hast thou done
In love to David – and his Son
   Shall ride the royal mule;
King David thy free choice appoints,
And from his loins thy seer anoints   305
   A man thy tribes to rule.

Psalm 24

The earth is God's, with all she bears
   On fertile dale or woody hill;
The compass of the world declares
   His all efficient skill.

For her foundations has he laid,   5
  The flowing waters to restrain,
And all her firm consistence made
  Upon the mighty main.

Who shall have strength and grace to climb
  Up to the sacred mount of God?   10
And for the holy place sublime,
  What pilgrim shall be shod?

Whose hands are clean, and heart is whole,
  Whose mind and tongue vain thoughts suppress,
Nor stain with perjury his soul,   15
  His neighbour to distress;

The Lord shall bless, and give him fruit
  In heav'n as his salvation speeds,
And God shall righteousness impute
  To his accepted deeds.   20

Such is the nature and reward
  Of all the children of his grace,
E'en them, who zealous for their Lord,
  O Jesus, seek thy face.

On golden hinges as ye swing,   25
  Ye gates, ye doors of endless mass,
Lift, lift your arches, and the king
  Of glory shall repass.

Who is the king of glory, who
  Is worthy of so great a name?   30
E'en Christ all pow'rful to subdue,
  Of vast victorious fame.

On golden hinges as ye swing,
  Ye gates, ye doors of endless mass,
Lift, lift your arches, and the king   35
  Of glory shall repass.

Who is the king of glory, say?
   'Tis Christ most worthily renown'd;
He whom the hosts of heav'n obey,
   Is king of glory crown'd.   40

Psalm 25

Lord and Master, to thine altar
   In the heav'ns by faith I scale,
Let no terror make me faulter,
   Nor let enmity prevail.

They shall never be confounded   5
   Who upon thy grace depend,
But false hearts, by conscience wounded,
   That without a cause offend.

In thy sacred institutions,
   Lord, be thou my gracious guide,   10
Strengthen my good resolutions,
   By thy canons to abide.

With a Christian education
   Give my soaring soul her scope;
For thou, God of my salvation,   15
   Art alone my daily hope.

Lord, with all their sweet effulgence,
   Beam thy mercies on thy fold,
And remember thine indulgence
   Shewn to thine elect of old.   20

Lord, upbraid not with the sallies,
   And offences of my youth,
But exert that love, which tallies
   With thy goodness and thy truth.

Gracious is the Lord, a lover   25
   Of the thing that's just and right;
He the wand'rers shall recover
   To the paths of life and light.

Men of gentle disposition
   By his judgments shall he sway;   30
And for hearts above ambition
   Shall facilitate his way.

Christ is truth with mercy treating
   All his congregated sheep,
Which his liturgy repeating   35
   All his ceremonies keep.

Lord, for Christ his intercession
   In the blood of every stripe,
Spare and pardon my transgression,
   Gross and for perdition ripe.   40

Where's the man dispos'd to centre
   All his views in God the word,
He shall by his guidance enter
   In the way that Christ preferr'd.

After death his soul surviving,   45
   Shall in peace her hours employ,
And his seed, thro' promise, thriving,
   Shall their native land enjoy.

All the mysteries and mazes
   Of the providential year,
To the man that fears and praises,   50
   Clear, as nature's laws, appear.

For the church and constitution
   I my soul by pray'r sublime,
From unequal distribution,   55
   And the snares of men to climb.

Turn again, O Lord, restore me,
   Let my breathings have access;
For the gloomy scenes before me
   Are desertion and distress.   60

Sorrows in my heart are heighten'd,
   And upon my spirit fall:
In afflictions am I straiten'd,
   Lord, deliver me from all.

Look upon the fierce invasion   65
   Of the powers that war within,
Mov'd from thence to take occasion
   Of forgiveness to my sin.

See my foes, how much recruited,
   To what swarms their musters swell,   70
Who my prowess have disputed,
   And in tyrant hate rebel.

From the fury, that has thirsted
   For my soul, O set me free,
Let me not be sham'd and worsted,   75
   Since I put my trust in thee.

Let fair dealing and perfection
   Steer me, as my course I run,
For my calling and election,
   And my hope is Christ, thy Son.   80

All thy flock, which travel weakens,
   Lord, by daily grace refresh;
Save the bishops, priests and deacons,
   From the devil, world and flesh.

Psalm 33

Rejoice in God, ye saints above
   The wiles and fire of fraud and lust;
For gratitude is fruitful love,
   And well becomes the just.

Praise with the harp the prince of grace,   5
   Let lutes accord to him that sings,
Adapt the mellow sounding bass
   With ten melodious strings.

Let novelty commend the strain,
   And sing, adoring, as ye kneel,   10
And swell with all your might and main
   The full resounding peal.

For Christ the word of his command
   Is truth in all its various terms,
And all th' atchievements of his hand   15
   His faithfulness confirms.

He has his righteousness at heart,
   And love and mercy hold his rod,
And earth abounds in every part
   With goodness and with God.   20

The firmament and all the host
   Of heav'n by Christ the word were form'd,
And quick'ning to the Holy Ghost,
   With active heat were warm'd.

In one great magazine compell'd,   25
   The waters of the main he heaps,
And, as a store by warders held,
   The briny depth he keeps.

Let earth in all her throng'd abodes,
   And ye, where'er your tents are spread,   30
Ye people, bless in all the modes
   Of reverence and dread.

With him the word and work are one,
   The moulds were made, the forms were cast,
As he commanded it was done,   35
   And stood for ever fast.

The Lord abolishes the schemes
   And purposes of heathen sects;
The people's murmurs, prince's dreams
   He quashes and rejects.   40

The councils of the Lord are sure,
  As infinitely just and sage,
And all his precious thoughts endure
  From age to rising age.

Blest are the people and the realm,   45
  Where Christ is seated on the throne;
For whom their Saviour holds the helm,
  Elected as his own.

The Lord from heav'n's imperial height
  Beholds the sons of men below,   50
And thence considers their estate
  Of transient wealth or woe.

By him their hearts are fram'd and turn'd,
  By him the vital fountain plays;
He knows whate'er is sought or spurn'd   55
  In all their works and ways.

There is no monarch therefore sav'd,
  Who has to multitudes recourse,
Nor is the stroke of conquest stav'd
  By numbers or by force.   60

The horses that the spearmen mount,
  When comes the trying hour of need,
Are of small service or account,
  With all their strength and speed.

Lo! God with fatherly concern,   65
  Looks down to see what course we steer,
And blesses those that live and learn
  A godly hope and fear;

Their souls from terror to redeem,
  And for their cup and social hearth   70
To raise the blade and fill the stream,
  Against the hour of dearth.

Our souls by patience we possess,
    Until the Lord his angel send;
For he's our helper to redress,   75
    Our buckler to defend.

Wherefore our spirits shall revive,
    Because our special end and aim
Is still to keep our hope alive
    By his most holy name.   80

Lord, let thy gracious love diffuse
    Its influence on our fervent vows,
Like as our faith all doubt subdues,
    And we thy cause espouse.

Psalm 68

Arouse—and let thy foes disperse
Thou master of the universe,
    Arouse thee from on high;
Take up the trumpet and alarm,
And at the terror of thine arm   5
    Let those that hate thee fly.

Like as afflicting smoke's dispell'd,
Let them be driv'n away and quell'd,
    As wax before the fire,
Let fraud at thine effulgence fail,   10
And let the multitudes in mail
    Before my God retire.

But let the men of righteous seed,
Accepted in their father's deed,
    Rejoice before the shrine;   15
Yea, let them shout till heav'n resounds,
There is no need of end or bounds
    To joyfulness divine.

Give praise—with songs your praises blend,
And as your thoughts to heav'n ascend,   20
  And leave the world beneath,
Extol his universal name,
Who rides on the celestial flame,
  In IAH, which all things breathe.

The father of the friendless child,   25
To keep the damsel undefil'd,
  And judge the widow's cause,
Is God upon his righteous throne,
Whence he the hands to rapine prone
  O'ersees and overawes.   30

Thy Lord domestic peace creates,
And those his Mercy congregates,
  Who solitary dwell;
The slave delivers from his chain,
But rebels in dry wastes remain,   35
  And where no waters well.

When thou Jehovah led the way,
Before thy people in array,
  From Egypt's barb'rous coast;
Thro' boundless wilds exposed and parch'd,   40
In pillar'd majesty thou march'd
  The captain of the host.

The earth in ecstasy gave place,
With vast vibrations on her base
  The present God she found;   45
Ev'n Israel's God—the heav'ns dissolv'd,
And Sinai's mount in clouds involv'd,
  Felt all his rocks rebound.

O God, thou bad'st the heav'ns dispense
The bread of thy benevolence,   50
  Down with the daily dew;
And fixt the people of thy pow'r,
Amidst their doubtings by a show'r
  Miraculous and new.

Therein thy congregation dwelt, 55
E'en midst the manna, which thou dealt
  So plentiful and pure;
Thy goodness to confirm the weak,
Thy charity to bless and break,
  The largess for the poor. 60

God, in stupendous glory deck'd,
His gracious covenant direct,
  Came down from heav'n to teach;
Great was the trembling and the fear
Of crowds, that rush'd that word to hear, 65
  They were enjoin'd to preach.

Each talking tyrant at the head
Of thousands and ten thousands fled,
  They fled with all their might;
And all Judea's blooming pride, 70
The spouse, the damsel and the bride,
  Dispos'd the spoil at night.

Though ye the bitter bondage wept,
And midst Rhamnesian tripods slept,
  Hereafter is your own; 75
Ye shall as turtle-doves unfold,
The silver plumage wing'd with gold,
  And make melodious moan.

When kings were scatter'd for our sake,
And God alarm'd his host to take 80
  His vengeance on the foe;
On Israel's countenance benign
He made his radiant grace to shine
  As bright as Salmon's snow.

Jehovah's hill's a noble heap, 85
And ev'n as Bashan's spiry steep,
  From which the cedars nod;
And Zion's mount herself sublimes,
And swells her goodly crest and climbs
  To meet descending God. 90

Ye haughty hills that leap so high,
What is th' exertion that ye try?
    This is God's hallow'd mount,
On whose blest top the glories play,
And where the Lord desires to stay   95
    While we his praise recount.

The chariots of the Lord are made
Of angels in a cavalcade
    Ev'n twenty thousand strong,
Those thousands of the first degree,   100
O'er Sinai — in the midst is HE,
    And bears the pomp along.

God is gone up from whence he rose
With gifts accepted for his foes,
    His loaded altars smoke;   105
Captivity, from chains repriev'd,
Is made his captive, and receiv'd
    To thy most blessed yoke.

God is our help from every ill,
And gives to every want its fill,   110
    For us and all our race;
By him we're every hour review'd,
To him the daily pray'r's renew'd
    For daily bread and grace.

God, that great God whom we profess,   115
Is all-benevolent to bless,
    Omnipotent to save;
In God alone is our escape,
From death and all the gulfs that gape,
    From terror and the grave.   120

God shall not send his blessing down
To rest upon the hoary crown
    Of those which grace resist;
But shall afflict the heads of all,
That after his repeated call   125
    To penitence, persist.

From Bashan, which they pass'd of yore,
Said God, I will my tribes restore,
   And bring them back again;
Where Abr'ham worshipp'd and was bless'd,   130
Of Canaan they shall be possess'd,
   Emerging from the main.

That thy baptized foot may tread,
Where proud blasphemers laid their head,
   By judgments unreclaim'd;   135
And that thy shepherd's dogs may chase
Thy flocks into their pleasant place,
   Who made the earth asham'd.

They've seen their errors to disprove
My God in blest procession move,   140
   The pomp of God my king;
Accordant to the train below,
The dances rise, the streamers flow,
   And holy flow'rs they fling.

The goodly shew the singers lead,   145
The minstrels next in place proceed,
   With music sweet and loud;
The damsels, that with wild delight,
The brisk-resounding timbrels smite,
   Are in the mid-most crowd.   150

O thou Jeshurun, yield thy thanks,
All ages, sexes, tribes and ranks,
   In congregated bands;
To God united thanks restore,
Brought from the heart its inmost core,   155
   And with protesting hands.

There Benjamin in triumph goes,
Least but in love the Lord of those
   That dwell in tents and bow'rs;
And Judah next to the most high,   160
With Zebulon and Naphtali
   Their princedoms and their pow'rs.

God to the sires of all the tribes
Some great peculiar gift ascribes,
   To each his talent's told;   165
The loan with such long-suff'ring lent,
Do thou establish and augment
   Ten thousand thousand fold.

From this thy temple which we lay,
To thee the homage they shall pay,   170
   To thee the praise impute;
Kings shall their annual gifts renew,
And give Melchisedec his due,
   The glory and the fruit.

Rebuke the spearmen with thy word,   175
Those calves and bulls of Bashan's herd,
   Which from our ways abhor;
Let them pay toll, and hew the wood,
Which are at enmity with good,
   And love the voice of war.   180

The nobles from the sons of Ham,
Shall bring the bullock and the ram,
   Idolatrous no more;
The Morians soon shall offer alms,
And bow their heads, and spread their palms,   185
   God's mercy to implore.

Ye blessed angels of the Lord,
Of nations and of kings the ward,
   That further thanks and pray'r,
To Jesus Christ your praise resound,   190
Collected from the regions round
   Your tutelary care.

In other days before the sev'n,
Upon that ante-mundane heav'n,
   In glorious pomp he rode –
He sends a voice, which voice is might,   195
In inconceivable delight
   Th' acknowledg'd word of God.

Ye heroes foremost in the field
That couch the spear, or bear the shield,   200
  Bless God that ye prevail;
His splendour is on Israel's brow,
He stands all-pow'rful on the prow
  'Midst all the clouds that sail.

O God, all miracle thou art,   205
Ev'n thou the God of Israel's heart
  Within thy holy shrine,
Thou shalt with strength and pow'r protect,
Thy people in the Lord elect,
  Praise, endless praise be thine.   210

Psalm 85

O Lord, thy land has favour found
  And mercy speeds again,
To loosen Israel ty'd and bound
  In Satan's irksome chain.

Thy grace to Jacob's chosen seed   5
  With their remorse begins,
And Christ, the merit that we plead,
  Has cover'd all our sins.

With them thou deignedst to betroth
  Thou art no more displeas'd,   10
And God the Father's righteous wrath
  Is thro' his son appeas'd.

O Lord, the Saviour of the poor,
  Anew our hearts create,
And make the world's salvation sure   15
  From its abandon'd state.

When Christ his tears our sins efface,
  Can goodness ever fail,
And after this stupendous grace
  Shall vice again prevail?   20

Wilt thou not reconcile our souls
   To their eternal rest,
And glad our hearts, as Christ enrolls
   Our name among the blest?

O Lord thy bounteous mercy shew   25
   And these thy people spare,
And with thy saving health endue
   The penitents at pray'r.

I will to my supreme content
   The word of Christ explore —   30
'The heavenly king's at hand, repent,
   And go and sin no more.'

Whene'er a faithful two or three
   Attend the warning peal,
There Christ himself delights to be   35
   His glories to reveal.

Thy truth and mercy for increase
   Of love have met in bliss,
Stern righteousness and gentle peace
   Have join'd the holy kiss.   40

From Christ the branch fair truth shall sprout
   And bloom again on earth,
And justifying grace come out
   From heav'n at Shilo's birth.

Yea, God's benevolence shall beam   45
   As Satan's pow'r he stops,
And men and earth reform'd shall teem
   With grace and fruitful crops.

A gracious message shall apprise
   The world of better days;   50
His sermons, precepts, pray'r revise
   And regulate our ways.

Psalm 98 (first version)

O Frame the strains anew,
Your grateful natures shew
  To Christ, the source of holy song;
For passing deeds he wrought,
Until to God he brought,   5
  By miracle, the faithless throng.

With hands which saints revere,
And arm without compeer,
  He has the vast atchievement done
And over death and hell,   10
With all the Fiends that fell,
  This day's immortal trophies won.

CHRIST JESUS has declar'd
That sinners shall be spar'd,
  And that through him salvation came;   15
The world could not convince
Of sin the righteous prince,
  So manifest his spotless fame.

He still has bore in mind
His mercies, loving kind,   20
  And truth to Jacob's house engag'd;
And all remotest earth
Have seen, in Shilo's birth,
  Salvation, as by seers presag'd.

Then, O ye peopl'd lands,   25
Unite in tuneful bands,
  And to the Lord your gladness tell,
For such a blest reverse
Your hymns of thanks rehearse
  Your songs of exultation swell.   30

Ye jocund harpers, kneel,
As you the impulse feel,
  And to the Lord your praise intend;

Ye holy psalmists join
In harmony divine,   35
  And all your grateful voices blend.

The cheerful trumpet sound,
And let the horns be wound,
  To yield thro' twisted brass their tone;
The choicest notes employ,   40
To prove your hearty joy
  In him that sits upon the throne.

Let ocean make a noise
With ev'ry isle he buoys,
  And all the life his floods contain,   45
The rounded world above,
And all that live and love
  Their Maker on the hills or plain.

The vast and briny broad
All hands aloft applaud,   50
  E'en as the mountain or the rock,
Which also have their ways,
In spirit God to praise,
  Who comes by Christ to judge his flock.

Descending from on high,   55
His people he shall try,
  In mercy, goodness, and in grace;
His merits we shall plead,
Till rigour must recede,
  And wrath to charity give place.   60

Psalm 127

If the work be not direct,
  And the Lord the fabric build,
All the plans that men project
  Are but labour idly spill'd.

If the Lord be not the guard, 5
    And the forts and tow'rs sustain,
All the city gates are barr'd,
    And the watchman wakes in vain.

Vainly for the bread of care
    Late and early hours ye keep, 10
For 'tis thus by fervent pray'r
    That he lays the blest asleep.

Lo! thy children are not thine,
    Nor the fruits of female love,
But an heritage divine, 15
    And a blessing from above.

Like as arrows in the grasp
    Of a valiant man of might,
Are the children that you clasp
    In some future hour of fight. 20

Blest! who in his quiver stows
    Darts like these, a goodly freight,
Nor shall blush when with his foes
    He shall parley in the gate.

Psalm 134

Attend to the music divine
    Ye people of God with the priest,
At once your Hosanna combine
    As meekly ye bow to the east.

Ye servants that look to the lights 5
    Which blaze in the house of the Lord,
And keep up the watch of the nights
    To bless each apartment and ward,

The holy of holies review,
    And lift up your hands with your voice, 10
And there sing your anthems anew,
    In praise to Jehova rejoice.

The Lord that made heav'n and earth,
  Which rules o'er the night and the day,
His blessing bestow on your mirth,   15
  And hear you whenever ye pray.

Psalm 135

O Praise the Lord, and bless his name,
  Ye servants of the Lord,
To God your anthems frame
  With swelling voice and chord.

You unto whom are stated posts   5
  Within God's hallow'd fane,
Who serve the Lord of hosts,
  And in his courts remain,

O to the Lord address your praise,
  Which is with grace replete,   10
His fair perfections blaze,
  For they are passing sweet.

For Jacob claims his Saviour's care
  As God's peculiar plant,
And Israel is his heir   15
  Assign'd by special grant.

I know the Lord our God is great
  And infinite, above
The measure or the weight
  Of other pow'r or love.   20

Whatever is the Lord's command
  Beyond, beneath the sun,
In ocean or by land,
  Or in the depth, is done.

He from the world's remotest ends   25
  The pregnant cloud explores;
With rain he lightning sends,
  The wind is from his stores.

His plagues th' Egyptian race consume
    From greatest to the least,   30
The firstlings from the womb
    Of man as well as beast.

Then institutes his paschal lamb,
    And triumphs o'er the waves,
And thee, O land of Ham,   35
    With Pharaoh and his slaves.

He smote with his Mosaic rod
    The realms of divers climes;
And he, th' almighty God,
    Slew tyrants for their crimes.   40

Sihon, who dwelt at Heshbon, fell,
    And Og, the world's disgrace,
And all the tools of hell,
    In Canaan's boundless space;

And gave their regions far and wide   45
    Of vineyards, fruits and flow'rs,
For Israel to divide,
    Proud domes and fragrant bow'rs.

O God, thy name and word endure
    In infinite renown;   50
From race to race secure
    Thy fame is handed down.

For God, in our behalf arous'd,
    Will strict reprisals make;
His people thus espous'd,   55
    His special grace partake.

As for the gods the heathen serves
    And true religion mocks,
They're mov'd by fictious nerves,
    Cast gold and silver blocks.   60

Their mouths are fram'd, from whence there comes
   Not e'en the breath of lies;
Ecstatic death benumbs
   Their glass-constructed eyes.

Their ears are fashion'd by the mould,   65
   Nor can they hear a sound;
Their molten lips are cold,
   In breathless fetters bound.

The founders of such gods as these
   Resemble their own dross,   70
And so do all whose knees
   Are bow'd to form and gloss.

Praise ye the Lord, each branch and bud
   Of Jacob's chosen root,
And you of Aaron's blood   75
   The praise to God impute.

Praise ye the Lord of Levi's line
   That in the temple keep;
In fear and praises join
   Ye congregated sheep.   80

The Lord be praised from Zion's brow
   Which dwells in Salem's dome,
And gives his people now
   The promis'd milk and comb.

Psalm 137

Pensive we sat the silent hours
Where by the Babylonian tow'rs
   At large the waters stray,
Till mem'ry brought thee to our eyes,
O Zion, then the tears and sighs   5
   Burst out and made their way.

No matter for our harps – our care
Was not on mirth and music there,
   All solace we declin'd;
We sate and suffer'd them in view   10
To hang as bended, or as blew
   The willows or the wind.

When they, that led our captive train,
Bade us our heavy hearts refrain
   From grief to joys extreme;   15
Thus they commanded their request,
'Sing us a song, and sing your best,
   And Zion be the theme!'

What, in a land by God abhorr'd,
Shall we profane unto the Lord   20
   The consecrated songs;
And Israel's harp and hands employ,
To strike up symphonies of joy
   'Mongst foreigners and wrongs?

Jerusalem! O blest in woe,   25
If I forget thee, or forego
   When heav'n and nature call,
May this right hand, and God's own heart
Forget his spirit, and her art
   To touch the strings at all!   30

May my tongue to my palate cleave
If I forget thee when I grieve;
   If to all realms on earth
I not Jerusalem prefer,
Jerusalem! and harp on her   35
   When most my might in mirth!

O Lord, when it shall be fulfill'd
That thou Jerusalem rebuild,
   Remember unto good,
How 'down with it,' th' insulting band   40
Cry'd, 'down with it, and mar the land
   Where all that splendour stood.'

Renown'd the man! that shall reward
And serve thee as thou'st serv'd the Lord,
   Thou shalt thy turn deplore;   45
There's desolation too for thee,
Thou daughter of calamity,
   And Babylon no more!

But he is greatest and the best,
Who spares his enemies profest,   50
   And Christian mildness owns;
Who gives his captives back their lives,
Their helpless infants, weeping wives,
   And for his sin atones.

Psalm 148 (second version)

Hallelujah! kneel and sing
Praises to the heav'nly king;
To the God supremely great,
Hallelujah in the height!

Praise him, archangelic band,   5
Ye that in his presence stand;
Praise him, ye that watch and pray,
Michael's myriads in array.

Praise him, sun, at each extreme
Orient streak, and western beam,   10
Moon and stars of mystic dance,
Silv'ring in the blue expanse.

Praise him, O ye heights, that soar
Heav'n and heav'n for evermore;
And ye streams of living rill,   15
Higher yet, and purer still.

Let them praise his glorious name,
From whose fruitful word they came,
And they first began to be
As he gave the great decree.   20

Their constituent parts he founds
For duration without bounds,
And their covenant has seal'd,
Which shall never be repeal'd.

Praise the Lord on earth's domains,   25
And the mutes that sea contains,
Ye that on the surface leap,
And ye dragons of the deep.

Batt'ring hail, and fires that glow,
Steaming vapours, plumy snow,   30
Wind and storm his wrath incurr'd,
Wing'd and pointed at his word.

Mountains of enormous scale,
Ev'ry hill, and ev'ry vale,
Fruit-trees of a thousand dyes,   35
Cedars that perfume the skies.

Beasts that haunt the woodland maze,
Nibbling flocks, and droves that graze;
Reptiles of amphibious breed,
Feather'd millions form'd for speed;   40

Kings, with Jesus for their guide,
Peopl'd regions far and wide,
Heroes of their country's cause,
Princes, judges of the laws;

Age and childhood, youth and maid,   45
To his name your praise be paid;
For his word is worth alone,
Far above his crown and throne.

He shall dignify the crest
Of his people rais'd and blest,   50
While we serve with praise and pray'rs
All, in Christ, his saints and heirs.

Psalm 149 (first version)

Hosanna! God be prais'd,
  The song of thanks pursue;
Let ev'ry thought be rais'd,
  And ev'ry note be new;
Let saints assembl'd in his fane   5
The chorus of applause sustain.

Let Jacob's heart be glad
  In his Creator's name,
Ev'n him which made and clad
  His soul in such a frame;   10
Let Zion's grateful sons be gay,
And bless his sempiternal sway.

Praise him, ye youthful pairs,
  As ye the dance complete,
Which to the quick'ning airs   15
  Has wing'd your active feet,
And strike the timbrel to the strings
Of him that plays the harp and sings.

Because there is increase
  To God's eternal bliss   20
When men exult in peace
  To such a tune as this,
And he shall in the spirit wait
On those, whose meekness makes them great.

Let those his holy saints   25
  That have put off their earth,
Whom spite no more attaints,
  Rejoice in glorious mirth,
And let their gladness be imprest
On those bright mansions, where they rest.   30

Let hymns, of praise compos'd
  In mirth and mystic skill,
To God began and clos'd,
  Their mouths with music fill,
And as they modulate their psalms,   35
Their hands present triumphant palms.

To meditate the good
  And glory of mankind,
That vice may be withstood,
  And heathens well inclin'd;   40
That vengeance, violence, and guile
No more the human race defile.

To make their princes bow
  To Christ's indulgent yoke,
And God's best name avow   45
  As they their sins uncloak;
To bid their noblemen unite
With Christians in the Lord of light.

That war, and hate, and pride,
  And ev'n the name of foe   50
May in that love subside
  Which Christian champions show;
For thus the holy Gospel runs,
Such honour have his saints and sons.

Psalm 150

Hosanna! praise the Lord, and bless
According to his holiness,
  And let your praises tow'r;
O bless him in sublimest strains,
Where in the firmament he reigns   5
  Of his exalted pow'r.

The works of his Almighty hand,
Which on eternal record stand,
  With hymns of thanks review;
On his majestic glory dwell,
Whose rays all excellence excel,   10
  And give the praises due.

The best and boldest blast be blown
From trumpet of triumphant tone
  Abroad his praise to send;
His name upon the lute be sung,   15
With citterns to his praises strung,
  The work of joy attend.

Take up the timbrel, let the sound
Extol him as the dances bound,   20
  And let the pipes conspire
To give his praises to the wind,
And let your organ's voice be join'd
  By minstrels on the wire.

Well order'd to a just degree   25
Of their most perfect melody
  With cymbals praise his name;
And let the cymbals full and strong
Together and with all their song
  Aloud his praise proclaim.   30

Let all things that have breath to breathe
From heav'n above, from earth beneath,
  To Christ's renown repair;
O give him back your breath again,
Put all the life into the strain,   35
  And soar by praise and pray'r!

Reason and Imagination

A FABLE

Address'd to Mr Kenrick.

Amidst the ample field of things,
The doubtful Muse suspends her wings;
While Thoughts, Imagination's host,
Keep hov'ring over Reason's post
Maintain'd, O *Truth*, upon thy base,   5
Whose voice, and whose Angelic face,
Are what the prudent love and hear,
And by no other star they steer.

   In vain fair *Fancy* decks her bow'rs,
And tempts with fruits, and tempts with flow'rs;   10
Her wiles in ev'ry mode express'd,
Or lewdly strip'd, or proudly dress'd;
Try all the little arts she can,
Firm stands the Attribute of Man;
And solid, weighty, deep and sound,   15
Asserts its right, and keeps its ground.

   'Twas in that famous *Sabine* grove,
Where Wit so oft with Judgment strove,
Where Wisdom grac'd th' Horatian lyre,
Like weight of metal play'd by fire;   20
Where Elegance and Sense conferr'd,
Just at the coming of the WORD,
Who chose his reasons to convey
A plain and a familiar way,

Then, would you taste the moral tale, 25
First bless the banquet, and regale.
IMAGINATION, in the flight
Of young desire, and gay delight,
Began to think upon a mate,
As weary of the single state; 30
For sick of change, as left at will,
And cloy'd with entertainment still,
She thought it better to be grave,
To settle, to take up, and save.
She therefore to her chamber sped, 35
And thus at first attir'd her head.
Upon her hair, with brilliants graced,
Her tow'r of beamy gold she placed;
Her ears with pendant jewels glow'd
Of various water, curious mode, 40
As nature sports the wintry ice,
In many a whimsical device.
Her eye-brows arch'd, upon the stream
Of rays, beyond the piercing beam;
Her cheeks in matchless colour high, 45
She veil'd to fix the gazer's eye;
Her paps, as white as Fancy draws,
She cover'd with a crimson gauze;
And on her wings she threw perfume
From buds of everlasting bloom. 50
Her zone, ungirded from her vest,
She wore across her swelling breast;
On which, in gems, this verse was wrought,
'I make and shift the scenes of Thought.'
In her right hand a Wand she held, 55
Which Magic's utmost pow'r excell'd;
And in her left retain'd a Chart,
With figures far surpassing art,
Of other natures, suns and moons,
Of other moves to higher tunes. 60
The Sylphs and Sylphids, fleet as light,
The Fairies of the gamesome night,

The Muses, Graces, all attend
Her service, to her journey's end:
And Fortune, sometimes at her hand,   65
Is now the fav'rite of her band,
Dispatch'd before the news to bear,
And all th' adventure to prepare.

    Beneath an Holm-tree's friendly shade,
Was REASON's little cottage made;   70
Before, a river deep and still;
Behind, a rocky soaring hill.
Himself, adorn'd in seemly plight,
Was reading to the Eastern light;
And ever, as he meekly knelt,   75
Upon the Book of Wisdom dwelt.
The Spirit of the shifting wheel,
Thus first essay'd his pulse to feel. –
'The Nymph supreme o'er works of wit,
O'er labour'd plan, and lucky hit,   80
Is coming to your homely cot,
To call you to a nobler lot;
I, *Fortune*, promise wealth and pow'r,
By way of matrimonial dow'r:
Preferment crowns the golden day,   85
When fair Occasion leads the way.'
Thus spake the frail, capricious dame,
When she that sent the message came. –

    'From first Invention's highest sphere,
I, Queen of Imag'ry, appear;   90
And throw myself at REASON's feet,
Upon a weighty point to treat.
You dwell alone, and are too grave;
You make yourself too much a slave;
Your shrewd deductions run a length,   95
'Till all your Spirits waste their strength:
Your fav'rite logic is full close;
Your morals are too much a dose;

You ply your studies 'till you risk
Your senses – you should be more brisk –   100
The Doctors soon will find a flaw,
And lock you up in chains and straw.
But, if you are inclin'd to take
The gen'rous offer, which I make,
I'll lead you from this hole and ditch,   105
To gay Conception's top-most pitch;
To those bright plains, where crowd in swarms
The spirits of fantastic forms;
To planets populous with elves;
To natures still above themselves,   110
By soaring to the wond'rous height
Of notions, which they still create;
I'll bring you to the pearly cars,
By dragons drawn, above the stars;
To colours of Arabian glow;   115
And to the heart-dilating show
Of paintings, which surmount the life:
At once your tut'ress, and your wife.' –
' – Soft, soft, (says REASON) lovely friend;
Tho' to a parley I attend,   120
I cannot take thee for a mate;
I'm lost, if e'er I change my state.
But whensoe'er your raptures rise,
I'll try to come with my supplies;
To muster up my sober aid,   125
What time your lively pow'rs invade;
To act conjointly in the war
On dullness, whom we both abhor;
And ev'ry sally that you make,
I must be there, for conduct's sake;   130
Thy correspondent, thine ally;
Or any thing, but bind and tye –
But, ere this treaty be agreed,
Give me thy wand and winged steed:
Take thou this compass and this rule,   135
That wit may cease to play the fool;

And that thy vot'ries who are born
For praise, may never sink to scorn.'

 O KENRICK, happy in the view
Of *Reason*, and of *Fancy* too;   140
Whose friendship of a few days' growth,
Is ripe, and greater than them both;
Who reconcil'st with Euclid's scheme,
The tow'ring flight, and golden dream,
With thoughts at once restrained and free,   145
I dedicate this tale to THEE.
But now, a vet'ran for the prize,
I claim a licence to advise.
Let not a fondness for the sage,
Decoy thee from a brighter page,   150
THE BOOK OF SEMPITERNAL BLISS,
The lore where nothing is amiss,
The truth to full perfection brought,
Beyond the sage's deepest thought;
Beyond the poet's highest flight;   155
Then let Invention reason right,
And free from prejudice and hate,
And false refinement's vain debate,
Since GOD's the WORD, that *Christians* read,
Be love their everlasting deed.   160

Ode to Admiral Sir George Pocock

When CHRIST, the seaman, was aboard
 Swift as an arrow to the *White*,
While Ocean his rude rapture roar'd,
 *The vessel gain'd the Haven with delight:
We therefore first to him the song renew,   5
Then sing of POCOCK's praise, and make the point in view.

* John vi. 21.

The Muse must humble ere she rise,
  And kneel to kiss her Master's feet,
Thence at one spring she mounts the skies
  And in *New Salem* vindicates her seat;   10
Seeks to the temple of th' Angelic choir,
And hoists the ENGLISH FLAG upon the topmost spire.

O Blessed of the Lord of Hosts,
  In either India most renown'd,
The Echo of the Eastern coasts,   15
  And all th' Atlantic shores thy name resound. –
The victor's clemency, the seaman's art,
The cool delib'rate head, and warm undaunted heart.

My pray'r was with Thee, when thou sail'd
  With prophecies of sure success;   20
My thanks to Heav'n, that thou prevail'd
  Shall last as long as I can breathe or bless;
And built upon thy deeds my songs shall tow'r,
And swell, as it ascends, in spirit and in pow'r.

There is no thunder half so loud,   25
  As God's applauses in the height,
For those, that have his name avow'd,
  Ev'n *Christian* Patriots valorous and great;
Who for the general welfare stand or fall,
And have no sense of self, and know no dread at all.   30

Amongst the numbers lately fir'd
  To act upon th' heroic plan,
Grace has no worthier chief inspir'd,
  Than that sublime, insuperable man,
Who could th' out-numb'ring *French* so oft defeat,   35
And from th' HAVANNAH stor'd his brave victorious fleet.

And yet how silent his return
  With scarce a welcome to his place –
Stupidity and unconcern,
  Were settled in each voice and on each face.   40
As private as myself he walk'd along,
Unfavour'd by a friend, unfollow'd by the throng.

Thy triumph, therefore, is not here,
   Thy glories for a while postpon'd,
The hero shines not in his sphere,   45
   But where the Author of all worth is own'd. –
Where *Patience* still persists to praise and pray
For all the Lord bestows, and all he *takes away*.

Not HOWARD, FORBISHER, or DRAKE,
   Or VERNON's fam'd *Herculean* deed;   50
Not all the miracles of BLAKE,
   Can the great Chart of thine exploits exceed. –
Then rest upon thyself and dwell secure,
And cultivate the arts, and feed th' *increasing* poor.

O NAME accustom'd and inur'd   55
   To fame and hardship round the globe,
For which fair Honour has insur'd
   The warrior's truncheon, and the consul's robe;
Who still the more is *done* and *understood*,
Art easy of access, art affable and good.   60

O NAME acknowledged and rever'd
   Where ISIS plays her pleasant stream,
Whene'er thy tale is read or heard,
   The good shall bless thee, and the wise esteem;
And they, whose offspring* lately felt thy care,   65
Shall in TEN THOUSAND CHURCHES make their
   daily pray'r. –

'Connubial bliss and homefelt joy,
   And ev'ry social praise be thine;
Plant thou the oak, the poor employ;
   Or plans of vast benevolence design;   70
And speed, when CHRIST his servant shall release,
From triumph over death to everlasting peace.'

* Alluding to the Admiral's noble Benefaction to the Sons of the Clergy.

Ode to General Draper

— Utcunque ferant ea facta minores
Vincat amor patriae, laudumque immensa cupido. VIRG.

Noble in Nature, great in arms,
  The Muses patron and thyself a bard,
Who sternly rushing from domestic charms
  And for thy country tow'ring upon guard,
As born against the foes of human kind,   5
Preced'st the march alone, and leav'st all rank behind.
A little leisure for a thankful heart,
  Its own peculiar workings to attend,
A little leisure to survey the Chart,
  Of all thy labours bearing to their end;   10
To hail Thee, at the head of all renown,
To plan thy private peace, and weave thy laurel crown.

The Fame of DRAPER is a pile
  Of God's erecting in th' embattled field;
An English fabric in the Roman stile,   15
  To which all meaner elevations yield;
What ho! ye brave lieutenants of the van,
Within a thousand furlongs not a single man.

My Muse is somewhat stronger than she was,
  In spite of long calamity and time,   20
Arouse, Arouse ye! is there not a cause?
  Arouse ye lively spirits of my prime!
Breathe, breathe upon the lyre thy parting breath,
There is no thought of him but triumphs over death.

Ye boys of Eton take your theme,   25
  That heroes from heroic fathers come;
Ye sons of learned Granta draw the scheme
  Of Archimedes, on the warrior's drum:
No more let champions scorn the man of parts,
For DRAPER comes like MARLBRO' from the school of arts.
O early train'd and practis'd in desert,   30
  The son of emulation from the womb,

In ancient arms and eloquence expert;
  And student of the themes of Greece and Rome,
Thou chose ACHILLES from th' *Homeric* throng,   35
Who sinks beneath thy deeds, tho' rais'd upon *thy song.

A CHRISTIAN HERO is a name
  To bards of Classic eminence unknown,
A hero, that prefers a higher claim
  To God's applause, his country's and his own;   40
Than those, who, tho' the mirror of their days,
Nor knew the Prince of Worth, nor principle of praise.
Advance, advance a little higher still –
  Th' Ideas of an Englishman advance!
Advance above his meaner strength or skill;   45
  Who solely grasps his pen or shakes his lance.
Thy talent ever flows to learning's hoard,
And bore to leisure fruit 'midst peril and the sword.

O ENGLISH aspect name and soul,
  All ENGLISH to our joyful ears and eyes!   50
Thy chariot cleanly risk'd upon the goal
  Has brought Thee winner for the Martial Prize;
And interval on interval succeeds,
Before thy second comes to signify his deeds.
A note above the Epic trumpet's reach   55
  Beyond the compass of the various lyre,
The song of all thy deeds, which sires shall teach
  Their children active prowess to inspire. –
Thou art a Master – whose exploits shall warm,
The valiant yet to come, and future heroes form.   60

It is an honest book, that writes
  Thy name as worthy honourable lot,
For fair and faithful† thy detail recites,
  The merits of thy brethren on the spot;

---

* Alluding to a famous Copy of Latin Verses, written by DRAPER at
Eton.
† See Gazette for the 16th of April, 1763.

From gallant MONSON foremost of th' array,   65
To him that came the last, yet help'd to win the day.
What tho' no sense of gratitude be shown
  As heretofore, to chiefs of meaner rank;
No mason hew thy figure from a stone,
  Or painter daub thee staring on a plank;   70
No group of Aldermen proclaim thee free,
And in the Tayler's College give thee thy degree?

What tho' no bonfires be display'd,   75
  Nor windows light up the nocturnal scene;
What tho' the merry ringer is not paid,
  Nor rockets shoot upon the STILL SERENE;
Tho' no matross upon the rampart runs,
To send out thy report from loud redoubling guns?
What tho' thy precious health does not go round,
  Where'er the gourmandizing sinner dines;   80
Thy name be kept in secrecy profound,
  O'er female converse and loquacious wines;
What tho' th' astonish'd rustic does not fawn,
On DRAPER made of wax, or on the bellows drawn?

No coin the medalists devise,   85
  With thankful captives crowding the *Reverse*;
Or *Plutus* leading *Merit* to the prize,
  Or ALBION wailing MORE's untimely hearse;
What tho' no bawling ballad singers rend
The skies with joy for thee, or dirges for thy friend?   90
Not monumental marble or the life
  Upon the rival canvas aptly feign'd,
Nor City-Speaker, licensed by his wife,
  To screw up panegyric, bridg'd and strain'd;
Not glass adorn'd with mottos and with boughs,   95
Nor fires that light the mob to roar and to carouse.

Not the round peal or guns' salute,
  Pronouncing still that DRAPER is the toast;
Not youth and blooming beauty, bearing fruit
  To Justice, as they make A MAN their boast;   100

Not Salmon's wax-work or the hackney muse,
Not all the prose and verse of all the Grub-street news.
Not anything they have denied to Thee,
  Is half so great as that which you possess;
The patriot's hand, the honest parson's knee,   105
  And the GREAT BRITISH MONARCH's love express;
And if I may presume upon my mite,
This rough unbidden verse, that aims to do thee right.

Stupendous, surely, is thy chance,
  If such a man as thou should be despis'd;   110
Advance – thy fav'rite word – advance, advance
  To take thy rank with worthies in the skies;
The Captain of ten thousand in the sphere,
Where *Michael* draws the sword or throws the
     glitt'ring spear.
Thyself and seed for which there is no doom,   115
  Race rising upon race in goodly pride,
Shall ever flourish root, and branch, and bloom,
  Shall flourish tow'ring high and spreading wide;
To carry God's applauses in their heart,
To shew an ENGLISH face, and act an ENGLISH part.   120

An Epistle to John Sherratt, Esq.

Haec mihi semper erunt imis infixa medullis,
Perpetuusque ANIMI debitor HUJUS ero.
Ovid de Trist. Eleg. iv.

  Of all the off'rings thanks can find,
  None equally delights the mind;
  Or charms so much, or holds so long,
  As gratitude express'd in song.
  We reckon all the BOOK of GRACE   5
  By verses, as the source we trace,
  And in the spirit all is great
  By number, melody and weight.

By nature's light each heathen sage,
Has thus adorn'd th' immortal page;   10
Demosthenes and Plato's prose,
From skill in mystic measure flows;
And ROLT's sublime, historic stile,
Is better that the Muses smile.
Take then from heartiness profest,   15
What in the bard's conceit is best;
The golden sheaf desertion gleans
For want of better helps and means.

    Well nigh sev'n years had fill'd their tale,
From Winter's urn to Autumn's scale,   20
And found no friend to grief, and *Smart*,
Like Thee and Her, thy sweeter part;
Assisted by a friendly *pair
That chose the side of CHRIST and PRAY'R,
To build the great foundation laid,   25
By one † sublime, transcendent maid.
'Tis well to signalize a deed,
And have no precedent to plead;
'Tis blessing as by God we're told,
To come and visit friends in hold;   30
Which skill is greater in degree,
If goodness set the pris'ner free.
'Tis you that have in my behalf,
Produc'd the robe and kill'd the calf;
Have hail'd the *restoration day*,   35
And bid the loudest music play.
If therefore there is yet a note
Upon the lyre, that I devote,
To gratitude's divinest strains,
One gift of love for thee remains;   40
One gift above the common cast,
Of making fair memorials last.

                      *

* Mr and Mrs ROLT.
† Miss A. F. S.—. of *Queen's-Square*.

Not He whose highly finish'd piece,
Outshone the chissel'd forms of Greece;
Who found with all his art and fame,   45
*A partner in the house I claim;
Not he that pencils CHARLOTTE's eyes,
And boldly bids for ROMNEY's prize;
Not both the seats, where arts commune
Can blazon like a word in tune;   50
But this our young scholastics con,
As warrant from th' *Appulian* Swan.
Then let us frame our steps to climb,
Beyond the sphere of chance and time,
And raise our thoughts on HOLY WRIT,   55
O'er mortal works and human wit.
The lively acts of CHRISTIAN LOVE,
Are treasur'd in the rolls above;
Where Archangelic concerts ring,
And God's accepted poets sing.   60
So Virtue's plan to parry praise,
Cannot obtain in after days;
Atchievements in the Christian cause,
Ascend to sure and vast applause;
Where Glory fixes to endure   65
All precious, permanent and pure.
Of such a class in such a sphere,
Shall thy distinguish'd deed appear;
Whose spirit open and avow'd
Array'd itself against the crowd   70
With cheerfulness so much thine own,
And all thy motive God alone;
To run thy keel across the boom,
And save my vessel from her doom,
And cut her from the pirate's port,   75
Beneath the cannon of the fort,
With colours fresh, and sails unfurl'd,
Was nobly dar'd to beat the world;

* Mr *Roubilliac*'s first Wife was a *Smart*, descended from the same
Ancestors as Mr *Christopher Smart*.

And stands for ever on record,
IF TRUTH AND LIFE BE GOD AND LORD.   80

Epitaph on Henry Fielding, Esq.

The Master of the GREEK and ROMAN page,
The lively scorner of a venal age,
Who made the public laugh, at public vice,
Or drew from sparkling eyes the pearl of price;
Student of nature, reader of mankind,   5
In whom the patron, and the bard were join'd;
As free to give the plaudit, as assert,
And faithful in the practice of desert.
Hence pow'r consign'd the laws to his command,
And put the scales of Justice in his hand,   10
To stand protector of the Orphan race,
And find the female penitent a place.
From toils like these, too much for age to bear,
From pain, from sickness, and a world of care;
From children, and a widow in her bloom,   15
From shores remote, and from a foreign tomb,
Call'd by the WORD of LIFE, thou shalt appear,
To *please* and *profit* in a higher sphere,
Where endless hope, unperishable gain,
Are what the scriptures *teach* and *entertain*.   20

On a Bed of Guernsey Lilies

Written in September 1763.

Ye beauties! O how great the sum
    Of sweetness that ye bring;
On what a charity ye come
    To bless the latter spring!
How kind the visit that ye pay,   5
Like strangers on a rainy day,

When heartiness despair'd of guests:
No neighbour's praise your pride alarms,
No rival flow'r surveys your charms,
   Or heightens, or contests!   10

Lo, thro' her works gay nature grieves
   How brief she is and frail,
As ever o'er the falling leaves
   Autumnal winds prevail.
Yet still the philosophic mind   15
Consolatory food can find,
   And hope her anchorage maintain:
We never are deserted quite;
'Tis by succession of delight
   That love supports his reign.   20

Munificence and Modesty

A POEM

The Hint from a Painting of Guido.

O VOICE of APPROBATION, bless
The spirits still demanding less,
The more their natures have to need,
The more their services can plead;
The more their mighty merits claim –   5
The voice of Approbation came.

   Fair MODESTY, divinely sweet,
With garb prepared, and lamp replete,
Lamented still from sun to sun
So much received, and nothing done.   10
Her abstinence was insincere,
Her studies not enough severe;
Her thoughts at fault, and still to seek,
Her words inadequate and weak;
Her actions wretched and restrain'd,   15
Her passions neither balk'd nor rein'd.

Her head she waved in meek distrust,
Her eyes were fix'd to read the dust;
Her cheeks were tinctured to receive
The blushes of the crimson eve,   20
Prophetic of a better day,
When thus she framed her hymn to pray.
'O Thou, whose bounties never fail,
Who smil'st upon the lowly vale,
And giv'st fertility and peace   25
Their flow'ry lawn and golden fleece;
Who send'st the spirit of the breeze,
To bend the heads of stately trees,
Till pines with all their state and rank,
Bow like the bullrush on the bank.   30
Who bid'st the little brook flow on,
And warbling soothe the silent swan,
And spreading form the shaded lake,
Untill th' emerging rays retake
The transcript of the scene to Thee,   35
O FATHER of SIMPLICITY.
As this thy glossy turf I press,
And prostrate on my forehead bless,
Consider for the poor infirm,
The harmless sheep, th' obnoxious worm,   40
The stooping yoke that turn the soil,
And all the children of thy toil.
In fine, of all the num'rous race,
Of all that crowd and ought to grace
Thy vast immeasurable board,   45
To me the lowest lot afford.'

   She bow'd, she sigh'd, and made her pause:
And instantly th' immense applause
Of thunder in the height was heard,
And all the host of Heav'n appear'd.   50
And thro' the great and glorious throng,
Of Seraphims, ten thousand strong
Came down that prince of high degree,
Th' archangel LIBERALITY.

A crown of Beryls graced his head,   55
His wings were closed, his hands were spread;
His stature nobler than the rest,
A sun and belt adorn'd his breast;
His voice was rapture to the ears,
His look like GRANBY in his geers;   60
When lighting on the dewy sod,
Thus spake the Almoner of God.
'Survey these scenes from east to west,
All earth in bloom and verdure drest;
Those olives planted by the line,   65
That forest after God's design.
Those naked rocks that rise to bound,
The vine-invested elms around;
The golden meads that far extend,
And to the silver streams descend.   70
Those fields of corn in youthful green,
Where larks prepare the nest unseen.
Or turn your eyes, immortal Fair,
To yon gay walks of art and care,
Where the throng'd hive their sweets augment,   75
And murmur not, but thro' content.
That long canal so clear and deep,
Unmoved, but by the Crusion's leap;
That Grotto, which from Gani's mines,
And Ocean's ransack'd bosom shines.   80
I, whose commission's to dispense
The meed of God's munificence,
To thy undoubted worth resign,
These joys of thought and sense, as thine.'

    I ask not (MODESTY replied)   85
For wealthy regions far and wide;
I rest content, if you but spare,
What is the utmost of my pray'r;
A little cot my frame to house,
With room enough to pay my vows.   90
'Then take a view of yonder tow'rs,
Where Fortune deals her gifts in showr's;

Where that vast bulwark's proud disdain
Runs a long terras on the main;
Whose strong foundation Ocean laves,   95
And bustles with officious waves,
To bring with many a thousand sail,
Whate'er refinement can regale;
Rich fruits of oriental zest,
Perfumes of Araby the blest,   100
With precious ornaments to wear,
Upon thine hands, thy neck, thy hair:
O Queen of the transcendent few,
All decoration is thy due.'
Remote from cities and their noise   105
Serenity herself enjoys,
And free from grandeur and expense,
Had best be cloth'd with innocence.
'If such thine elevated mind,
Choose pleasures for thy sex design'd;   110
A blooming youth I will provide,
To make thee a transported bride;
To give each day some new delight,
And bless the soft connubial night.'
I may not act a double part,   115
And offer a divided heart;
Let other nymphs their swains endear,
For my affections are not here.
'Accomplish then that great desire,
To which the wise and good aspire;   120
A name that no detraction knows,
Whose fragrance is as SHARON's rose;
Which makes the highest flight of fame,
By vast and popular acclaim.'
O rather may I still refrain,   125
Nor run the risk of being vain;
To peace and silence let me cleave,
And *give* the glory – not receive.
'Yet, yet accept a gift of love,
The royal Sceptre and the Dove;   130

All things on earth thou shalt command,
Whatever heart, whatever hand;
Why are those charming looks aground?
Arise, aspire, thou shalt be crown'd.'
Talk not of crowns – I have no will,   135
No power, no thought. – 'No more, be still.
'Who's there?' The vast Cherubic flight,
Of thousand thousands on the right.
'Who's there?' 'Tis ORIEL and his SONG,
Full eighty thousand legions strong. –   140
'Hand from the nether Zenith down
The chariot with the emerald crown
By Phoenix drawn. – Lo! this is SHE,
Which has atchieved the first degree;
And scorning MAMMON and his leav'n,   145
Has won Eternity and Heav'n.'

The Sweets of Evening

The sweets of Evening charm the mind,
    Sick of the sultry day;
The body then no more's confin'd,
But exercise with freedom join'd,
    When Phoebus sheathes his ray.   5

The softer scenes of nature soothe
    The organs of our sight;
The Zephyrs fan the meadows smooth,
And on the brook we build the booth
    In pastoral delight.   10

While all-serene the summer moon
    Sends glances thro' the trees,
And Philomel begins her tune,
Asterie too shall help her soon
    With voice of skilful ease.   15

A nosegay every thing that grows,
   And music every sound
To lull the sun to his repose;
The skies are color'd like the rose
   With lively streaks around. 20

Of all the changes rung by Time
   None half so sweet appear,
As those when thoughts themselves sublime,
And with superior natures chime
   In fancy's highest sphere. 25

Epistle to Dr Nares

Smart sends his compliments and pray'rs,
Health and long life to Dr Nares —
But the chief business of the card
Is 'come to dinner with the bard,'
Who makes a mod'rate share of wit 5
Put on the pot, and turn the spit.
'Tis said the Indians teach their sons
The use of bows instead of guns,
And, ere the striplings dare to dine,
They shoot their victuals off a pine. 10
The Public is as kind to me,
As to his child a Cherokee;
And if I chance to hit my aim,
I choose to feast upon the game;
For panegyric or abuse 15
Shall make the quill procure the goose;
With apple-sauce and Durham mustard
And codling pie o'er-laid with custard.
Pray please to signify with this
My love to Madam, Bob, and Miss, 20
Likewise to Nurse and little Poll,
Whose praise so justly you extoll.

P.S.
I have (don't think it a chimaera)
Some good sound port and right Madeira.

Lines with a Pocket Book

Of all returns in man's device
'Tis gratitude that makes the price,
And what Sincerity designs
Is richer than Peruvian mines.
Hence estimate the heart's intent,   5
In what the thankful hands present.
This volume soon shall worth derive
From what your industry shall hive.
Soon will it in each leaf produce
The tale of innocence and use.   10
O, what pleasure there appears
In a train of well spent years!
Think of this whene'er you look
On this small but useful book.
Here too let your appointments be,   15
And set down many a day for me.
Your Saviour shall himself record
The hours you lend unto the Lord;
Where angels sing and cherubs smile
And Truth's the everlasting style.   20
O may the year we now renew
Be stor'd with happiness for you!
With all the wealth your friends would choose
And all the praise yourself refuse.
The guise of diffidence profest   25
And meekness bowing to be blest.

To Mrs Dacosta

O fram'd at once to charm the ear and sight,
Thou emblem of all conjugal delight,
See Flora greets thee with her fragrant powers,
A group of Virtues claims a wreath of Flowers.

On Gratitude

To the Memory of Mr Seaton.

O Muse! O Music! Voice and Lyre,
  Which are together Psalm of Praise
From heav'n the kneeling bard inspire
  New thoughts, new grace of utt'rance raise,
That more acceptable with Thee   5
  We thy best service may begin
O thou that bent thine hallow'd knee,
  And bless'd to bleed for Adam's sin.
Then did the Spirit of a Man
  Above all height sublimely tow'r,   10
And then sweet Gratitude began
  To claim Supremacy from Pow'r.
But how shall we those steps ascend,
  By which the Host approach the Throne? –
Love thou thy brother and thy friend,   15
  Whom thou on earth hast seen and known.
For Gratitude may make the *plea
  Of Love by Sisterhood most dear –
How can we reach the first degree
  If we neglect a step so near?   20
So shall we take dear *Seaton*'s part
  When paths of topmost heav'n are trod,
And pay the talent of our heart
  Thrown up ten thousand fold to God.

* 1 John. iv. 20.

He knew the art the World despise   25
   Might to his Merit be applied
Who when for man he left the skies
   By all was hated, scorn'd, denied.
      *'The man that gives me thanks and laud
      Does honour to my glorious name'   30
Thus God did David's works applaud,
   And seal'd for everlasting fame,
And this for SEATON shall redound
   To praise, as long as *Camus* runs;
Sure Gratitude by him was crown'd,   35
   Who bless'd her Maker and her Sons.

When *Spencer* virtuous *Sidney* prais'd
   When *Prior Dorsett* hail'd to heav'n;
They more by Gratitude were rais'd
   Than all the *Nine* and all the *Sev'n*.   40
Then, O ye emulative tribe
   Of Granta, strains divine pursue;
The glory to the Lord ascribe,
   Yet honour *Seaton*'s memory too.
The *Throne* of *Excellence* accost   45
   And be the post of Pray'r maintain'd;
For Paradise had ne'er been lost
   Had heav'nly Gratitude remain'd.

* Psalm 1. 23.

THE WORKS OF HORACE,
TRANSLATED INTO VERSE

Odes, I. 1: To Maecenas

Different men have their several pleasures: Horace affects the
name of a poet, especially in the lyric cast.

Maecenas, of a race renown'd,
Whose royal ancestors were crown'd,
O patron of my wealth and praise,
And pride and pleasure of my days!
Some of a vent'rous cast there are,   5
That glory in th' Olympic car,
Whose glowing wheels in dust they roll,
Driv'n to an inch upon the goal,
And rise from mortal to divine,
Ennobled by the wreath they twine.   10
One, if the giddy mob proclaim,
And vying lift to *threefold fame;
One, if within his barn he stores
The wealth of Lybian threshing-floors,
Will never from his course be press'd,   15
For all that Attalus possess'd,
To plough, with sailor's anxious pain,
In Cyprian sloop th' Aegean main.
The merchant, dreading the south-west,
Whose blasts th' Icarian wave molest,   20
Praises his villa's rural ease,
Built amongst bowling-greens and trees;

* To the three greatest honours of Rome; to be either aediles, praetors,
or consuls.

But soon the thoughts of growing poor
Make him his shatter'd barks insure.
There's now and then a social soul   25
That will not scorn the Massic bowl,
Nor shuns to break in a degree
On the grave day's solidity;
Now underneath the shrubby shade,
Now by the sacred fountain laid.   30
Many are for the martial strife,
And love the trumpet and the fife,
That mingle in the din of war,
Which all the pious dames abhor:
The sportsman, heedless of his fair,   35
With patience braves the wintry air,
Whether his blood-hounds, staunch and keen,
The hind have in the covert seen,
Or wild boar of the Marsian breed,
From the round-twisted cords is freed.   40
But as for Horace, I espouse
The glory of the scholar's brows,
The wreath of festive ivy wove,
Which makes one company for Jove.
Me the cool groves by zephyrs fann'd,   45
Where nymphs and satyrs, hand in hand,
Dance nimbly to the rural song,
Distinguish from the vulgar throng.
If nor Euterpe, heavenly gay,
Forbid her pleasant pipes to play,   50
Nor Polyhymnia disdain
A lesson in the Lesbian strain,
That, thro' Maecenas, I may pass
'Mongst writers of the Lyric class,
My muse her laurell'd head shall rear,   55
And top the zenith of her sphere.

Odes, I.4: To Sextius, A Person of Consular Dignity

By describing the delightfulness of spring, and urging the
common lot of mortality, he exhorts Sextius, as an
Epicurean, to a life of voluptuousness.

A grateful change! Favonius, and the spring
  To the sharp winter's keener blasts succeed,
Along the beach, with ropes, the ships they bring,
  And launch again, their wat'ry way to speed.
No more the ploughmen in their cots delight,   5
  Nor cattle are contented in the stall;
No more the fields with hoary frosts are white,
  But Cytherean Venus leads the ball.
She, while the moon attends upon the scene,
  The Nymphs and decent Graces in the set,   10
Shakes with alternate feet the shaven green,
  While Vulcan's Cyclops at the anvil sweat.
Now we with myrtle should adorn our brows,
  Or any flow'r that decks the loosen'd sod;
In shady groves to Faunus pay our vows,   15
  Whether a lamb or kid delight the God.
Pale death alike knocks at the poor man's door,
  O happy Sextius, and the royal dome,
The whole of life forbids our hopes to soar,
  Death and the shades anon shall press thee home.   20
And when into the shallow grave you run,
  You cannot win the monarchy of wine,
Nor dote on Lycidas, as on a son,
  Whom for their spouse all little maids design.

Odes, I.38: To His Servant

He would have him bring nothing for the gracing of his
banquet but myrtle.

In the original metre exactly.

Persian pomps, boy, ever I renounce them:
Scoff o' the plaited coronet's refulgence;
Seek not in fruitless vigilance the rose-tree's
    Tardier offspring.
Mere honest myrtle that alone is order'd,   5
Me the mere myrtle decorates, as also
Thee the prompt waiter to a jolly toper
    Hous'd in an arbour.

Odes, II.14: To Posthumus

Life is short, and death inevitable.

Ah! Posthumus, the years, the years
  Glide swiftly on, nor can our tears
Or piety the wrinkl'd age forefend,
Or for one hour retard th' inevitable end.
    'Twould be in vain, tho' you should slay,   5
  My friend, three hundred beeves a day
To cruel Pluto, whose dire waters roll,
Geryon's threefold bulk, and Tityus to controul.
    This is a voyage we all must make,
  Whoe'er the fruits of earth partake,   10
Whether we sit upon a royal throne,
Or live, like cottage hinds, unwealthy and unknown.
    The wounds of war we 'scape in vain,
  And the hoarse breakers of the main;
In vain with so much caution we provide   15
Against the southern winds upon th' autumnal tide.

The black Cocytus, that delays
His waters in a languid maze,
We must behold, and all those Danaids fell,
And Sisyphus condemn'd to fruitless toil in hell.   20
Lands, house, and pleasing wife, by thee
Must be relinquish'd; nor a tree
Of all your nurseries shall in the end,
Except the baleful cypress, their brief lord attend.
Thy worthier heir the wine shall seize   25
You hoarded with a hundred keys,
And with libations the proud pavement dye,
And feasts of priests themselves shall equal and outvie.

Odes, II.15: Upon the Luxury of the Age He Lived in

So great our palaces are now,
They'll leave few acres for the plough.
Wide as the Lucrine lake canals extend,
And sterile planes in sum the wedded elms transcend.
Then violet beds, and myrtle bow'rs,   5
And all the nosegay-blending flow'rs,
Shall far and wide their spicy breath renew,
Where for their former lords the fertile olives grew.
There the thick laurel's green array
Shall ward the fervid beams of day.   10
Not so our founder's will, or Cato's lore,
And all our bearded sires commanded things of yore.
Their private fortunes were but small,
But great the common fund of all.
No grand piazzas did there then remain   15
To catch the summer breezes of the northern wain.
Nor did they, by their edicts wise,
The providential turf despise,
Those laws, which bade each public pile be grand,
And with new stone repair'd, the holy temples stand.

Odes, II.16: To Grosphus

All men covet peace of mind, which cannot be acquired either
by riches or honours, but only by restraining the appetites.

When o'er the Aegean vast he sails
   The seaman sues the gods for ease,
Soon as the moon the tempest veils,
    Nor sparkling guide he sees.
Ease by fierce Thracians in the end;   5
   Ease by the quiver'd Mede is sought;
By gems, nor purple bales, my friend,
    Nor bullion to be bought.
Not wealth or state, a consul's share,
   Can give the troubled mind its rest,   10
Or fray the winged fiends of care,
    That pompous roofs infest.
Well lives he, on whose little board
   Th' old silver salt-cellar appears,
Left by his sires – no sordid hoard   15
    Disturb his sleep with fears.
Why with such strength of thought devise,
   And aim at sublunary pelf,
Seek foreign realms? Can he, who flies
    His country, 'scape himself?   20
Ill-natur'd care will board the fleet,
   Nor leave the squadron'd troops behind,
Swifter than harts, or irksome sleet
    Driv'n by the eastern wind.
If good, the present hour be mirth;   25
   If bitter, let your smiles be sweet,
Look not too forward – nought on earth
    Is in all points complete.
A sudden death Achilles seiz'd,
   A tedious age Tithonus wore –   30
If you're amerc'd, fate may be pleas'd
    To give to me the more.

A hundred flocks around thee stray,
    About thee low Sicilian kine,
And mares apt for thy carriage neigh,   35
    And purple robes are thine.
Me, born for verse and rural peace,
    A faithful prophetess foretold,
And groundlings, spirited from Greece,
    In high contempt I hold.   40

Odes, II.18

He asserts himself to be contented with a little fortune, where
others labour for wealth, and the gratification of their desires,
as if they were to live for ever.

Gold or iv'ry's not intended
    For this little house of mine,
Nor Hymettian arches, bended
    On rich Afric pillars, shine.
For a court I've no ambition,   5
    As not Attalus his heir,
Nor make damsels of condition
    Spin me purple for my wear,
But for truth and wit respected,
    I possess a copious vein,   10
So that rich men have affected
    To be number'd of my train.
With my Sabine field contented,
    Fortune shall be dunn'd no more;
Nor my gen'rous friend tormented   15
    To augment my little store.
One day by the next's abolish'd,
    Moons increase but to decay;
You place marbles to be polish'd
    Ev'n upon your dying day.   20
Death unheeding, though infirmer,
    On the sea your buildings rise,
While the Baian billows murmur,
    That the land will not suffice.

What tho' more and more incroaching,   25
　　On new boundaries you press,
And in avarice approaching,
　　Your poor neighbours dispossess;
The griev'd hind his gods displaces,
　　In his bosom to convey,   30
And with dirty ruddy faces
　　Boys and wife are driven away.
Yet no palace grand and spacious
　　Does more sure its lord receive,
Than the seat of death rapacious,   35
　　Whence the rich have no reprieve.
Earth alike to all is equal,
　　Whither would your views extend?
Kings and peasants in the sequel
　　To the destin'd grave descend.   40
There, tho' brib'd, the guard infernal
　　Would not shrewd Prometheus free;
There are held in chains eternal
　　Tantalus, and such as he.
There the poor have consolation   45
　　For their hard laborious lot;
Death attends each rank and station,
　　Whether he is call'd or not.

Odes, III.12: To Neobule

Neobule, smitten with the love of young Hebrus, leads a life
of indolence and sloth.

'Tis wretched in earnest to live like a mope,
　　Nor wash down chagrin with sweet wine;
To yield an uncle all spirit and hope,
　　Who rails at your pleasures and mine.
The charms of young Hebrus, and love's flying boy,   5
　　Have stol'n your work-basket away,
And all that fine tap'stry that us'd to employ,
　　And give to Minerva the day.

This gay Liparean's a notable knight,
  Bellerophon's self he may seem,   10
Not beat in the battle, or match'd in the flight,
  When fresh from the cruse and the stream.
The same in each motion's as clean as a cat,
  To hurl at the deer in the park,
Thro' bushes and shrubs the wild-boar can come at,   15
  And his quickness ne'er misses the mark.

Odes, III.16: To Maecenas

All things are open to gold; but Horace is content with his
    lot, by which he remains in a state of happiness.

A tow'r of brass, whose doors were barr'd
With oak, while, howling, upon guard,
  Stood dogs, prepar'd to bite,
Had been sufficient, to be sure,
Imprison'd Danae to secure   5
  From rakes that prowl by night:
If Jove, and she of ocean born,
Had not Acrisius laugh'd to scorn,
  With all his anxious tribe;
A way they found was fair and free,   10
When once the god should make his plea,
  Transform'd into a bribe.
Gold through the sentinels can pass,
And break through rocks and tow'rs of brass,
  Than thunderbolts more strong: 15
That *Argive prophet lost his life,
And was undone, because his wife
  Was bought to do him wrong.

* Amphiaraus, a Grecian prophet, foreseeing that he should die at the
siege of Troy, kept himself concealed; but was betrayed by his wife, for
the sake of a golden necklace.

The Macedon of such renown,
With gifts the city-gates broke down,   20
    And foil'd his rival kings:
Gifts ev'n can naval chiefs ensnare,
Though rough and honest, they would care
    For more superior things.
Anxiety pursues increase,   25
And craving never like to cease –
    I have myself deny'd
With cause to lift my crest on high,
And with such men as thee to vie,
    O knighthood's peerless pride.   30
The more a man himself refrains,
The more from heav'n his virtue gains;
    I pitch my tent with those
Who their desires, like me, divest,
And, as an enemy profest,   35
    The slaves of wealth oppose.
More noble in my lowly lot,
Than if together I had got
    Whate'er th' Appulian ploughs;
And poor amongst great riches still,   40
The fruit of no mean toil and skill,
    Could in my garners house.
A wood of moderate extent,
And stream of purest element,
    And harvest-home secure,   45
Make me more happy than the weight
Of Africa's precarious state
    Of empire could ensure.
What tho' nor sweet Calabrian bee
Makes his nectarious comb for me,   50
    Nor Formian wine grows old
Within my cellars many a year,
Though from rich Gallic meads I shear
    No fleeces of the fold:
Yet want's remote, that wretched fate,   55
That makes a man importunate –
    If more I should require,

I should not be refus'd by you —
But I must raise my revenue
  By curbing my desire.   60
And better so, than should I add
The Lydian realm to what I had,
  And all the Phrygian land;
They that crave most, possess the least —
'Tis well where'er enough's the feast;   65
  Heav'n gives with frugal hand.

Odes, III.22: To Diana

He consecrates the pine, which hangs over his villa, to Diana,
whose offices he celebrates.

Queen of the mountains far and near,
  And of the woodlands wild,
Who, thrice invok'd, art swift to hear,
  And save the maids with child;
This pine, that o'er my villa tow'rs,   5
And from its eminence embow'rs,
  I dedicate alone to thee;
Where ev'ry year a pig shall bleed,
Lest his obliquity succeed
  Against thy fav'rite tree.   10

Odes, IV.2: To Antonius Julus, the Son of Mark Antony, of the Triumvirate

It is hazardous to imitate the ancient poets.

Whoever vies with Pindar's strain,
  With waxen wings, my friend, would fly,
Like him who nam'd the glassy main,
    But could not reach the sky.

Cascading from the mountain's height,   5
   As falls the river swoln with show'rs,
Deep, fierce, and out of measure great
    His verses Pindar pours.
Worthy to claim Apollo's bays,
   Whether his dithyrambics roll,   10
Daring their new-invented phrase
    And words, that scorn controul.
Or gods he chants, or kings, the seed
   Of gods, who rose to virtuous fame,
And justly Centaurs doom'd to bleed,   15
    Or quench'd Chimera's flame.
Or champions of th' Elean justs,
   The wrestler, charioteer records,
And, better than a hundred busts,
    He gives divine rewards.   20
Snatch'd from his weeping bride, the youth
   His verse deplores, and will display
Strength, courage, and his golden truth,
    And grudges death his prey.
The Theban swan ascends with haste,   25
   Of heav'n's superior regions free;
But I, exactly in the taste
    Of some Matinian bee,
That hardly gets the thymy spoil
   About moist Tibur's flow'ry ways,   30
Of small account, with tedious toil,
    Compose my labour'd lays.
You, bard indeed! with more applause
   Shall Caesar sing, so justly crown'd,
As up the sacred hill he draws   35
    The fierce Sicambrians bound.
A greater and a better gift
   Than him, from heav'n we do not hold,
Nor shall – although the times should shift
    Into their pristine gold.   40
The festal days and public sports
   For our brave chief's returning here,
You shall recite, and all the courts
    Of law contentions clear.

Then would I speak to ears like thine,   45
   With no small portion of my voice,
O glorious day! O most divine!
    Which Caesar bids rejoice.
And while you in procession hie,
   Hail triumph! triumph! will we shout   50
All Rome – and our good gods supply
   With frankincense devout!
Thee bulls and heifers ten suffice –
   Me a calf weaned from the cow,
At large who many a gambol tries,   55
    Though doom'd to pay my vow.
Like the new moon, upon his crest
   He wears a semicircle bright,
His body yellow all the rest,
    Except this spot of white.   60

Odes, IV.3: To Melpomene

Horace was born for poetry, to which his immortality is
entirely owing.

He, on whose natal hour you glance
   A single smile with partial eyes,
Melpomene, shall not advance
   A champion for th' Olympic prize,
Nor drawn by steeds of manag'd pride,   5
In Grecian car victorious ride.

Nor honour'd with the Delphic leaf,
   A wreath for high atchievements wove,
Shall he be shewn triumphant chief,
   Where stands the Capitol of Jove,   10
As justly rais'd to such renown
For bringing boastful tyrants down.

But pleasing streams, that flow before
  Fair Tibur's flow'ry-fertile land,
And bow'ring trees upon the shore,   15
  Which in such seemly order stand,
Shall form on that Aeolic plan
The bard, and magnify the man.

The world's metropolis has deign'd
  To place me with her darling care,   20
Rome has my dignity maintain'd
  Amongst her bards my bays to wear;
And hence it is against my verse
The tooth of envy's not so fierce.

O mistress of the golden shell!   25
  Whose silence you command, or break;
Thou that canst make the mute excel,
  And ev'n the sea-born reptiles speak;
And, like the swan, if you apply
Your touch, in charming accents die.   30

This is thy gift, and only thine,
  That, as I pass along, I hear –
'There goes the bard, whose sweet design
  Made lyrics for the Roman ear.'
If life or joy I hold or give,   35
By thee I please, by thee I live.

Odes IV.7: To L. Manlius Torquatus

All things are changed by time; one ought therefore to live
cheerfully.

The melted snow the verdure now restores,
  And leaves adorn the trees;
The season shifts – subsiding to their shores
  The rivers flow with ease.

The Grace, with nymphs and with her sisters twain,   5
    Tho' naked dares the dance –
That here's no permanence the years explain,
    And days, as they advance.
The air grows mild with zephyrs, as the spring
    To summer cedes the sway,   10
Which flies when autumn hastes his fruits to bring,
    Then winter comes in play.
The moons their heav'nly damages supply –
    Not so the mortal star –
Where good Aeneas, Tullus, Ancus lie,   15
    Ashes and dust we are.
Who knows if heav'n will give to-morrow's boon
    To this our daily pray'r?
The goods you take to keep your soul in tune,
    Shall 'scape your greedy heir.   20
When you shall die, tho' Minos must acquit
    A part so nobly play'd;
Race, eloquence, and goodness, from the pit
    Cannot restore your shade.
For nor Diana's heav'nly pow'r or love,   25
    Hippolytus revives;
Nor Theseus can Perithous remove
    From his Lethean gyves.

Odes, IV.10: To Phyllis

He invites her to a banquet, upon the birth-day of Maecenas.

     Full nine years old my cellar stows
      A cask of good Albanian wine,
     And parsley in my garden grows;
     For Phyllis chaplets to compose,
       Much ivy too is mine: 5

With whose green gloss you shall be crown'd;
  With burnish'd plate the house looks gay,
The altar, with chaste vervains bound,
Craves to be sprinkled from the wound,
    As we the lambkin slay.   10

All hands are busied – here and there
  Mixt with the lads the lasses fly,
The bustling flames, to dress the fare,
Roll up thick smoke, which clouds the air
    Above the roof on high.   15

But would you know what joy resides
  With me, to tempt you at this time –
You are to celebrate the ides,
The day which April's month divides,
    And Venus calls her prime: 20

A feast observable of right,
  Which I more heartily revere,
Than that which brought myself to light,
From whence my patron to requite,
    Flow many a happy year!   25

Young Telephus, at whom you aim,
  Is not for such as thee at all;
A rich and a lascivious dame
Upon his love has fixt her claim,
    And holds him in sweet thrall.   30

Let blasted Phaeton dissuade
  Presumptuous hope too high to soar;
And *he a dread example made
By Pegasus, who scornful neigh'd
    That he a mortal bore.   35

* Bellerophon.

Things worthy of yourself pursue,
   Nor go where vain desire allures;
'Tis lawless to extend your view
To one that's not a match for you –
     Hail! crown of my amours!   40

For, after this, I will be free
   From every other flame and fair –
Come, learn the song I made for thee,
And join, with charming voice and me,
     To banish gloomy care.

The Secular Ode

For the safety of the Roman empire.

Phoebus and Dian, queen of bow'rs,
   Bright grace of Heav'n, the things we pray;
O most adorable of pow'rs,
And still by adoration ours,
     Grant us this sacred day.   5

At which the Sybils in their song,
   Ingenuous youths and virgins warn;
Selected from the vulgar throng,
The gods, to whom sev'n hills belong,
     With verses to adorn.   10

O fost'ring god, whose fall or flame,
   Can hide the day or re-illume;
Which com'st another and the same,
May'st thou see nothing like the fame,
     And magnitude of Rome!   15

And thou, to whom the pray'r's preferr'd,
   The matrons in their throes to ease;
O let our vows in time be heard,
Whether Lucina be the word,
     Or genial goddess please.   20

Make fruitful ev'ry nuptial bed,
  And bless the conscript father's scheme,
Enjoining bloomy maids to wed,
And let the marriage-bill be sped,
    With a new race to teem.   25

That years elev'n times ten come round,
  These sports and songs of grave delight;
Thrice by bright day-light may resound,
And where the thickest crowds abound,
    Thrice in the welcome night.   30

And you, ye destinies, sincere
  To sing what good our realm awaits;
Let peace establish'd persevere,
And add to them, which now appear,
    Still hope of better fates.   35

Let fertile earth, for flocks and fruit,
  Greet Ceres with a wheaten crown;
And ev'ry youngling, sprout and shoot,
Let Jove with air attemper'd suit,
    While wholesome rains come down.   40

Serene, as when your darts you sheathe,
  Phoebus, the suppliant youths befriend;
And all the vows the virgins breathe,
Up to thy crescent from beneath,
    Thou, queen of stars, attend.   45

If Rome be yours, and if a band
  Of Trojans safely came by sea;
To coast upon th' Etrurian strand,
And change their city and their land,
    By your supreme decree.   50

For whom, unhurt, thro' burning Troy
  The chaste Aeneas way could find;
He whom the foes could not destroy,
But liv'd to make his friends enjoy,
    More than they left behind.   55

— Ye gods, our youth in morals train,
   With sweet repose old age solace;
On Rome, in general, O rain
All circumstance, increase, and gain,
    Each glory and each grace. 60

And he whose beeves were milky white,
   When to your shrine his pray'rs appeal'd;
Of Venus and Anchises hight,
O let him reign supreme in fight,
    But mild to them that yield. 65

By sea and land, the Parthians now
   Our arms and ax with dread review;
For terms of peace the Scythians bow,
And, lately arrogant of brow,
    To us the Indians sue. 70

Now public faith and honour dare,
   With ancient modesty and peace,
To shew their heads, and virtue rare,
And she that's wont her horn to bear,
    With plentiful increase. 75

The archer with his shining bow,
   The seer that wins each muse's heart;
Phoebus, who respite can bestow,
To limbs in weakness and in woe,
    By his salubrious art. 80

If, built on Palatine, the height
   Of his own tow'rs his eyes engage;
The Roman and the Latian state,
Extend he to a longer date,
    And still a better age! 85

And may Diana, who controuls
   Mount Algidus and Aventine;
To those great men that keep the rolls,
And to the youths that lift their souls,
    A gracious ear incline! 90

That Jove, and all the gods, will bless
  Or pray'rs, good hopes my thoughts forebode;
THE CHORUS, who such skill possess,
Phoebus and Dian to address,
    In this thanksgiving ode.   95

Satires, II.6

He declares himself to be content with such things as he is
    possessed of, and that he wishes for no more.

    This was the summit of my views,
    A little piece of land to use,
    Where was a garden and a well,
    Near to the house in which I dwell,
    And something of a wood above.   5
    The Gods in their paternal love
    Have more and better sent than these,
    And, Mercury, I rest at ease,
    Nor ask I any thing beside,
    But that these blessings may abide.   10
    If I cannot my conscience charge,
    That I by fraud my wealth enlarge,
    Nor am about by fond excess
    To make my little matters less;
    If I am not a fool in grain,   15
    To make such wishes weak and vain,
    'O that I could that nook command
    That mars the beauty of my land!
    O where there lies a pot of gold,
    Might I by some good God be told!   20
    Like him who having treasure found,
    No longer till'd, but bought the ground!
    With Hercules so much his friend!' –
    If for what I possess, or spend,
    No mean unthankful mind I bear,   25
    I supplicate you with this pray'r:

May every thing I have be fat,
My servants, cattle, dog, and cat,
All but my genius – and be still
My guardian, if it is your will!   30
Wherefore, when I from town retreat
To these my mounts, and lofty seat,
How can I of my time dispose
Better than in this measur'd prose?
Here neither worldly pride destroys,   35
Nor pressure of South wind annoys,
Or sickly Autumn, still the gain
Of Libitina's baleful reign.
O early sire, or Janus hight,
(If that name more your ears delight)   40
With whom men all their toils commence
In life (for so the Gods dispense)
Do thou thyself begin the song –
At Rome you hurry me along
To give in bail – dispatch me there   45
Lest some one else should do th' affair.
Well – tho' aground the North wind blow,
Or winter brings the days of snow
To shorter compass – I must go –
About myself to over-reach –   50
When I in form have made my speech,
At once determinate and loud,
Why I must bustle in the crowd,
Sure all slow-walkers to offend –
What are you mad? what mean you, friend?   55
(Some swearing fellow's apt to say)
You jostle all things in your way,
While in post-haste you must be sped,
With great Maecenas in your head –
This *does*, and is too by the bye –   60
A sugar-plum – I will not lie –
But ere I reach th' Esquilian gloom,
I'm charg'd with all th' affairs of Rome.

'Roscius desires you, as a friend,
The court-house early to attend;   65
The clerks beseech you would return,
Upon a thing of vast concern;
Take care Maecenas seal and sign,
To this same instrument of mine.'
I will *endeavour*, should one say,   70
They'll answer, if you will, you may,
And still keep urging, as before –
'Tis now the seventh year or more,
Since to Maecenas I was known,
And freely number'd as his own,   75
So far as one he chose to raise
Just to the honour of his chaise,
Conversing as he took his tour,
About such trifles – What's the hour?
Say is *Gallina, who's from Thrace,   80
A match for Syrus face to face?
These morning frosts are very bad
For those who are but thinly clad,
Or any thing, that comes in play,
Which one to leaky ears may say.   85
E'er since this fortunate event,
Th' invidious sons of discontent
Daily increase – 'This friend of ours,
On whom her favours fortune show'rs;
A place with great Maecenas claims,   90
With him was present at the games,
Plays in the field with him at ball.' –
Ah, lucky rogue! cries one and all –
Does any bad disheart'ning news,
Its influence thro' the streets diffuse: 95
Whoe'er I meet consults with me.
'Good Sir, (for sure you must be he,
Who all th' affairs of state must know,
As nearer to the gods below)

* Gallina and Syrus, two great gladiators.

Aught do you of the Dacians hear?'   100
No – not a syllable – 'you jeer:'
May all the gods afflict my heart,
If I know either whole or part. –
'Well – then will Caesar give the lands,
He promis'd to his chosen bands,   105
In Sicily or here, I pray?'
The more I swear, I cannot say –
The more they stare, they cannot sound
A man so close and so profound! –
Thus do I lose my time and ease,   110
Not without wishes such as these –
O rural scenes! when shall I see
Your beauties, and again be free
Now with those ancient books, I chose
With leisure now, and soft repose,   115
In grateful thoughtlessness to drown
The anxious business of the town?
When shall Pythagoras his beans,
With bacon, and well-larded greens
Be plac'd before me? O ye nights!   120
Of suppers and divine delights,
In which within my proper pale
I and my bosom friends regale;
And make ev'n saucy slaves partake
Of those libations that I make.   125
Each guest according as it suits
May take the glass, no one disputes,
Whether the strong the bumper choose,
Or weaker cheerfully refuse.
A conversation then begins   130
Not on our neighbours' wealth or sins,
Or whether Lepos preference claim
For dancing? – but what's more our aim,
And what 'tis evil not to know –
If happiness from riches flow,   135
Or be not rather virtue's prize,
And which it is cement the ties

Of friendship – rectitude or gain,
And what is real good in grain,
And how perfection to attain?   140
Mean time my neighbour Cervius prates
Old tales, that rise from our debates;
For if a man who does not know
The world, his eulogy bestow
On great Arellius' cumbrous store   145
He instantly sets off – 'Of yore
A country mouse, as it befell,
Received a cit into his cell,
One crony to another kind
As intimate time out of mind;   150
This mouse was blunt and giv'n to thrift,
But now and then could make a shift
(However rigid or recluse)
With open heart to give a loose:
In short he would not grudge his guest   155
Or oats or vetches of the best:
And bringing in some berries dried,
With nibbled scrap of ham beside,
Hop'd he variety might plead
To make his daintiness recede,   160
For our grandee would scarcely touch
The things, his squeamishness was such. –
Mean time the master of the treat
Extended on clean straw would eat
Nothing but tares and crusts, to spare   165
For his good friend the nobler fare.
At length the citizen made free
To speak his mind – my friend, (said he)
How can your mouse-ship hold it good,
To live here on a rugged wood,   170
And how have patience with the place!
Will you not rather turn your face
To view mankind, the town prefer
To these rough scenes that here occur?

Come take my counsel and agree 175
To make a tour along with me.
Since mortal lives must have an end,
And death all earthly things attend,
Nor is there an escape at all
For man or mouse, for great or small; 180
Wherefore, good friend, these matters weigh,
And let us for our time be gay,
Let life's contracted period teach
Mice to live jollily – This speech
Soon as it on the peasant wrought, 185
He nimbly springs from forth his grot,
Then both the destin'd journey take
By midnight gloom their jaunt to make:
And now about that time each mouse
Took refuge in a wealthy house, 190
Where gorgeous carpets crimson-red
Look'd splendid on each ivory bed:
Where many a bit, in many a tray,
Was left from feast of yesterday.
He having then the peasant set 195
Upon a purple coverlet,
Runs like my landlord here and there –
Dish after dish with dainty fare,
And like a handy footman serves,
First tasting every thing he carves. 200
The clown by no means making strange
Begins to chuckle at the change,
And lying on the couch at ease
Lives merrily on all he sees.
But on a sudden, with a roar, 205
Bang open flies the folding door,
And fright our gutlers from their cheer –
Now round the room half-dead with fear,
They scout – new terrors still abound,
With barking dogs the roofs resound. 210
Then (quoth the clown) I have no call
For such a life as this at all;

> My cave and wood be still my share,
> There rather let me skulk from care,
> And live upon a single tare.'   215

Epistles, I.4: To Albius Tibullus

He addresses Albius Tibullus, to whom he seems to commend
the study of Philosophy, and recount the talents with which
he was adorned from heaven.

> Tibullus, whom I love and praise,
> Mild judge of my prosaic lays,
> Can I account for your odd turn,
> Who I Pedanian groves sojourn:
> Are you now writing to out-please   5
> The works of Cassius, or at ease,
> And silence, range the healthy wood,
> Studious of all things wise and good?
> Thou'rt not a form without a heart,
> For heav'n was gracious to impart   10
> A goodly person, fine estate,
> Made for fruition, fortunate.
> What more for her most fav'rite boy,
> Could a nurse image, to enjoy,
> Than to be wise, and ably taught,   15
> To speak aloud his noble thought,
> To whom grace, fame, and body sound,
> Might to pre-eminence abound,
> With table of ingenious fare,
> And purse with money still to spare?   20
> – 'Twixt hope and care, 'twixt fear and strife,
> Think every day the last of life.
> Beyond your wish some happy day,
> Shall come your grief to over-pay.
> Me sleek and fat, as fat can be,   25
> I hope you'll shortly come to see:
> When you've a mind to laugh indeed
> At pigs of the Lucretian breed.

Epistles, I.20: To His Book

You seem to cast, my vent'rous book,
Towards the town a wishful look,
That thee the chapmen may demand,
Where Janus, and Vertumnus stand;
When polish'd by the binder's art. –   5
Both keys and seals, with all your heart,
You hate, and every thing refuse
Which all your modest volumes choose.
You grudge that you are shewn to few,
Desirous of the public view,   10
On other principles compil'd –
Away then, since you are so wild –
When once set off there's no return –
Soon shall you say with much concern –
Ah! wretch, what would I, when your pride   15
Is by some reader mortified,
And in some narrow nook you stick,
When curiosity is sick.
But if the augur do not dream,
In wrath for this your desp'rate scheme   20
At Rome you'll be a welcome guest,
As long as you are new at least.
But when all dirty you become,
In witness of the vulgar thumb,
Or groveling book-worms you must feed,   25
Or for us Utica shall speed;
Or bundled up in packthread chain,
Be sent a transport into Spain.
The good adviser, all the while,
To whom you gave no heed, will smile: 30
As he who from the mountain threw
The sulky ass, that would not do
His bus'ness – 'then go down the hill –
Who'd save an ass against his will.'
This destiny too must remain –   35
Thee fault'ring dotage shall detain

About the city-skirts to teach
The boys their rudiments of speech.
And when the fervency of day
Brings you more hearers, you must say,   40
That poor and meanly born at best,
I spread my wings beyond my nest,
And what you from my birth subtract,
You for my virtues must exact;
That peace or war, I still was great,   45
With the first pillars of the state,
Short-siz'd, and prematurely grey,
Form'd for th' intensity of day,
With passion ev'n to phrenzy seiz'd,
But very easily appeas'd.   50
If any person by the bye
Should ask how old I am, reply,
That when the fasces were assign'd,
To Lepidus and Lollius join'd
I was full out, and fairly told,   55
Four times eleven Decembers old.

HYMNS FOR THE AMUSEMENT
OF CHILDREN

Hymn 1: Faith

The Father of the Faithful said,
   At God's first calling, 'Here am I;'
Let us by his example sway'd,
   Like him submit, like him reply,

'Go take thy son, thine only son,   5
   And offer him to God thy King.'
The word was giv'n – the work begun,
   'The altar pile, the victim bring.'

But lo! th' angelic voice above
   Bade the great Patriarch stop his hands;   10
'Know God is everlasting love,
   And must revoke such harsh commands.'

Then let us imitate the Seer,
   And tender with compliant grace
Ourselves, our souls, and children here,   15
   Hereafter in a better place.

Hymn 2: Hope

Ah! Hannah, why should'st thou despair,
   Quick to the Tabernacle speed;
There on thy knees prefer thy pray'r,
   And there thy cause to mercy plead.

Her pious breathings now ascend,   5
    As from her heart the sighs she heaves;
And angels to her suit attend,
    Till strong in hope she now conceives.

Then Samuel soon was brought to light
    To serve the Lord, as yet a child –   10
O what a heart-reviving sight!
    Sure Cherubims and Seraphs smil'd.

Thus yet a child may I begin
    To serve the Lord with all my heart;
To shun the wily lures of sin,   15
    And claim the prize, or e'er I start.

Hymn 3: Charity

O Queen of virtues, whose sweet pow'r
Does o'er the first perfections tow'r,
Sustaining in the arms of love
All want below, all weal above.

With thee O let my thoughts conceive,   5
For all the very best believe;
Predict, pronounce for all the best,
And be by bearing all things blest.

To suffer long and still be kind
In holy temperance of mind,   10
Rejoice that truth is on my side,
As free from envy as from pride.

Both tongues and prophecies shall cease,
And painful knowledge cede to peace;
And time and death o'er all prevail,   15
But Charity shall never fail.

Then guide, O Christ, this little hand,
To deal thy bounties round the land;
To clothe and feed the hungry poor,
And to the stranger ope my door.   20

My cup of water, Christ, is free.
For all that love and thirst for thee;
With wisdom many a soul to win,
And loose the irksome bonds of sin.

Make me, O Christ, tho' yet a child,   25
To virtue zealous, errors mild,
Profess the feelings of a man,
And be the Lord's Samaritan.

Hymn 4: Prudence

O best oeconomist of life,
Tho' all the passions were at strife;
Yet thou, fair Prudence, could'st assuage
The storm, and moderate its rage.

With Dove and Serpent at thy call,   5
As caution'd by the Lord of all,
Thou art in Christ full well aware,
Of open force or secret snare.

To check thy thoughts divinely meek,
To weigh thy words before you speak,   10
To make the day's demand secure,
To be the treas'rer of the poor.

All these, Prudentia, these are thine;
And God thro' Christ shall make them mine;
To do my best till life shall end,   15
Then on futurity depend.

Hymn 5: Justice

O let not fraud 'gainst me prevail,
  My God, my Christ avow'd;
Which weigh'st the mountains in thy scale,
  And balancest the cloud.

And still peculiar on my side,   5
    Keep me from rigour free;
Make me forgive in manly pride,
    All that exact on me.

Pay my demander more than due,
    With measure heap'd and press'd;   10
And rather welcome than pursue,
    My brother when distress'd.

O give me sense and grace to know
    Thy will and check my own;
In heav'n above, in earth below,   15
    The Lord is judge alone.

Hymn 6: Mercy

O sweet – attentive to the pray'r,
Ye forward hope and stave despair;
Thro' Christ his blood divinely spill'd,
Tremendous ruin to rebuild.

Tho' high above the great and just,   5
Yet thou descendest to the dust;
Both to the sovereign and the slave,
Nor quit'st the monument and grave.

O let me like the righteous die,
And so I shall if thou art by!   10
The vial in thy hand uprears,
My Saviour's blood, my Saviour's tears.

Come, Cherub, come, possess my soul,
All wrath and bitterness controul;
If thou thy charming pow'rs bestow,   15
I'll shew thee to my veriest foe.

Hymn 7: Temperance

For forty days the Lord abstain'd,
  (The subtle tempter near)
And greatly every bait disdain'd,
  Self-aw'd and self-severe.

This is the pattern that I set,   5
  To keep the flesh in awe;
I will not gross desires abet,
  Withdraw, foul fiend, withdraw!

The fiend withdrew, the Angels came,
  And worship'd at his feet;   10
'O great Jehovah, word and name
  Inestimably sweet!

'How could that cursed serpent dare,
  Thine honour to offend?'
Says Christ, a little while forbear,   15
  'Tis for a glorious end.

O may I keep the body cool,
  By fasting on my knees;
And follow strict religion's rule,
  Those days the church decrees.   20

Keep, keep intemp'rance far away,
  'Tis duty and 'tis love;
Or how shall I my breast display,
  To nest my Saviour's dove?

Hymn 8: Fortitude

Stand fast, my child, and after all.
Yet still stand fast, says holy Paul,
Thy resolution be renew'd,
For this is Christian Fortitude.

Repeat the Lord's own pray'r for grace,   5
At ev'ry hour in ev'ry place;
Spring up from human to divine,
For strength invincible is thine.

Then, as the great Apostle saith,
'Bove all things take the shield of Faith,   10
Salvation's helm, and for thy sword,
E'en God's good spirit and his Word.

And now in dang'rous giddy youth,
Your loins begirt about with Truth;
Your feet with Gospel-peace be shod,   15
Your breast-plate Righteousness from God.

When to the ghostly fight alarm'd,
Know, soldier, thou'rt completely arm'd,
And free from terror or dismay,
March on, engage, and win the day.   20

Hymn 9: Moderation

Tho' I my party long have chose,
    And claim Christ Jesus on my side,
Yet will I not my peace oppose,
    By pique, by prejudice, or pride.

Blessed be God that at the font,   5
    My sponsors bound me to the call
Of Christ in England to confront
    The world, the flesh, the fiend and all.

And yet I will my thoughts suppress,
    And keep my tongue from censure clear;   10
The Jew, the Turk, the Heathen bless,
    And hold the plough and persevere.

There's God in ev'ry man most sure,
    And ev'ry soul's to Christ allied;
If fears deject, if hopes allure,   15
    If Jesus wept, and pray'd, and died.

Hymn 10: Truth

'Tis thus the holy Scripture ends,
   'Whoever loves or makes a lie,
On heav'n's felicity depends
   In vain, for he shall surely die.'

The stars, the firmament, the sun,   5
   God's glorious work, God's great design,
All, all was finish'd as begun,
   By rule, by compass, and by line.

Hence David unto heav'n appeals,
   'Ye heav'ns his righteousness declare;'   10
His signet their duration seals,
   And bids them be as firm, as fair.

Then give me grace, celestial Sire,
   The truth to love, the truth to tell;
Let everlasting sweets aspire,   15
   And filth and falsehood sink to hell.

Hymn 11: Beauty

FOR A DAMSEL

Christ, keep me from the self-survey
   Of beauties all thine own;
If there is beauty let me pray,
   And praise the Lord alone.

Pray – that I may the fiend withstand,   5
   Where'er his serpents be:
Praise – that the Lord's almighty hand
   Is manifest in me.

It is not so – my features are
   Much meaner than the rest;
A glow-worm cannot be a star,   10
   And I am plain at best.

Then come, my love, thy grace impart,
    Great Saviour of mankind;
O come, and purify my heart,   15
    And beautify my mind.

Then will I thy carnations nurse,
    And cherish every rose;
And empty to the poor my purse,
    Till grace to glory grows.   20

Hymn 12: Honesty

I have a house, the house of prayer,
    (No spy beneath my eaves)
And purring gratitude is there,
    And he that frights the thieves.

If I of honesty suspend   5
    My judgment, making doubt,
I have a good domestic friend,
    That soon shall point it out.

'Tis to be faithful to my charge,
    And thankful for my place,
And pray that God my pow'rs enlarge,   10
    To act with greater grace.

To give my brother more than due,
    In talent or in name;
Nor e'en my enemy pursue,   15
    To hurt, or to defame.

Nay more, to bless him and to pray,
    Mine anger to controul;
And give the wages of the day
    To him, that hunts my soul.   20

Hymn 13: Elegance

'Tis in the spirit that attire,
  Th' investiture of saints in heav'n,
Those robes of intellectual fire,
  Which to the great elect are giv'n.

'Bring out to my returning son,   5
  The robes for elegance the best;'
Thus in the height it shall be done,
  And thus the penitent be blest.

'Tis in the body, that sweet mien,
  Ingenuous Christians all possess,   10
Grace, easy motions, smiles serene,
  Clean hands and seemliness of dress.

Whoever has thy charming pow'rs,
  Is amiable as Kidron's *swan,
Like holy Esdras feeds on flow'rs,   15
  And lives on honey like St John.

* David.

Hymn 14: Loveliness

Good-nature is thy sterling name,
  Yet loveliness is English too;
Sweet disposition, whose bright aim,
  Is to the mark of Jesus true.

I've seen thee in an homely face,   5
  Excel by pulchritude of mind;
To ill-form'd features give a grace,
  Serene, benevolent and kind.

'Tis when the spirit is so great,
  That it the body still controuls,   10
As godly inclinations meet,
  In sweet society of souls.

It is that condescending air,
    Where perfect willingness is plain,
To smile assent, to join in pray'r,   15
    And urg'd a mile to go it twain.

To grant at once the boon preferr'd,
    By contrite foe, or needy friend;
To be obliging is the word,
    And God's good blessing is the end.   20

Hymn 15: Taste

O guide my judgment and my taste,
    Sweet SPIRIT, author of the book
Of wonders, told in language chaste,
    And plainness not to be mistook.

O let me muse, and yet at sight   5
    The page admire, the page believe;
'Let there be light, and there was light,
    Let there be Paradise and Eve!'

Who his soul's rapture can refrain
    At Joseph's ever-pleasing tale,   10
Of marvels, the prodigious train,
    To Sinai's hill from Goshen's vale?

The Psalmist and proverbial Seer,
    And all the prophets, sons of song,
Make all things precious, all things clear,   15
    And bear the brilliant word along.

O take the book from off the shelf,
    And con it meekly on thy knees;
Best panegyric on itself,
    And self-avouch'd to teach and please.   20

Respect, adore it heart and mind,
    How greatly sweet, how sweetly grand,
Who reads the most, is most refin'd,
    And polish'd by the Master's hand.

Hymn 16: Learning

Come, come with emulative strife,
To learn the way, the truth, and life,
　　Which Jesus is in one;
In all sound doctrine he proceeds,
From Alpha to Omega leads,   5
　　E'en Spirit, Sire, and Son.

Sure of th' exceeding great reward,
'Midst all your learning learn the Lord –
　　This was thy doctrine, Paul;
And this thy lecture should persuade,   10
Tho' thou hadst more of human aid,
　　Than thy blest brethren all.

Humanity's a charming thing,
And every science of the ring,
　　Good is the classic lore;   15
For these are helps along the road,
That leads to Zion's blest abode,
　　And heav'nly muse's store.

But greater still in each respect,
He that communicates direct   20
　　The tutor of the soul;
Who without pain, degrees or parts,
While he illuminates our hearts,
　　Can teach at once the whole.

Hymn 17: Praise

Tho' conscience void of all offence,
　　Is man's divinest praise,
A godly heart-felt innocence,
Which does at first by grace commence,
　　By supplication stays: 5

Yet I do love my brother's laud,
  In each attempt to please;
O may he frequently applaud,
'Good child, thou soon shalt go abroad,
  Or have such things as these. –   10

'This silver coin'd by sweet queen Anne,
  This nosegay and these toys,
Thou this gilt Testament shalt scan,
This pictur'd Hymn-book on a plan,
  To make good girls and boys.'   15

O may they give before I ask,
  Suggest before desire,
While in the summer-house I bask,
The little lab'rer at his task
  Is worthy of his hire.   20

Hymn 18: Prayer

Pray without ceasing (says the Saint)
Nor ever in the spirit faint;
With grace the bloom and faith the root,
The pray'r shall bring eternal fruit.

When the great Seer sad news did bring   5
To Ahab, e'en that wicked king!
Hear what the word of mercy says,
Spare thou the man, 'behold he prays.'

Our hopes Christ Jesus to elate,
Has bid us be importunate,   10
And with the bustling widow vie,
That triumph'd over tyranny.

'Tis peace, 'tis dignity, 'tis ease,
To bless the Lord upon our knees;
The voice and attitude of fear,   15
For God's own eye, for God's own ear.

Christ Jesus when the Twelve besought
His aid, the PATER NOSTER taught;
By giving glory we begin,
And end in deprecating sin.   20

Then give the glory yet again,
For who would be in grief or pain,
Or brook anxiety and care,
When the quick remedy is pray'r.

Hymn 19: Patience

By sin and Satan un-intic't,
JOB, type of our Emmanuel Christ,
With all the gems he had in store,
None half so bright as Patience wore.

JOB, son of Issachar, at length   5
Proves Patience is the child of Strength;
Yet Jesus could new pow'rs create,
And e'en in weakness made her great.

Long-suff'ring God, whose goodness can
Bear with, and bless provoking man;   10
Let us like thee attempt our parts,
And 'gainst false brethren arm our hearts.

Teach us in sickness to adore
Thine hand, and all our ills restore:
Or let us meditate in death   15
On Thee – poor man of NAZARETH.

Teach me in poverty to think
Of Him who drank on Cedron's brink;
But had nor mansion-house, nor bread,
Or to repose him, or be fed.   20

Teach me 'midst all the griefs below,
This transient state, this world of woe,
Submissive on my bended knee,
To take my cross and follow Thee.

Hymn 20: Watching

At every tempter's first essay,
Be sure to watch, be sure to pray;
For this great requisite the Lord
Has strongly urg'd upon record.

Yea this he strongly urg'd to all,   5
A warning common as his call;
Then who can his behest revere,
And not obey in heed and fear?

Had the good man been on his guard,
His doors and windows duly barr'd,   10
He would not, by the Lord advis'd,
Have lost his all, and been surpriz'd.

Had this command been fully weigh'd,
Peter his Lord had not betray'd;
But spite of all his mighty boast,   15
He fail'd and slept upon his post.

Sleep not – but watch the chamber well,
By sleeping Holofernes fell;
And Jael's memorable nail,
Did o'er a sleeping king prevail.   20

'Behold, I come' – come quickly then,
Thou Saviour of the souls of men;
For pray'r and hymns are mine employ,
Who long for ever-wakeful joy.

Hymn 21: Generosity

That vast communicative Mind,
That form'd the world and human kind,
    And saw that all was right;
Or was Thyself, or came from Thee,
Stupendous Generosity,   5
    Above all lustre bright.

'Not *for themselves the bees prepare
Their honey, and the fleecy care,
   Not for themselves are shorn:
Not for themselves the warblers build,   10
Not for themselves the lands are till'd,
   By them that tread the corn.'

The Lord shed on the Holy Rood
His infinitely gen'rous blood,
   Not for himself, but all;   15
Yea e'en for them that pierc'd his side,
In patient agony he died,
   To remedy the Fall.

O highly rais'd above the ranks
Of Angels – he could e'en give thanks   20
   Self-rais'd, and self-renew'd –
Then who can praise, and love, and fear
Enough? – since he himself, 'tis clear,
   Is also Gratitude.

* Virgil.

Hymn 22: Gratitude

I upon the first creation
   Clap'd my wings with loud applause,
Cherub of the highest station,
   Praising, blessing, without pause.

I in Eden's bloomy bowers   5
   Was the heav'nly gard'ner's pride,
Sweet of sweets, and flow'r of flowers,
   With the scented tinctures dy'd.

Hear, ye little children, hear me,
   I am God's delightful voice;   10
They who sweetly still revere me,
   Still shall make the wisest choice.

Hear me not like Adam trembling,
  When I walk'd in Eden's grove;
And the host of heav'n assembling,   15
  From the spot the traitor drove.

Hear me rather as the lover
  Of mankind, restor'd and free;
By the Word ye shall recover
  More than that ye lost by Me.   20

I'm the Phoenix of the singers,
  That in upper Eden dwell;
Hearing me Euphrates lingers,
  As my wond'rous tale I tell.

'Tis the story of the Graces,   25
  Mercies without end or sum;
And the sketches and the traces
  Of ten thousand more to come.

List, my children, list within you,
  Dread not ye the tempter's rod;   30
Christ our gratitude shall win you,
  Wean'd from earth, and led to God.

Hymn 23: Peace

The Mount of Olives was thy seat,
  O Angel, heav'nly fair;
And thou, sweet Peace, didst often meet
  Thy Prince and Saviour there.

But now abroad condemn'd to roam,   5
  From Salem lov'd and bless'd;
A quiet conscience is thine home,
  In every faithful breast.

Thou didst Augustus first inspire,
  That bloody war should cease;   10
And to Melchisedec retire,
  The Sov'reign of our peace.

O come unto the Church repair,
   And her defects review;
Of old thou plantedst olives there,   15
   Which to redundance grew.

Sustain the pillars of the state,
   Be health and wealth conjoin'd;
And in each house thy turtles mate,
   To multiply mankind.   20

Hymn 24: Melancholy

O pluck me quick the raven's quill,
   And I will set me down,
My destin'd purpose to fulfil,
But with this interrupted skill,
   Of thought and grief profound.   5

How to begin, and how depart,
   From this sad fav'rite theme,
The man of sorrow in my heart,
I at my own ideas start,
   As dread as Daniel's dream.   10

As soon as born the infant cries,
   For well his spirit knows,
A little while, and then he dies,
A little while, and down he lies,
   To take a stern repose.   15

But man's own death is not th' event,
   For which most tears are due;
Wife, children, to the grave are sent,
Or friends, to make the heart repent,
   That it such blessings knew.   20

O Thou who on the mountain's brow,
   By night didst pray alone;
In the cold night didst pay thy vow,
And in humiliation bow,
   To thrones and pow'rs thine own.   25

Tell us, for thou the best can tell,
   What Melancholy means?
A guise in them that wear it well,
That goes to music to dispel
   Dark thoughts and gloomier scenes.   30

Say, didst thou solitude desire,
   Or wert thou driv'n away,
By rank desertion to retire,
Without or bed, or food, or fire,
   For all thy foes to pray?   35

Yet thou didst preach of future bliss,
   Peace permanent above,
Of Truth and Mercy's holy kiss,
Those joys, which none that love thee miss,
   O give us grace to love.   40

Hymn 25: Mirth

If you are merry sing away,
   And touch the organs sweet;
This is the Lord's triumphant day,
Ye children in the gall'ries gay,
   Shout from each goodly seat.   5

It shall be May to-morrow's morn,
   Afield then let us run,
And deck us in the blooming thorn,
Soon as the cock begins to warn,
   And long before the sun.   10

I give the praise to Christ alone,
   My pinks already show;
And my streak'd roses fully blown,
The sweetness of the Lord make known,
   And to his glory grow.   15

Ye little prattlers that repair
   For cowslips in the mead,
Of those exulting colts beware,
But blithe security is there,
   Where skipping lambkins feed.   20

With white and crimson laughs the sky,
   With birds the hedge-rows ring;
To give the praise to God most high,
And all the sulky fiends defy,
   Is a most joyful thing.   25

Hymn 26: Mutual Subjection

Some think that in the Christian scheme
   Politeness has no part;
That manners we should dis-esteem,
   And look upon the heart.

The heart the Lord alone can read,   5
   Which left us this decree,
That men alternate take the lead
   In sweet complacency.

When his Disciples great dispute
   Christ Jesus reconcil'd,   10
He made their sharp contention mute,
   By shewing them a child.

If I have got the greater share
   Of talents – I should bow
To Christ, and take the greater care   15
   To serve and to allow.

This union with thy grace empow'r
   More influence to supply;
Hereafter, he that lacks this hour,
   May be as great as I.   20

Hymn 27: Good-Nature to Animals

The man of Mercy (says the Seer)
    Shews mercy to his beast;
Learn not of churls to be severe,
    But house and feed at least.

Shall I melodious pris'ners take   5
    From out the linnet's nest,
And not keep busy care awake,
    To cherish ev'ry guest?

What, shall I whip in cruel wrath
    The steed that bears me safe,   10
Or 'gainst the dog, who plights his troth,
    For faithful service chafe?

In the deep waters throw thy bread,
    Which thou shalt find again,
With God's good interest on thy head,   15
    And pleasure for thy pain.

Let thine industrious Silk-worms reap
    Their wages to the full,
Nor let neglected Dormice sleep
    To death within thy wool.   20

Know when the frosty weather comes,
    'Tis charity to deal
To Wren and Redbreast all thy crumbs,
    The remnant of thy meal.

Tho' these some spirits think but light,   25
    And deem indifferent things;
Yet they are serious in the sight
    Of CHRIST, the King of Kings.

Hymn 28: Silence

Before thy betters with suspense,
    Into thyself withdraw;
Silence denotes superior sense,
    And shews superior awe.

Keep blessing still within thy heart,   5
    In meditation meek;
Thus thou'rt prepar'd to act thy part,
    When urg'd at length to speak.

When words break forth not duly weigh'd
    From out the babbler's tongue,   10
Full many a mournful mischief's made,
    Full many a conscience stung.

Then pray with David, that the Lord
    Would keep himself the door;
And all things from thy lips award,   15
    That make thy brother sore.

But if there be a point to praise
    Some godly deed of price,
With all thy might thy plaudits raise,
    Here silence were a vice.   20

Hymn 29: Long-Suffering of God

One hundred feet from off the ground
    That noble Aloe blows;
But mark ye by what skill profound
    His charming grandeur rose.

One hundred years of patient care   5
    The gard'ners did bestow,
Toil and hereditary pray'r
    Made all this glorious show.

Thus man goes on from year to year,
    And bears no fruit at all;   10
But gracious God, still unsevere,
    Bids show'rs of blessings fall.

The beams of mercy, dews of grace,
    Our Saviour still supplies —
Ha! ha! the soul regains her place,   15
    And sweetens all the skies.

Hymn 30: Honour

In man it is the truth affirm'd,
    Mean craft and guile withstood,
And variously by various term'd,
    Is both by grace and blood.

Courage and patriot zeal thou art,   5
    An ardour for the whole,
At once munificence of heart,
    And magnitude of soul.

In women 'tis that jealous fear,
    Which tends to parry shame;   10
It is their Chastity's barrier,
    And bulwark of their fame.

It is sweet dignity and ease,
    Reserve without disdain;
Pleasing, tho' negligent to please,   15
    Bearing, not giving pain.

Then kneel, ye little prattlers down,
    I'll bless, if you will pray,
And one shall wear the laurel crown,
    And one be Queen of May.   20

Hymn 31: Immortality

'Be of good cheer, for I, ev'n I,
  Have overcome the world;' –
The wind and tide are yours – apply
  Your oars with sails unfurl'd.

Sure Immortality was known   5
  To few, but very few,
Before I came, the corner-stone,
  To build my work anew.

But now ye know it in your hearts,
  Ye hear it with your ears;   10
Not by dark visions, or by starts,
  Its evidence appears.

Sheep, blessed sheep, ye shall be brought
  To pleasures how divine!
To joys surpassing human thought,   15
  And such as equal mine.

How brilliant past conceit each star
  Shall shine before the Lamb:
'Tis bliss to know not what ye are,
  By knowing what I AM.   20

Hymn 32: Against Despair

OLD RALPH IN THE WOOD

A Raven once an Acorn took
  From Bashan's tallest stoutest tree;
He hid it by a limpid brook,
  And liv'd another oak to see.

Thus Melancholy buries Hope,   5
  Which Providence keeps still alive,
And bids us with afflictions cope,
  And all anxiety survive.

Hymn 33: For Saturday

Now's the time for mirth and play,
Saturday's an holyday;
Praise to heav'n unceasing yield,
I've found a lark's nest in the field.

A lark's nest, then your play-mate begs   5
You'd spare herself and speckled eggs;
Soon she shall ascend and sing
Your praises to th' eternal King.

Hymn 34: For Sunday

Arise – arise – the Lord arose
    On this triumphant day;
Your souls to piety dispose,
    Arise to bless and pray.

Ev'n rustics do adorn them now,   5
    Themselves in roses dress;
And to the clergyman they bow,
    When he begins to bless.

Their best apparel now arrays
    The little girls and boys;   10
And better than the preacher prays
    For heav'n's eternal joys.

Hymn 35: At Dressing in the Morning

Now I arise, impow'r'd by Thee,
    The glorious Sun to face;
O clothe me with humility,
    Adorn me with thy grace.

All evil of the day forefend, 5
  Prevent the Tempter's snare;
Thine Angel on my steps attend,
  And give me fruit to pray'r.

O make me useful as I go
  My pilgrimage along; 10
And sweetly soothe this vale of woe
  By charity and song.

Let me from Christ obedience learn,
  To Christ obedience pay;
Each parent duteous love return, 15
  And consecrate the day.

Hymn 36: At Undressing in the Evening

These clothes, of which I now divest
  Myself, ALL-SEEING EYE,
Must be one day (that day be blest)
  Relinquish'd and laid by.

Thou cordial sleep, to death akin, 5
  I court thee on my knee;
O let my exit, free from sin,
  Be little more than Thee.

But if much agonizing pain
  My dying hour await, 10
The Lord be with me to sustain,
  To help and to abate.

O let me meet Thee undeterr'd,
  By no foul stains defil'd!
According to thy holy word, 15
  Receive me as a child.

[Hymn 37]: Pray Remember the Poor

I just came by the prison-door,
I gave a penny to the poor:
Papa did this good act approve,
And poor Mamma cried out for love.

Whene'er the poor comes to my gate,   5
Relief I will communicate;
And tell my Sire his sons shall be
As charitably great as he.

[Hymn 38]: Plenteous Redemption

David has said and sung it sweet,
That God with mercy is replete;
And thus I'll say, and thus I'll sing,
In rapture unto Christ my King.

King of my heart and my desires,   5
Which all my gratitude inspires,
Bids me be great and glorious still,
And so I must, and so I will.

[Hymn 39]: The Conclusion of the Matter

Fear God – obey his just decrees,
And do it hand, and heart, and knees;
For after all our utmost care
There's nought like penitence and prayer.

Then weigh the balance in your mind,   5
Look forward, not one glance behind;
Let no foul fiend retard your pace,
Hosanna! Thou hast won the race.

THE END

NOTES

Poems 1735–1756

TO ETHELINDA

First published in *Poems on Several Occasions* (1752), but written in 1735 according to the subtitle. 'Ethelinda' was identified by Smart's daughter, Elizabeth Le Noir, as Anne Vane, daughter of Henry Vane (later Earl of Darlington) of Raby Castle, Staindrop, where Smart spent much of his childhood. Anne Vane was nine at this time. According to Elizabeth Le Noir, 'this very spirited ode had taken such effect that these young lovers had actually set off on a runaway match together', but were 'timely prevented' (letter to E. H. Barker, *c.* 1825, Bodleian Library).

ON TAKING A BATCHELOR'S DEGREE

First published in the *Student* (September 1750) with the Horatian allusions printed as footnotes, but presumably dating from January 1744 when Smart received his BA.

ON AN EAGLE CONFINED IN A COLLEGE-COURT

First published in the *Student* (June 1751), but presumably written between 1744 and 1746 when an eagle was kept in a quadrangle at Trinity College. Text from *Poems on Several Occasions* (1752).

TO MISS H— — WITH SOME MUSIC

First published in the *Gentleman's Magazine* (June 1754) with the signature 'S', but not printed in collections of Smart's poems in the eighteenth century. It was attributed to Smart by Brittain, who recognized it as one of the poems concerning Harriote

Pratt, of Downham Market, Norfolk. Smart 'entertained a long and unsuccessful passion' for Harriote, according to his nephew, Christopher Hunter (Life of Smart in *Poems of the late Christopher Smart* (1791), vol. I). The poem was presumably written before August 1751, when Smart announced the transfer of his allegiance from 'Harriote' to Anna Maria Carnan in his song 'The Lass with the Golden Locks'. In July 1749 Smart wrote from Downham to his friend, the composer Charles Burney, that he had been listening to Harriote playing 'on her spinnet & organ at her ancient mansion' (letter reproduced in Sherbo's *Christopher Smart: Scholar of the University*). Either Downham or Norfolk would fit the lacuna in line 10. The spelling 'Harriote' is always used in Smart's manuscripts (cf. *Jubilate Agno*, B531).

ODE TO LADY HARRIOT

First published in the *Gentleman's Magazine* (February 1755), but presumably written before August 1751: see previous note. Text from *Poems of the late Christopher Smart* (1791).

INSCRIPTIONS ON AN AEOLIAN HARP

First published in the *Student* (August 1750), but reprinted without Smart's name in the *Gentleman's Magazine* (April 1754) in a letter about Aeolian harps signed 'Philo-Musicus' (probably a pseudonym for Smart himself). The Aeolian harp was a recent innovation in England, although it had been invented in the seventeenth century by Athanasius Kircher. Kircher's description of his instrument in *Musurgia Universalis* (Rome, 1650) is summarized in the *Gentleman's Magazine*, but the earliest English references are accredited to James Thomson in *The Castle of Indolence* and 'Ode on Aeolus's Harp' (both 1748). The allusion to Memnon's 'harp' is based on the common but erroneous assumption that the ancient statue of Memnon, which was said to emit music in response to the sun's rays at dawn and sunset, represented Memnon holding a harp or lyre. Smart had already used the image of Memnon's lyre, with almost identical phraseology, in his Tripos verses, *Mutua osci-tationum propagatio solvi potest mechanice* (1743). But 'Inscriptions' is one of the first poems to use the Aeolian harp as a trope for spontaneous lyrical utterance. The motto, 'Waft some part, O winds, to the ears of the gods', is from the singing contest in Virgil's third pastoral.

THE AUTHOR APOLOGIZES TO A LADY

First published in the *Student* (October 1750); text from *Poems on Several Occasions* (1752). The mottoes from Pliny ('Nature is never more complete than in her smallest creature') and Homer ('small and dear') accentuate the mock-heroic element in Smart's self-justification.

TO MY WORTHY FRIEND, MR T. B.

First published in the *Midwife* (June 1753). Mr T. B. was Timothy Bevan (1704–86) who, with his brother Silvanus, established an apothecary's business in London. He lived in Hackney in a large Georgian villa with well-kept gardens and shrubberies. His only daughter, Priscilla, was born in 1737; Cicero's love for his daughter Tullia was legendary.

TO THE REV. MR POWELL

First published in the *Gray's-Inn Journal* (May 1753) as 'An Epistle to the Reverend Mr Evan Pritchard of — in Glamorganshire'; reprinted in the *Midwife* (June 1753) with the name in the title left blank but the text substantially the same as in *Poems of the late Christopher Smart* (1791), the version reproduced here. Morgan Powell, a Cambridge friend of Smart, came from Carmarthenshire; Evan Pritchard has not been identified. The 'Act' (line 19) refers to the game laws, under which only possessors of specified property qualifications were allowed to hunt hares and other game. Line 31 refers to the fable of the cock who rejected a pearl found in a dunghill (Phaedrus III, 11).

APOLLO AND DAPHNE

First published in the *Midwife* (December 1750); text from *Poems on Several Occasions* (1752).

THE MISER AND THE MOUSE
First published in April 1751 in both the *Student* and the *Midwife*; text here from the *Student*. The poem is an imitation of an epigram attributed to Lucilius in the *Greek Anthology*.

DISERTISSIME ROMULI NEPOTUM
First published in *Poems on Several Occasions* (1763), but presumably written before 1756, when William Murray became Lord Mansfield. A distinguished lawyer, Lord Chief Justice from 1756 to 1788, Murray was renowned especially for his powers of oratory. He was one of Smart's first patrons, encouraging the young poet to write to Pope in 1743 with a sample of his translation of Pope's *Essay on Criticism* (1711) into Latin. The epigram is an imitation of Catullus.

CARE AND GENEROSITY
First published in the *Midwife* (September 1751); text from *Poems on Several Occasions* (1752).

THE COUNTRY SQUIRE AND THE MANDRAKE
First published in the *Gentleman's Magazine* (April 1755); text from *Poems of the late Christopher Smart* (1791). The moral of the fable (lines 53–6) depends on the supposed resemblance of the root of the mandrake plant to the human form.

A STORY OF A COCK AND A BULL
First published in the *Literary Magazine* (May/June 1756). The jingoist sentiments (lines 1–10) are not wholly tongue-in-cheek; the boast that Englishmen were superior to Frenchmen, by varying ratios, was proverbial. Cf. Garrick, *Upon Johnson's Dictionary*: 'Talk of war with a Briton, he'll boldly advance,/ That one English soldier is worth ten of France.' A 'main' (line 42) was a cock-fight.

'HAIL, ENERGEIA! HAIL, MY NATIVE TONGUE'
First published in the *Universal Visiter* (January 1756) at the conclusion of a prose essay, 'Some Thoughts on the English Language'. The essay ends with the contention that iambic metre

gains a 'weight and dignity' in English, which it lacks in Latin, because of the abundance of monosyllables and consonants in the English language. English iambics therefore are 'extremely animated and majestic'. Smart's opening lines challenge Milton's description of the 'sinews weak' of his 'native tongue' ('At a Vacation Exercise in the College', 1–2); his own description of the resources of the language (lines 5–10) is indebted to Pope's *Essay on Criticism*, 366–71.

Seatonian Poems

ON THE ETERNITY OF THE SUPREME BEING

Published in Cambridge in April 1750 by the university printer, this was the first of Smart's winning entries for the annual Seatonian Prize (established in that year), awarded to a member of the university for a poem on 'the Perfections or Attributes of the Supreme Being'. Smart's Seatonian poems were generally regarded in the eighteenth century as both the best of their kind and the crowning achievement of his poetic career. He was said to have been inspired by the elevated language of the Psalms (*Gentleman's Magazine*, May 1751), to have achieved a manner 'truly Miltonian' (*English Review*, May 1792) and to have 'written with the sublimest energies of religion, and the true enthusiasm of poetry' (Hunter, *Poems of the late Christopher Smart*, 1791, vol. I), but the boldness of his aspirations was also seen as the cause of his breakdown: 'Wrapt in a vision, he presum'd to sing/The attributes of Heav'n's eternal King:/But O! approaching tow'rds the Throne of light,/Its flashing splendors overpow'r'd his sight' (John Lockman, 'A Thought, on reading a Bill for the acting of Merope', *Daily Advertiser*, 29 January 1759).

Both in form and in subject-matter, the Seatonian Prize poems belong to a sub-genre already well-established by 1750, the religious-didactic verse essay, usually in heroic couplets or blank verse. Such poems commonly attempted to reconcile modern scientific concepts with traditional theology, by celebrating the order, variety and infinite extent of the universe as evidence of

NOTES

the wisdom and power of God, the great 'Artificer' (line 33);
they also acknowledged the incapacity of human reason to
comprehend his purpose and the impropriety of questioning his
ways (lines 43–61). Exercises on eschatological themes in ele-
vated language were another common feature of the genre:
Smart's description of the Day of Judgement (lines 62–120) was
particularly admired as a sample of 'sublime' expression. The
only unusual element in 'On the Eternity' is the idea, found in
various forms in occult writings, that natural objects are
inscribed with the divine signature (lines 2–5; cf. *Jubilate Agno*,
B477–91). This is the earliest intimation in Smart's poetry of his
sacramental conception of nature.

The appeal for divine assistance in his poetic endeavours (lines
13–21) is more than conventional rhetoric. It represents Smart's
developing idea of the consecrated poet who, though *uninspired*
in theological terms (i.e., not actuated directly by divine influ-
ence, as were the authors of the Scriptures), may yet overcome
the limitations of human language (lines 6–12). This requires
the intervention of God, Great Poet of the Universe, whose
inspiring word was the agent of creation (lines 21–5). The
concept of God as *Poet* (from the Greek word ποιητής which
means 'maker'), and hence of the universe as his *Poem*, was a
common Renaissance trope; the implication that the human
poet replicates the work of divine creation is not far below the
surface. Smart's mottoes, from Horace ('We attempt lofty
themes') and Virgil ('Neither the gods nor his own strength
suffice'), reflect a sense of his own audacity, but the emphasis is
still on the deficiency of the 'human tongue' until it is 'new-
tun'd' after death (lines 127–30).

ON THE IMMENSITY OF THE SUPREME BEING
First published in Cambridge in April 1751. The poem recapi-
tulates the 'Argument from Design' tirelessly reiterated by
'physico-theologians'; i.e., that the existence of God is proved
by the evidence of purpose and design in the physical universe,
including the human form itself. Smart's increasing self-confi-
dence manifests itself in his adoption of the language of the

Psalter: lines 2–5 are a paraphrase of Psalm 57:9. As a contemporary critic noted, 'Mr Smart has kept that most divine poet the *Psalmist* in his eye, almost through the whole of this work' (*Monthly Review*, May 1751). Along with his Davidian stance, goes the idea of a spontaneous language of praise which the natural creation already utters and which it is the task of the poet to emulate (lines 6–11). The poem makes a significant advance on the first Seatonian essay: the attunement of the soul required to enable the poet to join in the universal chorus of adoration is now represented as an accomplished fact (lines 140–45).

ON THE OMNISCIENCE OF THE SUPREME BEING

First published in Cambridge in November 1752. Urania, the Muse of Astronomy, had been appropriated for divine poetry since the Renaissance, but Smart was doubtless influenced particularly by Milton's Urania, who 'with eternal Wisdom didst converse' (see *Paradise Lost*, VII, 1–39). The contrast (lines 31ff) between instinctive knowledge, communicated to animals immediately by God (their 'science', line 86), and the limited, uncertain knowledge laboriously acquired by man, was frequently made by 'physico-theologians' (see W. Derham, *Physico-Theology* (1713) vol. IV, chs. xi and xiii, but cf. also Prior, *Solomon* (1708), vol. I, and Pope, *Essay on Man*, III, 83–98). Smart's scientific references come from a mixture of ancient and modern sources. The need for a reliable means of measuring longitude at sea (line 91) had led to the appointment of a parliamentary committee in 1714, to which Newton submitted a paper enumerating various possible methods (for Smart's continuing interest in this topic see *Jubilate Agno*, B169). While still a young graduate at Cambridge, Smart had read Newton's *Opticks* (1704), in which the rainbow was explained in terms of refraction (lines 101–2). On the other hand, the 'scale of being' (line 163), i.e., the concept of a graduated scale or chain linking all creatures, from microscopic organisms up to man and thence through supernatural beings ultimately to God himself, developed in the Middle Ages out of ideas originating with Plato and

Aristotle, though it reached its widest dissemination as a scientific principle in the eighteenth century. The tailpiece, *TΩ ΘΕΩ ΔΟΞΑ*, is a liturgical formula, 'Glory to God', but it could also be interpreted as 'Knowledge [be ascribed] to God.'

ON THE POWER OF THE SUPREME BRING

First published in Cambridge in January 1754, but written by 5 December 1753 when it was awarded the Seatonian Prize. Although the Psalms remain a strong influence, the poem differs from its predecessors both in its emphasis on the specifically Christian manifestation of God's power (lines 108–45) and in its topicality. Lines 51–6 refer to severe earth tremors which shook London in 1750, causing great alarm and prompting the Bishop of London to issue an admonitory *Letter to the Clergy and People of London* (1750) interpreting the event as a warning to the citizens against their sins and a summons to repentance. Lines 83–4 refer to recent experiments with electricity reported in contemporary periodicals. On the other hand, the description of magnetism as 'sympathetic love' (line 80) reverts to pre-Newtonian explanations of attraction, in keeping with Smart's depreciation of modern philosophy (85–90).

ON THE GOODNESS OF THE SUPREME BEING

First published in Cambridge in March 1756, but written by 28 October 1755 when it was awarded the Seatonian Prize. The invocation is full of Miltonic echoes (cf. *Paradise Lost*, I, 17–23 and VII, 12–14), but Smart, unlike Milton, deliberately merges his classical and Christian sources of inspiration. Orpheus, son of Apollo and the Muse Calliope, whose skill as a lyre-player was said to be so consummate that his music could move inanimate nature (lines 1–5), was traditionally the archetype of the inspired poet. But where Milton dissociates 'the Orphean lyre' from his 'heavenly Muse' (*Paradise Lost*, III, 17–19), Smart reclaims Orpheus for divine poetry by identifying him with David. His authority, indicated in the footnote, is Patrick Delany's *Historical Account of the Life and Reign of David King of Israel* (1740–42). The description of light (lines 23–44) is notable for its fusion of Miltonic and Newtonian elements.

HYMN TO THE SUPREME BEING

Published by John Newbery in June 1756, with a dedication to Dr James, inventor of a well-known fever powder, whose judgement and medicines are claimed to have rescued Smart three times from the grave 'in a manner almost miraculous' (since Newbery had exclusive rights over the distribution of James's Fever Powders, the dedication should not be taken altogether at face value). Both the date and the precise nature of the illness that occasioned the poem are uncertain (Smart had suffered illnesses serious enough to attract notice in the press twice previously, in 1752 and 1753), but there is no reason to doubt the reality of the spiritual crisis it precipitated. Although not formally connected with the Seatonian poems, 'Hymn to the Supreme Being' is linked with them by title and by allusion to the divine attributes treated in them (lines 55–7). The experience it describes is the culmination of a process that can be traced through these earlier poems: a steady progression from generalized theism, in 'On the Eternity', to the specifically Christian emphasis of 'On the Power'. Simultaneously there is a growth in the poet's sense of attunement to the harmony of all creation: the Herbertian imagery in line 74 (see Herbert's *Easter*) looks back to the 'tuning' metaphor in the first two Seatonian poems. Contemporary critics, however, thought Smart's expression of religious feeling too effusive, finding in the 'Hymn' 'more gratitude than genius, and more piety than poetry' (*Critical Review*, June 1756).

Jubilate Agno

Jubilate Agno was written over a period of about four years during Smart's incarceration in a private madhouse from 1758/9 to the end of January 1763. The manuscript remained unknown to the public until 1939, when it was published by W. F. Stead under the title *Rejoice in the Lamb: A Song from Bedlam*. A radically revised edition was published in 1954 by W. H. Bond, who was the first to discover the arrangement of the text evidently intended by Smart.

The manuscript consists of a quantity of loose sheets, covered on both sides with a series of closely written, unnumbered verses, each beginning with the word *Let* or *For*. *Let* and *For* verses are never combined on the same sheet, but it seems that the sheets were numbered in pairs. Originally there must have been eleven pairs of double-sheets, folded to produce four pages each (making a total of eighty-eight pages); what remains are seven double-sheets (some of which have become disjoined) and two single sheets (a total of thirty-two pages). Of these, four are *Let* double-sheets, numbered 1, 3, 10 and 11 respectively, and three are *For* double-sheets, numbered 3, 4 and 5 respectively. The single sheets, one *Let*, one *For*, are the unnumbered halves of original double-sheets. The surviving sheets fall into four groups, labelled alphabetically by Bond. The following table shows the relationship of the text printed here to the manuscript:

A1–113 *Let* sheet no. 1
B1–295 *Let* sheet no. 3   B1–295 *For* sheet no. 3
                                         B296–512 *For* sheet no. 4
                                         B513–768 *For* sheet no. 5
C1–162 *Let* [sheet no. 7?]   C1–162 *For* [sheet no. 7?]
D1–128 *Let* sheet no. 10
D129–237 *Let* sheet no. 11

Fragment C comprises the pair of unnumbered single sheets, the cognate leaves of which would have carried the verses preceding and following the surviving C text. Fragment D breaks off before the end of sheet 11, and the work was clearly discontinued at this point.

Where both sets of verses survive, concurrence of folio numbers, dates within the text, and other evidence indicate that they were intended to correlate, each *Let* verse answered by a *For* verse. The model may well have been the antiphonal pattern of Hebrew poetry as explained in Robert Lowth's *De sacra poesi Hebraeorum* (1753), a work which Smart knew well. At the same time, however, both *Let* and *For* verses have their own sequentiality, formal or thematic: there is thus a network of linkages, giving scope for a complex interplay of meaning. In practice, both *Let–For* correspondences and internal continuities frequently break down. Nevertheless, in spite of its disjunctions, its heterogeneity, its obscurities and the seemingly bizarre juxtaposition of orders of experience normally felt to be discrete, *Jubilate Agno* is neither hopelessly incoherent nor lacking in a logic of its own. Its disparate elements are held together by a comprehensive evangelical purpose, and an underlying scheme of ideas.

The work proclaims itself at the start as a vast hymn of praise. It is in accord with the exhortation in 'On the Goodness of the Supreme Being' to 'join in the general chorus of all worlds', and fulfils Smart's vow in 'Hymn to the Supreme Being': 'Deeds, thoughts, and words no more his mandates break,/But to [God's] endless glory work, conceive, and speak.' The *Let* verses are modelled on the canticle sung at mattins in the Church of England, *Benedicite omnia opera*: 'O all ye works of the Lord, bless ye the Lord: praise him, and magnify him for ever' (echoed in D73). The *Benedicite* provides the pattern both for the catalogue of creatures or objects in their classes who are called upon to praise the Lord, and for the use of individual names ('O Ananaias, Azarias, and Misael, bless ye the Lord: praise him, and magnify him for ever'). Names of persons in Fragments A–C are all taken from the Bible (including the Apocrypha), with the one unexplained exception of Campanus (B166), a mad apocalyptic prophet whom Smart could have read about in the translation of Pierre Bayle's *Dictionnaire historique et critique*, which he used at Cambridge. The non-Biblical names in fragment D, it has been shown, were probably taken from obituary listings in current periodicals (see Arthur Sherbo, *Modern Language Notes*, 71 (1956), pp. 177–82). Names of animals, plants, gems and so on are drawn from a variety of sources, including contemporary works of natural history, travel books and herbals, but the main authority is Pliny's *Natural History*; for, Smart asserts, 'all the creatures mention'd by Pliny are somewhere or other extant to the glory of God' (B620).

The *For* verses reveal the evangelical motive of the work: Smart presents himself as a Christian warrior (B19–21), preaching the Gospel (B9) and uttering prophecies (C57ff) to recall mankind, but especially the English people (B332), to Christian worship and redemption. His ideas about the genealogy of races, the origins and nature of language, music and sounds, the history of the early Church, reform of the liturgy and so on, as well as his notions of the final destiny of mankind and the universe, are all related to his evangelical mission.

It also involves a thorough-going revision of current principles of natural philosophy. Smart sets out to defend the 'philosophy of scripture' against the 'vain deceit' of modern philosophy (B130, B219). His phrasing echoes the words used by St Paul to warn Christians against the enticements of secular philosophy, for 'in [Christ] are hid all the treasures of wisdom and knowledge' (Colossians 2). On this basis, Smart develops his own cosmology, in which the mathematical laws of Newtonian science are replaced by animistic forces sustained and directed by God (B160ff). In an age of scientific materialism, as he perceived it, Smart vindicates the creed that things of the spirit are the true reality (B258). A wide and eclectic range of reading is pressed into the service of this ambitious project. Smart was acquainted not only with the standard works of classical learning, philosophy, theology, science, literature, and ancient and modern history, but also with hermetic and cabbalist lore. The influence of occult writings is seen in such ideas as the concept of 'intelligences' informing the universe (B234, B317–8, B677), of 'spiritual' water (B207), of the air as a repository of human voices and spirits (B221, B224, B348), and in the alphabetical and numerological schemes in Fragments B and C. The most important source of *Jubilate Agno*, however, remains the Bible. The Word of God is for Smart the key to all knowledge and truth, *Word* being used in its triple sense of Logos, the creative principle; Christ, the voice of truth (B288, D84); and the Scriptures. Newton's error in Smart's eyes was caused by neglect of this fact (B195, B220, B648).

Smart's linguistic ideas and experiments are intimately connected with his philosophy. Language for him is not a Lockean system of arbitrary signs, but a complex symbolic code at every level: syntax, words and letters (B477–91, B513ff, B624–47). Puns and other forms of word-play, often involving two or more languages, are vitally functional as well as a manifest source of delight. Not since the Metaphysical Poets had the potential for polysemy inherent in linguistic forms been so tirelessly and creatively exploited as it is in *Jubilate Agno*. Smart's linguistic experiments are also related to his concern to give language greater concreteness or 'impression' (B404; the metaphor comes from the process of type-founding: see note on *The Works of Horace, Translated into Verse*). To this end, grammar and syntax are freely adapted for the sake of conciseness, emphasis or figurative force. Smart uses archaisms, such as 'earning' for 'yearning' (B672), northern dialect words, new formations and coinages, or unfamiliar applications of familiar words, such as 'jeopardy' for captivity (B1, B560), and the expressive noun 'prank' for the antics of a cat (A57, B628–9). Smart's Cat Jeoffry (B695–768) has a significant place in the whole scheme of things: his actions demonstrate one of Smart's most fundamental ideas, first developed in the Seatonian poems, that all creatures worship God simply by manifesting their individual natures to the full (cf. B228–30).

Jubilate Agno is richer in personal and topical allusions than any other of Smart's major works. The names of individuals mentioned in the text provide a roll-call of Smart's family; his friends from childhood up to the time of his confinement (the reference to Samuel Johnson in D74 provides a footnote to the visit to Smart reported in Boswell's *Life of Johnson*); his patrons and publishers; his literary, political and military heroes; his 'fellow-prisoners'; and subscribers to the *Translation of the Psalms* which he was already preparing.

One group of names represents his childhood and family connections with Kent and Durham. He mentions with pride the Welsh origins of his mother (B91), who came from Radnorshire. Smart's father came from Co. Durham but moved to Kent as steward to Lord Vane (D22) of Fairlawn in Shipbourne where Smart spent his first eleven years (B119, B168). After his father's death the family moved back to Co. Durham where they came under the patronage of the Vanes of Raby Castle. Anne Vane, the object of Smart's juvenile love poem, 'To Ethelinda', is remembered with particular feeling, both by her maiden name and by her married name Hope (B534, C104, D186; B666–7 probably also refers to her). The reference in B46–52 is more obscure, but it presumably relates to the estate on Staindrop Moor, formerly belonging to his uncle, to which Smart was heir-at-law (cf. B23). He appears to have signed away his claim on the estate in favour of his mother but to have had continuing doubts about the prudence of his action: the birds in the *Let* verses are all terms for a fool, dupe or cheat. Other Durham names include the Master of Durham School in Smart's time, Richard Dongworth, and his successor, Thomas Randall (D28–9); his patrons, George Bowes (B609), and the Duke of Cleveland (B683) who helped pay for his Cambridge education; John Gordon (B286) and Thomas Bowlby (B254) who were at school with him; churchmen Henry Bland (D176), Prebendary of Durham, and Cornelius Harrison (D88), Perpetual Curate of Darlington.

A large number of the names that can be confidently identified relate to Smart's years at Cambridge. These include pupils and fellow undergraduates, Thomas Anguish (B288), John Bird (C43), Richard Chase (D113), Leonard Cutting (C134), Richard Gulstone and Francis Halford (D115), John Higgs (B66) and the four, all from Christ's College, named in D24; Fellows of Pembroke and other colleges, Richard Atwood (B226), Francis Burton (D109), John Delap (B655), Richard Lyne (B288), Charles Mason (B282), John Peele (C150), John Rust (D59), Robert Tilson (D122) and Stephen Whisson (B312). Jermyn Pratt, whose sister Harriote (B531) Smart courted for some years (see 'To Miss H— —' and note), was also a friend in Smart's undergraduate days; their father, Roger Pratt of Ruston (Ryston), is commemorated in D105.

Smart's years in London and his hectic activities in popular journalism and the theatre are reflected in the numerous names of writers, musicians and entertainers: composers Charles Burney (Smart's most loyal friend), Thomas and Michael Arne (D196), all of whom wrote settings for Smart's songs; musicians Baumgarden (B592), a bassoon-player, and Benjamin Hallet (B243), a celebrated boy-flautist; a troupe of French dancers, the Graniers (D160), whom, typically, Smart wants to be 'Englished' (i.e., naturalized); the proprietor of Sadler's Wells, Thomas Rosoman (D156), and the proprietor of Vauxhall Gardens, Jonathan Tyers (B455, D144). Contemporary poets and writers include Smart's friends Christopher Anstey (D104), Charles Churchill (B295), Robert Lloyd (D62), William Mason (D80) and William Whitehead (B660). Also named are printers or booksellers with whom Smart had dealings: Crockatt (D210), Flexney (D62), Fletcher (B263) and Gosling (B684).

Smart's references to his wife, Anna Maria, and children, Marianne ('Polly') and Elizabeth ('Bess') provide telling hints of the breakdown of his marriage and his anxieties about its consequences (B7, B55–6, B59, B75–6; see also C73, C108, C128). Anna Maria was a Roman Catholic, and hence, like Ruth, a 'Moabitish woman' (B56; 'Moabite' was a Puritan term of abuse for Roman Catholics; also used by Smart for the French in B399). Smart's wish is that Polly should be brought up in the Church of England (identified with the 'house of David' in B55) rather than in her mother's faith. The children were in fact sent away to a French convent.

Smart evidently kept abreast of current events while he was in the madhouse by reading newspapers and periodicals, and he followed the progress of Britain and her allies in the war against France (1756–63) with keen interest. By July 1759, when the first references occur, the war was beginning to swing in Britain's favour, and Smart readily assimilated the victories of Britain and her allies into his prophecies. References to 'the West' (B8) probably allude to the capture of French settlements on the Guinea coast of West Africa in 1758, and the capture of Guadeloupe in the West Indies in April 1759. By the late summer, the navy was involved in important actions at Le Havre, Lagos Bay and Brest (B260); victories in 1759 were so frequent that Horace Walpole complained that the church bells were worn out from ringing (B353), and Smart interpreted England's success as the beginning of the millennium (B382). He greeted the news of the capture of Havana in September 1762 with enthusiasm (D112), deplored its restoration under the terms of the peace treaty signed by Britain, France and Spain

in November (D191), and commemorated one of the sailors
who died in the action (D157).

Four textual changes should be noted: the insertion of
'nothing' in B258, 'I' in B282, 'at' in B290 (all suggested by
Stead) and 'the' in D212 (Stephen the Preacher').

FRAGMENT A

The single sheet in the manuscript that corresponds to Fragment
A contains no clue to its date, but inference based on the dating
of Fragment B would suggest that it was written some time
between June 1758 and April 1759, i.e., after Smart's discharge
from St Luke's Hospital, and probably after his admission to
the private madhouse.

The creatures are more systematically related to their
accompanying Biblical characters than in the following frag-
ments. The connections are made sometimes by direct allusion
to biblical stories (Balaam and the Ass in A11; Daniel and the
Lion in A13), sometimes by oblique reference (A26; Joshua is
compared to a unicorn in Numbers 24:8). Other connections
are generic. An important theme is the supersession of Judaic
rigour by Christian mercy. Thus a series of creatures that are
'unclean' by Jewish law culminates in A63 with the swine,
associated with Cornelius, a Christian convert (the only New
Testament name in Fragment A): as a gentile, Cornelius was
'unclean' but was baptized by Peter after a vision in which Peter
was warned not to despise the creatures whom God had cleansed
(Acts 10). In A90 a reference to the Christ-child prefigured in
Isaiah 11:6 follows after a series of predatory animals, and
recalls Isaiah's prophecy of harmony among all creatures at the
coming of the Messiah, to the confounding of Satan ('the
Adversary').

Most of the verses can be elucidated, where necessary, with
the help of a biblical concordance, but A49 probably contains a
private allusion to Smart's hereditary claim to an estate on
Staindrop Moor (see B23), formerly in the possession of his
uncle: Shallum similarly was owner of land to which his nephew
had reversionary rights (Jeremiah 32:6–12).

FRAGMENT B

Dates in Fragment B indicate that *Let* sheet 3 and *For* sheet 3
(B1–295) were written at the rate of three verses a day from 27
July to 29 October 1759; sheet 4 (B296–512) at one a day from
30 October 1759 to 1 June 1760; sheet 5 (B513–768) again at
three a day from 2 June to 26 August 1760. The creatures in
B1–122 (*Let* sheet 3) are also usually grouped in threes: two
birds followed by an animal or other creature. With the switch
to New Testament names at B123, Smart embarks on a long
catalogue of fish, obviously with reference to the idea of the
apostles as 'fishers of men' (Matthew 4:19): cf. B110, B131,
B142.

In the opening *For* verses, Smart adopts the stance of an
Ezekiel, prophesying from captivity: his abstinence (B5) is in
accord with his priestly role (see Ezekiel 44:21). Modern events
are persistently associated with events in biblical history, by
puns, analogy or other means: e.g., the prayer for peace (B4) is
linked with Jael, whose assassination of Sisera with a nail
ushered in a period of peace for Israel; the 'host' in the west
(B8) relates British victories in West Africa and the West Indies
to Isaiah's prophecy of victory over the Philistines 'toward the
west' (Isaiah 11:14). A more elaborate typology links Israel with
both Rome and England through Joab (B62, B433–4); hence
the collocation of Ehud, Mutius Scaevola and Colonel Draper
(B19), heroes of their respective nations (see 'Ode to General
Draper'), and hence also Smart's boast of descent from Abraham
(B73). His genealogical fantasies are tied up with his sense of a
special calling as Christian champion: in deleted passages in B54
and B58 he equates Agricola, the Roman governor of Britain,
with St George, both names meaning 'farmer'. B58 originally
read: 'For Agricola is SAINT GEORGE, but his son CHRIS-
TOPHER', etc. 'Pheon', the heraldic term for arrow, formed
part of the Smart coat of arms.

Verses in this fragment are often linked with dates in the
Church calendar: B16 was written on 1 August, Lammas Day,
a harvest festival: Smart plays on the idea of late harvest. B139
was written on the eve of 8 September, the Feast of the Nativity
of the Virgin Mary: Smart links Mary's freedom from original

sin (her Immaculate Conception according to Roman Catholic doctrine) with the virgin birth of Christ. B162 was written on Holy Cross Day: St Christopher ('Christ-bearer') is identified with Simon of Cyrene, the bearer of Christ's cross. B31, written on 7 August, the Feast of the Name of Jesus, prompts one of Smart's most complicated exercises in allusion (the choice of 'Convolvulus' is not fortuitous). The linking idea is that of divine blessing, symbolized by 'girth' (i.e., girdle or cincture, hence the association with 'ring'), as in the proverb 'ungirt, unblessed'. Smart's specific reference is to God's exhortation in Job 38:3 ('Gird up now thy loins like a man; for I will demand of thee'), but the girdle is a common biblical symbol for righteousness and faithfulness. The girdle/ring association leads on to the 'signet', which is a symbol of God's blessing in Jeremiah 22:24. The 'Stone' refers both to the biblical designation of Jesus as the corner-stone of the true faith, and to the patristic identification of him as the 'pearl of great price' (Matthew 13:46): cf. *Hymns and Spiritual Songs*, 2.48.

B45 is one of several entries that reflect Smart's High Church leanings: 'great mess' is the archaic form for High Mass, a term frowned on by strict Protestants. Note also Smart's concern with fasting (B117; cf. C70), observance of the Sabbath as distinct from the Lord's Day (B212), reservation of the Sacrament (B206) and reform of the Liturgy (B252, B511–12; cf. C100). His ideas about Church history (B225, B231–4) are more eccentric, but not mere caprice. In *Origines Britannicae* (1685), Edward Stillingfleet contended that St Paul was the founder of the Christian Church in England. Similarly, the legend recorded by William of Malmesbury that the church at Glastonbury was dedicated by Christ himself was still being quoted in Rapin's *History of England* (1725–31). Smart's doctrinal principles, however, are generally orthodox, with the exception of his eschatological speculations, which appear to be based on some of the controversial doctrines attributed to Origen (B170–176; cf. B291–5, B329–31, B420). Smart's notion seems to be that the history of creation consists of a succession of 'Eternities' (corresponding to Origen's 'aeons') destined to culminate in a purgative fire, which will purify even

the basest sinners (B330). Eternity is a 'creature' (B170), in the
sense that it is a property of the physical creation, not inherent
in the divine order of things: καταβολη επι τη διαβολη ('foun-
dation upon [or downfall after] Satan') is a punning condensa-
tion of Origen's argument that Creation is a consequence of the
Fall, or is itself the Fall. God himself is 'beyond Eternity' (B331)
and so is Hell (B322).

Smart's attack on modern science and exposition of his own
animistic principles begin at B160. His scientific learning was
broad rather than profound. Library records at Pembroke
College show that he used Newton's *Principia* and *Opticks*,
Woodward's and Burnet's cosmogonies and Van Musschen-
broek's *Experimental Physics*. He also knew Chambers's *Cyclo-
paedia* (1728), which alone would be sufficient to account for
most of the knowledge displayed in *Jubilate Agno*. Through
periodicals like the *Gentleman's Magazine* he would moreover
have seen regular reports of the *Philosophical Transactions* of
the Royal Society. On some topics, such as electricity (B260–67,
B760–62) and the properties and uses of mica, for which he
coins the term 'Gladwick', i.e., 'benign light' (B199–203), he
draws on recent experiments and discussions. But on other
issues he is out of date. The problem of determining longitude
at sea (B169, B190, B349) had become a matter of keen public
interest since the establishment in 1714 of an official committee
to consider the question and the offer of a substantial reward
for the discovery of a practicable solution. Smart, however,
seems unaware of, or was perhaps uninterested in, the develop-
ment of an accurate marine chronometer, by means of which
the problem was already being overcome. He follows the old
percolation theory of the origins of fountains, springs and rivers
(B206), which had been superseded in the 1730s by the conden-
sation theory. He subscribes to the idea of the circulation of sap
(B341), which had been discredited by Stephen Hales in 1727.
Interest in barometers and air-pumps (B213–20) was keen in
Smart's time, but he rejects the contemporary discussion of the
principles involved in favour of the concepts of 'sympathy' and
'life', derived from scholastic philosophy; this is in accord with
his belief in the essentially 'spiritual' nature of reality (B258).

Theories then current about the speed of light (B284–5), the apparent magnitude of the moon on the horizon (B426–30) and the precession of the equinoxes (B347) are similarly ignored or rejected in favour of mystical explanations of such phenomena.

FRAGMENT C

This fragment is the most esoteric, the one most indebted to occult writings and Smart's personal fantasies and obsessions. It appears to have been written from 21 February to 12 May 1761. Biblical names come mainly from Ezra and Nehemiah, and the botanical names from eighteenth-century herbals and medical handbooks.

The alphabetical and numerological passages (C1–49) resume the exercise begun in Fragment B, but with more specific reference to occult ideas, such as the notion of hidden languages (C40–48): C41 describes the secret language of the Cabbalists called 'notaricon', in which sentences are formed by using single words as acronyms; C45 probably refers to the 'Unwritten Cabbala', the corpus of traditions transmitted orally from generation to generation on which cabbalistic lore is said to be based. C46–7 seems to refer in a confused way to the Tetragrammaton (the four-lettered Hebrew name of God), which is regarded as the foundation of knowledge in the Cabbala. The symbol in C47, however, is not Hebrew but Arabic *lam*, *'alif* as it is represented in Walton's Polyglot Bible (1657), which Smart used at Cambridge. Smart was apparently trying to equate the Hebrew and Arabic names of God, which are then linked in C48 with the 'Unknown God' worshipped by the Athenians ('Aeolians'). According to St Paul this was in reality the Christian God (Acts 17:22–31).

Smart's interest in number-symbolism may have dated from his reading of Iamblichus' life of Pythagoras at Cambridge, but Pythagorean numerology was incorporated into Masonic ritual (for Smart's membership of the Freemasons, see B109), and various other numerological systems were current in the Renaissance. C20–24 follow Pythagorean symbolism as explained in Henry Cornelius Agrippa's *Three Books of Occult Philosophy* (1651), but Smart's symbolism is not consistently Pythagorean, or specific enough to assign to any source. C34–8 may be original: 'Cipher' (nought) 'augments' numbers by multiplying them by ten; a chain of noughts can be seen as a series of mathematical symbols for infinity. Smart identifies this chain of infinites with the chain of being, thus making Christ the summation of all things by number, as by letter (cf. C18 and Revelation 1:8: 'I am Alpha and Omega, the beginning and the ending, saith the Lord').

Smart's extended sequence of prophetic verses (C57ff) is licensed by reference to Orpheus (C52–4), not only a type of David (cf. 'On the Goodness of the Supreme Being', 1) but also the supposed origin of the mystic cult of Orphism. The elaborate discourse on horns (C118–62) has some basis in Old Testament symbolism and traditional biblical exegesis, but many of the notions are too arcane or too deeply embedded in Smart's private preoccupations to be intelligible.

FRAGMENT D

This fragment was written from 12 June 1762 to 30 January 1763 when Smart was rescued from the madhouse by John Sherratt and other friends (D235; see also 'Epistle to John Sherratt'). The Latin names of precious stones, herbs and creatures come from Pliny, but the descriptions are mostly taken (often verbatim) from the standard Latin dictionary of the time, Ainsworth's *Thesaurus linguae latinae* (1736), even when Ainsworth deviates from Pliny or is incorrect. The birds in D187–208 are all so described in Albin's *Natural History of Birds* (1731–8). The Tunal-Tree and Copec (D213–14) are both described in Daniel Coxe's *Description of Carolana* (1722). Some of the names, however, are Smart's invention or error, suggesting that he was working partly from memory. Engalacton (D95), 'milk-producing', and Neottophora (D185), 'young-bearing', are Smart's own coinages from Greek. Murrion (D147) is not a creature but a variant of 'morion', a helmet without a beaver. Shag-green (D184) is not an animal but the leather itself. The Albicore (D193) is a fish.

Many of the comments arise directly from the personal names, by word-play or other association. In D17, for example, defence of the Tory 'landed interest' (landowners), is associated with the name 'Freeman': Ralph Freeman was a leading Hanoverian Tory. The comments in D39–40 refer to Thomas Pelham, who adopted the name 'Holles' on inheriting the Holles estate and was afterwards created Duke of Newcastle. John Rust (D59) was tutor to the son of Sir Richard Hoare. The name 'Close' (D73) signals the end of the catalogue of precious stones with the refrain from the *Benedicite*. William Hunter (D133), Smart's brother-in-law and father of Christopher (B65), was a doctor, hence his association with Balsam. Hogarth (D193) married the daughter of Sir James Thornhill whose paintings decorated the interior of Adgecomb House. James Merrick (D203) was known to be preparing a translation of the Psalms. By this stage, Smart was working on his own version, and on the *Hymns and Spiritual Songs* (see D148, D199, D208): many of the people named in Fragment D were subscribers to his volume. The Latin quotations in D84 probably also refer to Smart's Psalms and *Hymns*: the first ('A way must be found . . .'), from Virgil's third Georgic, is about trying new ways of writing; the second ('The way, the truth, the life are Christ', adapted from John 14:6) could allude to Smart's Christianizing of the Psalms.

The fish surreally named in D11 is probably a recollection of the 'large kind of flat fish' described in George Anson's *Voyage Round the World* (1748), which Anson thought was 'the fish that is said frequently to destroy pearl-divers, by clasping them in its fins'; Smart associates it with the injunction, 'Let the floods clap their hands' in Psalms 98:8 (Book of Common Prayer version). The idea of applause had a special place in his theology: see B343–4. To clothe a horse (D158), i.e., cover with a blanket, was a term used in eighteenth-century farriery (for 'cloath'd' as the correct reading of this word in the manuscript, see Cecil Price, *Review of English Studies*, NS 34 (1983), p. 344).

Hymns and Spiritual Songs for the Fasts and Festivals of the Church of England

References to the *Hymns and Spiritual Songs* and to feasts and saints' days in Fragment D of the *Jubilate* (D132, D144, D148, D199), a possible allusion in *Hymns and Spiritual Songs*, 17.13–14 to a late stage in the construction of Blackfriars Bridge, and probable references in *Hymns and Spiritual Songs*, 21.27–8 and 26.17–20 to the war against Spain and Naples (declared 4 January 1762) suggest a composition date of 1762–3. The *Hymns and Spiritual Songs* were published, in *A Translation of the Psalms of David*, in August 1765.

The English Church from the Reformation adopted the metrical psalm rather than the hymn in its worship. At the beginning of the eighteenth century Isaac Watts, an Independent, argued the devotional need not only for a modern and Christianized versification of the Psalms, but also for an original hymnody. Watts's *Hymns and Spiritual Songs* (1707) provided a model and impetus for the remarkable rise of hymn-writing which was amongst the most significant literary developments of the eighteenth century. The hymn-writers included Charles Wesley, Philip Doddridge, Augustus Toplady, William Cowper and John Newton. Hymn-singing became a central element of the public worship of Independents and other dissenting groups, of Methodists, and of the Evangelical party within the Church of England. It had not, however, by Smart's time become part of the official practice of the Church of England, whose congregations continued to sing the metrical psalm.

It is clear that Smart felt, as Watts had done, the necessity in worship of an original hymnody: 'a NEW SONG also is best, if it be to the glory of God' (*Jubilate Agno*, B390; cf. *Hymns and Spiritual Songs*, 9.25–6). What is distinctive about Smart's hymn-cycle is that, unlike any Evangelical or Methodist collection, it is immediately and insistently concerned with the formal liturgy and worship of the established Church. Smart's *Hymns and Spiritual Songs* are in some ways a verse companion to the Book of Common Prayer, celebrating the feasts and fasts of the

Church calendar, with the addition of the four civic 'Solemn Days'. They are thematically and verbally related to the Scripture passages prescribed for each holiday in the eighteenth-century lectionary. Their most important source, after the Bible and the Book of Common Prayer, is Robert Nelson's *Companion for the Festivals and Fasts of the Church of England*, first published in 1704, a much reprinted and widely read commentary. Parallels or precedents for Smart's celebratory cycle of hymns on the Church year are to be found in the works of seventeenth-century devotional poets rather than eighteenth-century hymnodists. There are significant collections of hymns or poems on the Church occasions in George Wither's *Hymnes and Songs of the Church* (1623), George Herbert's *The Temple* (1633), and Jeremy Taylor's 'Festival Hymns According to the Manner of the Ancient Church' (appended to his *Golden Grove*, 1655). Perhaps the closest model is Thomas Ken's *Hymns for all the Festivals of the Year* (published in Ken's posthumous *Works*, 1721).

The theology of Smart's *Hymns and Spiritual Songs* is essentially orthodox Anglican, with some emphases of Smart's own. The text of Scripture states fully and plainly all truths essential to Christian belief, and is not to be distorted by scholastic reasoning (5.1–8, 16.49–50). The Trinity is defended in the Trinity hymn (16), and in the affirmation of the divinity of Christ the Word which begins and ends Smart's cycle. The possibility of human generosity, faithfulness and love, as well as the value and merit of charity and practical benevolence, is regularly asserted (3.61–2, 17.118, 18.34–6); but there is little reference to the doctrine of saving grace which is a common theme in Smart's *Psalms*, and none of that firm dismissal of 'idol works' so characteristic of the Evangelical hymnody. Where Evangelical hymn-writers regularly warned of the worthlessness of the fallen created world, Smart by contrast celebrates the gifts of a fruitful and innocent nature, whose beauty is an argument for and an incentive to praise and prayer (12.9, 13.11–12), and whose very function is thanksgiving (1.25–6, 2.36, 13.4, 32.29–30). In this, Smart's *Hymns and Spiritual Songs* are an especially powerful expression of the growing tendency of the eighteenth century to find in the imaginative enjoyment of nature not only pleasure but even a means of grace. Less likely to find sympathy today is Smart's anti-Romanism, especially in the four hymns on the 'Solemn Days' (5, 17, 26, 29), an attitude to some extent authorized in the Church's prescribed Forms of Prayer, and common in previous hymns and poems on these occasions.

Isaac Watts, John and Charles Wesley, and many other hymn-writers of the eighteenth century deliberately aimed at a clarity and plainness of expression appropriate to hymns designed for use in public worship by men and women of all classes and educations. There are important statements on the proper style of the popular hymn in Isaac Watts's Preface to his *Hymns and Spiritual Songs* (1707) and in John Wesley's Preface to *A Collection of Hymns, for the Use of the People Called Method-ists* (1780). Smart's *Hymns and Spiritual Songs* make far fewer concessions to the requirements of a typical congregation, and in style, as often in theme, are closer to the seventeenth-century devotional lyric. Biblical allusions are often covert (1.14), and often imaginatively integrated into the poetry (32.25–8). Smart's world of reference expands beyond the Bible to mythology (the phoenix in 6.79–80); botany (the tree of chastity in 2.40–41); history (Charles I's cryptic last word 'Remember!' in 17.98); and secular literature (the pastoral elements in 32). Many eighteenth-century hymnodists, and particularly the Evangeli-cals, preferred an often familiar and explicit imagery (the sinner's heart of stone, man as a worm, the washing away of sins in the blood of the Lamb). Smart, by contrast, frequently works with a synthesizing, associative, figurative logic, as in the image of God's ring (2.48), or the anemones ('wind-flow'rs') played upon by the sunbeams (12.10–12).

Smart's *Hymns and Spiritual Songs* are presented, and struc-tured, as a 'wreathed garland' (1.10) of praise, the conclusion of each hymn being linked by some theme or association to the beginning of the next, the cycle closing in Christ the Word. Analogues for this circular form may be found in the religious verse of the seventeenth century, in Donne's *La Corona*, for example, or in Herbert's 'Sinnes round' and 'A Wreath'.

HYMN 1

Smart makes the beginning of the Church year coincide with the beginning of the natural year. Christ leaves the angelic 'guiltless natures' in heaven to save the world from the 'rod' of wickedness (lines 14–15; see Ezekiel 7:10–11). The English are presented from the beginning of Smart's cycle as a chosen people (line 42); cf. 5.11, 17.11.

HYMN 2 (1 JANUARY)

The Circumcision is presented as a symbol of purity, as in Colossians 2:11. The hymn has two heroes. Abraham appears explicitly in lines 1–5, and is alluded to in line 41 ('chastity', the tree known in Latin as *Agnus Castus* and in English as Abraham's Balm). Christ is referred to as Shilo (cf. Genesis 49:10), and imaged as the saving 'gem' of the 'Father's ring' (cf. Jeremiah 22:24). The 'device' on the ring (lines 51, 53–4) is an adaptation of Matthew 3:17.

HYMN 3 (6 JANUARY)

The hymn's two topics, pilgrimage and childhood, are provided by Matthew 2:1–12, the Gospel for the day.

HYMN 4 (25 JANUARY)

For each of the Old Testament miracles listed in the first four stanzas, Smart offers in the concluding four a surpassing equivalent from the New Testament history of Paul (see Acts 9, 22).

HYMN 5 (30 JANUARY)

One of the four 'Solemn Days', which were formally celebrated by the Church of England from the Restoration until the nineteenth century; cf. hymns 17, 26, 29. Sermons on the martyrdom of Charles I were popular; cf. Fielding, *Joseph Andrews*, bk. 1, ch. 17.

HYMN 6 (2 FEBRUARY)

The first half of the hymn asserts the superiority of the new covenant, the temple or Church of Christ's body (see John 2:21; 1 Corinthians 3:16; Ephesians 1:22–3), over the old covenant of the law, represented by Solomon's temple. 'Hiero' (line 6) is probably a playful variation (cf. Greek: ἱερόν, 'temple'; ἱερός, 'holy') on 'Hiram' (1 Kings. 7:13ff.).

HYMN 7

Smart chooses texts on the theme of timely repentance from Luke 23:39–43 (lines 1–8), 3:8–9 (lines 21–4) and 22:61–2 (lines 31–2).

HYMN 8 (24 FEBRUARY)

Acts 1:15–26, the Epistle for this day, relates the choosing of Matthias as an apostle to replace Judas Iscariot. Other biblical allusions in this hymn are in line 33 to Christ the 'living stone ... chosen of God, and precious' (1 Peter 2:4); in line 51 to the escape of Shadrach, Meshach, and Abed-nego from the 'fiery furnace' (Daniel 3); and in line 52 to Christ's coming as a 'refiner's fire' (Malachi 3:2).

HYMN 9 (25 MARCH)

'Mary's key' (line 44) is the Magnificat (Luke 1:46–55). Her three sisters in celebratory song (43–8) are Hannah (1 Samuel 2:1–10), Deborah (Judges 5), and Judith (Judith 13, 16).

HYMN 10

Smart's emphasis on the miracles of Christ's life, rather than on the redemptive and sacramental aspects of his death, makes this unusual amongst English lyric poems on the Crucifixion.

HYMN 11

The hymn begins by calling Christians in the morning to praise and prayer, then celebrates the choral and instrumental music of an English church (lines 97–117), and ends the day of worship with the evening bells. The body of the hymn (lines 9–96) is a poetic sermon which takes its 'text' from 'sacred writ' (7–8). Lines 65–92 refer to the Harrowing of Hell; cf. 1 Peter 3:18–20; Acts 2:25–7.

HYMN 12 (25 APRIL)

The spring flowers offer a harmony of sight, parallel to the harmony of music (7–8). The pairing birds and blooming flowers of this season of the natural year serve as a calendar for the Church's year of worship (lines 16–17).

HYMN 13 (1 MAY)

The homeless and ascetic life of Philip and James is set against the riches of an English natural scene, created by God the master painter (lines 15–16) and overflowing with God's blessing (lines 19–20; cf. Luke 6:38).

HYMN 14

The hymn's central theme, Christ's infinite works and mercy, is stated in the paraphrase of John 21:25 which forms the first stanza.

HYMN 15

Always fascinated by language and its divine origins, Smart concentrates here on the gift of tongues which enabled the apostles to preach Christ's word to the nations (see Acts 2:4, 2:6). He avoids the emphasis on the pentecostal gifts of the Holy Ghost to individual believers characteristic of Evangelical and Methodist hymns on Whitsunday.

HYMN 16

Smart defends the position that the Trinity is a mystery which must be accepted against philosophic scepticism and the quibbling disputes of scholasticism (lines 7–12, 37–42). Belief in the divinity of Christ (the key issue in Trinitarian controversies) is both essential and sufficient for salvation (lines 1–6). Smart insists that the doctrine of the Trinity is clearly and unequivocally expressed in Holy Scripture. The point is made by repeated allusion to, and often by near quotation of, key texts: Matthew 18:19–20 (lines 15–18), Ephesians 4:5 (line 19), Genesis 1:26 (line 36), 1 Corinthians 12:3 (lines 51–2), 1 John 5:7 (lines 55–6).

HYMN 17 (29 MAY)

The anniversary of the Restoration of Charles II, one of the four 'Solemn Days'; known as 'Oak-Apple Day' (see line 106). The hymn is a thanksgiving for the gifts that God has bestowed upon England: the naval heroes of the past (line 28) and present (line 35); the military victories of Edward III, the Black Prince, and Henry V (lines 37–48); Anne's triumphs at war and her programme of church-building (lines 49–50); the English Reformation, the English Bible and the English Universities – the 'eyes of science' (lines 79–80). The English are the true seed of Abraham through Sarah the 'free woman' (line 11; see Genesis 16, 21:1–3; Galatians 4:28–31), sponsored in their patriotic achievements by Christ. The French, on the other hand, are 'Moab's spurious seed' (line 18; see Genesis 19:36–7). The 'dome of CHRIST' (line 15) is St Paul's Cathedral. 'Cam' (line 43) is David Gam, a hero of Agincourt. 'Stall' (line 48) is a Scottish dialect word, meaning 'body of armed men'.

HYMN 18 (11 JUNE)

The hymn focuses on the charitable generosity of Joses, 'surnamed Barnabas ... The son of consolation', who forsook worldly possessions to follow Christ (Acts 4:36–7; cf. lines 6–12).

HYMN 19 (24 JUNE)

The miraculous fertility of the Baptist's mother Elizabeth (lines 21–4; cf. Luke 1) parallels the divine benefaction of the fruits of midsummer.

HYMN 20 (29 JUNE)

Peter, dissociated from the secular power and show of Rome, is claimed as a proper saint of the sea-going Protestant English (lines 45–60). The 'sons of YEA and NAY' (line 28) were Christ's disciples; see Matthew 5:37.

HYMN 21 (25 JULY)

James the fisherman, son of Zebedee, called the 'son of thunder' (line 21; see Mark 3:17), is an evangelical prototype of the English mission, as Smart sees it, of naval trade and conquest.

HYMN 22 (24 AUGUST)

Lines 1–2 quote John 1:47. The personification of Sincerity in Smart's hymn, especially in the imagery of the last four stanzas, probably draws on the personification of Wisdom in Ecclesiasticus 24, the first Lesson for Morning Prayer.

HYMN 23 (21 SEPTEMBER)

Smart's architectural image of the Evangelists as the four pillars of the Church, at each of the points of the compass, probably derives from Irenaeus (see Migne, *Patrologia Graeca*, 7.885). Cf. Galatians 2:9, 1 Timothy 3:15, Revelation 3:12. According to patristic tradition, the Gospel of Matthew was originally written in Hebrew.

HYMN 24 (29 SEPTEMBER)

Smart's examples of the ministry of Angels are from Jude 9 (lines 13–16), Tobit 12:8–15 (lines 17–24), and Luke 1:5–19 (lines 25–8). In the last two stanzas Smart distinguishes between angels of God's presence and angels who minister and reveal knowledge to men.

HYMN 25 (18 OCTOBER)

Luke is portrayed here as doctor and artist. In Colossians 4:14 he is called 'the beloved physician'; in the Prayer Book collect for the day he is 'Physician of the soul'. According to a tradition which arose about the sixth century he painted an icon of the Virgin.

HYMN 26 (25 OCTOBER)

One of the four 'Solemn Days'; George III came to the throne on 25 October 1760.

HYMN 27 (28 OCTOBER)

This hymn is a further appropriation of saints to the English Church and people, making use of the tradition that Simon preached and was martyred in Britain (cf. Samuel Johnson, 'Upon the Feast of St Simon and St Jude', written in 1726). Lines 3–4 are explained by Romans 12:20. 'Ten thousand' (line

23) was generally accepted as the approximate number of churches in England.

HYMN 28 (1 NOVEMBER)
Smart's imagery of constellations is from Job 38:31–2, of stars and grains of sand from Genesis 15:5, 22:17.

HYMN 29 (5 NOVEMBER)
One of the four 'Solemn Days'. In Smart's time 5 November was an occasion not only for popular celebrations but also for sermons, tracts and hymns whose common themes were the Satanic promptings and wickedness of the Papist plot, and the spiritual sloth that made England vulnerable to it. The images of lazy godlessness of stanzas 2 and 3 derive from Ecclesiasticus 22:1–2 (Ecclesiasticus 22 was the first Lesson for Morning Prayer on this day) and Isaiah 22:13.

HYMN 30 (30 NOVEMBER)
Christ prophesies the crucifixion of his prophets (line 30) in Matthew 23:34. The mosques (line 43) are those of Constantinople, whither, according to tradition, Andrew's body was removed from Patrae in Greece. Edom (line 45) is the non-Christian world, the false line of Jacob's brother Esau (see Genesis 36:1, Jeremiah 49:15).

HYMN 31 (21 DECEMBER)
As in John 20:29, the doubt of Thomas is contrasted with the faith of later Christians.

HYMN 32 (25 DECEMBER)
To call (line 2) the shepherds of Judaea (Luke 2:8–20) the 'swains of Solyma' (i.e., of Jerusalem), and to turn the Archangel Michael into a player on the shepherd's pipes (line 14), is to add to the biblical account of the nativity some of the resonances of classical pastoral. Here, however, the 'loves' (cupids, amoretti) of a pagan pastoral scene are replaced by the Christ-child who is love itself (line 16; cf. 1 John 4:8, 4:16). Christ's new covenant

of love similarly replaces (lines 25–8) the Old Testament covenant of the angry God of hosts, who comes in the whirlwind (Jeremiah 25:32) and whose vengeance against the proud is figured in the destruction of oaks (Isaiah 2:13; Zechariah 11:2). The use of classical pastoral imagery in connection with the Nativity places Smart's hymn in a tradition that includes Milton's *Nativity Ode* and Pope's *Messiah*. The insistent use of paradox in stanzas 1–3 is a rhetorical feature, and the representation of the nativity as a miraculous moment of spring in winter (stanzas 6–8) is a thematic feature of many sixteenth- and seventeenth-century poems on the subject.

HYMN 33 (26 DECEMBER)

Stephen, the first martyr, is represented in lines 19–20 as the victorious runner in the spiritual race (1 Corinthians 9:24–5), one of Smart's favourite images, and in line 27 as the 'faithful servant' of the parable of the talents (Matthew 25:14–30). To gem (line 24) is 'to put forth the first buds' (Johnson, *Dictionary*).

HYMN 34 (27 DECEMBER)

Traditionally John was 'the disciple whom Jesus loved' (see John 13:23, 19:26, 20:2, 21:20).

HYMN 35 (28 DECEMBER)

Jeremiah prophesied Rachel's 'weeping for her children' (Jeremiah 31:15; cf. lines 9–16). The prophecy was fulfilled, according to Matthew 2:17–18, in the Slaughter of the Innocents. The 'hope which prophets give' (line 25) is 'that thy children shall come again to their own border' (Jeremiah 31:17). Jeremiah 31:1–18 is the first Lesson for Morning Prayer on this day.

A Song to David

The *Song* was written either during Smart's confinement in the madhouse between January 1759 and January 1763 or immediately after his release. The first edition appeared in April 1763, the second in August 1765 in the volume entitled *A Translation of the Psalms of David*.

Even in its own time the *Song* was thought obscure and irregular, melancholy evidence of its author's madness. Analysis of the poem's sources and generic affiliations, however, shows it to be probably the most coherent and carefully worked extended lyric poem of its period.

Smart's *Song* probably relates to a contemporary controversy concerning the character of David. At a number of points the *Song* shows Smart's knowledge of Patrick Delany's *Historical Account of the Life and Reign of David King of Israel* (1740–42). Part of the purpose of Delany's extended eulogy had been to answer the criticisms of David made in Pierre Bayle's *Dictionnaire historique et critique* (1697; English translation, 1711). The debate broke out once more in England immediately before the composition and publication of Smart's *Song*, notably in the comparison of the virtues of David and George II in Samuel Chandler's *Character of a Great and Good King Full of Days* (1760), and in the vilification of David in the anonymous *History of the Man after God's own Heart* (1761).

But the *Song* is not primarily controversial. David is for Smart in every way the ideal man, embodying (lines 19–96) all of the twelve virtues or gifts of Jacob's sons (see Genesis 30 and 49; cf. *Jubilate Agno*, B355–8, B601–13). He is exemplary as king, warrior, scholar and priest. Above all Smart found in David a model of the divine poet. In the *Song* David is 'the minister of praise at large' (line 14), singing in adoration of God and his Creation. For Smart David's Psalms were 'the Book of Gratitude'. It is clear that Smart the poet sought and identified himself with this Davidic role, declaring himself in the *Jubilate Agno* the 'Reviver of ADORATION amongst ENGLISH-MEN' (B332). 'ADORATION' (the capitals are indispensable) is the key word of a long central passage in the *Song* (lines 301–426) celebrating the divine gifts of the seasons and the senses. Of all the Psalms, those which most powerfully influenced the *Song* were the great hymns in praise of God's created world, Psalms 104 and 148.

Psalms is only one of the many biblical books upon which Smart drew in writing the *Song*. The accounts of David's life in 1 and 2 Samuel and 1 Chronicles are a major source. The decalogue passage (lines 229–88) is based not only on Exodus 20:1–17, but also on several other passages in the Old Testament laws, as well as on Christ's teachings, especially in the Sermon on the Mount (Matthew 5–7). Job 39 and 41 provide a number of the images of sublimity in the animal world in the *Song*'s concluding 'amplification' (lines 427–516). 'Alba' in line 485 is an allusion to the 'white stone' in Revelation 2:17 which is the promised reward of those who triumph in Christ. Much of the pleasure the *Song* offers (and some of its difficulty) arises out of the suggestive brevity and complexity of its biblical reference. Christ's closing of 'th' infernal draught' in line 222, for instance, is a resonantly compressed allusion to Matthew 13:47–50. The 'sparrows' and 'swallows' (lines 422–4) have a psalmistic reason for being in God's Church (cf. Psalms 84:6), and the olive-tree on which they perch is a covert reference to David himself (Psalms 52:8). The *Song*'s rich variety of allusion comprehends natural history as well as the Scriptures, and often combines the two. Amongst the constellations spied by 'the Lord's philosopher' (392–3) is 'the Dog', Canis Major, to which the astronomer Schiller had, in the early seventeenth century, given the name 'David'. The 'crusions' and 'silverlings' (line 341) are gold and silver fish, fashionable recent introductions to English ponds and basins: Smart chooses word-forms that invest both with another kind of value (cf. Greek χρυσίον, gold coin; 'silverlings', i.e., shekels, Isaiah 7:23).

The *Song*'s most involved passage concerns the 'pillars of knowledge' (175–222). These seven pillars are those of the House of Wisdom (Proverbs 9:1), though they probably owe something to the cabbalistic idea that God established the world on seven pillars, corresponding with the seven firmaments. Each of the seven pillars is associated with a day of the creating week

(Genesis 1, 2:1–3), and each is assigned its own Greek letter. The letters probably refer to God: certainly Alpha and Omega are Christ (Revelation 1:8, 21:6). The pillars, and their associated 'arches' and 'vaults', are a favourite complex of images for Smart; they may be found also in the *Psalms* (e.g., 18:88–90) and the *Jubilate Agno* (e.g., B158).

Smart's choice of a religious subject for his high ode is part of his explicit purpose in his poetry of the 1760s to turn the muse to 'lore of sacred writ' (*Hymns and Spiritual Songs*, 11.8). It is a fulfilment of a call made in his own century by many writers, including Joseph Addison, James Thomson, and John Dennis, for a return of poetry to the divine. Smart had been particularly impressed and inspired by Robert Lowth's detailed account of biblical poetry in his Oxford lectures *De sacra poesi Hebraeorum* (1753). Generic analogues for Smart's sacred ode include Adam's hymn exhorting the Creation to praise God in *Paradise Lost* (V, 153–208), James Thomson's *Hymn on the Seasons* (1746) and lyrics by Isaac Watts in his *Horae Lyricae* (1709). Formally, the closest analogues may be found among eighteenth-century verse paraphrases of biblical texts, some examples of which aspire to the independent status and sublimity of the ode; notable are Isaac Watts's 'David's Lamentation over Saul and Jonathan, 2 Sam. i.19' (*Reliquiae Juveniles*, 1734), and Robert Lowth's 'Ode Prophetica', a Latin version of Isaiah 14:4–27 (reprinted, from Lowth's Oxford lectures, by Smart himself, in the *Universal Visiter*, January 1756). Of all the possible models the closest of all (as Robert Brittain pointed out in *Publications of the Modern Language Association*, 56, 1941) is 'The Benedicite Paraphrased', a poem written by James Merrick in the same stanza as Smart's *Song*, and published in Dodsley's *Museum* in 1746:

> Ye works of God, on him alone,
> In Earth his Footstool, Heaven his Throne,
>   Be all your Praise bestow'd;
> Whose Hand the beauteous Fabrick made,
> Whose Eye the finish'd Work survey'd,
>   And saw that All was Good.

In the Advertisement for the *Song* printed in *Poems on Several Occasions* (1763), Smart spoke of the poem's 'exact Regularity and Method'. The prefatory 'Contents' explain how the *Song* is given shape by division into thematic groups of stanzas: the twelve virtues of David (stanzas 5–16), the seven 'pillars of knowledge' (stanzas 31–7), the ten commandments standing at the centre of the poem (stanzas 39–48), three stanzas on each of the four seasons (stanzas 52–63), a stanza on each of the five senses (stanzas 65–9). These topics are articulated about recurrent returns to David himself (stanzas 4, 17, 38, 49, 51, 64, 71). This structure is given further emphasis by a rich variety of rhetorical means. Thus, each of the twelve stanzas on David's virtues begins with an epithet from the summarizing list provided in stanza 4. The 'exercise' on the seasons, where the word ADORATION cycles twice through the six lines of the stanza, is distinguished from the exercise on the senses where ADORATION remains in the first line. The fifteen stanzas of the concluding 'amplification' work up, through the positive and comparative degrees of the five adjectives, to the surpassing glory of the salvation wrought by Christ. The structural organization of the high ode was a problem that many mid-eighteenth-century poets, among them William Collins and Thomas Gray, confronted. Smart's solution in *A Song to David* might well be thought the most successful of his time.

A Translation of the Psalms of David

Smart may have conceived the idea of a verse translation of the Psalms early in the 1750s. References in the *Jubilate Agno* show that he was busily engaged on it during the madhouse years. The *Translation of the Psalms* was published, by subscription, in August 1765.

During the course of the eighteenth century many voices were raised in favour of a new Anglican psalmody, to replace the Old Version (first published complete in 1562) and New Version (by Tate and Brady, 1696), which together dominated the worship of the Church. Isaac Watts had provided Independent congregations with both a metrical version of the *Psalms of David* (1719), and a set of original hymns (*Hymns and Spiritual Songs*, 1707). Later in the eighteenth century the clearest call within the English Church for a new, Christianized, metrical psalter came from John Jones, author of *Free and Candid Disquisitions Relating to the Church of England* (1749). Jones's radical advocacy of Anglican liturgical reform gave rise to a furious and lasting public debate during Smart's early years as a writer in London. Perhaps responding to this controversy, and with Watts's example almost certainly in his mind, Smart set out to write, for Anglican congregations, both a new metrical psalter, the *Translation of the Psalms of David*, and a collection of 'new songs', the *Hymns and Spiritual Songs for the Fasts and Festivals of the Church of England*. Smart's prefatory note to his *Translation of the Psalms* insists that they are 'written with an especial view to the divine service', and aim to be 'useful and acceptable to congregations'. Since the old tunes to which the congregation familiarly sang the Old Version could not be used with many of the wide variety of metres Smart employed, melodies were written for his *Translation of the Psalms* by a number of eminent composers, notably William Boyce and James Nares (*A Collection of melodies for the Psalms of David, According to the Version of Christopher Smart, A.M., 1765*).

Smart's is distinctly an Anglican translation of the Psalms, with its 'sundry allusions to the rites and ceremonies of the Church of England', and its approval of 'th' establish'd church and king' (74.43). He made a point, in Proposals soliciting subscriptions, of claiming that his enterprise had received 'the Encouragement of many of the Bishops'. Smart's choice of the Psalter in the Book of Common Prayer as his main text for translation (though he no doubt also had the Authorized Version open as he worked) similarly seems to be the decision of a Church of England man. The Prayer Book version had been attacked by Nonconformists since the Savoy Conference of 1661, and as steadily defended by Anglican writers. More specifically, when he wrote the *Translation of the Psalms* Smart's sympathies seem to have lain, in an important area of belief, with the Evangelical wing of the Church. In a number of Psalms he introduces, in terms familiar in eighteenth-century Evangelical hymnody and apologetics, the doctrine that our merit is not our own but Christ's, by whose 'justifying grace' we are saved (see 85.5, 7, 43; 98(1).57, 58).

Formally, Smart's *Psalms* are imitations, rather than close verbal translations. Abraham Cowley had argued, a century earlier, that some of the power of such high-lyric poets as Pindar and David inevitably lies in particularities of expression, custom and religion scarcely comprehensible to a general modern audience, and that modern versifiers of the Psalms must therefore 'supply the lost Excellencies of another *Language* with new ones in their own' (Preface, *Poems*, 1656). Attempts to interpret David's Hebraic expression for a modern Christian audience may be found in the glosses, and to limited and varying degrees in the poetic texts, of Matthew Parker's *Whole Psalter Translated into English Metre* (1567?), George Wither's *Psalmes of David Translated into Lyrick-Verse* (1632) and John Patrick's *Psalms of David in Metre* (1691). In the early eighteenth century Isaac Watts expounded the argument for a more consistently Christianized psalmistic 'imitation', in which the New Testament elements are a thoroughly integrated part of the verse. It was no longer enough, Watts insisted, for an English congregation to 'sing the words of *David*, and apply them in our meditation to the things of the new testament'; rather, the Psalms must be rewritten in the words David might have used had he been our contemporary, to 'speak the present circumstances of the church, and that in the language of the new testament' ('A Short Essay toward the Improvement of Psalmody', *Hymns and Spiritual Songs*, 1707). In his *Psalms of David Imitated in the Language of the New Testament, and Apply'd to the Christian State and Worship* (1719) Watts provided an authoritative model: 'I have chosen rather to *imitate* than to *translate*; and thus to compose a *Psalm-book for Christians* after the Manner of the *Jewish Psalter*.'

Converting each verse of his original into a stanza, Smart allowed himself in his *Translation* space for the most thoroughgoing evangelical imitation of the Psalms attempted in English.

The whole project is 'attempted in the Spirit of Christianity'. David's curses of his enemies are removed, or are transformed into pleas for Christian forgiveness and salvation. Where David blessed the man who would dash the children of Babylon against the stones, Smart applauds him whose 'Christian mildness' spares the 'helpless infants' of his enemies (137.49–54). The voice of David often becomes the voice of Christ or of the Christian believer. The Old Testament law becomes the word of Christ. New Testament imagery and reference are pervasive, to the extent that some at least of the Psalms are remade as evangelical lyrics. Many passages are poetic allusions to, and some are original syntheses of, New Testament texts. *Psalms*, 18.151–6, for example, owes less to the verse of the Psalter (18:26) it nominally translates than to the Gospels of John (3:3, 3:5, 4:10–14) and Matthew (18:3). The following notes to individual Psalms concentrate on Smart's incorporation in his translation of New Testament materials.

Smart's *Translation of the Psalms* did not, as he had hoped, find acceptance in regular Anglican worship, though evidence survives that 'hymns' made up of selected stanzas from his translation were sung at special services in London in 1765, 1772 and 1780. Smart's thoroughly evangelical method, and modestly Evangelical message, no doubt led more conservative members of the Church to think his version too great a deviation from established practise.

PSALM 18

Line 150 is an Evangelical modification of 1 Corinthians 13:13.

PSALM 24

Lines 19–20 may be an Evangelical modification of Acts 10:35.

PSALM 25

Line 47 alludes to Romans 4:16. There are other New Testament echoes in lines 37 (cf. Hebrews 7:25) and 79 (cf. 2 Peter 1:10). 'Bishops, priests and deacons' (line 83) is a phrase from the Litany in the Book of Common Prayer.

PSALM 33

New Testament expressions are used in lines 68 (cf. Hebrews 12:28) and 73 (cf. Luke 21:19). The Lord will send his angel (line 74) at the end of the world; see Matthew 13:41, 24:31.

PSALM 68

With Smart's lines on the gifts of the twelve tribes (163–5) compare *A Song to David*, 19–96, and *Jubilate Agno*, B355–8, 601–13. 'Melchisedec' (line 173) is a reference to Christ (cf. Hebrews 7:17).

PSALMS 85

The New Testament texts drawn on here include Romans 5:9 and 1 Thessalonians 1:10 (lines 11–12); Matthew 4:17 and John 8:11 (lines 31–2); Matthew 18:20 (lines 33–6); Romans 3:24 (line 43).

PSALM 149

'Mansions' (line 30) is from John 14:2, 'palms' (line 36) from Revelation 7:9.

Poems 1763–1771

REASON AND IMAGINATION

First published in *Poems. By Mr Smart* (July 1763), and in a shorter form (lines 17–18, 27–138) in the *Gentleman's Magazine* (July 1763). The version printed in *Poems by the late Christopher Smart* (1791) comprised lines 27–138 only, with Kenrick's name omitted from the title. It may be that the core of the fable was written before Smart's confinement and subsequently expanded for the 1763 volume: a collection of *Tales and Fables in Verse* by Smart was repeatedly advertised from 1755 onwards but never published. The shorter versions leave out the specifically Christian references (lines 22–4, 149–60). In the *Gentleman's Magazine*, the debate between Reason and Imagination is located in the classical context of Horace's famous Sabine grove (lines 17–18), but lacks the date provided in the full version: the advent of Christ, the 'WORD'. Whether or not the frame passages were a later addition to the fable proper, they materially affect its interpretation. The dedication suggests that the poem was intended partly as a friendly riposte to William Kenrick's *Epistles Philosophical and Moral* (1759), a set of verse essays arguing for the primacy of reason and demonstrative science as the criteria of truth. Like Kenrick, Smart presents imagination as an essentially inventive faculty (line 54), whereas reason is founded on truth (lines 4–5). Where he differs from Kenrick is in his implicit redefinition of both truth and reason in Christian terms. Truth with its 'Angelic face' (line 6) suggests the truth revealed by Christ himself (John 14:6; see *Jubilate Agno*, B288, D84) while Reason, personified as a pious hermit conversant with the Book of Wisdom, perhaps the Wisdom of Solomon (lines 69–76), is both the faculty that enables man to comprehend revelation, and the measuring and ordering power ordinarily denoted by the term (line 135). The concluding admonition (lines 149–60) seems to be directed against Kenrick's final epistle, on the immortality of the soul, which claims that knowledge ('Science') is the means by which man may aspire to the kingdom of heaven.

ODE TO ADMIRAL SIR GEORGE POCOCK

First published in *Poems. By Mr Smart* (July 1763). George Pocock (1706–92) was knighted and made Admiral of the Blue in 1761 after a distinguished naval career with successful commands on both East and West Indian stations (lines 14–16). His most notable and recent achievement was the capture of Havana in 1762 (line 36). He returned to England in January 1763, but there is no factual corroboration for Smart's account of his poor reception (lines 37ff): it may reflect Pocock's own sense of grievance over his failure to secure promotion to First Commissioner in the Admiralty, for which he had been nominated in 1762. He was MP for Plymouth from 1760 to 1768 (line 58), and was renowned for his public benefactions as well as his private generosity (lines 61–72).

Like all the commendatory poems of 1763–4, this ode is closely linked in ideas and expression with Smart's *Hymns and*

Spiritual Songs, and in particular with the concept of the 'Christian hero'. Christian heroism, exemplified by the saints and martyrs of the early Church, is manifested in modern times by men and women, especially Englishmen and women, of outstanding virtue. Their reward is the accolade of 'God's applauses' (line 26); cf. *Hymns and Spiritual Songs*, 18.19–20 and 'Ode to General Draper', 37–42. Since the fountainhead of Christian heroism is Christ himself (*Hymns and Spiritual Songs*, 17.1–6), Smart makes him the archetype of all heroic seamen through his feat on the Sea of Galilee (lines 1–4). The '*White*' is an archery term, referring to the white band on the target.

For the roll-call of British naval heroes (lines 49–51), cf. *Hymns and Spiritual Songs*, 17.25–36 and 65–6. The names chosen here are all of commanders famous like Pocock for victories against Spain.

ODE TO GENERAL DRAPER

First published in *Poems. By Mr Smart* (July 1763). The word 'hew' in line 69 was printed as 'knew' but corrected immediately in the *Daily Advertiser*. William Draper (1721–87), a friend of Smart, was educated at Eton and King's College, Cambridge, where he held a Fellowship before joining the army in 1744 (lines 25–36). He served as aide-de-camp to the third Duke of Marlborough (line 30), commanded a regiment at the siege of Madras, 1758–9, and led the expeditionary force that captured Manila in 1762 (lines 61–6). Colonel Monson (line 65) was officer in charge of a landing party in the assault on Manila, in the course of which Major More (line 88) was killed.

The motto, adapted from Virgil's *Aeneid* ('However lesser men may report those deeds, patriotism and passion for renown shall prevail'), anticipates the patriotic theme. For the idea of the Christian hero (lines 37–42), cf. 'Ode to Admiral Sir George Pocock'. Lines 71–2 allude to the custom among city companies such as the Merchant Taylors of conferring freedom of the company on distinguished citizens. A 'matross' (line 77) was a gunner's mate.

AN EPISTLE TO JOHN SHERRATT

First published in *Poems. By Mr Smart* (July 1763). Sherratt (1718–82?), a London businessman and entrepreneur, was manager of Marylebone Gardens in the 1750s (the capacity in which Smart may first have known him). He became self-appointed reformer of private madhouses and engineered Smart's escape from confinement in January 1763 (see B. Rizzo, 'John Sherratt, Negociator', *Bulletin of Research in the Humanities*, 86 (1983–5), pp. 373–429.) He was assisted by Richard Rolt (co-editor with Smart of the *Universal Visiter*), Rolt's wife and Anna Sheeles, whose mother kept a boarding-school in Bloomsbury at which Charles Burney was music-master.

The main theme of the poem, gratitude, is introduced by the motto, 'These things will always be fixed in my heart, and I shall be indebted to him for my life forever.' For the conception of gratitude as the inspiration for lyrical poetry (lines 1–4) cf. *Hymns and Spiritual Songs*, 3.25–8. Smart's claim for the supremacy of verse (lines 5–14) rests on a famous text from Wisdom 11:21 ('thou hast ordered all things in measure and number and weight') which was the basis of Renaissance analogies between divine and artistic order; Smart's examples, the Bible ('Book of Grace') and the prose of Demosthenes and Plato, illustrate his interest in cadence, as well as metre, as a source of 'mystic measure' (cf. *Hymns and Spiritual Songs*, 3.31). The work of Rolt referred to (line 13) is presumably *Cambria* (1749), a lengthy historical poem in blank verse.

Smart returns to the subject of gratitude in line 37, contending that the most lasting memorial to deeds of love is poetry written in a spirit of Christian devotion (lines 37–56). Smart's compressed and allusive style makes the argument of lines 43–52 difficult to follow, but his point appears to be that intellectuals ('young scholastics') quibble futilely about the relations between poetry and painting, encouraged by Horace ('th' *Appulian* Swan'); Horace's dictum *ut pictura poesis* licensed endless debate on the two arts in the eighteenth century. Best of all is 'a word in tune', i.e., song infused with Christian spirit: 'in tune' is a Smartian pun, signifying both lyrical quality and a state of harmony with God's purpose (see 'On the Eternity', 129–30, and 'On the Immensity', 143).

The sculptor Louis Roubiliac and the portrait-painter George Romney (lines 43–8) were at the height of their fame at this time. The artist said to rival Romney is probably Allan Ramsay, whose celebrated portrait of Queen Charlotte was painted about 1762. Lines 73–80 probably owe their nautical imagery to Sherratt's part-ownership of a privateer which was involved in the capture of a French prize-ship in 1756.

EPITAPH ON HENRY FIELDING
First published in *St James's Magazine* (July 1763), afterwards in *Poems on several Occasions* (1763), from which the text is taken. Smart was associated with Fielding in the Paper War against John Hill in 1752–3. Fielding died in 1754 in Lisbon, where he had gone in the hope of recovering his health (lines 14–16), but the epitaph must have been written later because the plan for a reformatory for penitent prostitutes alluded to in line 12 (i.e., the Magdalene Hospital; see *Jubilate Agno*, B128) was not published until 1758 (actually by Henry Fielding's half-brother, Sir John). Fielding was commissioned as JP for Westminster in 1748 (lines 9–10), and lent his support to the Foundling Hospital for Orphans (line 11).

ON A BED OF GUERNSEY LILIES
First published in *Ode to the Right Honourable the Earl of Northumberland* (July 1764).

MUNIFICENCE AND MODESTY
First published in *Poems on several Occasions* (November 1763). Two manuscript corrections, in Smart's hand, appear in every known copy, and have been incorporated: 'read' for 'reach' in line 18 (this correction was notified in the *Daily Advertiser* on 4 November 1763), and 'won' for 'one' in line 146.

The poem is an allegory at two levels, moral and religious. The key to the first is the painting referred to in the subtitle, which Moira Dearnley identified as Guido Reni's *Liberality and*

Modesty (see Dearnley's *The Poetry of Christopher Smart*, 1968, plate IV). It depicts two female figures on a terrace, with an expanse of water and well-wooded headland in the background: one is offering a bowl of jewels which the other is bashfully fingering, while a *putto* flies overhead. This painting supplies the moral theme and some of the iconology of Smart's poem, but leaves unexplained the ornate description of Liberality (lines 47–60) and the grandeur of Modesty's final reward (lines 119–46), which led Christopher Devlin to suggest that Reni's *Coronation of the Virgin* was the painting in question (see *Poor Kit Smart*, p. 157). That painting was not known in England at the time, but Smart does indeed elevate the straightforward allegory of Reni's *Liberality and Modesty* into a spiritual drama in the high baroque style, turning the simple tableau of moral virtues into an encounter between the archangel (line 54) and the Holy Virgin (lines 115–18), which culminates in her Assumption. In the Roman liturgy, Mary is identified with 'the rose of Sharon' (line 122), the bride in the Song of Songs. The sceptre and the dove (line 130) are traditionally associated in Christian iconography with the archangel Gabriel and the Virgin Mary at the Annunciation. Smart draws on the traditional stock of images and concepts relating to the Feast of the Assumption of the Blessed Virgin Mary (cf. poems on this subject by Southwell and Crashaw). Some details, however, are more individual: Modesty's address to God as Father of Simplicity (line 36) may be explained in conjunction with her vow of chastity (lines 115–18) by reference to St Paul's address to Christian converts in 2 Corinthians 11:2–3: 'I have espoused you to one husband, that I may present you as a chaste virgin to Christ. But I fear, lest . . . your minds should be corrupted from the simplicity that is in Christ.' Oriel (line 139) looks like Smart's coinage as a name for Christ, from the title 'Oriens' used for him in the Great Advent Antiphons in the Roman liturgy: these are sung before and after the Magnificat, the Virgin's proclamation of her modesty. Smart's celebration of a Roman Catholic dogma is curious, in view of his sometimes virulent anti-Romanism, but the Virgin Mary evidently occupied a special place in his imagination (cf. *Jubilate Agno*, B139, B664).

The Marquis of Granby (line 60), one of the most dashing and successful of Britain's generals in Europe in the Seven Years' War, had recently returned to England in a blaze of glory; 'geers' (armour) was an archaism by this date, probably chosen for its chivalric associations.

THE SWEETS OF EVENING

First published in *Ode to the Right Honourable the Earl of Northumberland* (July 1764). The names Philomel and Asterie (the quail) both come from Ovid's *Metamorphoses*.

EPISTLE TO DR NARES

First published in April 1765 in the *Universal Museum*, but the original invitation, in Smart's hand, survives in Pembroke College Library, Cambridge, with a note dating it '1764 or 5'. James Nares (1715–83), a Doctor of Music from Cambridge, was choir-master at the Chapel Royal. He contributed several settings to the *Collection of Melodies for the Psalms of David According to the Version of Christopher Smart, A.M.* (1765).

LINES WITH A POCKET BOOK

First published in the *Monthly Magazine* (March 1804), but printed here from a letter in the Bodleian Library from Elizabeth Le Noir to E. H. Barker, *c.* 1825, in which she says the lines were addressed to one of Smart's sisters but gives no date.

TO MRS DACOSTA

First published in the *Gentleman's Magazine* (August 1818) but dated 7 June 1770, which is probably correct, although the contributor assigns it to 1758. Mrs Dacosta was the wife of Emmanuel Mendez Dacosta, Clerk of the Royal Society, who was Smart's fellow-prisoner in the King's Bench in 1770.

ON GRATITUDE

First printed by John Drinkwater in *A Book for Bookmen* (1926) from Smart's manuscript (the text followed here).

Thomas Seaton (1684–1741), Fellow of Clare College, Cambridge, and vicar of Ravenstone, Northamptonshire, was founder of the Seatonian Prize for poems on the divine attributes of the Supreme Being for which Smart successfully competed in 1750–56. Seaton was himself the author of hymns and other religious works. The date of composition of *On Gratitude* is unknown, but it has closer affinities in subject and style with Smart's later religious poetry than with his Seatonian poems.

The tortuous syntax of lines 17–18 and the curious placing of the footnote make this passage ambiguous. The text cited ('If a man say, I love God, and hateth his brother, he is a liar: for he that loveth not his brother whom he hath seen, how can he love God whom he hath not seen?') relates more immediately to the preceding couplet. The general sense of lines 17–18 seems to be that Gratitude to fellow humans has the same claim ('plea') as Love (i.e., Christian charity) to be a step towards love of God, by virtue of their 'Sisterhood' (both *caritas* and *gratitudo* are feminine nouns). Lines 37–8 refer to eulogistic poems addressed by Spenser and Prior to their respective patrons, Sir Philip Sydney and the Earl of Dorset. Line 40 refers to the nine Muses and the seven Sciences, i.e., the traditional branches of learning.

The Works of Horace, Translated into Verse

When John Hawkesworth visited Smart in October 1764 in the lodgings overlooking St James's Park to which Smart moved after his release from the madhouse, he saw on his table 'a quarto book, in which he had been writing, a prayer book and a Horace' (letter quoted in *Poems of the late Christopher Smart*, 1791). Although it was not published until 1767, Smart was already engaged on his verse translation of Horace which, he told Hawkesworth, was intended to supersede the prose translation for Latin students he had written, as a pot-boiler, in 1756. The earlier translation was none the less very successful, remaining popular as a crib throughout the eighteenth and much of the nineteenth century, but Smart was never proud of it and feared, as he told Hawkesworth, that it 'would hurt his memory'.

Smart had used Horace as a model for his own verse – as had most aspiring poets of the time – from at least 1744 (see 'On Taking a Batchelor's Degree'), but his devotion intensified after his confinement. In the Preface to the 1767 translation, Horace is equated with David as 'the *Heathen Psalmist*', called 'one of the most thankful men that ever lived', and credited with the Smartian understanding that 'the business of poetry is to express gratitude, reward merit, and promote moral edification'. More specifically, Smart attributes Horace's distinction as a poet to his unrivalled peculiarity of expression. Only through some 'affinity in the spirit' can a translator hope to render the 'lucky risk of the Horatian boldness' which, he says, stems partly from 'choice diction' (Horace's *curiosa felicitas*), partly from the force of '*Impression*', that 'talent or gift of Almighty God, by which a Genius is impowered to throw an emphasis upon a word or sentence in such wise, that it cannot escape any reader of sheer good sense, and true critical sagacity' (cf. *Jubilate Agno*, B404). This power, he notes, 'is always liveliest upon the eulogies of patriotism, gratitude, honour, and the like'. In his pursuit of Horatian boldness, Smart does not hesitate to take liberties with the original, doubtless feeling that his freedoms were justified by the fact that the verse translation was supported by a literal prose gloss. But he is given to unexpected, and sometimes arresting, literalism on occasion, as in 'grave day's solidity' (*Odes*, I.1.28) for *solido die* ('busy day'). Smart's translation is notable also for its metrical variety and dexterity, ranging from the strict Sapphics of Ode 1.38 to the casual iambic tetrameters of the Epistles: Smart claimed with some justice that his 'familiar measure' was more appropriate to these conversation pieces than the heroic couplets more often used for them by translators.

ODES, I.1

Smart cites this as one of the odes most rich in *curiosa felicitas*, but also comments that 'however amiable for its gratitude, and special for its phrase', it is 'written *Stylo mediocri*. I have endeavoured to raise it all the way, particularly at the conclusion.' Lines 55–6 expand Horace's brief phrase, *sublimi feriam sidera vertice* ('I shall raise my exalted head to the stars').

ODES, II.14
Smart comments on lines 1–4 of the original: 'what affectionate tenderness with a cast of melancholy are *impressed* on this stanza!'

ODES, II.18
Another of the Odes singled out in the Preface for its *curiosa felicitas*.

ODES, III.12
There is no 'cat' in the original: Smart's prose version of lines 13–16 is: 'the same is adroit [*catus*] to spear at the stags flying through the open plain in herds full of consternation, and active to surprise the wild boars, lurking in the deep underwood.'

ODES, III.22
Lines 8–10: 'obliquity' represents Horace's *obliquum ictum*. The literal translation of these lines is, 'Through the years I shall offer it the blood of a pig practising on it his sidelong attack.'

ODES, IV.2
Lines 5–8 of the original are quoted in the Preface as an example of *Impression*, for their 'strength and grandeur'.

ODES, IV.3
Lines 17–24 of the original (25–36 here) are quoted in the Preface as an example of *Impression*, for their 'amazing sweetness'; Smart's lines 27–30 expands on the literal translation, 'O you who could lend the music of the swan even to mute fishes, if you desired'. Cf. *Jubilate Agno*, B24.

ODES, IV.10
Ode 11 in modern editions of Horace.

SATIRES, II.6
Line 28 expands *pecus . . . et cetera* ('my flocks and the rest'). Lines 60–61 are cryptic even in the original: *hoc iuvat et melli*

est ('that pleases me and is like honey'); i.e., Horace is glad that his intimacy with Maecenas is recognized.

EPISTLES, I.20

Line 56: Smart passed his forty-fourth December in 1766, when his translation of Horace was ready for the press.

Hymns for the Amusement of Children

Although the first edition is dated 1771, publication was announced on 27 December 1770. Smart was arrested for debt in April 1770, and most if not all of the poems therefore may well have been written in the King's Bench prison where he spent the last year of his life. Hymn 32 was published in a newspaper in June 1770 with the signature 'A Prisoner' (see note below). Thanks to the intervention of his brother-in-law, Thomas Carnan, publisher of these hymns, Smart lived in relative comfort under the 'Rules', which allowed him decent quarters and free movement within a limited area outside the prison.

Hymns for the Amusement of Children was Smart's third collection of poems written for young people, after his translation of the *Fables of Phaedrus* (1765) and versified *Parables* (1768). The edition was dedicated to the seven-year-old son of George III, Prince Frederick, and furnished with simple woodcuts (one for each hymn) on the pattern of John Bunyan's *Book for Boys and Girls* (1686). Virtually the only other hymnals for children published before 1770 were Isaac Watts's *Divine Songs Attempted in Easy Language for the Use of Children* (1715) and Charles Wesley's *Hymns for Children* (1763). Smart's hymns are closer in style to Watts than to Wesley, but differ markedly in emphasis, stressing the mercy of God and the bounteousness of his blessings on earth and hereafter, rather than the sinfulness of man and the fear of eternal punishment. Smart's intention, like Watts's, was to provide moral instruction in simple language; but simplicity of diction in Smart's hymns does not always reflect simplicity of thought. Because of his compressed style, abrupt transitions and unexpected associations of ideas, together with his habit of covert allusion (usually to biblical sources, not all of which would have been immediately recognized even by eighteenth-century readers) these hymns make more demands even on the adult reader, but also offer more rewards, than most hymns designed for children.

Although less tightly organized than the *Hymns and Spiritual Songs*, the *Hymns for the Amusement of Children* also has a general design. The 'plan' of the book (see 17.14−15) is a scheme of Christian doctrine, beginning with 'Faith' (Hymn 1) and culminating in 'Plenteous Redemption' (Hymn 38). The sequence is figuratively unified by the Pauline metaphor of the 'race' (Hymns 2.16 and 39.8; cf. *Hymns and Spiritual Songs*, 33.20). Hymns 1−8 deal with the three Theological Virtues, followed by the four Cardinal Virtues, together with Mercy. Hymns 9−14 (perhaps intended for the six Sundays of Lent) deal with the moral duties of a Christian. Hymn 15 introduces a sequence of ten hymns centred on the Gospel. The abundance of allusions to the Passion in Hymns 19−25 suggests that they may have been designed for Holy Week. Once again, Gratitude is a cardinal concept (Hymns 21−2), for which there is good liturgical authority: the Eucharist is the supreme act of Christian thanksgiving (the literal meaning of Eucharist), and re-enacts the Last Supper at which Christ himself 'gave thanks' (Matthew 26:27; cf. Hymn 21.20).

HYMN 1

The allusion is to God's instruction to Abraham to sacrifice his son Isaac (Genesis 22:1−14): Abraham's obedience is cited by St Paul as a notable example of faith (Hebrews 11:17).

HYMN 4

Lines 5−8 refer to Christ's warning to the disciples, 'Behold, I send you forth as sheep in the midst of wolves: be ye therefore wise as serpents and harmless as doves' (Matthew 10:16).

HYMN 13

The controlling metaphor comes from Revelation 19:8: 'For the fine linen is the righteousness of saints'. Lines 5−8 refer to the parable of the prodigal son.

HYMN 15

The theme is the supremacy of the Bible both as a guide to conduct and a model of language: the association of 'taste' with spiritual enlightenment and the scriptures comes from Hebrews 6:4–5.

HYMN 18

Lines 5–8 allude to Elijah, who denounced the wickedness of Ahab but was instructed by God not to punish him when he was found doing penance (1 Kings 21:17–29). Lines 9–12 allude to the parable of the widow who won justice from an ill-disposed judge by the persistence of her pleading (Luke 18:1–8).

HYMN 19

For Smart's association of Job of Uz with Job, son of Issachar (Genesis 46:13), cf. *Jubilate Agno*, B405; it has no biblical authority. Strength is Issachar's special attribute according to Genesis 49:14.

HYMN 20

This hymn seems to be intended for the Easter Vigil: the biblical context is the night before the Crucifixion, when the disciples were bidden to watch and pray in order to avoid temptation (lines 1–4), and when Peter fell asleep and denied Jesus (lines 13–16). Smart links this sense of 'watching' with that of watching for the second coming of Christ. Lines 9–12 allude to the story of the man who was robbed because he failed to keep watch (Matthew 24:42–4: 'Watch therefore: for ye know not what hour the Lord doth come'). Lines 21–4 allude to similar prophecies and injunctions in Mark 13:24–37.

HYMN 23

'Salem' (line 6) means 'peace'. Augustus was celebrated for bringing internal peace to Rome (lines 9–10). Melchisedec, King of Salem, is identified as 'King of peace' (and hence a type of Christ) in Hebrews 7:1–3 (lines 11–12).

HYMN 26
Lines 9–12 refer to Mark 9:33–7.

HYMN 31
Lines 1–2 are Christ's words after the Last Supper (John 16:33); he is called the 'corner-stone' of the Church (lines 7–8) in 1 Peter 2:6–7.

HYMN 32
First published in a series of epigrams in the *London Chronicle* (16 June 1770), signed 'A Prisoner', and given a secular context with 'Romney' in place of 'Bashan' (line 2). It was frequently reprinted as a separate poem (see B. Rizzo, 'Christopher Smart: A Letter and Lines from a Prisoner of the King's Bench', *Review of English Studies*, NS 35 (1984), pp. 509–16.

HYMNS 33–6
The last of the hymns designated as such: Smart follows Watts in concluding the main series with four occasional pieces (the last four in Watts's *Divine Songs* are for Morning, Evening, Sunday Morning, and Sunday Evening).

HYMNS 37–9
Numbered in the Contents but not on the page, these are clearly part of the doctrinal 'plan', but perhaps because of their brevity not regarded as 'hymns' proper.

INDEX OF TITLES

INDEX OF FIRST LINES

FOR THE BEST IN PAPERBACKS, LOOK FOR THE 🐧

In every corner of the world, on every subject under the sun, Penguin represents quality and variety – the very best in publishing today.

For complete information about books available from Penguin – including Puffins, Penguin Classics and Arkana – and how to order them, write to us at the appropriate address below. Please note that for copyright reasons the selection of books varies from country to country.

In the United Kingdom: Please write to *Dept E.P., Penguin Books Ltd, Harmondsworth, Middlesex, UB7 0DA.*

If you have any difficulty in obtaining a title, please send your order with the correct money, plus ten per cent for postage and packaging, to *PO Box No 11, West Drayton, Middlesex*

In the United States: Please write to *Dept BA, Penguin, 299 Murray Hill Parkway, East Rutherford, New Jersey 07073*

In Canada: Please write to *Penguin Books Canada Ltd, 2801 John Street, Markham, Ontario L3R 1B4*

In Australia: Please write to the *Marketing Department, Penguin Books Australia Ltd, P.O. Box 257, Ringwood, Victoria 3134*

In New Zealand: Please write to the *Marketing Department, Penguin Books (NZ) Ltd, Private Bag, Takapuna, Auckland 9*

In India: Please write to *Penguin Overseas Ltd, 706 Eros Apartments, 56 Nehru Place, New Delhi, 110019*

In the Netherlands: Please write to *Penguin Books Netherlands B.V., Postbus 195, NL-1380AD Weesp*

In West Germany: Please write to *Penguin Books Ltd, Friedrichstrasse 10–12, D–6000 Frankfurt Main 1*

In Spain: Please write to *Longman Penguin España, Calle San Nicolas 15, E–28013 Madrid*

In Italy: Please write to *Penguin Italia s.r.l., Via Como 4, I-20096 Pioltello (Milano)*

In France: Please write to *Penguin Books Ltd, 39 Rue de Montmorency, F-75003 Paris*

In Japan: Please write to *Longman Penguin Japan Co Ltd, Yamaguchi Building, 2–12–9 Kanda Jimbocho, Chiyoda-Ku, Tokyo 101*

PENGUIN CLASSICS

Netochka Nezvanova   Fyodor Dostoyevsky

Dostoyevsky's first book tells the story of 'Nameless Nobody' and introduces many of the themes and issues which dominate his great masterpieces.

Selections from the Carmina Burana   A verse translation by David Parlett

The famous songs from the *Carmina Burana* (made into an oratorio by Carl Orff) tell of lecherous monks and corrupt clerics, drinkers and gamblers, and the fleeting pleasures of youth.

Fear and Trembling   Søren Kierkegaard

A profound meditation on the nature of faith and submission to God's will which examines with startling originality the story of Abraham and Isaac.

Selected Prose   Charles Lamb

Lamb's famous essays (under the strange pseudonym of Elia) on anything and everything have long been celebrated for their apparently innocent charm; this major new edition allows readers to discover the darker and more interesting aspects of Lamb.

The Picture of Dorian Gray   Oscar Wilde

Wilde's superb and macabre novella, one of his supreme works, is reprinted here with a masterly Introduction and valuable notes by Peter Ackroyd.

A Treatise of Human Nature   David Hume

A universally acknowledged masterpiece by 'the greatest of all British Philosophers' – A. J. Ayer